Praise for Joan Johnston

"Joan Johnston does short contemporary Westerns to perfection."
—*Publishers Weekly*

"Like LaVyrle Spencer, Ms. Johnston writes of intense emotions and tender passions that seem so real that the readers will feel each one of them."
—*Rave Reviews*

"Johnston warms your heart and tickles your fancy."
—New York *Daily News*

"Joan Johnston continually gives us everything we want . . . fabulous details and atmosphere, memorable characters, a story that you wish would never end, and lots of tension and sensuality."
—*Romantic Times*

"Joan Johnston [creates] unforgettable subplots and characters who make every fine thread weave into a touching tapestry."
—*Affaire de Coeur*

Montana Bride

Joan Johnston

DELL • NEW YORK

A Dell Mass Market Original

Copyright © 2014 by Joan Mertens Johnston, Inc.

Published in the United States by Dell, an imprint of The Random House Publishing Group, a division of Random House LLC, a Penguin Random House Company, New York.

DELL and the HOUSE colophon are registered trademarks of Random House LLC.

ISBN 978-0-345-52748-6
eBook ISBN 978-0-345-52749-3

Cover design: Lynn Andreozzi
Cover illustration: Alan Ayers

Printed in the United States of America

www.bantamdell.com

9 8 7 6 5 4 3 2 1

Dell mass market edition: January 2014

This book is dedicated to
Roseanna J. Dirmann

Montana Bride

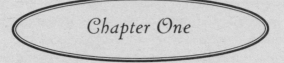

Chapter One

"Don't you dare strike that child!" Henrietta Wentworth set her plate of hardtack and beans aside and rose from her seat on a fallen log beside the campfire.

"He's my son. I'll hit him if I want." Mrs. Lucille Templeton had grabbed her seven-year-old son, Griffin, by the arm as he tried to escape after "accidentally" dropping a plate of beans into her lap.

"Look at my dress!" Mrs. Templeton wailed, staring down at a green-velvet-trimmed traveling dress that was clearly ruined. She tightened her grip until the boy grimaced and said, "This fiendish brat spilled that plate on purpose. He deserves the whipping he's going to get."

Hetty balled her fists and took three steps to put herself toe-to-toe with Mrs. Templeton. "You will beat that child over my dead body. Let him go."

"Hah!" Mrs. Templeton snorted. Nevertheless, she loosened her grip, and Griffin jerked free and fled. He disappeared behind the Conestoga wagon in which they'd all been traveling from Cheyenne, in the Wyoming Territory, to Butte, in the Montana Territory, where Mrs. Templeton was destined to become a mail-order bride.

The hodgepodge Templeton family included the widow Templeton, her nine-year-old daughter, Grace, and her seven-year-old son, Griffin. Hetty had trouble imagining how Mrs. Templeton had produced a daughter as kind as Grace, although she had no doubt how she'd spawned a hellion like Griffin.

Nevertheless, not one of the three Templetons looked like any of the others or seemed anywhere near their professed ages.

Mrs. Templeton, with her dyed blond hair, muddy brown eyes, and substantial figure, looked considerably older than twenty-eight.

Grace was plump, had flyaway red hair and green eyes, and was already sprouting small buds on her chest, which told Hetty she was more likely twelve or thirteen than the nine she professed to be.

Her brother, Griffin, was a skinny stripling with dark brown eyes and tangled black hair that made Hetty itch to take a brush to it. Hetty figured he'd last seen the age of seven three or four years ago.

No less odd was the short, slender, but very strong young Chinese man who was their guide, protector, and driver, Mr. Lin Bao, who said he'd come to America ten years ago to work on the transcontinental railroad. Hetty had learned that the Chinese put their family name first, so Mr. Lin's first name was Bao, which he'd told her rhymed with cow. Mr. Lin now worked for the man who would become Mrs. Templeton's husband, Mr. Karl Norwood.

"If I'd had my way, Miss High-and-Mighty," Mrs.

Templeton muttered as she lifted her skirts to dump beans from its folds, "we would have left you to rot in that wagon where we found you."

Hetty had no doubt of that. She'd never met a lazier or more selfish person in her life than Lucille Templeton. It was appalling that she owed this woman her life.

Mrs. Templeton had forced Mr. Lin to stop near the apparently abandoned Conestoga wagon because she'd wanted to scavenge whatever remained inside, but someone had already looted the wagon. All she'd discovered was Hetty, dehydrated, weak from loss of blood, and with a wound that had become infected from the arrow deeply embedded in her shoulder.

If not for Mrs. Templeton's avarice, Hetty would be dead.

Although, honestly, it was Mr. Lin's doctoring that had kept her alive. He'd used mysterious medicines from the Orient to bring Hetty back to life over the past seven weeks as they'd traveled north. Mrs. Templeton claimed to be a nurse, but she didn't seem to know much about caring for anyone. Hetty shot a quick look at the young Chinaman, who was sitting quietly beside the fire smoking a long, curved white clay pipe.

"If it had been up to you, Lucy," a young female voice accused, "you would have left Hetty in that wagon to die."

Hetty hadn't seen Grace approaching from the opposite side of the campfire, but she'd seen the girl defend her brother from their mother's slaps often enough to know that where Griffin was, Grace was never far behind.

"I'll take care of this, Grace," Hetty said, knowing that Mrs. Templeton was still angry enough to lash out at her daughter.

Her warning came too late. Mrs. Templeton reached out her arm like a lizard's tongue, grabbed a handful of Grace's tumbled red curls, and yanked hard. "You're the one to blame for this. I never should have brought the two of you along."

Grace shot a fearful look in Hetty's direction.

Hetty couldn't imagine having a mother who wished she'd left her children behind. A mother who felt free to slap faces and yank hair. A mother who considered her children a nuisance. No wonder Grace looked so scared.

Hetty's heart went out to the girl. Hetty's own wonderful, loving parents had been lost three years ago in the Great Chicago Fire, when Mrs. O'Leary's cow had kicked over a lantern and burned down most of the city, including the Wentworth family mansion and her father's bank.

Overnight, Hetty had gone from being the pampered daughter of wealthy parents to being an orphan stuck in the Chicago Institute for Orphaned Children. Her uncle, Stephen Wentworth, had left Hetty and her three sisters and two brothers at the orphanage even after they'd begged him to rescue them from the cruelty of the headmistress, Miss Iris Birch.

Miss Birch, like Mrs. Templeton, seemed to find joy in brutality against those weaker than herself. Every infraction at the Institute had been punished with three—"You're lucky it's only three!" Miss Birch was fond of saying—vicious strokes of a birch rod.

Hetty forced her thoughts away from her five siblings, who were all lost . . . or dead . . . but certainly gone. She couldn't do anything to help them. But she could help Grace.

"What I said about Griffin goes for Grace, too," Hetty said. "Let her go."

Mrs. Templeton twisted Grace's hair until the girl whimpered and stood on tiptoes to avoid the pain. "This is my kid. I'll do with her as I like."

"Not while I'm here, you won't." Hetty obeyed a sudden impulse, and her balled fist struck Mrs. Templeton in the nose.

"Ow!" Mrs. Templeton released Grace and grabbed her bloodied nose. "You'll pay for that!"

Instead of running like Griffin had, Grace stood and watched with anxious eyes. "Please, Lucy," the girl pleaded. "I'm sorry. Griffin's sorry."

"Shut up, you ungrateful whelp!" Mrs. Templeton snarled.

That was another strange thing about the Templeton family. Hetty couldn't imagine calling her own mother by her first name, yet both children called their mother "Lucy." Nor could she imagine any mother calling her daughter an "ungrateful whelp."

Hetty should have known better than to think Mrs. Templeton wouldn't strike back. A moment later she felt nails claw their way across her face, narrowly missing her left eye. One of the scratches across her brow bled profusely, blurring Hetty's vision on that side, so she almost missed seeing Mrs. Templeton bend to pick up a heavy dead branch.

"Lucy, don't!" Grace cried. And then, to Hetty, "Look out!"

As Mrs. Templeton swung the unwieldy weapon Hetty bent backward but then lost her balance and fell into a clump of buffalo grass. Hetty made the mistake of trying to push herself upright with her injured shoulder and yelped in pain. Even after seven weeks, it wasn't healed enough to support her. She was stuck on the ground, a sitting duck the next time Mrs. Templeton swiped at her with that heavy branch.

Mrs. Templeton must have realized Hetty's predicament, because she uttered a shout of triumph. However, the ponderous weight of the branch, as it continued its sweeping arc, had dragged her sideways. Instead of letting go to regain her balance, she held on to the branch, and her momentum forced her several steps backward.

Hetty heard Mr. Lin yelling something behind her, but she was too busy trying to avoid being brained by the tree branch to pay attention. She heard Mrs. Templeton cry out and wondered if Grace had somehow intervened to save her.

Hetty looked up in time to see Mrs. Templeton's arms flailing as she tripped backward over a large stone. She finally let go of the branch, which flew several feet upward before it began falling, falling, disappearing from sight before ever hitting the ground.

As Hetty struggled to her feet, she realized at last what Mr. Lin had been shouting. "Be careful!" she cried. "The cliff!"

She got one last look at Mrs. Templeton's face in the firelight—a ghoulish mask of fury—before the woman fell backward out of sight.

Her shrill scream seemed to go on endlessly. Then it stopped.

Hetty dashed with Grace toward the edge of the hundred-foot rock cliff that had been visible in the daylight when they'd camped, but which had disappeared beyond the light of the campfire after dark. She felt sick with grief and regret. She'd only wanted to protect Grace and Griffin. Instead she'd made them orphans. She couldn't do anything right! Mr. Lin should have let her die.

"Watch out!" Hetty gasped as she put a hand across Grace's waist to keep the girl away from the edge. She could see nothing in the blackness below.

Grace kept repeating, "Oh, no. Oh, no. Oh, no."

"What happened?" Griffin called out. "Did the witch hurt herself?"

Grace turned on her brother angrily as he appeared in the light of the campfire and said, "The witch is *dead*."

Hetty stared at the two children, dismayed at what they were saying about the woman who'd borne them. "What's wrong with you?" she asked Grace. "Your mother has just died a ghastly death."

"She wasn't our ma!" Griffin retorted.

"Griffin," Grace warned. "Don't say another word."

"There's no reason to lie anymore. Lucy's dead. We're *DOOMED*."

Hetty remembered her twin sister, Hannah, using that precise term, *DOOMED*, when their eldest sister, Miranda, had turned eighteen and could no longer remain at the orphanage. Miranda was the one who'd protected them from Miss Birch's terrible temper. Without her, they were *DOOMED* to suffer under the iron discipline of the horrible headmistress.

In the end, Miranda had stolen away, along with their two younger brothers, Nick and Harry, to become a mail-order bride in Texas. At least, Hetty hoped that was what had happened. The three sisters left behind—Hetty, her identical twin Hannah, and Josie—had never heard from Miranda again.

When Miranda had failed to contact them, they'd taken desperate measures to escape Miss Birch. Hannah had followed Miranda's lead and become the mail-order bride of an Irishman, Mr. McMurtry, and Hannah, Hetty, and Josie had journeyed west with him to the Wyoming Territory.

That trip had ended in a disaster that was all her fault. Because of her behavior, they'd been forced to leave the safety of the wagon train. Their lives had quickly unraveled. Mr. McMurtry had died of cholera, Hetty had been sorely wounded in an Indian attack, Josie had been taken captive by the savages, and Hannah had gone for help and never returned.

By the time Hetty had come to her senses, after weeks and weeks of being nursed back to health by Mr. Lin, they'd been closer to Butte than Cheyenne. She'd been forced to continue the journey to the Montana Territory. Once she got to Butte, Hetty planned to find some way to get back to Cheyenne, locate Hannah, if she was still alive, and begin a search for Josie.

Now she'd caused another disaster! What was wrong with her? Why did she always do exactly the wrong thing? How would she ever make amends for the wrong she'd done to these two poor orphaned children?

It suddenly dawned on her what Griffin had blurted.

She wasn't our ma! Hetty's brow knit in confusion. So what were the two children doing with Mrs. Templeton?

She suddenly understood so many things that had seemed strange about Mrs. Templeton's behavior toward her supposed children. About Griffin's pranks, which often had Mrs. Templeton as their victim. About Grace's wariness around her pretend mother. About the disparities in ages and appearances of the entire fake family. But how had the three of them ended up together on this journey to Butte?

Hetty turned to Grace and Griffin, who were now standing beside each other. She crossed her arms over her chest because she could feel her body beginning to tremble, and it was all she could think of to do to keep herself from flying into a million pieces.

Mrs. Templeton was dead on the rocks at the bottom of the cliff. Hetty was at least partly responsible for someone dying. Again.

She forced her mind away from memories of the calamity she'd caused on the journey west. There was nothing she could do to change the past. She closed her eyes to shut out the awful vision of two men fighting because of her, and the vivid blue eyes of the man she'd loved as he lay dying in her arms. When she opened them again, she said to the two children, "Is there something you'd like to tell me?"

"Mrs. Templeton worked upstairs at the saloon where we were living," Griffin said. "Before our mom died, she used to work there, too, and some of the ladies made sure we had a place to sleep and food to eat. But Grace was getting older, and they wanted her to—"

"Griffin, that's enough," Grace interrupted.

"Anyway," Griffin continued, "Mr. Norwood's advertisement for a mail-order bride said that he'd consider a widow with children, so Grace went to Lucy with this crazy idea that we could all get out of there if Lucy became this guy Norwood's mail-order bride."

"And Mrs. Templeton went along?" Hetty asked.

Grace grimaced. "As soon as I agreed to pay her, she did."

"You *paid* her to bring you along and she treated you that badly?" Hetty said.

"Why do you think I dumped those beans in her lap?" Griffin said.

"I wrote all the letters to Mr. Norwood," Grace said. "But Lucy insisted that I tell him she was twenty-eight, so Griffin and I had to pretend to be younger, too. I'm thirteen. I'll be fourteen in a couple of months."

Hetty turned to Griffin and asked, "How old are you?"

"I'll be ten in the spring."

Hetty glanced at Mr. Lin, who was listening to this confession, and wondered what he was thinking. His dark eyes remained inscrutable.

"We're *DOOMED,* all right," Grace said.

Hetty watched tears pool in Grace's eyes before they slid onto her freckled cheeks. Her heart went out to the two children.

Grace glanced at her brother and said, "I can always get work at a saloon in Butte."

Griffin's eyes narrowed, and his mouth flattened to a hard line. "Not that kind of work. Not if I have anything to say about it."

"What other choice do we have?" Grace said quietly.

It took Hetty a moment to realize what kind of work Grace was considering. At seventeen, Hetty was still naive enough, even after hearing the escapades of a girl at the orphanage who'd previously taken a lover, to be shocked. "There must be a better alternative," she said.

"Not unless we go to some orphanage," Griffin replied bitterly. "We ended up in one right after our ma died, but we ran away. We've been hiding out at the saloon ever since. I'm never going back. I'll starve first."

Hetty shuddered. Grace working in a brothel? Grace and Griffin at the mercy of some cruel headmistress like Miss Birch? "There has to be a way for the two of you to avoid either of those choices."

"There is way," Mr. Lin said.

Hetty, Grace, and Griffin all turned to find the Chinaman tapping out the contents of his long clay pipe.

"What do you suggest?" Hetty asked.

"I think *you* be mail-order bride," Mr. Lin said. "Two kids be your kids. Mr. Norwood get bride, kids get home, you get husband help you look for missing sisters." He smiled and said, "Work out happy for everybody. Okay?"

Hetty stared at Mr. Lin for a moment in astonishment, then glanced at the two children, who were staring back at her with hopeful eyes. Hetty wanted to help, truly she did. But she'd caused so much pain and suffering, she wasn't worthy of being anyone's bride. She'd had her chance at love, and she'd utterly destroyed it. She didn't deserve another.

Besides, the deception would never work. She could never pass for twenty-eight. She knew nothing about being a mother or a nurse. And she was a virgin.

Then she thought of what Grace might be forced to do if she refused. And pictured mischievous Griffin in an orphanage, facing some heartless headmistress.

Hetty looked from one young, worried face to the other and said, "Okay. I'll do it. I'll become Mr. Norwood's mail-order bride."

Chapter Two

"If this ruse is going to succeed," Hetty said to the two children, "we have a lot of work to do over the next week before we arrive in Butte."

"Like what?" Grace asked.

"You need to start calling me Mom, for a start," Hetty said.

"No way!" Griffin shot back. "You're not my ma. And I sure as hell don't have to do what you say."

Hetty met the boy's gaze across the morning campfire and held it. "And that sort of language must stop."

"The hell you say," Griffin snapped.

"I do," Hetty said.

"We'll see about that," Griffin muttered. He was whittling, and splinters of wood were flying as fast as he could shave them with his knife.

Mr. Lin had climbed down the cliff to bury Mrs. Templeton, leaving Hetty alone with the children. She'd spent the time before Grace and Griffin awoke this morning discussing the situation with the China-man.

Hetty had been surprised that Mr. Lin was willing

to go along with the planned deception. "Shouldn't your first loyalty be to Mr. Norwood?" she'd asked.

"Confucius say: 'Never force on another man what you not choose for yourself.' Not choose that wife for any man. Responsible to boss, so bring woman, but that woman no good for wife."

"And I am?" Hetty asked doubtfully.

"Better choice for sure," Mr. Lin said.

"Mr. Lin, I'm not so certain I agree."

"Please. We partners now. Name is Bao. Rhymes with cow," the Chinaman said with a smile.

Hetty felt strange calling any man who wasn't a relative by his first name, but since Mr. Lin had requested it, she began again. "Bao, I don't think you realize how difficult it will be to convince Mr. Norwood that I'm twenty-eight and a nurse, but especially that I'm the mother of those two half-grown children."

Mr. Lin pulled at the long, scraggly black beard growing from his chin, straightened his waist-length braid down his back, then rearranged the Oriental black silk cap he always wore low on his brow. Hetty had been on the trail long enough with the savvy Chinaman to know he performed the ritual to give himself time to think before replying.

More than once over the past seven weeks, Mr. Lin's sage advice had come from Confucius, a Chinese philosopher whose writing Mr. Lin said he'd studied as a young man in China.

Hetty was waiting patiently for Mr. Lin to begin his speech with "Confucius say . . ."

Instead, he said, "Long time past, I save Boss's life. I now responsible for Boss's happiness. I think you make Boss more happy than other woman. Boss see you so pretty, he not care about age. He like kids. Make respectable father. I teach you be nurse."

Hetty was still deciphering what Mr. Lin had said, when he rose. "I go bury other lady. You tell kids call you Mom. Tell Griffin no do bad things. Tell him comb hair. Tell Grace wear bigger dress, hide bumps on chest, look younger. I teach you medicine next few days on trail. You be nurse very soon."

A moment later he was gone. Hetty had stayed by the fire, waiting for the shadowy grays to turn pink, and then orange and yellow as the sun rose. She wasn't so sure it was going to be as easy as Mr. Lin seemed to think for her to take Mrs. Templeton's place.

Hetty had been too embarrassed to discuss with Mr. Lin the one difference between herself and Mrs. Templeton that she couldn't fix over the next week on the trail. Mr. Norwood was expecting a bride who'd already been bedded. Hetty was an innocent—and ignorant—virgin.

She'd been *in love*. She'd even shared several quick, furtive kisses with her beau in the dark. But Hetty had never been held close in a man's arms. She'd never lain with a man. She was still untouched.

It was hard to believe Karl Norwood wouldn't notice.

Hetty was simply going to have to figure out a way to deceive him. Surely she could fake whatever it was she was supposed to know. Surely she could follow his lead, so he wouldn't realize she had no idea what she was doing.

Assuming they got that far. First Mr. Norwood had

to accept his substitute bride. Once he got a look at this motley band of misfits, there was no telling whether he would follow through and marry her. Especially if the children wouldn't do their part to help convince him she was their mother.

"Please cooperate, Griffin," Grace implored. "Hetty's marrying a perfect stranger so I won't have to go to work doing you-know-what when we arrive in Butte." She turned to Hetty and said, "What else do you need from us, Mom?"

Hetty felt a lump form in her throat. This was going to be much harder than she'd ever imagined. From now on, she would be the only mother these two children had. She wondered if she would be able to do as wonderful a job, and be willing to make as many personal sacrifices, as her eldest sister, Miranda, had when she'd taken over for their absent mother.

"Do you have a hairbrush?" she asked Grace.

Grace shook her head. "Mrs. Templeton had one. I suppose we could borrow it."

Hetty hadn't thought about what they should do with Mrs. Templeton's possessions. "Do you know if she had any family?"

"None that I know of," Grace said.

"Then we might as well make use of her things," Hetty said. "Starting with that hairbrush. Do you think you could find it?"

While Grace was retrieving the hairbrush, Hetty watched Griffin whittling. "What are you making?" she asked.

"Same thing I always make," the boy replied.

"What is that?"

Griffin held up the piece of birch. "A horse."

It wasn't the entire horse, just the head, but it had visible ears and a mane and its mouth was open as though it was neighing. It was amazingly lifelike. Hetty had often watched Griffin pick up wood along the trail and then whittle something from it, but she'd been too caught up in her own problems to really look at what he was carving.

"Why a horse?" she asked.

Griffin shrugged. "I like horses."

"Have you ever owned one?"

"No."

Hetty figured the boy had always wanted a horse. Apparently, his mother hadn't been able to afford one. "What do you do with your figures when you finish?"

Griffin smirked. "This." He threw the half-finished horse head into the fire.

"Oh, no!" Hetty rushed to retrieve it, but it had fallen into the center of the hot coals and burst into flame. "Why did you do that?"

"Why not?" Griffin said. "There are plenty of sticks around. And I've got all the time in the world to whittle. Why keep it?"

"To enjoy it," Hetty said with asperity.

Griffin shrugged again. "I can always make another one when I want."

"Then give it away and let someone else enjoy it," Hetty suggested.

Griffin was digesting that advice when Grace returned with the brush. "Here it is."

Hetty realized that the girl thought she wanted to use it herself. "Come sit here, Grace," she said, gesturing to a spot beside her on the log.

Grace sat down and tightened the knot on the wool shawl around her shoulders.

Hetty realized Grace was wearing a calico dress, which wasn't warm enough for the cold weather. "Don't you have something warmer to put on?"

"I've got a dark brown wool dress, but I'm saving it for when it gets really cold."

Hetty noticed the girl's breath in the frigid air and smiled. "I think it's time, Grace. You can change after I finish brushing your hair."

"All right, Mom."

Hetty was still trying to grasp the reality of this thirteen-year-old girl calling her *Mom* when Grace said, "You're going to brush my hair?"

"Of course." Miranda had often brushed and braided both Hannah's and Hetty's hair at the orphanage. It seemed the most natural thing in the world for her to do that service for Grace. She started at the bottom, where Grace's red curls were most tangled and worked her way up until she could pull the brush from the crown of Grace's head all the way down without encountering a tangle.

Grace looked over her shoulder at Hetty and said, "That feels nice. You didn't pull my hair once, not like my—"

Grace stopped talking abruptly, and Hetty realized that the girl hadn't wanted to say anything bad about her mother. Hetty admired her for it. Grace's mother must have been busy and perhaps brushed through the snarls in a hurry to get done.

Hetty's heart bled for this girl who'd become a parent of sorts herself when her mother died. If Grace's mother had been as occupied with her work as Hetty suspected, Grace had probably been taking care of Griffin long before that.

"Would you prefer one braid or two?" Hetty asked.

"Two would make me look younger, don't you think?" Grace said.

That was another thing Hetty admired about Grace. The girl was always thinking ahead. Perhaps not so admirable was how adept she was at using her intelligence to deceive others. Hetty could understand that, too, considering the life Grace must have led. The girl had been smart enough to get herself and Griffin out of that saloon. Smart enough to get almost to Butte. And winsome—and pitiful—enough to get Hetty to agree to become her mother.

There was no pretense about that part of the deal. Hetty intended to become the best parent she could be to both children. That was the least she could do to salve her conscience for the hoax she was perpetrating on Mr. Karl Norwood.

"Two braids it is," she said as she divided Grace's bountiful curls into two handfuls. "You hold this one while I braid the other," she said, handing Grace the hair on the left.

Hetty began at Grace's brow and braided her red hair all the way down to the end, tying it off with a piece of string Grace handed her. Then she did the other half. When she was finished, she turned Grace around and surveyed her from the front.

Hetty smiled and said, "You're right. With those wide green eyes, and that gamine smile, and those braids, you could pass for a girl of nine." She leaned close and whispered, "Just be sure to keep that shawl draped over your budding chest."

Grace's face turned beet red. "What am I supposed to do? I can't help growing up."

Hetty discovered a stray curl that had already fought its way loose and tucked it behind Grace's ear. "Just be yourself. Everything will work out fine."

Grace turned to Griffin and said, "Your turn."

"No thanks!" Griffin said, leaping to his feet. "I'm not having some *girl* brush my hair."

Hetty held out the brush. "You're welcome to do it yourself."

"No thanks," Griffin repeated.

"No thanks, *Mom,*" Hetty said.

"You're not my ma. My ma's dead!"

Griffin turned and stalked toward the wagon, bumping into Mr. Lin on the way. He said something to Mr. Lin that Hetty didn't hear, then hurried away in the direction Grace had gone.

"How you do?" Mr. Lin asked Hetty as he kicked dirt over the fire to put it out.

Hetty made a face. "I believe I made some progress with Grace. Griffin is a disaster waiting to happen."

"Misunderstand," Mr. Lin said. "I ask how *you* do."

"Oh. I'm fine."

"You not fine. You sad in heart."

Hetty stared at the Chinese man, wondering how he could be so perceptive. She was sad for so many reasons she probably couldn't name them all in a single breath. "I've caused so much heartache, Mr. Lin. You can't imagine how much. I want to help those children. I want to be a good wife to Mr. Norwood. I don't want to fail either of them."

Mr. Lin surveyed the fire to be sure it was out, then turned to her, stroked his beard, ran his hand down his braid, and settled his silk cap. "Confucius say: 'Glory not in never falling, but in always getting up again.'"

Hetty smiled. Simple advice. If only it worked. But if she wasn't going to die of her wound, or from heartbreak or loneliness, and it looked like she wasn't, she could at least try to live a better life from now on.

"All right, Mr. Lin—Bao," she corrected herself. "I'll pull myself up by my bootstraps and get back in the game."

Mr. Lin tipped his head sideways and said, "Not understand *bootstraps*."

Hetty laughed and realized it was the first time she'd done so in months. She was going to have to pretend joy until she actually felt it again. She was going to have to pretend a lot of things until they became real.

"I don't know enough to pass as a nurse," Hetty pointed out.

"Confucius say: 'Real knowledge is to know one's ignorance.' I teach you."

"I thought you said we're only a week away from Butte."

"I teach good." Mr. Lin smiled and added, "You learn quick."

Hetty laughed again. "I'm glad you think so."

"Necessary to learn, so you learn."

He was right, Hetty realized. She'd done a lot of things lately she'd never imagined herself capable of doing.

Grace reappeared in a blousy brown dress with the

shawl tied in a knot to camouflage her chest. She twirled in a circle and said, "How's this, Mom?"

Hetty crossed to the girl and gave her a quick hug. "You look beautiful, Grace. Except for that smudge on your nose."

"What smudge?" Grace said, rubbing at her nose.

Hetty smiled. "I was teasing."

"Oh." Grace looked surprised. Then she grinned. "That was perfect, Hetty. I mean, Mom. Be sure you do something just like that when we meet Mr. Norwood. That way, he'll believe you're my mom for sure."

Hetty felt her stomach flutter with fear. She hoped it would be that easy to deceive her bridegroom.

Chapter Three

Karl Norwood paced the boardwalk in front of the Copper Mine Hotel, unable to make himself go inside. He was eager to meet his mail-order bride. And anxious and nervous and a little worried. What if he didn't like the look of her? What if she didn't like the look of him, which was far more likely? A man couldn't be more ordinary than Karl was. Average height, average build, brown hair, brown eyes, a face that had nothing to make it particularly noticeable in a crowd.

He hoped Mrs. Templeton appreciated intelligence. He was well educated, with a doctorate from Harvard, and had traveled the West, especially the Wyoming and Montana Territories, doing research in botany. His articles about the Indians' use of native plants for food and medicinal purposes had been published in several prestigious university journals.

Karl would never be wealthy, like his older brother Jonas, who owned a piece of the Union Pacific Railroad. But he was willing to work hard to make a good life for his wife and be a good father to her two children and several more he hoped they would have together.

He straightened his tie yet again, pulled down his gray wool vest, shifted his shoulders in his gray-and-black herringbone suit, adjusted his flat-brimmed, flat-crowned black hat, then shot a troubled glance at his friend, Dennis Campbell, who grinned back at him.

"What's so funny?" Karl asked.

"You," Dennis said. "Stop pacing. Settle down. You're as nervous as a long-tailed cat in a roomful of rocking chairs."

"It's not every day a man meets his bride," Karl said.

"Especially on his wedding day," Dennis added. "You don't have to marry the woman today, Karl. You can give yourself a little time—a week—to get to know her. What if she's a harpy? Or a crone? I can't believe you didn't demand a photograph."

There was a simple reason why he hadn't. Mrs. Templeton might have demanded one in return. Karl didn't want to be judged for his plain looks any more than he planned to judge his bride by her appearance. To be honest, he'd been found wanting too many times in the past. As far as he was concerned, it was a point in Mrs. Templeton's favor that she'd never demanded a picture of him.

Dennis ground out a cigarette under his boot and said, "This lady comes with a couple of kids. You sure you want that kind of responsibility right from the start?"

"I don't think two little kids will be much of a burden," Karl replied.

Dennis snorted.

"They won't!" Karl insisted. "I'm hoping we'll have

a few more. Mrs. Templeton is an educated woman, so she'll be able to teach our kids. Her letters have been intelligent and—"

"You don't even know the lady's first name," Dennis pointed out. "You haven't seen a picture of her. In my experience, people—especially women—lie. What if you're disappointed when you see her?"

"I'm thirty years old."

Dennis rolled his eyes, but Karl kept speaking.

"I may be stuck in the back of beyond for a couple of years. I want a family, the sooner, the better."

"It's sooner, all right," Dennis said. "I'm not so sure about the better. You might end up with the ugliest woman in the Montana Territory. Last chance to change your mind."

"It doesn't matter what Mrs. Templeton looks like, Dennis. I'm going to marry her," Karl said, tugging at his silk tie, which seemed to have gotten tighter around his throat. "I promised my brother I'd get to the Bitterroot Valley before winter sets in to start logging. It's already mid-November. If I don't leave now, I might have trouble getting there at all."

"You could wait and marry when the job is done," Dennis suggested.

"It could take a couple of years to prove this logging operation can produce the kind of lumber quotas Jonas expects," Karl replied.

"You should have married that debutante back in Connecticut," Dennis said. "She liked you."

"And I liked her. But how do you think she would have fared here in Butte?" Karl gestured at the muddy, wheel-rutted street, at the land surrounding the mining town that had been stripped of all vegetation in order to dig for copper and silver and gold, at the filthy, unshaven miners, and the rowdy saloons. "I need a woman who's proven she can survive a life as bleak as this."

That was not the truth, the whole truth, and nothing but the truth. Karl would have snapped up the Connecticut debutante in an instant, if she'd shown even a flicker of attraction to him. Her eyes had glazed over when Karl mentioned his work. They'd brightened only when she'd spied a better-looking swain, at which point she'd excused herself and left him standing alone. Karl had never shared with his handsome friend how often that sort of thing happened to him.

Karl wanted a beautiful bride as much as the next man. But he'd long ago realized that he had no right to hope for beauty when he didn't have good looks to offer in return. For a while he'd hoped that some more-than-handsome woman might be captivated by his intelligence. But that had never happened.

Karl sometimes wondered if he'd studied so long and hard to improve his knowledge because he'd known his looks were so unimpressive. "I don't think a debutante could deal with the isolation and primitive conditions of a place like the Bitterroot Valley," Karl continued, giving a good reason, other than his plain features, why he hadn't chosen a debutante for his bride. "I have to bite the bullet. I need to go in there and meet my mail-order bride, walk her to the church, and marry her."

"I think you're crazy," Dennis said.

"Mrs. Templeton has proven she can give birth to healthy children. And you've got to admit, it'll be helpful to have a nurse on hand. When men are working with axes, there are bound to be accidents."

"Not if I can help it," Dennis said. "That's why I'm here, Karl. To help you complete this job with the fewest complications. That includes injuries."

Karl had mixed feelings about his childhood friend's assignment as his second-in-command. Dennis's father was the head gardener on the Norwood estate in Connecticut, where the two boys had grown up together. Dennis had gone right to work for Karl's elder brother at seventeen. There was no question his friend had far more experience being a boss than Karl.

But Karl had pleaded for the chance to show Jonas he could do the job. He'd wanted to prove to his brother that the years he'd spent studying, and then traveling the American West doing research, hadn't been a total waste, as Jonas so often muttered they were. His brother had eventually given Karl the job, but he'd sent Dennis along to "help."

Karl had never been in charge of anything like this proposed logging operation, and frankly, the project was daunting. They would be working in the middle of nowhere, and it was his job to supervise a team of a dozen loggers while they cut as many ponderosa pines as they could over the winter. In the spring, he had to find a site for a millpond and build a mill.

Meanwhile, Jonas hoped to convince his partners of the benefits of building a rail line to the valley, so the lumber Karl produced could be shipped east.

Karl was most worried about his ability to manage the lumberjacks, unruly ruffians who judged a man entirely on his physical strength and stamina, two things

Karl lacked. Two things Dennis had. So maybe his brother had known best after all.

"I'll tell you what, Karl," Dennis said, setting a friendly hand on Karl's shoulder. "I'll go in first. If she's a hag, I'll wave you off."

Before Karl could stop him, Dennis opened one of the double doors leading into the Copper Mine Hotel and stepped inside. Karl quickly followed after him. He was dwarfed by his friend, who was six foot four to Karl's five foot ten, so his view of the red-silk-covered Victorian sofa in the center of the lobby was blocked.

He presumed his bride was sitting there alone, since he'd sent a note to her room at the hotel asking her to meet him first without her two children present. He ran into Dennis when his friend stopped in his tracks. Karl took a step back as he heard Dennis whistle appreciatively and whisper over his shoulder, "You are one lucky son of a bitch."

Karl peered around Dennis's shoulder and felt his heart jump. *She's breathtaking.*

His mail-order bride was perched on the edge of the sofa. A riot of blond curls surrounded a perfect, heart-shaped face. Her perfect, bashful smile had produced, heaven help him, perfect dimples. Her perfect, sky-blue eyes were focused unerringly on Dennis.

She wasn't alone on the sofa. To her left sat two children he presumed were hers.

His next thought came unwilling. *Those two children had different fathers.*

Karl was familiar with both Mr. Darwin's *On the Origin of Species* and Gregor Johann Mendel's study of genetics with pea plants. Karl doubted that a blue-eyed, blond mother and one individual father could have produced both a green-eyed redhead and a dark-brown-eyed child with black hair.

His mail-order bride had been pregnant before she'd married Mr. Templeton. Or she'd been unfaithful to him.

Maybe he was wrong. Maybe there was some combination of genes in Mrs. Templeton and her late husband that could have produced two such dissimilar children. Karl didn't want to believe such a beautiful face concealed such a deceitful heart.

Mrs. Templeton's letters, which had been both witty and smart, and the fact that she was the mother of seven- and nine-year-old children, had led Karl to think of his mail-order bride as a mature woman. But the waif with lost-looking eyes and tumbled blond curls who sat before him, fidgeting nervously with a torn string on her ill-fitting dress, didn't look even close to the twenty-eight years she'd claimed. Which was a problem, because the two children looked considerably older than their stated ages.

Karl smelled a rat.

"Are you Mr. Norwood?" Mrs. Templeton asked Dennis.

He heard Dennis laugh. Then his friend stepped aside and gestured at Karl. "Here's your groom."

Karl watched the hopeful smile on his bride's face ebb as she surveyed him from flat-brimmed black hat to muddy black boots. He felt his heart squeeze as he realized he'd been compared to his tall, good-looking, broad-shouldered, blue-eyed, black-haired friend and found wanting.

"I'm—" Karl cleared his throat of the frog that had caught there and said, "I'm Karl Norwood. You must be Mrs. Templeton."

His bride rose, but the two children stayed seated next to each other on the sofa. She extended her hand with a hesitant smile and said, "My name is Henrietta, but I've never liked it. My sis—" She cut herself off and lowered her eyes timidly, so her lashes sat on cheeks the color of peaches and cream.

Karl was enchanted. He felt his insides twist with sudden desire, felt his heart pound so hard he feared she might hear it. How had he chosen a bride so beautiful sight unseen? Her face was flawless except for several small scabs near one eye. It looked like a cat had swiped her with its paw.

In a low, tremulous voice that shivered along his spine, she said, "Please, call me Hetty."

Karl had to swallow again before he could speak. "All right. Hetty."

At the sound of her name, she blushed, painting her cheeks a rosy pink.

All the suspicious inconsistencies should have put him on guard, but Karl was too captivated to complain. He still had concerns about Mrs. Templeton's basic honesty, but he could forgive what had happened before they'd met. Lots of people came West hoping to put a shadowed past behind them. What mattered was Mrs. Templeton's—Hetty's—behavior from now on. Karl was willing to give her the benefit of the doubt.

Assuming she still wanted to marry him, now that she'd seen what she was getting.

"This is my friend, Dennis Campbell." Karl gestured to Dennis.

"Nice to meet you, Mr. Campbell," Hetty said.

Dennis touched a hand to his hat brim, smiled so that an entire mouthful of perfectly straight white teeth became visible, and said, "The pleasure is entirely mine."

Karl noticed that Hetty's blush deepened under Dennis's intense perusal. Karl felt a flare of jealousy and tamped it down. It wasn't Dennis's fault he was so good-looking. But the girl seemed entranced. His voice was sharper than he'd intended as he asked, "Would you introduce me to your children?"

"Oh, of course." Hetty appeared flustered as she tore her gaze from Dennis's face and focused it on her children. The girl jumped up immediately, then reached down and tugged on the boy's elbow until he got to his feet. "Mr. Norwood, these are my children, Grace and Griffin."

"Please, call me Karl," he said to Hetty.

She dipped her chin to her chest, then glanced up at him from beneath lowered lashes. "Very well. Karl."

He felt himself flushing. It was disconcerting to be so attracted to a woman he suspected had told a few whoppers in order to become his bride. He gritted his teeth in an effort to slow the thundering beat of his heart and turned to observe the children more closely.

"It's nice to meet you," Grace said, dipping a small curtsy. Her pale eyelashes fluttered nervously, and he could see she was trembling. She bumped her shoulder hard against the surly boy standing next to her, who kept his gaze on his feet as he muttered, "Yeah. Nice to meet you."

It was not an auspicious beginning, but they had the rest of their lives to become a family. Assuming Mrs. Templeton agreed to marry him.

"Do you need some time to acquaint yourself with me before we're wed?" Karl wasn't sure why he'd asked the question, especially since, given time, she might change her mind about the whole thing.

She shook her head so vigorously her curls bounced. "I don't want to wait. I want to be married today. I'm ready right now. I mean, if you are," she added lamely. "All I have to do is change into my wedding dress."

Karl smelled a rat and the cheese. What was her hurry? What else was she hiding?

"You can always call it off," Dennis said in his ear.

He'd forgotten his friend was standing there. "It's too late," he whispered back.

"It's never too late until you say 'I do,'" Dennis countered.

But it was too late to go hunting for another bride before he left for the Bitterroot Valley. Hetty was young and beautiful. And the children looked healthy, if a bit anxious and surly, respectively.

Karl knew himself to be an intelligent and patient man. If there were problems, he was smart enough to work them out. How hard could it be? Especially with such a stunning wife.

"All right," he said, crossing to his mail-order bride and holding out his arm for her to take. "I'll escort you to your room. Once you've changed, we can be married."

As they headed toward the hotel stairs, Karl thought he heard a deep, exhaled sigh of relief from the little girl trailing behind them.

Karl smelled a rat and the cheese and heard the trap snapping shut. Somehow he'd been had. But he glanced at the beautiful woman who held his arm and shoved all reservations aside. Today was his wedding day. To-morrow would be soon enough to worry about the passel of lies Henrietta Templeton had told to become his mail-order bride.

Chapter Four

Hetty was certain she would have been content with Karl Norwood as a husband, if only she'd seen him first. But her heart had leapt at the sight of his friend, Dennis Campbell, and then crashed to the ground when Dennis stepped aside to reveal the very ordinary man standing behind him. If it hadn't been for Grace perched beside her, gazing up at Hetty with fearful eyes and chewing on a fingernail that had already been bitten to the quick, she might have backed out of the wedding.

Hetty had tried not to let her disappointment show. But she'd seen the light die in Karl's brown eyes as the light had died in her own blue ones. She'd wanted to smile at him, but the muscles in her mouth wouldn't obey. She thought maybe such a plain-looking groom was fate paying her back for the way she'd squandered her first chance at love.

To make matters worse, it appeared that the very handsome Dennis Campbell would be going with them to the Bitterroot Valley. Hetty would have to face her attraction to the other man—and deny it—every day from now on. Fortunately, she'd grown up a great deal over the past few months. She knew the consequences of duplicity and jealousy. Men fought. And men died.

Once they were married, Karl had a right to expect her fidelity. Hetty knew better than to tempt fate by even glancing in Dennis Campbell's direction. Flirting with two men at the same time on the wagon train had resulted in the deaths of both men, including the one she loved.

Hetty fully intended to be faithful to her husband, but she wondered why God had played such an awful trick on her. If only she hadn't seen Dennis first!

The two men were as different as roses and crab-grass. Hetty felt a spurt of guilt at comparing her future husband to something so universally undesired. Karl seemed like a very nice man, but his looks paled in comparison to his friend. Hetty was tall, and while she might have looked up at Dennis, she looked directly into Karl's very plain brown eyes.

And that was another thing. From the first day she'd started playing bride with Hannah, Hetty had been determined to marry a man with blue eyes. Blue eyes were striking and compelling. Brown eyes were common and uninteresting.

Hetty realized now, standing at the altar in a small church with whitewashed wooden walls and a small stained-glass window, that Grace must have suspected she might balk. That was why the girl had insisted on coming downstairs with her when she met the groom for the first time. One glance at the worried look on Grace's face and the sulking glare on Griffin's, as they'd sat on the sofa beside her at the hotel, had been enough for Hetty to realize she couldn't back out.

"Hetty?" Karl said.

Hetty realized she'd been daydreaming while the ceremony had been going on. "I do?"

"Do you?" Karl said.

His gaze was so solemn Hetty felt the knot in her stomach tighten. She realized she'd made her response a question, rather than a statement. Her nose burned and her throat ached. She blinked to keep the threatening tears from falling. One slid down her cheek anyway.

Karl gently brushed it away with the rough pad of his thumb. His eyes asked for her answer, but he said nothing.

Hetty lowered her lashes, unable to meet his gaze as she agreed to become the wife of a man she didn't want to marry.

"I do," she croaked.

The preacher moved on as though she'd said the words with delight. A short while later she heard the cleric say, "You may kiss your bride, Mr. Norwood."

Hetty held herself steady, afraid she'd bolt if Karl Norwood came anywhere near her face with his lips. He must have sensed her reluctance, because he merely lifted her left hand, which he'd been holding, and gently kissed the simple gold ring he'd put there, as though he were some knight suing for the love of his lady fair.

Hetty did look at him then, surprised that she'd thought of Karl Norwood and a knight in shining armor in the same moment. Karl was no Lord Lochinvar, like the one in Sir Walter Scott's poem. That daring knight had stolen the bride he wanted from a Scottish castle—on the day of her wedding to another man—and escaped with her on his charger.

Karl hadn't even taken the trouble to come to Cheyenne to collect his bride. He'd sent Mr. Lin in his stead. Karl hadn't asked for a father's blessing and been denied, like Lochinvar. There had been no obstacle at all to wedding his mail-order bride, nothing at all to fight against. Not even a bride who had the guts and gumption to say, "I don't."

"My turn to kiss the bride," Dennis said.

Before Hetty could say a word in protest, Dennis Campbell had taken her by the shoulders, turned her to face him, and planted his lips right on hers. Hetty was too surprised to do anything but stand there. Dennis pulled her body close for an instant, so she felt every hard muscle in his chest against her breasts, which peaked against her will.

When he let her go, Hetty drew back in shock and put a hand to her mouth, not quite sure what had just happened. She stared up, wide-eyed, at Dennis.

He winked at her with one of those unbelievably blue eyes and said, "My very best wishes for a long and happy life, Mrs. Norwood," seeming blissfully unaware that he'd turned her world upside down, leaving her feeling upset and confused.

Hetty was afraid if she said anything at all she would babble. She wished Dennis hadn't kissed her, especially since she'd been tempted to kiss him back.

Even that fleeting urge to respond to a man who wasn't her husband made her feel sick to her stomach. And angry with Dennis. And even angrier at Karl, who should have been the first man to kiss her lips on her wedding day.

She glanced at her new husband, to see what he thought about what Dennis had done.

His brown eyes had darkened and looked stark, but he managed a smile. "I hope Dennis didn't embarrass you. We've been friends all our lives."

"Not at all," Hetty said, aware that she was lying to her husband only moments after their marriage.

Hetty turned to Grace, who was standing beside her, and saw the girl scowling at Dennis. Hetty realized that she'd better do something quick, or Grace was liable to say something to make matters worse. She turned her gaze back to Karl and asked, "What comes next?"

Dennis laughed and slapped his friend on the back. "She wants to know what comes next, Karl."

Hetty saw the embarrassed flush on Karl's face at his friend's teasing and said, "I meant, is there something we need to sign, now that the ceremony's over?"

Karl cleared his throat. "The church register."

The register showed Henrietta Wentworth Templeton had married Karl Frederick Norwood. Hetty refused to worry about whether the marriage was legal when she hadn't used her real last name. The point was, they'd said the words before God. She was married all right. *Till death us do part.*

"What happens now?" Griffin asked.

Dennis laughed and winked at Hetty again. "The honeymoon, of course."

Griffin snorted, turned to Karl, and said, "I mean, what happens to us? Me and Grace? Are we your kids now, or what?"

"Yes, you are," Karl replied as he settled a white woolen shawl, his wedding gift to Hetty, over her shoulders.

Hetty was wearing the white silk-and-lace wedding

gown Mrs. Templeton had brought with her, which Mr. Lin, who'd turned out to be pretty good with a needle, had altered for her during their last week on the trail. Karl's gift, the shawl, had been delivered to her hotel room after he'd escorted her there.

As Mr. Lin draped the shawl around Hetty's shoulders before they left for the church, Grace had remarked that she really appreciated Hetty marrying Karl, especially when he wasn't much to look at.

Mr. Lin had stepped in front of Hetty, looked up at her with his dark, inscrutable eyes, and said in a quiet voice, "Confucius say: 'Everything have beauty. Not everyone see it.'"

Hetty had pondered that thought ever since. She glanced at her brand-new husband, looking for the beauty Mr. Lin had suggested was there somewhere. She didn't see it.

"I'm hungry," Griffin said. "When do we eat?"

"Right now," Karl replied. "I've got dinner planned at the hotel."

"I wish I could join you," Dennis said, "but there's some business that needs to get finished if we're going to leave for the Bitterroot first thing tomorrow morning." He grinned at Karl. "Or rather, whenever the two of you are up and ready to get moving."

Hetty watched her husband flush again at such a blatant reference to the fact that Karl might want to linger in bed the morning after his wedding. She couldn't believe Dennis was abandoning his best friend on his wedding day—for business. Worst of all, she couldn't imagine sitting through a dinner at the hotel alone with Karl. Or rather, alone with Karl and Grace and Griffin.

"You married good now, Boss," Mr. Lin said.

Hetty had forgotten about the Chinaman, who'd come to the church and sat in a back pew to watch the ceremony.

Mr. Lin focused on Hetty, then Karl, and said, "Confucius say: 'Whatever you do, do with whole heart.'"

Easy for him to say, Hetty thought bleakly. He wasn't the one who'd just given up any hope of ever having that fairy tale ending. On the other hand, she was entirely responsible for ruining her chance at finding love and happily ever after, so what did it matter who she married? She was getting exactly what she deserved.

Karl's brown eyes crinkled at the corners as he smiled. "That seems like easy advice for a newly married man to take." He put a hand on Bao's shoulder and added, "Thank you again for bringing my bride safely here to me."

Mr. Lin shared a surreptitious glance with Hetty, then bowed his head. "Just doing job, Boss."

Hetty wasn't ready to be alone with her husband. Maybe Mr. Lin could provide the buffer she needed this first evening between herself and Karl. After weeks on the trail, she knew the Chinaman far better than the stranger she'd wed. She blurted, "Will you join us for supper, Bao?"

Mr. Lin shook his head. "So sorry. Have work. You enjoy first supper with husband."

Hetty watched with a sinking heart as he turned and marched back down the aisle.

"Are we gonna eat or what?" Griffin asked.

"Griffin," Grace said in a soft voice. "Don't be a brat."

"I'm hungry, too," Karl said. "Shall we all go?" He

gestured down the center aisle toward the door to the church.

Griffin dashed for the door, with Grace yelling, "Don't run in church!" as she sprinted after him.

Hetty saw Karl was smiling as he watched the two rambunctious children charge down the aisle. It was a beautiful smile, one that traveled from his mouth, with its slightly crooked front tooth, all the way to his brown eyes, which—Hetty would have sworn— shimmered with dazzling golden flecks in the light streaming through the stained-glass window.

A moment later Karl turned to her, the smile gone, the golden flecks gone, his face as ordinary as it had been when she'd promised to be his wife for as long as she lived.

"Shall we go, Mrs. Norwood?"

"I prefer Hetty."

Another smile flickered on his lips but never appeared there. "I wanted to hear how it sounded. Mrs. Norwood, I mean."

Mrs. Norwood. Married to plain Mr. Norwood.

Hetty felt sad. Bad. Frustrated. Irritated. Why, oh, why had she agreed to marry this stranger when she wasn't the least bit attracted to him? How was she going to allow him the liberties of a husband? And why did he have to be so *nice*?

Most grown-ups would have yelled at the two kids for galloping down the aisle. Karl had *smiled* at them, accepting their exuberance as part of what made them Grace and Griffin. She couldn't help liking him, even if she wasn't attracted to him.

Hetty hoped mere liking was going to be enough to get her through the night to come. There was no going back now. She slipped her arm through Karl's and said, "I'm starved. I was too nervous to eat before the ceremony."

The smile appeared on his face again, and she found herself fascinated by that slightly overlapping front tooth. He pulled her close as he admitted, "I couldn't eat anything, either. I was nervous, too."

"You were?"

"It's not every day a man is lucky enough to marry the most beautiful woman he's ever seen."

"Oh." Hetty stared into Karl's brown eyes and realized the golden flecks were there again. "What a lovely thing to say."

He kept his gaze focused on hers, and Hetty felt her empty stomach fill with butterflies. She had no idea how to respond to such a compliment. She didn't want to lie and say she was happy with his looks, too, but it seemed she needed to say something.

His stomach growled, and Hetty was surprised into laughter.

Karl shot her a rueful look. "So much for impressing my new bride. Shall we go, Hetty? Supper awaits."

"Of course." Hetty refused to think about what came next. At least, not until after she'd filled her stomach. Maybe then there'd be no room left for the butterflies to take flight.

Chapter Five

"I'm so sorry," Hetty said.

"It was an accident," Karl replied as he dabbed at the wine staining his vest and trousers with the red-and-white-checked napkin he'd carried away with him when they'd left the hotel restaurant and headed upstairs to their room. "The boy didn't mean to do it."

The problem was, Hetty was pretty sure Griffin had known exactly what would happen when he'd reached for a bowl of butter in the center of the table. She suspected Griffin had tipped over the crystal glass simply to see what reaction Karl would have. If the boy was hoping for outrage, or a punishing slap, he'd been disappointed. Karl had laughed.

"I'm glad you did that," he'd said to Griffin as he swabbed his vest with his napkin. "I couldn't refuse Dennis's offer of a bottle of wine to celebrate, but I've never really liked the stuff."

"Your poor suit!" Grace had exclaimed before shooting daggers at Griffin.

Karl had merely shrugged. "I don't expect to be wearing this suit much. It'll be Levi's and plaid wool shirts and boots from now on."

Hetty had seen the smirk come and go on Griffin's face and realized she couldn't let the boy get away with such a prank. "Nevertheless, we shouldn't allow the stain to set," she said. "I believe we're all finished with supper."

"We're supposed to get apple pie for dessert!" Griffin protested.

"Yes, we *were* going to have apple pie," Hetty said. "Now I think you'll agree it would be unwise to force Karl to sit here while his suit gets ruined." She turned to Karl and said, "Shall we go?"

Hetty could see Karl was going to relent and stay for dessert, so she rose and said, "Time for bed, children."

"Serves you right," Grace muttered under her breath to Griffin as she got up from her chair.

Griffin said nothing, simply made a moue in acceptance of how he'd been outmaneuvered.

Hetty realized that by making Karl's suit a priority, she'd denied herself the opportunity to escape into the children's room to ready them for bed, thereby postponing the start of her wedding night. She did pause momentarily by the door to their room and said to Grace, "Don't stay up late. We have a very long day on the trail tomorrow."

"I wish we could stay here a little longer," Grace said, gazing wistfully at the soft, four-poster bed she and Griffin would be sharing. "I'm so tired of traveling."

"Our journey will be over soon," Hetty promised. "You heard Karl say our new log home will have soft beds for everyone."

"I can't believe Griffin did that," Grace whispered after Karl had moved across the hall to unlock the door to his and Hetty's room. "Or that Karl was so nice about it."

"It seems we've all been very fortunate," Hetty said. "But if you have any sway at all with Griffin, tell him he shouldn't push his luck."

"I will," Grace said fervently.

Hetty hugged the girl, then turned to join Karl, who'd been waiting patiently by the open door to their room, the wine-stained table napkin pressed against his wine-stained vest.

Her heartbeat ratcheted up as they entered the room and Karl closed the door behind them. The hotel room seemed small, perhaps because so much of it was taken up by the bed. After all the weeks of sleeping under the sky, Hetty felt trapped within the four stifling walls.

She hadn't noticed it when she'd changed out of her wedding dress before supper, but she suddenly became aware of the smell of woodsmoke pervading Mrs. Templeton's navy-trimmed, light blue traveling dress, which the other woman had often worn while sitting by the fire. Hetty suddenly found the smoky smell unbearable.

Unfortunately, to get rid of the smell, she'd have to remove the dress, and she wasn't willing to do that. At least, not until it was absolutely necessary.

Hetty turned away from the waiting, turned-down covers toward Karl, brushed the lapel of his suit coat, and said, "There's wine on this, too."

Karl shrugged out of the jacket and draped it over a nearby ladder-back chair in the corner, then began unbuttoning his vest.

Hetty realized that if Karl took off everything with a

wine stain, he'd soon be standing before her in his smalls. She quickly crossed the room to the pitcher and bowl sitting on a clothes chest, poured some water, then dampened the cloth sitting beside the bowl and crossed back to Karl, who stood at the foot of the bed.

"Let me help you with that," she said, pressing the damp cloth against his wool vest before he could remove it.

Karl took the cloth from her and threw it on a pillar table beside the door, along with the napkin he'd been using. "There's a very good Chinese laundry in town. I'll drop the whole suit off before we leave and have it returned to me the next time supplies are delivered to the Bitterroot."

"But—"

"There's something I'd much rather be doing than worrying about this suit," he said in a soft voice.

Hetty fought the panic she felt as Karl reached out to brush a handful of golden curls back over her shoulder. She shivered as his fingertips trailed down to rest at the base of her throat.

He met her gaze with those plain brown *earnest* eyes of his and said, "I can feel your pulse racing. You don't have to be afraid of me, Hetty. We have all night. We can take our time."

Hetty was pretty sure all the time in the world wasn't going to make her feel any less terrified. It would have been frightening enough to face a wedding night. But she would be spending it with a stranger she'd met that very day. Even that might have been bearable if her husband had been someone for whom she felt a spark of physical attraction. But that was not the case.

She immediately felt guilty for wishing Karl was more good-looking. Or even a little good-looking. *Oh, Hetty, how can you be so shallow?*

If that had been the extent of it, Hetty might have made it through the night. But she was mortally afraid Karl would discover that she couldn't possibly be the parents of those two children because she was a virgin. Could a man always tell? Was there any way to keep him from finding out?

The whole point of this mail-order marriage had been to save those two precious children from abandonment. Hetty had no choice except to bluff her way through her wedding night. She tried to smile and felt her mouth wobble. She tried again and didn't think she'd done much better until Karl said in a low, rumbling voice that sent a shiver down her spine, "I love your dimples."

Hetty lowered her gaze, unable to look at the man she planned to dupe—if he could be duped. Maybe he had no more experience than she did. Maybe he wouldn't realize she was a virgin. Hetty blurted, "Have you ever . . . uh . . ." She felt her throat tightening but swallowed over the knot and continued, "That is, do you know much about . . . I mean, have you . . ."

Karl looked more and more uncomfortable, and Hetty realized there was no way to ask what she wanted to know.

"Have you ever been in love before?" she finished.

She saw the flare of surprise—and relief—in his eyes before he said, "As a matter of fact, I haven't. Have you?"

Hetty hadn't expected him to turn the question back on her. Tears immediately filled her eyes as she thought of Clive Hamm, of his beautiful blue eyes, of his powerful shoulders, of his flashing smile. And of his last words of love to her as he lay dying in her arms, the victim of a gunshot wound he'd received in a confrontation with the man Hetty had been flirting with in order to make Clive jealous enough to propose.

"That was foolish of me," Karl said. "Of course you've been in love."

Because she'd supposedly been married. Only she hadn't. How different her life, and her sisters' lives, might have been if only she'd been willing to wait patiently for that proposal from Clive, instead of provoking that showdown. Mr. McMurtry and the Wentworth sisters would never have been forced to leave the wagon train, with all the disaster that had followed.

And Hetty wouldn't have ended up married to a man she didn't love. She sobbed and pressed her fisted hands against her mouth to keep from wailing aloud. She had no one to blame but herself for her current predicament. And the only way to make amends for all the harm she'd done was to be as good a wife to this man, and as good a mother to those children, as she possibly could.

"Please don't cry," Karl said, reaching for her fisted hands and opening them and taking them in his.

She blinked her eyes to force back the tears. "I'm sorry to be such a crybaby," she choked out.

"I know this must be difficult for you."

Hetty could see Karl was torn between exercising his rights as a husband and leaving the consummation for later. Hetty knew she ought to give in. Time wasn't going to change anything. She was still going to be a virgin a month from now. But wouldn't it be safer not to give Karl an excuse to leave her and the children behind in Butte when he discovered the truth?

She had to give him something. It was his wedding night, too, after all. She decided to offer kisses. That seemed safe and surely wouldn't be as difficult to bear as allowing Karl the more intimate rights of a husband. Hetty decided to speak before she lost her nerve.

"Would you kiss me, Karl?"

For once, what Karl was thinking wasn't revealed in his eyes, which remained focused steadily on hers.

Hetty closed her eyes, pursed her lips as she'd practiced in the mirror growing up, and waited.

She felt Karl's fingertips frame her face and then tilt it slightly sideways. She quivered in expectation when she felt his warm breath against her skin.

A moment later, the warmth was gone, and she heard him say, "Open your eyes, Hetty."

Hetty's eyelids felt heavy, and it took a great deal of effort to lift them. When she did, she found Karl's face close to her own. Why hadn't he kissed her?

The question must have been there in her eyes because he said, "How long since your husband died, Hetty?"

Hetty felt the flush start at her throat and steal onto her cheeks as she formulated the necessary lie. "It's been . . . uh . . . ."

"It isn't important how long ago you were widowed except—"

"He died after Griffin was born," Hetty blurted. "Of cholera," she added, because she'd watched Hannah's husband, Mr. McMurtry, die of cholera and could describe the symptoms if Karl asked.

"I'm sorry for your loss." Karl cleared his throat and added, "So it's been a great many years since you've . . . been a wife."

What a tactful substitution for *had intimate relations,* Hetty thought. She cleared her own throat and answered, "Yes, it has."

"Perhaps we should wait a while. What do you think?"

Hetty couldn't imagine any other man being so considerate on his wedding night as to offer his bride the option of forgoing the whole thing. If that was, indeed, what Karl was doing. "What are you saying?"

Karl let go of her and took a step back. "I'm proposing we postpone the wedding night."

Hetty felt enormous relief. And a startling amount of disappointment. What kind of man didn't want to make love to his bride on his wedding night?

A weak one.

A considerate one.

The warring thoughts led her to ask, "Is there something wrong with me?"

"Lord, no!" he said. "I want to take you in my arms and—"

"Then why don't you?" Hetty interrupted.

Karl looked taken aback, but that only lasted a second.

Hetty found herself encircled by astonishingly confident arms. She felt Karl's large hand—she'd noticed he had very large hands—on the back of her head, angling it for a kiss, and then felt his mouth capture hers.

She wasn't sure what she should feel, how she should act, so she followed Karl's lead.

It was a kiss that presumed experience. A kiss filled with need. A kiss that demanded a response.

Hetty fought panic as a frisson of desire skittered up her spine. Her body felt taut and ached with wanting . . . something.

Clive is barely cold in his grave. I shouldn't be feeling so much pleasure. I don't deserve a good man and a good marriage and a happy life.

Her arms were caught between their bodies, which made her feel trapped. She resisted the urge to struggle free, but her body mirrored the tension she felt in Karl's.

He was breathing hard.

She was afraid to take a breath.

His lips were soft.

Hers had pressed flat.

His arms pressed her close.

Her arms slid up to keep them apart.

Hetty was aware that she was fighting Karl at every turn. Subtly. Slightly. But surely.

She had to swallow, and did, but the kiss continued. This kiss was nothing like the two she'd exchanged with Clive. They'd both been short and furtive, a bare touching of lips in the darkness behind Clive's wagon, the risk of discovery too great for more intimacy.

This kiss seemed to go on forever, leaving her more and more terrified. She couldn't catch her breath. Her knees wanted to buckle. Her hips strained toward Karl's. Her breasts felt full, the tips hard and aching. Her heart pounded hard in her chest.

When Karl finally broke the kiss, Hetty felt relieved.

She was panting, breathless. And disappointed. And then relieved again. She kept her eyes lowered, unwilling to let him see either emotion.

She quivered when she felt his knuckle beneath her chin, gently urging her face upward. She resisted only a moment, then met his searching gaze. She wondered what he was looking for. She wondered whether she ought to say something. She wondered if he could tell it was only the fourth time she'd ever been kissed. She wondered if he had any inkling how scared she'd been.

And still was.

He released her and took a step back. "It's too soon."

Hetty knew she'd failed her first test as a wife. "I can do better." Her voice sounded as uncertain as she felt.

Karl shook his head, let out a deep sigh, and took another step back. "I can wait. Our first time together will be all the sweeter if you're willing."

How could he tell that she wasn't? "Are you sure you don't mind waiting?"

His features transformed into something quite extraordinary as his mouth tilted in a lopsided smile. "I keep reminding myself of something Bao once told me. Or rather, Bao quoting Confucius."

"What's that?" Hetty asked.

" 'The cautious seldom err.' "

Hetty's brow furrowed. Then she smiled at Karl and said, "Oh. I see. Better safe than sorry."

"Exactly. Which means I need to ask, do you need privacy to get ready for bed?"

Hetty felt her cheeks burning with embarrassment. She looked around the hotel room, which had a lacquered Chinese screen in one corner. She thought of how embarrassing it might be for Karl if he should run into Dennis downstairs, especially after all the jibes his friend had poked at Karl after their wedding. "I can change behind the screen," she said.

Was that relief she saw on Karl's face?

"Fine," he said. "Let me know when you're done, and I'll turn my back while you slip under the covers."

Hetty glanced sideways at the bed, which Karl still apparently intended to share with her. She hoped her concern didn't show on her face. After all, if Karl had wanted to consummate the marriage, he could have proceeded without stopping at a single kiss. He was her husband. It was his right to make her his wife. He'd said he was willing to wait. There was no reason to fear he would not.

Except this man was a stranger. Who knew whether he would pounce once she was wearing only a nightgown and lying in bed beside him?

"Karl," she began, determined to clarify the situation before she undressed. "How long did you have in mind that we should take to get to know each other?"

Karl shrugged. "I thought we'd let things progress naturally."

Hetty's heart took an extra, panicked beat. "Naturally?"

"You know, take one day at a time and see how we feel."

Hetty had no doubt how she'd feel tomorrow and the day after that and the day after that. *Reluctant.* "How will you know when the time is right?"

It took all Hetty's willpower to stand still as Karl took the few steps to close the distance between them. He reached out and cupped her cheek, smoothing his callused thumb over the blush that had risen there. She felt caught like a fish on a hook, desperate to escape, but held fast by the look in his serious brown eyes. Finally he said, "The time will be right when you tell me it's right."

Hetty heard herself swallow loudly over the painful knot in her throat. "You're leaving the decision up to me?"

"Entirely."

He turned her by the shoulders, gave her a friendly pat on the rump, and said, "Now go get ready for bed."

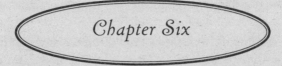

Chapter Six

Karl lay stiffly on his back on his side of the bed, so he wouldn't accidentally touch his brand-new wife. It had taken a long time for Hetty to fall asleep. Even so, she wasn't sleeping restfully. She tossed and turned and made soft, anxious noises. Conscience bothering her, he supposed, from all the lies she'd told.

Some wedding night. Not at all what he'd hoped, especially considering the fact that he wasn't marrying a woman who could be expected to have the normal fears of an unbroached bride. Pretty disappointing, actually.

The more Karl thought about it, the more he questioned why a girl—Hetty could only barely be called a woman—as beautiful as Hetty had been so willing to travel so far to marry a stranger. He felt sure she could have had her choice of men in Cheyenne, someone who would have provided a comfortable home for her and her children.

Why had she chosen to become a mail-order bride? What demons had forced Hetty to leave Cheyenne? From what—or whom—had she needed to escape? What had happened to the two different men he was more and more certain had fathered her two children?

Hetty must have been very, very young when she'd borne her daughter. And the boy must have gotten all his looks from his father, since he bore no resemblance whatsoever to his mother, or to his sister, for that matter.

Karl wished he wasn't so analytical. A really smart man would close his eyes to all the anomalies he'd found in his bride and simply enjoy her. Karl couldn't do that. Especially when it was so obvious that his bride found him wanting.

He'd felt her resistance to his kiss. It had been devastating. It had seemed wiser—safer for his ego—to back off than to continue. She'd agreed so quickly to postpone their wedding night that he hadn't tried to persuade her otherwise.

Karl knew he could please his wife in bed, given the chance. He'd had a good teacher, an older woman who'd tutored him in all the ways he could bring exquisite pleasure to his partner. But he wasn't going to force Hetty to accept his attentions. She'd clearly been reluctant even to kiss him, let alone venture into the sort of touching required to consummate their marriage.

It was true they barely knew each other. The few letters they'd exchanged had only given him a suggestion of what she might be like, and he was sure the reverse was equally true. A wedding night could be daunting even when the parties were well acquainted.

But Hetty was no virgin bride. She'd been married before. She wasn't unaware of what a husband might expect from her. Shyness he would have understood and respected. But Hetty's behavior had gone a step beyond that.

Karl hated to attribute her recoil to his looks, but that seemed the most obvious answer to the way she'd flinched from him. He knew physical attraction was a big part of sexual desire. How could he expect someone as beautiful as Hetty to find someone like him to her liking?

The problem was, there was nothing he could do to change his appearance. It was what it was. His only hope was to show his wife that he had other attributes that would make him a good spouse. To have her learn to like and, if possible, love him, so that his looks became irrelevant.

Karl made a disgusted sound, then looked at Hetty to see if he'd woken her. Looks were never unimportant, at least, not until old age. He and Hetty were both young, and she was even younger, he believed, than she'd claimed to be in her letters. He snorted softly. If she was twenty-eight, he was a cornstalk.

I have to be patient, he told himself. *I have to give her time.*

That solution was disturbing because of the evidence he had before him, in the persons of those two disparate children, that Hetty had a wandering eye. Was that why she'd wanted—needed—to leave Cheyenne? Had she been involved in some scandal with yet another man? What if she found someone more attractive to love, or make love to, before she fell in love with him?

Like Dennis.

Karl felt anew the *annoyance*—no, that word didn't begin to describe his feelings—the *anger* he'd experienced when his friend had kissed his bride so soundly.

Kisses meant nothing to Dennis. By the time his friend was seventeen and had left to seek his fortune as Jonas's man, Dennis had cut a wide swath through the willing girls in their neighborhood. Dennis had never questioned whether a woman found him attractive. He knew he was.

To Dennis, kisses were like stones along a riverbed, plentiful and common. To Karl, they were something precious, to be shared with someone special, like your brand-new wife. Karl hadn't kissed Hetty on the lips at the church because he'd wanted their first kiss as husband and wife to be savored between them in private.

Or maybe you had some inkling she might be unwilling, and you didn't want to be embarrassed if she turned her head.

That hadn't stopped his friend. Dennis had simply *given* her the kiss, as though Hetty would be happy to have it. Or maybe *taken* the kiss, as though Hetty wouldn't mind having it stolen.

Karl resented the hell out of having it stolen. Not that he'd ever say anything to Dennis. His friend would only laugh at him for being ridiculous. Dennis didn't take much of anything seriously. Except work. He took his work very seriously. His impressive physical appearance he simply took for granted.

Karl had compared himself all his life to Dennis and inevitably found himself wanting. Nevertheless, he'd kept Dennis as a friend because he would have felt petty cutting the acquaintance simply because he felt self-conscious—usually invisible—standing next to Dennis in a roomful of people.

Intellectually, Karl knew that looks didn't define a person. Character and kindness and intelligence and imagination and a hundred other things were far more meaningful in a relationship. Except, even in his chosen life's work, the study of flowers and trees and plants of every kind, appearance counted. The most colorful flowers attracted the most birds and butterflies and bees, which pollinated them, thus guaranteeing survival of the most stunning examples of the species.

Nature knew what it was doing.

Karl fisted his hands and clenched his teeth. He had to stop worrying about something over which he had no control. His wife would either fall in love with him, or she wouldn't.

Hetty moaned again in her sleep, and Karl carefully turned on his side to observe her in the moonlight streaming through the hotel window.

Her skin was flawless. Her nose was small and straight. Her eyelashes were long and lush and lay on high, wide cheekbones. Her lips were full and tempted him to taste them. A riot of curls framed her heart-shaped face on the pillow. Her shoulders, one of which was bared by the too-large nightgown were . . .

He was forming the words *creamy smooth* in his mind but stopped when he saw a puckered area of skin just below the line of her nightgown. He reached out and carefully moved the flannel lower, so he could see better in the moonlight.

It was a scar all right, a bad one. He surveyed the jagged circle of shiny, raised skin, which appeared to be only part of a terrible, newly healed wound. Bullet? Knife? The possibility that his new wife had recently been attacked seemed preposterous. Except, right there before his eyes was the wound to prove it had happened.

More alarming than the disfiguring wound was the fact that Hetty had chosen not to mention it. Surely such an assault would have merited a sentence in one of her letters. Unless this mutilation was the reason she'd needed to leave Cheyenne. It seemed more and more certain to Karl that his mail-order bride was running from someone in her past.

He wondered when and how Hetty planned to explain the wound. Maybe she wasn't planning for him to see it. Maybe she intended to stay garbed like a nun for the rest of their marriage. It was only by accident that he'd noticed the ragged, raised flesh in the moonlight. Ordinarily her nightgown would have hidden it.

Well, they would just see about that. When he made love to his wife, he planned to do it without a lot of clothing between them. He would see what she had to say about that scar when she had nothing left to hide behind.

Hetty rolled over and her nightgown fell open to reveal the luscious swell of her breast.

Karl groaned softly when he realized his body had responded urgently—and predictably—to the sight. If only his bride had kissed him back. It was agony to have this beautiful woman lying next to him and know it might be a very long time before he would be able to make love to her.

He slowly rose up on an elbow, leaving one hand free to reach for the curls on the pillow. Her hair was silky soft. He brushed a knuckle against her cheek, and she shifted her head back and forth, as though she'd been tickled by a feather.

Then he heard her say quite clearly, "No."

He withdrew his hand abruptly, then noticed she was repeating the word, even though she was still sound asleep.

"No no no No No NO!"

Her voice rose and became increasingly distraught. Her head moved from side to side, tears streamed from her eyes, and her hands and feet struggled beneath the covers.

Karl sat upright, laid a hand on one of her shoulders to shake her gently, and said, "Hetty, wake up. Hetty!"

But she was lost in whatever misery held her spellbound in her dreams. Karl lifted her into his arms to comfort her, holding her despite her efforts to be free. "Shh," he said. "It's all right, sweetheart. I have you."

Hetty's cries grew more frantic, her struggles more desperate, and Karl wondered if he'd made a mistake by taking her in his arms. But it was too late to back away. She was still sound asleep, and writhing as she was, she might fall off the bed if he let her go.

"Clive!" she cried. "Clive!"

She grabbed Karl around the neck, sobbing and making keening sounds of mourning. He heard pounding at the door, heard Grace begging to know what was wrong, but there was no way he could let go of Hetty to answer the door. "Come in!" he called.

Both children tumbled through the door. The boy kicked the door shut with his bare foot and stood there with his hands balled into fists. The girl crossed all the way to the bed, her eyes wide with fright, and demanded, "What are you doing to my mom?"

Instead of answering, Karl asked, "Who's Clive?"

The girl frowned, rubbed her nose, and shrugged.

Apparently, Clive wasn't one of the two fathers. He turned to the boy and said, "Griffin?"

"How the hell should I know?"

"Don't use that language," Karl said in a voice made harsh by the children's inability, or unwillingness, to identify the mysterious Clive. Whoever the man was, Hetty was grieving the loss of him. Karl wondered if Clive had wounded Hetty and run or whether Hetty had left an angry paramour behind in Cheyenne.

"She's wailin' like somebody died," Griffin said belligerently. "What did you do?"

Karl noticed that despite the boy's concern for his mother, he stayed out of reach. He wondered if Clive, or some other man, had hit Griffin in the past. He wanted to say, *I won't hurt you, boy,* but the painful knot in his throat made it difficult to speak. At last, he was able to clear his throat and said, "She's having a bad dream."

"So wake her up," Griffin replied.

Karl began, "I don't know if I—"

Grace simply took action. She grabbed her mother's shoulder, shook her hard, and said, "Wake up, Mom! Wake up!"

Hetty awoke with a cry of alarm. Her hands jerked defensively, and she hit Karl hard in the nose.

"Ow!" He used one hand to rub at his nose to ease the sting, while he kept the other wrapped around her.

She looked confused, and then startled to find herself in his embrace.

He let her go completely and said, "You were having a bad dream."

"Oh." She scooted away from him, then took in the presence of Grace and Griffin. "What are you two doing in here?"

"You were crying pretty loud," Grace said.

Hetty slid her bare feet over the edge of the bed, then reached out and pulled Grace into her arms. "I'm so sorry I worried you, Grace."

Karl got out of bed on the opposite side, found a handkerchief in his coat pocket, and handed it to Hetty.

She swiped at her eyes then blew her nose. When she was done, she turned her gaze to her son and said, "Griffin, are you all right?"

He grimaced. "I ain't gettin' any sleep."

"I'm *not* getting any sleep," Hetty corrected with a smile.

"Yeah. I kinda figured that when I heard you bawlin'," he said, misunderstanding, obviously on purpose, the correction to his grammar.

Karl wondered why the boy had such poor grammar if Hetty always made a point of correcting him. Maybe he did it as a means of rebelling against his mother's authority, although he was awfully young for that. Karl glanced at Grace, who crossed her arms tightly to cover what he now saw was a budding chest, undeniable without the shawl that had concealed it earlier in the day.

Karl frowned. He had to stop believing anything

these three had told—or were telling—him. It was all a pack of lies.

Griffin was clearly older than seven. Grace was definitely older than nine. Chances were good they had different fathers, one of whom had not been named Clive. And Hetty, his supposedly perfect and perfectly beautiful wife, was most likely a harlot.

Chapter Seven

Hetty hadn't slept much the rest of the night. She'd been afraid of dreaming again. Clive's blue eyes had been so piercing in her dream, it was as though he was right there, dying in her arms. She could hear his voice as though he were in the room with her, hear his awful death rattle as he whispered, "I love you, Hetty."

In the morning, as they began their journey to the Bitterroot Valley, Hetty had tried several times to engage Karl in conversation in order to banish Clive from her mind. Karl answered with one word or not at all. He seemed lost in thought. She wondered if he was usually so taciturn. She hoped not. The thought of living the rest of her life with this stern, silent man was disheartening.

It didn't help that Griffin was acting so prickly. Karl had told the boy that it was his job to collect firewood and put it in the sling under the Conestoga wagon. Even though Griffin had done the same job during the journey from Cheyenne to Butte, he'd objected by retorting, "I'm not your slave."

"No firewood, no supper," Karl had replied.

"That seems a bit harsh," Hetty had argued.

Karl had turned to her and said, "No firewood, no supper. And that's final."

Griffin had shot Karl a look of pure loathing and hadn't picked up a single piece of firewood all day. Grace, of course, had made up for it by filling the canvas tarp slung under the wagon to overflowing. Hetty wondered if it would make a difference to Karl. She dreaded the confrontation she could see coming when they stopped for supper.

Unfortunately, Karl's reticence and Griffin's defiance weren't her only problems. Karl and Dennis were riding horseback alongside the covered wagon, which was being driven by Mr. Lin. She and the two children were walking behind the wagon. Karl frequently rode ahead to scout the trail, leaving her alone with Dennis. An hour ago, Dennis had dismounted and tied his horse to the back of the wagon so he could walk beside her.

Hetty would have preferred to avoid the attractive man entirely. Dennis was as talkative as Karl was quiet. She kept hoping to find something offensive or boastful in his behavior that would make him unlikable. But Dennis didn't talk about himself. He told funny, engaging stories about Karl.

Hetty couldn't help noticing the way Dennis's blue eyes crinkled at the corners when he laughed. How his laugh created deep creases around his mouth. How white and straight his teeth were. How the hint of a beard darkened his cheeks and chin and made him look ruggedly handsome. How he stood head and shoulders above her, making her feel protected by his size and strength.

The result was that she felt awful. Guilty and ashamed. She shouldn't be admiring Dennis Campbell so much. She shouldn't be wishing she was married to him instead. She shouldn't be wondering what it would have been like if *he* had been the one to take her in his arms last night and kiss her. Why did he have to be so charming and funny and amiable? Why couldn't he have told mean stories about Karl, so she could detest him for being disloyal to his friend?

"We were at this fancy dress ball in New York, and Karl reached into his pocket and pulled out a pressed pink and white flower," Dennis said. "Karl said it was a bitterroot blossom. Apparently, it's what this valley we're headed to is named for, because so many of them grow there."

"Why would he take something like that to a ball?" Hetty wondered aloud. What she really wanted to know was *for whom* Karl had brought a pressed flower to the ball.

"Who knows?" Dennis said. "Karl proceeded to give us a lecture about the dried-up thing. He said Meriwether Lewis had collected a bunch of bitterroot specimens in 1806, which is why this famous botanist, Frederick Pursh, gave it the scientific name *Lewisia rediviva*. And you won't believe this. Karl said that the Flathead and Kootenai and Nez Perce eat it!"

"Are you sure he said the Indians *eat* it?" Hetty asked. "With a name like bitterroot it can't taste very good."

From behind them, Hetty heard Karl say, "They remove the inner core—the heart, if you will—before they cook it, which is supposedly the bitter part. Or they let it sit for a year or two, which makes it less bad tasting."

Hetty turned and stared up at Karl, who'd ridden up behind them, but she kept walking backward to keep up with the wagon. "How did you end up behind us? I thought you rode out to check the trail ahead of us."

"I was looking for a stream that's supposed to be north of here, so we'll have water when we stop for supper."

"Did you find it?" Dennis asked.

"It's a mile or so ahead," Karl replied. "Would you like to take a ride and see it?" he asked Hetty.

"What would I do for a horse?"

"You can ride behind me," Karl suggested.

"Take mine," Dennis offered, untying his horse's reins from the back of the wagon and handing them to Hetty. Instead of asking her if she could mount on her own, he simply put his hands on either side of her waist and lifted her so she could throw a leg over the buckskin.

The instant she was in the saddle, Dennis removed his hands. There was nothing disrespectful about what he'd done. She might have been his sister or some stranger he was helping. Nevertheless, Hetty felt breathless. Her skin felt scorched where his hands had touched her. She glanced quickly at Karl and saw that his lips had become a thin, censuring line.

I didn't ask Dennis to help me, she felt like saying. *What was I supposed to do? Complain? I'm on the horse, so let's go.*

Hetty realized the reason she felt compelled to defend herself against that look of disapproval was because she was, in fact, guilty of finding Dennis attractive. Of feeling something when he touched her, even if it was only his hands at her waist to set her on a horse. It wasn't her fault Dennis had walked with her and talked to her. He couldn't help being charming and entertaining and handsome.

She'd ignored her feelings of attraction as best she could because she knew the consequences of jealousy. Unless Karl could read her mind, there was no reason for him to feel suspicious, because his friend had done nothing wrong.

"You said in your letters that you were a competent horsewoman," Karl said. "Are you all right on that mount?"

Hetty realized that Grace must have written in one of her letters to Karl that his mail-order bride knew how to ride, and he wanted to confirm that she actually could. Hetty didn't blame him for checking. Karl might not be handsome, but he was a long way from stupid. Hetty wondered how long she and the two children were going to get away with all the lies they'd told.

Luckily, before the Great Chicago Fire, Hetty had spent long hours riding with her twin in Lincoln Park, which was renamed after the assassinated president. "I can ride," she said.

"Then let's go."

Karl kicked his horse into an easy lope, and Hetty did the same, keeping pace with him.

"Did you have a nice talk with Dennis?" he asked.

"He told a lot of funny stories. About you."

Karl eyed her askance. "That must have been entertaining."

Hetty lifted her chin and said, "It was." She wasn't going to apologize for enjoying Dennis's banter. Karl could learn a thing or two from his friend. Hetty shivered and decided the cold was more noticeable because she was moving faster on horseback, or perhaps because the wagon was no longer cutting off the brisk wind.

"You need a warmer coat," Karl said.

"It seems so," she agreed. Hetty waited for Karl to continue the conversation, but he said nothing more. The silence was uncomfortable, so she said, "What kind of dangers were you expecting to find ahead on the trail?"

"The Salish signed a treaty a couple of years ago, but there's still the occasional renegade out there. And the terrain is tricky. There are gullies and cliffs we'll need to avoid."

Hetty had a sudden memory of Mrs. Templeton falling backward, of that long scream that had suddenly stopped. She shuddered and made a sound of distress.

"Are you all right?" Karl asked.

Hetty bit the inside of her cheek to keep from confessing everything. It was horrible to have tricked Karl into marriage. Horrible to be lying to him so much and so often. But the consequences of telling the truth might be dire for Grace and Griffin, so instead of spilling her guts, she said, "I'm fine."

"You had a look on your face like you were in pain."

"I'm all right," Hetty insisted.

Karl frowned, and Hetty felt her heart sink. Lies upon lies. All this deception weighed heavily on her conscience. She wondered whether Karl would really abandon the children if she simply told him the truth. All of the truth.

Hetty realized immediately that she couldn't do that until the marriage was consummated, and they were truly husband and wife. She couldn't take the chance that Karl would call the whole thing off. Grace and Griffin had nowhere else to go. She would never—could never—abandon them, but she was unable to support them on her own.

But an accounting was coming. She'd learned in Sunday school that houses built on sand could never stand in a storm. Disaster lay ahead, unless she could figure out some way to square things with Karl.

Out of the blue, Karl asked, "How many men have there been in your past?"

Hetty yanked her horse to a stop so abrupt he reared. It took her a moment to get the buckskin under control. Once she did, she stared wide-eyed and white-faced at Karl. "What do you mean?"

"Let's clear the air," Karl said in a harsh voice. "I know Grace and Griffin had different fathers. I want to know how many other men have enjoyed your favors."

Hetty stared at him, aghast. She'd known Grace and Griffin weren't Mrs. Templeton's children, but she'd never imagined they had different fathers. Then she realized what else he'd suggested. She'd never let any man into her bed, let alone an army of them! "How dare you accuse me—"

"Who's Clive?" he interrupted.

Hetty's heart suddenly began beating so hard she thought Karl must be able to hear it. "How do you know about Clive?"

"You were yelling his name in your sleep."

"Oh."

"So you're not denying he exists?"

"He's dead," she said flatly. "He was killed."

"By another one of your lovers?"

Hetty thought she might faint. She'd never had a lover, but she'd flirted with another man to make Clive jealous. She kicked her horse to escape back to the wagon, but Karl caught the reins and pulled her mount to a halt.

"Were you in love with him?"

"Yes, I loved him! So what? Clive's dead, and I'm married to you."

That shut him up for a moment. But only a moment. He shot back, "How long ago did he die?"

Hetty knew to the day when Clive had died, but she didn't think she should share that with Karl. "A few months ago," she hedged.

Karl winced. "You were corresponding with me a few months ago."

"After Clive died I was looking for a new start." Hetty was tempted to add more, to embellish the lie. But her stomach was churning, and she was afraid it would erupt if she kept telling whoppers.

"So you're still grieving." Karl made it a statement rather than a question. Then he muttered, "Well, I suppose that answers one question."

"What's that?"

He met her gaze and said, "Why you resisted my kiss last night."

"Oh." Hetty's throat had swollen closed, preventing more speech. She hung her head, feeling anew the overwhelming remorse for what she'd done. And for what she was doing. She wished fervently she could go back and give Mr. Lin a different answer. But it was too late to make some other choice. She was trapped.

"Look at me, Hetty."

She lifted her gaze and glared resentfully into Karl's brown eyes, which glowered back at her. She felt a shudder of fear run through her. The man looking at her now was different from the one she'd married. There was nothing ordinary or mild mannered about this formidable man.

"I don't care what you did in the past," he said. "That's over and done. We start new from here. But I want the whole truth. What else haven't you told me?"

Hetty wanted so much to tell him about Grace and Griffin. But she didn't dare. "Nothing."

"There's nothing else? Everything's out in the open?"

Hetty wondered what else it was he expected her to confess. She decided to tell him how difficult life had been for all of them in the past, and began, "The children had—"

"I know they had different fathers," Karl interrupted. "I don't care whether you got pregnant before you were married, or cheated on your former husband. That's between you and him."

Hetty stared at Karl aghast. "Is that what you think?"

"I'm a botanist, Hetty. I study the biology of plants. Which is how I know Grace and Griffin are at most half siblings and likely older than the ages you gave me."

Hetty didn't know what to say. All those lies brought into the open should have cleared the air, but she felt suffocated by the truth. Or at least, as much of the story they'd concocted as Karl had been able to unravel. Luckily, he still seemed to believe she was Grace and Griffin's mother.

"What do you want from me?" she asked.

"I want you to stop lying," he said bluntly.

Hetty's face felt hot. She was having trouble meeting Karl's gaze, but she made herself look him in the eye when she said, "All right. Is that all?"

"Do your grieving, Hetty. Get over Clive. Because there's only room for one man in this marriage."

Chapter Eight

Karl offered a tin plate of beef and beans to Hetty that Bao had prepared and said, "Eat up."

She stared at the plate without taking it. They'd stopped for the day at the stream, even though the sun hadn't yet started down. "If Griffin can't eat supper, I'm not eating, either."

Karl shot a look in Griffin's direction. The boy was sitting on a dead log whittling hard and fast so the shavings landed in the fire, creating flares of yellow light.

"Griffin's being punished for not doing his chores," Karl said. He held the plate out to her. "Here. Take it."

Hetty crossed her arms over her chest. "No."

"If Mom and Griffin aren't eating, neither am I," Grace chimed in, crossing to stand beside Hetty.

"If nobody else is eating, guess I'd better put down my plate," Dennis said, grinning at Karl from his seat on a flat stone as he set his plate down.

Karl felt frustration welling up inside him. The wind hissed angrily through the evergreens and he felt like joining in. He was being treated like the bad guy here, when he was only trying to instill a sense of responsibility in a growing boy. He glanced toward Bao, who sat on the other end of the same log as Griffin, calmly smoking his long clay pipe. "I know you have an opinion, Bao. Let's have it."

"Confucius say: 'To go beyond is as wrong as to fall short.'"

Karl's balled fists landed on his hips. "What the hell does that mean?"

"It means your punishment doesn't fit the crime," Hetty said. "It's too harsh. I know what it feels like to go to bed hungry, and no child of mine is ever going to suffer like that."

Karl wondered again about the woman he'd married. Going to bed hungry? What kind of desperate life had Hetty been leading before she'd become his bride?

"And I wish you wouldn't swear in front of the children," she added.

"Hell and damnation," Karl muttered under his breath.

Hetty glared at him, her arms still crossed over her chest like a schoolmarm, and tapped her toe in disapproval.

Karl looked to Dennis for support, but his friend had settled a booted ankle on the opposite knee and was focused on rolling a smoke. Karl glanced toward Griffin and saw the boy was smirking at him in triumph.

He turned to Hetty. "Am I that boy's father now, or not?"

Hetty looked startled by the question. "What do you mean?"

"I think the question was pretty simple," Karl said. "Yes? Or no?"

"Yes," Hetty said. "But—"

"But nothing," Karl interrupted. He crossed to Griffin and said, "Put that knife away and come with me."

The boy didn't look nearly so confident with Karl towering over him. Griffin glanced toward Hetty, who was too far away to be any help, then up at Karl and blustered, "I don't have to do what you say."

Karl turned to Hetty again. "Yes? Or no?"

It was easy to read the myriad emotions crossing Hetty's face: fear, anxiety, hope, reluctance, anxiety, fear, and finally hope again. "Griffin, put away your knife and do as your father says."

Griffin's chin took on an angry, stubborn tilt as several more shavings flared in the fire. "He's not my pa."

Karl was watching Griffin as Grace said quietly, "This is what we dreamed about Griffin. A mother *and* a father. A real family." Grace's eyes brimmed with tears that glittered in the setting sunlight.

Griffin took one look at her and snapped, "Fine!" He threw the piece of wood, which Karl realized had become a horse's head with a flying mane, into the fire. Then the boy stood, stuck the sharp knife into a worn leather sheath tied to his belt, and said, "Let's go."

"Karl!" Hetty called out to him.

He stopped and glanced at her over his shoulder. "What?"

Her heart was in her eyes. *Don't hurt him. Be gentle. He needs love, not pain.* But she only said, "He's just a little boy."

The sudden knot in his throat surprised Karl and kept him from saying anything as he followed Griffin away from the fire. There was still enough sunlight to see in the grassy circle where they'd camped, but Griffin kept going until they reached a Douglas fir at the edge of the clearing, where the boy's sullen face was lost in the deepening shadows.

Griffin searched out a white-trunked aspen among the stand of pungent evergreens, peeled a switch from one of the bare, wind-whipped branches, and handed it to Karl. "Here. Go ahead and give me some licks. I deserve it."

Karl took the switch without thinking, then searched out the gleam of the boy's dark eyes in the shadows and said, "I know it must have been difficult for you and Grace to leave your home in Cheyenne to come to the Montana Territory."

Griffin snorted. "Not hardly."

"Why not? What was wrong with it?"

Griffin opened his mouth to speak and snapped it shut again.

Karl waited him out.

Finally, Griffin said, "Grace is the one who wanted a pa, not me. I was happy with the way things were."

"With just you and Grace and your mother, you mean," Karl said.

Griffin kicked at a pile of rotten leaves with the toe of his boot. "Yeah. With just us."

"Your ma said your father died shortly after you were born, and that you haven't had a father for most of your life. I'd like to be your pa if you'll let me."

"I don't see the big deal about having a pa. All you've

done so far is order me around and ask me to work like a dog."

Karl choked back the laugh that sought voice because he knew it wouldn't help his efforts to discipline the boy. He tried to remember what role his own father had played in his life. Mostly, he'd been absent. Or absorbed in projects with Karl's older brother.

Karl had never really thought much about parenting his mail-order bride's children, because they were supposedly seven and nine—still young enough to be tied to their mother's apron strings. Whatever his age, Griffin was already clever enough to manipulate the world around him. He needed a man to guide him and set an example for him.

Karl had thought about the kind of father he wanted to become, which was the kind of father he'd wished he had. "Fathers teach their sons to be men of character and honesty," he said. "They teach the importance of working hard to get what you want, of being responsible for yourself, and taking good care of those you love."

"I take care of myself just fine," Griffin retorted. "I don't need help from anyone."

"What about taking care of those you love?"

"Grace is pretty good at taking care of herself, too," Griffin said.

"What about your mother?" Karl said. "If I'm not mistaken, she gave up her supper to make sure you didn't go without. Seems to me your sister joined her without a second thought. I figure they're both pretty hungry right about now because you were too proud to accept your punishment."

Griffin hung his head and shuffled his toe over the golden pile of aspen leaves again. In a low voice he mumbled, "You can whip me now if you want."

Karl broke the switch in half and threw it aside. "I have a far worse punishment than that in mind for you."

Griffin looked up at him, the whites of his eyes visible, his shoulders braced for whatever blow was on the way. "I'm not afraid. Do whatever you want."

"Fine. Since Grace did your job for you today, you can do her job for the rest of the week."

It took Griffin a moment to process what he'd said. Then he blurted, "You want me to *wash dishes*? That's a girl's job!"

"Bao does it all the time. I intended for Grace to help him, but I think under the circumstances, you should take her place for a week."

"I hate washing dishes."

"All the better," Karl said. "I'll expect you to fill up that tarp under the wagon with wood this coming week as well."

"You want me to do my job *and* Grace's job? That's not fair!"

"I suspect you've already figured out that life's not fair." Karl didn't know what he'd do if Griffin refused to accept his punishment. He didn't think a beating would do much good, and he was plumb out of other ideas.

Griffin's lower lip was caught in his teeth. He shot a glance at Grace, who sat on the log he'd vacated, along with Hetty, whose arm was around his sister. At last, his chin came up and he said, "All right. I'll do your stupid chores. I won't even eat any supper tonight. But you gotta let Grace eat. She used to go without a lot, and now she kind of panics when there's nothing for supper."

Karl's eyes narrowed, and he glanced toward Hetty. What kind of life had this family been leading? A hard one, for sure. It had never occurred to him that Hetty's beauty wouldn't have been a solution to any and all problems. Apparently not.

"Go ahead and eat," Karl said. "You'll need your strength to wash all those dishes." He put out his hand. "Do we have a deal?"

Griffin spat on his palm, accepted the offered hand, and said, "Deal."

Karl put a hand on Griffin's shoulder to head him back toward the fire, but the boy shrugged out from under it and scampered back to join his mother and sister. Hetty bent down to listen as Griffin spoke with Grace.

Karl felt his heart jump when Hetty smiled at him. She spoke to the children, then turned and walked to meet him at the edge of the forest. She reached out both of her hands, which he took in his own.

"You are so wise," she said in a voice soft enough not to be heard by the children.

"It was all I could think of to do."

"It's perfect," Hetty said. "Griffin will surely think twice before he refuses to do his share in the future."

Hetty suddenly seemed to realize that her hands had found their way to his chest, with his hands closed around them. She flushed as she pulled free.

Karl opened his hands and let her go. It felt as though

he were releasing a wild bird, startled to find itself captive and equally surprised to realize it was free to fly away.

As she turned to leave he blurted, "I want this marriage to work, Hetty."

She turned back to him, her face filled with concern. "So do I."

He wished he hadn't started this conversation, but now that he had, he might as well finish it. "Fidelity is important to me."

He watched her swallow hard before she replied, "To me, too."

"You'll be surrounded by men at the camp," he continued. "Bao will do most of the cooking, but he'll need your help serving the men. And, of course, if any of the loggers is injured, you'll be tending to his wounds."

"I expected all of that," Hetty said.

Karl was stuck. Hinting wasn't going to do the job. He didn't want to accuse Hetty outright of being promiscuous, even though that was his fear. He needed to make his feelings plain before they arrived in the valley. "I guess what I'm saying is, there will be plenty of temptation to stray."

The blood left Hetty's face in such a rush that he thought she might faint.

"I would never . . . You can't believe that I . . . Why would you think . . . ?"

When she finished sputtering, Karl said, "What happened, Hetty? Why did you do it?"

He was asking for an explanation of why she'd gotten pregnant before her marriage to the one husband she'd supposedly had. Or why she'd cheated on him. Or both.

Karl waited for her to speak. And waited. She seemed to be struggling with some terrible inner turmoil.

At last, she looked into his eyes and said, "Haven't you ever done anything you regretted?"

Karl was silent for a moment, absorbing the remorse on her face. Then he said, "Yes. I have."

Hetty sighed. "Then you know how futile it can be to wish you'd done things differently. You can't undo what's done. You can only move forward and hope to be a better person."

Karl reached out and caught her hand. She tried to pull free, but he held on and drew her closer. He swallowed over the painful lump in his throat and said, "That's all I can ask."

Her voice was so soft he could barely hear her as she said, "I promise I will never give you cause to mistrust me, Karl."

It was too late for that. He wasn't absolutely certain he'd heard two honest sentences in a row since he'd met her. But there were other things far more important to him than her past.

Will you ever be glad to be my wife? Will you ever be able to love me?

Karl knew better than to ask. He was very much afraid there was nothing about him that caused Hetty's heart to take an extra beat.

He caressed her cold hand. "I'm looking forward to getting to know you, Hetty." He opened her clutched fingers one by one as he continued, "To unfolding the petals of a beautiful blossom one by one, until I know everything there is to know about you."

She laughed nervously. "There's no need to court me, Karl. I'm already your wife."

"Precisely," he said. "I plan to keep my vows, too, Hetty. To honor you. And to cherish you."

Her eyes were focused on his mouth. He wondered if it was his mouth, or the words coming out of his mouth, that she found so entrancing. He leaned down, closing the distance between them.

He heard her gasp as their lips met and waited for her to pull away. But she didn't. He was afraid to breathe, afraid he would break the spell.

Her lips pressed back against his, and her breathing became erratic. Her body began to tremble.

He wanted to take her in his arms and hold her and promise her everything would be all right. That he would love her and take care of her and their children for the rest of their lives.

Abruptly, she ended the kiss and stared into his eyes, looking unhappy and confused.

He wanted to say something to comfort her, but he had no idea what she wanted or needed or expected to hear.

She freed herself from his grasp and said, "I've got to make sure the children get fed." Then she turned and hurried back toward the fire.

Karl stayed where he was. He'd never imagined that being married, and becoming an instant stepfather, would be so full of complications. He wished he knew more about Hetty's life before he'd met her. The letters she'd written, filled with wit and humor, had carefully concealed the dire life she and her children must have been leading.

Karl was filled with curiosity about his new family. And with concern that he would never be able to win his wife's love.

Patience. Persistence. Karl had both qualities. It looked like he was going to need them. He wanted Hetty willing when he finally made her his wife. He wanted her as eager to consummate their marriage as he was. He wanted their joining to be joyful and exciting and immensely pleasurable.

He wanted the moon and the stars.

Karl shook his head as he laughed at himself. It never hurt to reach for what you wanted. Sometimes, a lot of the time, if you tried hard enough, you got it. Karl wasn't sure how he was going to manage it, but somehow, he was going to make his wife fall in love with him.

Chapter Nine

"What is this one called, Karl?" Grace asked, holding up a yellowed leaf she'd plucked from a stalk growing near the trail.

"You're never gonna stump him, Grace," Griffin said in disgust. "He's probably been making up names for all these plants, anyway. How would we know any different?"

"You can give up if you want, Griffin," Grace said, skipping along beside Karl's horse as he examined the two-inch-wide, heart-shaped, coarsely-toothed leaf she'd handed up to him. "But I plan to win the prize."

"We don't even know what the prize is," Griffin scoffed. "Or if there even is a prize. He's probably making that up, too."

Hetty stopped her own search for a leaf long enough to say, "You can't win if you won't play, Griffin."

"It's getting hard to find anything Karl hasn't already identified," he grumbled.

Karl wondered if Griffin realized what he'd admitted by that statement. Even if the boy wouldn't play, he'd been watching and learning. Bao had suggested the game one morning two weeks ago, and Karl had gone along with it. The children would present Karl with leaves which he had to identify. Whoever stumped him would win a prize. Dennis had promised to provide the prize, confident that it wouldn't be necessary, since Karl was an exceptional botanist. And, indeed, Karl hadn't yet been baffled by anything he'd been shown.

"This is *Heuchera cylindrica*," he told Grace.

"*Heuchera cylindrica*," Grace repeated.

Griffin snorted. "Which is a fancy name for what?"

"The common name for this plant is alumroot," Karl said, handing the leaf back to Grace.

"What is it used for, Karl?" Grace asked.

"The Flatheads chew it to relieve stomach cramps."

"I'll just bet they do," Griffin muttered.

"Stomach cramps," Grace said as she studied the leaf.

Griffin made a face. "You don't have to repeat everything he says like it was handed down from on high."

"I want to learn," Grace said. "Don't you?"

"Why would I want to know that gumweed is a remedy for poison ivy, when I don't even know what poison ivy looks like? Or that pipsissewa tea breaks a fever? I ain't gonna be no doctor."

The boy might not want to learn, Karl thought with an inward smile, but his words proved he was absorbing a great deal of information.

"It's fun to know the way all these plants can be used," Grace argued.

"I'm gonna try that kinnikinnick for sure," Griffin said with a grin. "Soon as I can find some tobacco to mix it with."

Grace grimaced and shook her head, then loped off to look for another leaf.

Trust the boy to remember a plant that the Indians mixed with tobacco to make it taste less strong when smoked, Karl thought. He was amused, rather than upset, because the chances of Griffin encountering wild tobacco in the Bitterroot Valley to mix with kinnikinnick were slim to none.

"I've got one!" Hetty announced triumphantly, running up to Karl.

Despite his supposed disinterest, Griffin asked, "Are you sure it's a new one?"

Finding something Karl hadn't already identified was getting harder and harder the closer they got to their destination, but even Karl was surprised that no one had yet found a plant he didn't know. He'd studied hard, but he hadn't realized just how well he knew the plant life in the Montana Territory.

Karl took the withered leaf from her and examined it carefully. At last he said, "You win the prize, Hetty."

"I do?"

"She does?" Grace said, stopping in her tracks, her face crestfallen.

"We finally found one you don't know?" Griffin said with a combination of disbelief and satisfaction.

"Oh, I know this one, all right," Karl said.

"Then why does Mom win?" Grace demanded.

"Because this plant proves we're near the end of our journey." Karl stopped his mount and stepped down to share Hetty's discovery with the two children, who'd crossed to stand beside her, anxious to learn what was so special about the rotted brown leaf he held in his hand. He perused it carefully, front and back.

"What is it, Karl?" Hetty asked.

Karl knew Hetty had been as avid in her search for leaves as the two children, and she looked giddy at the prospect of winning the contest. Her delight in the game had given her face a glow each morning and put stars of excitement in her blue eyes throughout each day. Karl had been enchanted. Or maybe bewitched. He was sorry to see the game come to an end.

Dennis rode up and asked, "Why the powwow?"

"Mom won the prize," Grace announced, disappointment in her voice.

Dennis dismounted and joined the group. "Don't tell me someone's found a leaf you can't identify, Karl."

"Then I won't," Karl said with a grin.

"What have you got there?" Dennis asked.

"A sign that our journey's nearing its end," Karl replied.

"I know what it is!" Griffin announced.

"You do not," Grace said, confronting him, hands on hips. "How could you?"

"I do, too! Because of what Karl said. It's a bitterroot leaf, isn't it, Karl?" Griffin said triumphantly.

Karl held out the dried-out, one-inch leaf, which had once been fleshy, but which had withered away and fallen off the plant in early June when the bitterroot flower appeared. "Yes, it is."

Griffin smirked at Grace and said, "Told you so!"

"What's the prize, Karl?" Grace asked.

"You'll have to ask Dennis," Karl replied.

"I didn't think I'd have to provide a prize," Dennis

said, chagrined. "Let me think a minute. Oh, by the way, who won?"

"I did," Hetty said, smiling broadly. She turned to Karl and said, "It's incredible how knowledgeable you are, Karl. How on earth did you learn all this? It seems you know every plant, flower, bush, and tree in the Montana Territory."

Karl felt himself flushing at the compliment. "It's simple, really. I studied."

"But it's *not* simple," Hetty replied. "More than once I've brought you a leaf that looked nothing like anything I'd seen before, but it turned out to be something you'd already identified."

"Leaves of the same plant can come in a lot of shapes and sizes," Karl said.

"I can't imagine how you remember it all," Hetty said, admiration plain in her voice.

"It seems to me like a pretty big waste of a perfectly good brain," Dennis interjected. "Why bother remembering so much useless information?"

"It's not useless," Karl said, stung by his friend's surprising criticism.

Dennis made a disparaging face. "It's not? Give me one good way you can use it."

Karl opened his mouth to defend himself, but Hetty beat him to it.

"You must not have been listening very closely, Dennis. Karl could feed us with his knowledge if we were hungry. He could treat us with his knowledge if we were sick. He knows which trees are best for building or burning. He knows which bushes will bear sweet fruit and which will bring forth the most beautiful flowers. And he knows which plants are harmful and should be avoided."

Karl was astonished to hear Hetty make the same argument he'd made so many times to his elder brother, who'd disdained the time Karl had spent learning about plants.

Unfortunately, Dennis had been present for too many of those arguments, and he responded exactly as Jonas so often had.

"Only a savage still uses leaves and roots for medicine. We don't need those native remedies," Dennis said snidely. "We have better, more effective ones. And we can grow wheat and corn to feed ourselves. We don't need to eat the damned bitter root of some flower."

Karl hadn't realized until this moment that Dennis shared Jonas's feelings about his work. It was shocking to hear him speak so rudely and crudely about Karl's study of plants and to dismiss his life's work so completely. He knew better than to argue. He'd never changed Jonas's mind. He wasn't likely to change Dennis's, either.

But it seemed Hetty wasn't done. "Maybe back East this sort of information isn't important," she said heatedly. "But you seem to forget we're heading into a wilderness where we have to expect the unexpected. Those savages you're condemning have managed to survive in this wilderness a very long time. So I don't see how anyone could call Karl's amazing knowledge about the plants that grow in the Montana Territory *useless*."

Dennis clapped, grinned at Karl, and said, "Bravo! I haven't heard such an impassioned defense of your work since the last time you argued with Jonas."

"I mean it!" Hetty said.

"I'm sure you do, sweetheart, but—"

"I'm not your sweetheart!" Hetty snapped, cutting him off. "And I'll thank you not to make fun of my husband."

Dennis looked thunderstruck by the attack. He shot a look at Karl that said, *What's going on? Where's that sweet, shy bride you married?*

Karl wasn't quite sure himself. But he felt his heart skip a beat when he looked into Hetty's admiring blue eyes.

She turned to Dennis and said, "When you're considering what to give me for a prize, Dennis, be sure it's something I can split three ways." She put an arm around Grace's waist, then tousled Griffin's eternally shaggy hair. "We all three deserve to share in the reward."

Griffin's chin dropped, and he murmured, "I don't."

"Of course you do!" Hetty said.

Griffin shook his head. "I didn't play, so I don't deserve to win. And I ain't taking charity."

"I'm *not* taking charity," Hetty corrected softly. "And it isn't charity when you earn it."

Karl could see the boy was only a moment from bolting. He put a hand on Griffin's shoulder to keep him in place. "Tell me, Griffin, what is *Populus balsamifera*?"

For a moment, the boy didn't answer, and Karl wondered if he'd made a mistake about how closely Griffin had been listening for the past two weeks. Then the boy's head came up, and he said almost defiantly, "That's the Latin name for cottonwood."

"How do the Indians use it?" Karl asked.

"They make a poultice of the leaves for bruises and sores and boils."

"Anything else?"

"Yeah. They make tea from the bark for whooping cough."

"Anything else?"

Griffin's eyes brightened. "They mix the buds in springtime with blood to make black paint that won't wear off."

"Anything else?" Karl repeated.

Griffin glanced at Dennis, then said, "Yeah. Cottonwood sap is sweet to eat, and so is the inner bark. And you can feed cottonwood twigs and bark to horses, 'cause they like it."

"Is that all?" Karl asked.

Griffin shot Dennis a cheeky look. "Cottonwood makes a good fire. It doesn't crackle, and it gives off a clean smoke."

"You were playing, Griffin, whether you knew it or not," Karl said. "You absolutely deserve a share of the prize."

Griffin jerked himself free and mumbled, "If you say so."

"I'm convinced," Dennis said. He turned to his saddlebags, reached inside, and came out with a leather pouch. He opened it and handed a long, thin strip of black licorice to Hetty and then to Grace. Finally, he offered one to Griffin, whose hands were stuck in his pockets. "Take it, kid. You earned it."

Griffin glanced toward Hetty, who nodded, then to Karl, who nodded and smiled encouragement. Finally, he looked at Grace and said, "You can have my share."

"I couldn't remember half what you did about cottonwoods," Grace said. "Take it, Griffin."

Karl could tell the boy didn't trust Dennis not to snatch the prize back at the last moment. He finally reached out, grabbed the licorice strip, and ran pellmell toward the front of the wagon. Grace shot an anxious look at Hetty and hurried after him.

"What the hell's wrong with that boy?" Dennis asked.

"Watch your language," Karl said.

"What the hell's wrong with *you*?" Dennis replied irritably. "You never minded my language before."

"It's not just you and me anymore. I have a wife and kids to think about."

Dennis snorted and muttered, "Son of a bitch." Then he held up his hands in surrender. "You win. I'll watch my language."

Karl met Hetty's gaze and saw approval there. His throat constricted with emotion. He shouldn't care what she thought. Henrietta Wentworth Templeton Norwood was a liar.

Over the past two weeks he'd begun to speculate that she must not have been much older than Grace when she'd gotten pregnant for the first time. Had she even been married when Griffin was born? If she'd had a child out of wedlock, it would explain her willingness to move West.

Maybe she'd never been married. Or maybe she'd been married twice before. If so, what had happened to those two previous husbands? And who the hell was Clive?

Whatever Hetty's past, he didn't want to know any more than he already did. The only thing that mattered was her behavior from now on. And it had felt awfully good to have his wife take his side.

"If you're through playing games," Dennis said, mounting up, "you might want to help find us a place to camp tonight." He kicked his horse and headed off toward the sunset.

Karl flushed at the censure. He'd stayed close to the wagon the past two weeks to play the game, letting Dennis do most of the scouting. Apparently, Dennis was more than ready to hand that duty back to him.

He mounted up without another word. Before he could ride away, he felt Hetty's hand on his thigh. He looked down, startled by her touch.

"Karl?"

"What?" His voice was harsh with the need to restrain his sudden desire. It took all his willpower to resist the urge to pull her up onto the horse with him, to hold her tight and kiss her silly.

He wanted to make love to his wife.

Hetty looked taken aback for a moment, but she smiled up at him and said, "Thank you for the game."

"It was Bao's idea."

"You were the one who ended up doing all the work. The children loved it. So did I. You were wonderful."

Karl thought, *To hell with it*. He looped the reins around the saddle horn, leaned down and caught Hetty under the arms, and lifted her up onto his lap. He looked into her eyes and saw that she was stunned at what he'd done. He couldn't have explained the impulse that had made him act. But as long as he'd gone this far, he followed his instincts and kissed his wife.

He was expecting resistance, but there was none. Her mouth opened at the press of his tongue, and he felt his heart pound as her hand caressed his neck. Karl pulled her tight against him, but there was no way to feel her body beneath the bulk of their coats, so he sought the connection to her that he wanted and needed through their kiss.

He'd barely begun tasting her sweetness when he heard a shout from Bao.

"Boss! Come quick!"

Karl broke the kiss, slid Hetty off his lap to the ground, and spurred his horse, all in the same instant. In the wilderness, moments could make the difference between life and death. As he galloped to catch up to the wagon, regretting the abrupt end to their kiss, he thought, *This had damned well better be one hell of an emergency!*

Chapter Ten

Hetty stood stunned for a moment, unsteady on her feet, her fingertips pressed against her lips. She couldn't believe what had just happened. First, that Karl had pulled her up onto his lap and kissed her in broad daylight, his tongue intruding into her mouth so she could actually taste him, and second, that he'd abandoned her so suddenly.

Her body was still discombobulated from the kiss, her breathing erratic, her heart thumping hard in her chest, but she forced her legs to work as she stumbled after him.

She heard Grace screaming. And Dennis yelling. And Bao's shrill, broken English. And finally, Karl's furious bellow above them all.

Hetty broke into a run.

What she saw when she reached the front of the wagon made her gasp and halt in her tracks. Karl and Dennis were engaged in a bout of fisticuffs! The fight between Clive Hamm and Joe Barnett passed before her eyes, along with its devastating conclusion.

"Stop!" she cried. "Oh, please, stop!"

The two men ignored her. It quickly became clear that Karl was outmatched by his larger, stronger friend. The skin around his puffed-up left eye was red and raw.

Karl ducked under Dennis's swing and punched him in the gut. Dennis grunted and caught Karl in a crushing bear hug. Karl slipped a foot behind Dennis's ankle and shoved, and Dennis tumbled to the ground with Karl on top of him. The two men began pummeling each other again.

Hetty was desperate to stop the fight, but she had no idea how. Maybe if she knew what had caused it, she would be able to end it. She turned to Grace and demanded, "What happened? Why are they fighting?"

Between sobs, Grace said, "Mr. Campbell hit Griffin."

Hetty's mouth fell open. "Why on earth would he do such a thing?" When Grace didn't answer, she turned to Griffin and asked, "What happened, Griffin?"

"It was an accident!" Griffin protested.

"What was?" Hetty demanded.

Griffin snarled, "What happened!"

Frustrated that she didn't know any more than she had before she'd started questioning Griffin, Hetty turned to Grace and asked, "Did you see what happened?"

"A stone from Griffin's slingshot hit Mr. Campbell's horse and made him buck and Mr. Campbell fell off and his horse ran away," Grace said all in one breath.

"Oh, Griffin, no!" Hetty cried. "Where did you get a slingshot?"

"I made it."

"Give it to me," Hetty said.

Griffin pulled the wooden slingshot out of his belt and smacked it into her waiting hand, but his chin took on a brash tilt as he said, "Nobody slaps me. Not for nothin'!"

Hetty's breath caught in her throat. "Dennis must have been sorely provoked. What else did you do?"

Griffin shot her a look of betrayal. "I should have known you'd take his side."

Grace interceded to say, "Mr. Campbell grabbed a handful of Griffin's coat—"

"So I kicked the son of a bitch in the shin!" Griffin finished.

"Karl arrived in the nick of time," Grace sobbed. "That son of a bitch would have choked Griffin senseless for sure!"

Hetty opened her mouth to complain about the children's use of that ugly term to describe Dennis Campbell and shut it again. Dennis was a grown man. He should know better than to attack a child, no matter what the provocation.

She turned back to the two snarling and grunting men wrestling on the ground, wondering how she could break up the furious fight without coming to serious harm herself.

Suddenly, Bao doused the two men with an entire bucket of icy water. They broke apart and came up spluttering and swearing.

Both men rose like shaggy, lumbering bears, turning to threaten Bao, who dropped the bucket, crossed his arms inside his wide sleeves, and said, "Confucius say: 'Without feelings of respect, what is there to distinguish men from beasts'?"

The two men stared at the Chinaman with jaws agape.

Hetty seized the opportunity to step between them. Since Karl was on top when the water got dumped, he'd gotten soaked. Water dripped from his hair and spiked his eyelashes. She put her hands on his wet coat, her back to Dennis, and said, "Enough. That's enough, Karl. Dennis is your best friend. You've done enough to punish him for a slap." She didn't mention the apparent attempt to choke Griffin, since that was likely to enrage Karl all over again.

Then she turned around, keeping herself between the two men, and said, "Enough, Dennis. This is no way for best friends to treat each other. Griffin is sorry. It was an accident."

"Like hell it was! That brat spooked my horse on purpose."

"Did not!" Griffin retorted.

Hetty turned to Griffin and said, "You'd better get moving if you're going to find Mr. Campbell's horse before dark."

"Me?" Griffin glanced at the surrounding wilderness with a look of trepidation, and Hetty almost changed her mind about sending him out to recover the horse. But she knew if there were no consequences for Griffin's behavior, it would only get worse.

She pointed west and said, "Get moving."

"I'll go with him," Grace offered.

Hetty almost stopped her, but it would be safer for the two children to be together. "Fine. We'll camp right here. Be sure you're both back before dark, whether you find Mr. Campbell's horse or not."

"You'd damn well better find him," Dennis said.

"I told you to watch your language," Karl warned, swiping at a cut on his cheek with the back of his hand and smearing blood across his face.

"Get moving!" Hetty ordered sharply. The sooner Griffin was out of Dennis's sight, the better. As the children trotted away, Hetty turned back to the two men.

She gave her attention first to Dennis, hoping to calm him down. "Let me see your face."

Dennis stood still as Hetty grasped his chin and gently turned his face back and forth so she could survey the damage. Dennis had a nasty bruise on his right cheekbone and a bleeding cut on his chin. She turned to Bao and said, "Mr. Lin, I'll need your medicine kit."

"What about me?" Karl demanded, hands on hips.

Hetty glanced over her shoulder and said, "Get out of those wet clothes before you catch pneumonia. I don't want to find myself a widow before I've had a chance to be a wife."

Karl looked disgruntled.

"Bao can take care of you while I doctor Dennis," she told him. Hetty wished there was a way she could explain to Karl that she was nursing Dennis because she wanted a chance to question him further about his behavior toward Griffin. She tried meeting Karl's gaze and sending a message with her eyes, but he turned and stomped away toward the back of the wagon.

"Come over here and sit down, Dennis," Hetty said, leading him by the hand to a tree split by lightning that had fallen beside the trail. There was an awkward moment when she tried to free her hand and Dennis held on.

"I appreciate you taking the time to doctor me," he said, caressing her palm with his thumb.

Hetty wished Dennis had been the one with his eye nearly swollen shut, because there was nothing to protect her from the look of admiration in his incredible blue eyes. She knew she shouldn't feel flattered, but she couldn't help it.

Oh, she was a horrible, fickle girl. Hetty would forever regret flirting with one man to make another jealous. She would never, for the rest of her life, do anything so foolish again. So she didn't understand how she could be feeling like this with Dennis, when Karl's recent kiss had almost caused her to swoon. What was wrong with her? How she wished for her twin! Hannah would have known how to put this rascally charmer in his place.

Luckily, Bao arrived at that moment with his medicines and a wet cloth. He set down the box and handed Hetty the rag. He took one look at Dennis and said to Hetty, "No need stitches. You remember which salve for bruises?"

Hetty opened the box and found the small jar with the salve Bao had told her would ease swelling. "This one," she said certainly as she picked it out of the many jars inside the box.

Bao nodded. "I go take care of Boss."

Hetty caught the Chinaman by the elbow and asked, "Is Karl badly hurt?" In hindsight, she realized she should have doctored him and let Bao take care of Dennis. Next time she would know better.

"No bad," Bao said. "Black eye. Cheek bleed. Be well soon."

Before she could ask more, the Chinaman was gone. She turned back to Dennis, who was sitting on the split log staring up at her with a frown between his brows.

"I didn't think you cared about Karl," Dennis said. "In fact, I would have bet my bottom dollar you dislike your husband."

Hetty was startled into blurting, "You're wrong. I admire Karl enormously."

"Ah. But will you ever love him? That's the question."

Hetty flushed. "That's between me and Karl."

Dennis yelped as she dabbed at the blood on his chin with the damp rag.

"Don't be a baby," she chided.

"That hurts!"

She looked him in the eye and said, "I'm sure Griffin's face hurts, too. Where you slapped him."

Dennis had the grace to look ashamed. "I'm not used to dealing with kids. Especially not a brat like—"

"Don't you dare call my son a brat!" Hetty said. "He's a little boy who made a mistake."

"That kind of mistake can be fatal out here," Dennis countered. "What if I'd broken my neck coming off that horse? What if those kids can't find my buckskin? A man on foot in this wilderness is a dead man. There's no room for mistakes, Hetty. Not even for kids."

Hetty dabbed more gently at Dennis's chin and caught her lower lip between her teeth as she contemplated what he'd said. "I guess we all have a lot to learn," she said at last. Most especially her.

She set the rag down on the log, then opened the jar and smoothed salve on the darkening bruise on Dennis's cheek. "I've taken away Griffin's slingshot, and I'll admonish him to be more careful in the future." She stopped what she was doing and looked into Dennis's startlingly blue eyes. "But I give you fair warning. I won't tolerate anyone striking a child of mine. Not for any reason."

Dennis grimaced as he pursed his lips, which pulled on his injured chin. All signs of romance were gone from his face as he said, "You keep a tight rein on those kids of yours, and we'll all get along fine."

Hetty realized that was likely all the apology he was going to make. She was glad. She needed reasons to dislike Dennis, to keep her from so readily feeling the physical attraction that arose whenever he was near.

She closed the jar of salve and put it away in the box. "I'm done. You should change your wet clothes, too. It'll be dark soon, and the temperature is brutal once the sun goes down."

He grinned crookedly, a look so charming it made her breath catch, then saluted her and said, "Yes, ma'am."

Hetty grabbed the box of medicines and hurried toward the back of the wagon almost at a run, searching for her husband. She would have to keep her distance from Dennis. She didn't want to give him the wrong idea. Apparently, she couldn't even take his hand to lead him to a seat without it being misconstrued or look into his eyes without him seeing an invitation that she didn't intend.

She found Karl standing at the tailgate of the wagon in dry clothes, a sticking plaster on his cheek, but Bao was missing. "Where's Mr. Lin?"

"I asked him to go keep an eye on the kids."

She studied Karl's damaged face. "Is your eye badly injured?"

"Bao says not," he replied, reaching up to gently probe the swelling around his eye.

"Does it hurt?"

He laughed, then groaned and grabbed his ribs. "Don't make me laugh. Everything hurts."

"Your poor eye!"

He reached up toward his awful-looking left eye again but never touched it. "Bao says it's going to snow tonight. I'll be able to put something cold on it tomorrow morning to get the swelling down."

"What are you doing for the swelling right now?"

"Bao said you have some kind of salve that'll make it feel better."

"Oh. I do." She set the box down on the open tailgate and retrieved the jar of salve. She put a dab of salve on her finger, then hesitated. "Your eye looks tender. I don't want to hurt you."

"If that stuff will help, go to it."

She was as gentle as she knew how to be, but he still winced as she applied the salve. He looked at her the whole time with the one brown eye he could see through. Hetty felt aware of his gaze, warmed by it. It was a totally different experience from what she'd felt when Dennis had gazed at her. Less threatening, she decided at last. More comfortable. More appropriate. Because he was her husband and had a right to look his fill.

Dennis did not, but he'd looked anyway. So why had she felt thrilled by his regard?

Hetty didn't understand herself. She was frightened by her feelings. Was she doomed always to court disaster? Her head told her that encouraging Dennis in even the smallest way was a bad idea, but she couldn't control her beating heart, which speeded up whenever Dennis Campbell looked her way.

And yet, she'd found Karl's kiss thrilling, enthralling, exciting. What kind of person was she? Why couldn't she confine her romantic responses to *one man*?

Hetty gestured Karl to sit on a nearby stump so she could reach his face better, then took her time with his eye, making sure every swollen inch of it was covered with salve. "Is that better?" she asked when she was done.

"Not much."

Hetty was surprised by the discordant sound of his voice and looked into his one good eye. It was focused on her right breast, which was exposed as she leaned over to tend to him. She hastily backed away, her face flushed. "I'm so sorry."

"No need to move on my account," Karl said with a smile. He groaned as his left eye tried to crinkle and couldn't. "I should get into a fight more often, if it means this kind of attention."

"Karl," Hetty began. She wasn't sure where to go from there. She didn't want him ever to fight Dennis again, but she wasn't sorry he'd stood up for Griffin. She wasn't sure whether to applaud or admonish him.

"What?" he said when she didn't speak.

"I'm glad you defended Griffin," she said at last.

"That boy deserves a walloping," Karl replied. He held up his hands when he saw the horror on Hetty's face. "But I suppose he's getting enough punishment hunting down Dennis's horse. On the other hand, a spanking wouldn't kill the kid. And it might do him some good."

Hetty shook her head. "I took away his slingshot and—"

"He can make another one," Karl interrupted.

"I'll have a talk with him. Dennis explained how dire the situation might have become if he'd been hurt worse. Or might become if the children can't find his horse. Griffin isn't a bad boy—"

"He sure as hell is an angry one," Karl interrupted again. "What happened to him, Hetty? Why is he so mad at the world?"

Hetty didn't know why Griffin was so angry with everyone and everything. She could guess. She'd spent a lot of time herself being mad. At the Great Fire for taking away the wonderful life she'd known. At her parents for dying. At her uncle for abandoning her and her siblings in an orphanage. At the dreadful Miss Birch for being so cruel. At herself for being so selfish and stupid. And at God for tearing her family apart.

Tears welled in Hetty's eyes as she thought of the family she'd lost and might never see again. "Griffin's life hasn't been easy."

"Yours either, from the look on your face," Karl said.

"What look is that?"

Karl brushed away a tear that had fallen with the rough pad of his thumb. "Those beautiful eyes of yours had such a look of pain just now. Can you tell me about it?"

Not without spilling the beans, she couldn't. She swallowed over the sudden knot in her throat. "It doesn't matter anymore. It's over and done."

Karl's hand dropped, and his voice sounded curt as he said, "I'd better get the fire started. Those kids'll be cold and hungry when they get back."

Then he was gone.

Hetty felt abandoned. And yet, Karl's only thought had been for the comfort and well-being of her supposed children. She wished she could tell him the truth. She wished she'd never started this charade. She wished she could go back and tell Mr. Lin, *No, I won't pretend to be a mother. And I don't want to be anyone's mail-order bride.*

It was too late for that. For better or worse, she was Karl's bride. And she was the only mother those two children had. She would have a talk with Griffin when he returned. She would explain everything Dennis had told her. And she would ask Griffin to try harder to be a good boy.

Hetty stopped herself right there. That sort of lecture was liable to have the opposite effect of the one she intended. She had a better idea. She would tell Grace what she'd learned from Dennis, and let Grace advise her brother to curb his behavior. Griffin seemed to have a soft spot where Grace was concerned.

Hetty wondered if she would ever become a good wife to Karl or a good mother to Grace and Griffin.

All she could do for the present was pretend and hope that by pretending and pretending, she would one day become the real thing.

She was drawn from her reverie by a shout. She listened hard and heard the same word again. Her blood froze when she realized what it was.

Indians!

Chapter Eleven

It was one Indian. And he was friendly. But it took a long time for Hetty's heartbeat to return to normal.

The Salish brave, appearing out of the bushes on a pinto pony with Dennis's horse in tow, had frightened the wits out of Grace, who'd shrieked "Indians!" at the top of her lungs.

As Hetty ran toward her child's fearful cry, she relived the Indian attack the day Hannah's husband, Mr. McMurtry, had died of cholera. Because they'd been forced to leave the wagon train when Clive and Joe had fought over her, she and Hannah and Josie had been alone, unable to defend themselves, although Josie had given a good account of herself with the bullwhip used to drive the oxen. The Indians had laughed at her efforts, until she'd managed to knock one off his pony.

Hetty's throat was choked with the remembered terror of standing in the back of the wagon and seeing a war-painted face staring back at her, and she shuddered recalling the horrific pain of the arrow that had pierced her flesh. Hannah had been crouched in the back of the wagon beside her husband, who'd died only moments before. Apparently, the sight of her identical twin suddenly standing up beside her had spooked the Indians, who'd grabbed Josie, freed the oxen, and galloped away.

Hetty felt anew the guilt and grief over the unknown fate of her sisters and for Mr. McMurtry's death, which might not have occurred if they'd still been traveling with the wagon train.

The wagon master had already warned Mr. McMurtry once to curb Hetty's flirtatious behavior toward Clive and Joe, which had caused a previous altercation between the two men. Hannah had spoken to her as well.

Hetty had felt only the power of her beauty and the exhilaration of finally being free of the oppressive rules under which she'd lived at the orphanage. She'd been giddy with the knowledge of Clive's fierce attraction to her and determined to make him bow to her will and marry her before they reached Cheyenne.

Hetty wore her guilt like a millstone around her neck. She was oppressed by the catastrophe she'd caused, which had ended with three men dead, one sister lost in the wilderness, and one captured in a vicious Indian attack that had left her family scattered.

Her whole body shivered as she stared at the savage sitting across from her. The two children were huddled as close to her as possible, the three of them crouched on a wool blanket not five feet away from the dark-skinned, sharp-nosed man. He had two long, grease-laden black braids with black-and-white feathers attached and wore a long-sleeved, beaded buckskin shirt, fringed buckskin leggings, and knee-high moccasins.

To Hetty's amazement, Karl was able to converse with the Salish brave in his native tongue.

"What does he want?" Dennis asked Karl.

"Two Feathers says he found this buckskin running free, so it belongs to him. He wants us to trade for it, if we want it back."

Dennis shot a dark look at Griffin. "What's that going to cost us?"

Hetty put an arm around the boy, but he shrugged it off and glared back at Dennis.

"He wants sugar, tobacco, and whiskey," Karl said.

Dennis raised his eyebrows. "Now I understand why you brought along so much tobacco when you don't smoke."

Karl shrugged. "The Indians asked for it all the time last summer."

"I'm not so sure it's a good idea to give him any whiskey."

"I told him we don't have any."

Dennis glanced at the Salish and said, "Did he believe you?"

"I offered him a Bowie knife instead. He seems willing to bargain."

Grace leaned close and said to Hetty, "That Indian doesn't look so frightening sitting there beside Karl. I thought my heart was going to stop when I first saw him."

Hetty hoped Grace couldn't tell she was still trembling. She was supposed to be the strong one, but her stomach was cramped so hard she thought she might be sick.

The savage spoke again in guttural tones.

"What does he want now?" Dennis asked.

Karl glanced at Hetty. "If we don't have whiskey, he's willing to forgo the sugar and tobacco and give up the horse in exchange for Grace. He likes her red hair."

Hetty lurched to her feet in horror and cried, "No!"

The Indian remained where he was and calmly spoke again.

Karl replied in the strange language.

Hetty was trying desperately to control the hysteria that made her want to grab the children and run. "What did he say?" she demanded. "What did you say?"

"He said if I wanted to keep the red-haired girl, he'd be happy to have the yellow-haired woman instead," Karl replied. "I told him he can have sugar and tobacco and a sharp knife. Or nothing."

"Oh," Hetty said. That sounded like an ultimatum. She felt Grace tugging on her skirt and sat down, hugging the girl tightly to her. She would never give her up. Never.

What if the Salish wouldn't accept Karl's offer? The Indian wasn't tall, but he looked strong, and he had an old-fashioned rifle that had never left his side. What if he decided to try and take Grace anyway? And how would they retrieve Dennis's horse if the Indian wouldn't take trade goods for it? Would they have to fight him?

Hetty was beginning to understand the enormous, far-reaching consequences of Griffin's small bit of mischief. They'd lost half a day of travel and perhaps

Dennis's horse, or at the very least a quantity of sugar and tobacco and a knife. Their very lives had been put in jeopardy by the appearance of this savage. No wonder Dennis had been so angry. Perhaps she'd judged him too harshly. He'd apparently foreseen difficulties of this sort, even if he hadn't known the exact form they would take.

Karl and the Salish were conversing again, and Hetty waited with bated breath and a hurting heart to see the result of their discussion.

Karl and the Indian grasped arms, and Karl nodded. The Indian rose and crossed to the wagon wheel where he'd left Dennis's horse tied. Meanwhile, Karl retrieved a ten-pound sack of sugar, a five-pound bag of tobacco, and a Bowie knife from the back of the wagon. The Indian handed Karl the reins, and Karl handed off the items he'd collected.

The Indian grunted an assent and disappeared into the forest beyond the fire.

"Do you suppose that's the last we'll see of him?" Dennis asked.

"I hope so," Karl said, staring off into the darkness. "I'm glad we'll be where we're going before he has time to get home and show off his loot. The last thing I want is a band of Salish braves catching us on the trail." He turned and said, "Griffin, come here."

Griffin sat where he was for a moment before Hetty gave him a surreptitious shove. The boy rose and crossed to Karl, his chin upthrust.

Karl handed Griffin the reins and said, "This poor animal needs some attention. Unsaddle him and give him a good rubdown, then feed him some corn before you picket him."

To Hetty's surprise, Griffin accepted the reins without a word of protest.

"I'm not sure I want that kid handling my horse," Dennis said. "How do I know he won't scare him off again?"

Hetty held her breath, waiting to see how Griffin would react. She knew Grace had spoken to her brother about behaving better, but Hetty wondered if Griffin had listened to anything his sister had said.

"I'd never hurt your horse on purpose, Mr. Campbell," Griffin said sullenly. "I told you, it was an accident." He glanced at Grace, then turned back to Dennis and mumbled, "I'm sorry for the trouble I caused."

"You should be!" Dennis said.

Hetty didn't give either Griffin or Dennis a chance to start a quarrel. She rose abruptly and said, "That stew should be ready by now. Griffin, go take care of Dennis's horse. You can eat when you're done. Grace, come help me dish up plates for everyone."

"Oh!" Grace said.

Hetty whirled to find out what was wrong now. She found Grace staring up into a sky where the sunlight had disappeared behind lowering gray clouds, her hands held out before her.

"What is it, Grace?"

Grace turned her gaze back to Hetty, her eyes alight with wonder. "It's snowing."

Hetty shivered as a gust of wind lifted her skirt and tiny icicles of snow blasted her cheeks.

Bao said, "Much snow tonight."

"Let's eat fast and get these dishes washed and everything packed up," Karl said.

Everyone except Griffin sat down to eat, racing to get the warm stew into their stomachs before the snow cooled it off. Then they scattered to do all the chores necessary to prepare for the storm Bao had predicted.

As Hetty crossed to the wagon to stow away the cooking pot and utensils, her shoulders sagged at the thought of how the storm might delay their journey. She wondered how the Chinaman knew there would be a lot of snow and whether he was going to be right. She was so mortally tired of traveling. She'd left Chicago in March, and Thanksgiving was around the corner. She was more than ready to have a solid roof over her head again.

Karl finished tying off a tarp that would keep the snow from blowing under the wagon. The two kids were already inside the closure when Hetty joined him.

"That should keep you and the kids from getting buried under a drift," he said.

Hetty glanced toward the canvas tent that had been set up for the three men, where Dennis and Bao had already retired. "How long do you think we'll be stuck here?"

"As long as the snow stops sometime tonight, we should be able to travel tomorrow. It'll be slow going, and we'll have to be careful of drifts, but I see no reason why we can't reach the logging camp tomorrow evening or early the next day."

Hetty tied the wool scarf around her head a little tighter as the wind whipped up. "We're that close?"

Karl smiled, winced as his injured eye crinkled, then said, "Yeah."

Hetty shivered and tucked her hands under her arms to warm them. Once they arrived at their new home, Karl would expect their marriage to move forward. She didn't know how long she could hold him off. She had no idea how she was going to fake experience in bed she didn't have. She didn't know how she was going to make love to a man she didn't love.

Hetty was tired of pretending, and there was no end of it in sight. She felt sad and lonely and so alone. A small sound of distress escaped as a wave of homesickness washed over her.

"You all right?" Karl asked.

Hetty started, unaware that Karl had moved and was standing right behind her. She turned to him and said, "I'm just tired of traveling."

Karl pulled her snug against him, encircling her in his arms, making her feel safe and secure.

Hetty leaned her head against his shoulder, yearning to share the burden she carried with someone else. Unfortunately, that someone couldn't be Karl, not until this marriage was consummated and it was too late for him to back out. She shivered as she thought of the wedding night to come.

"You're cold," he said. "You should get under cover."

He put an arm around her waist and kept her close as they headed toward the opening in the canvas covering the base of the wagon. Hetty realized that in the short time since they'd finished supper, the gently falling snow had become something decidedly more malevolent.

"Karl, I wish . . ."

He stopped and turned her so they were facing, his hands at her waist. "What do you wish?"

Hetty wished she'd been able to wait for an answer to the letter she'd sent to Hannah from Butte, care of General Delivery in Cheyenne, just in case Hannah had ended up there. It was awful not to know what had happened to her twin. Awful to think she might never see any of her family again.

Hetty felt a sob building and swallowed it down. She felt Karl's lips against her brow and pressed her body closer to his, seeking the only comfort to be had. Perhaps Karl sensed her feelings of regret for the situation in which she found herself. Oh, how awful for him if he did!

Hetty's arms found their way up around Karl's neck, and she hugged him tight, offering back the comfort he'd given to her. She both craved the end of their journey and feared it. She worried about what he would do when he discovered that she'd been lying all along. What would happen to the three of them if he ever found out the truth?

Then Karl spoke, and she knew for sure that he'd sensed what she hadn't been able to say.

He spoke into her ear, so she heard him easily over the fierce, howling wind. "If you want out of this marriage, Hetty, tell me now."

Hetty stared up at him, shocked at his suggestion. "Do you want out?" she blurted.

"This is about what you want."

She could have her freedom. She could head back to Cheyenne to discover what had happened to Hannah and Josie. If she couldn't find them, she could head to Texas to hunt for her eldest sister, Miranda, and two younger brothers, Nick and Harry. She could try to reunite with her family.

Or she could stay where she was. And go on with her life. And remain Karl Norwood's wife.

The temptation to leave was strong. There was nothing holding her here. Except two children she'd come to love.

Hetty looked into Karl's shadowed brown eyes and saw the worry there. She wondered just how much he would be hurt if she took him up on his offer. And realized she would never know, because she could never leave the children. She was their mother, for now and always. But Karl didn't need to know she was making her decision based on *them* rather than *him*.

"I'll stay, Karl, if that's all right with you."

She hadn't realized quite how anxious he was until she felt his shoulders relax. For a moment she thought he would kiss her. But he didn't.

Then he changed his mind.

His lips were cold when they touched hers but quickly warmed. His tongue came searching, and Hetty opened to him. It was a kiss of possession, fierce despite its brevity. When Karl ended the kiss, Hetty's nerves felt shattered.

How could a simple kiss from such an ordinary man create such havoc inside her? She didn't love Karl. In fact, she found his best friend far more physically attractive. She'd remained in Karl's arms and sought comfort from him under false pretenses, and she'd agreed to stay married to him for reasons that had nothing to do with love.

Hetty didn't want to consider what her response to Karl's kiss might mean. How had she become a woman who so callously flirted? Who relished attracting the attention of more than one man? Who needed and wanted to be adored . . . and didn't seem to care who did the adoring?

Hetty had a great deal to think about. She wished her mother was still alive. She wished her sisters were near. She felt inadequate, young and inexperienced and *stupid*. She wanted someone older and wiser to tell her what to do.

But she had nowhere else to turn. She was going to have to look into her own heart and follow it.

She met Karl's gaze, tugged her wool coat tight, and said, "Good night, Karl."

He put a finger to the brim of his hat in acknowledgment. "Good night, Hetty."

Hetty scooted under the wagon through the opening Karl had left in the tarp and sought her pallet beside Grace. To her surprise, the girl was awake.

"I saw you," Grace whispered.

"What?"

"I saw you kissing him," the girl said, her voice dripping with accusation.

"Karl is my husband, Grace," Hetty said in her defense.

"Just be careful, Hetty," the girl warned. "Men always want more than kisses."

Hetty opened her mouth to ask what Grace meant and shut it again. Poor Grace. She'd obviously seen far more of her mother's business activities than any child should have. Hetty knew she should explain to

Grace that what happened between a husband and wife was far different from what Grace's mother had experienced with her customers. But the girl had already turrned her back on Hetty.

It took a very long time for Hetty to fall asleep. Before she could explain to Grace the difference between selling one's body for money and sharing one's body for love, she was going to have to make peace with her decision to marry Karl Norwood. Because love would likely be no part of it when she finally gave herself to her husband.

Chapter Twelve

Karl was the first one up the next morning. He hadn't, in fact, done much sleeping. The roiling questions in his head had kept him awake. In another day, or at most two, they would reach the cabin. He probably shouldn't have asked Hetty whether she wanted to stay married to him. Her answer had come with enough hesitation to make him wonder how close she'd come to giving him a different answer.

The thought of making love to a reluctant woman had given him nightmares. He wasn't sure whether he felt relieved or more anxious now that his wife had agreed to continue the marriage.

Karl had always been realistic about his looks. He would never have had the courage to court such an incredibly lovely woman. A great deal of his reluctance to accept the unexpected gift of a beautiful wife was the knowledge that Hetty might always yearn for a husband equal to her in good looks. In short, that she might never be able to love him.

But had love ever been a realistic expectation when he'd acquired a bride sight unseen? Karl had been pleased that his mail-order bride had never requested details of his appearance. Now he questioned why a woman as beautiful as Hetty had wanted to become a mail-order bride. Which brought him back to square one.

Did he want to be married to Hetty? It didn't matter, really, because unless Hetty wanted out—and she'd said she didn't—it would be difficult to undo the wedding. And Karl was honest enough, and human enough, to admit he was looking forward to the day when he could make love to his bride.

Bao appeared at Karl's side, wading through the two feet of snow that had drifted to six feet around the wagon, and said, "Storm not over."

"Of course it is," Karl replied, glancing up at an almost clear blue sky.

Bao shook his head. He pointed to the dark, lowering clouds in the distance. "More snow coming."

Karl didn't know how the Chinaman was able to predict the weather, but he'd been right more often than not. "Guess that means we'd better get everyone up and moving."

"I make breakfast," Bao said. "You wake wife and kids."

Karl untied the tarp wrapped around the wagon and let it fall down to reveal the three inside. Except, there were only two heads—one blond, one redheaded—visible under a pile of blankets. The third pallet was empty.

Karl looked for footsteps in the snow or any sign that Griffin might have woken up early and gone to answer a call of nature. The snow was pristine. The kid must have left sometime during the night.

"Son of a bitch," he muttered. "Hetty, wake up! Grace, where's your brother?"

Grace was startled awake and looked bleary-eyed at Karl. "What do you mean?" She glanced around long enough to realize Griffin wasn't under the wagon with them and said, "Isn't he outside with you?"

"Would I be asking where he is if he was out here with me?" Karl replied acerbically. "There are no tracks in the snow. Did he say anything about taking off on his own?"

Neither female had undressed except to pull off her shoes, and both Hetty and Grace quickly pulled their shoes back on, tied the laces, grabbed their coats, and bounded from beneath the wagon.

Grace looked in every direction without moving. Hetty looked only at him.

"Are you sure he's missing?" Hetty said. "Maybe he just—"

"Look around you," Karl interrupted. "Do you see any footprints leading away from the wagon?"

Hetty searched the ground. "Maybe there are some at the back of the wagon."

"I already looked. There's no sign of anybody leaving the wagon after the snow stopped."

Hetty's eyes were wide with shock. She turned to Grace and asked, "Why on earth would he run away?"

Grace sobbed once before she could control herself enough to speak. "Griffin told me that he didn't tie down Mr. Campbell's horse. That when Dennis went looking this morning his horse would be gone. I told him I was sick and tired of his games, and he'd better find that horse and get him back before morning or he wasn't my brother anymore. But I was angry. I didn't mean it!"

"Of course you didn't," Hetty said, taking the girl in her arms. She looked up at Karl with desperate eyes. "You have to find him, Karl."

Karl knew the horse would have wandered with its tail to the wind. There was no telling how far Griffin had gone while hunting for it, or whether he'd even gone off in the same direction as the horse. If Bao was right, there was more snow and cold on the way. The boy might slide into a deep drift, freeze to death in the cold, and not be found until spring. "I'll do my best, Hetty. The rest of you need to finish the journey without me."

"We can't leave!" Hetty said. "What if Griffin comes back here and we're all gone? He won't know where to look for us."

"Bao says there's more snow coming. I want you and Grace out of the weather. Once you arrive at the logging camp, Dennis and Bao can get mounts and come help me with the search. That is, if I haven't already found Griffin."

Hetty's worried gaze told him that she suspected how slim the chances were that he would find the missing boy, especially if the weather worsened.

"Please let me help you look for him," she begged.

"Take me, too," Grace pleaded.

"You can both help me best by getting to the logging camp safe and sound," Karl said, steeling himself against the tears in both sets of eyes.

"Breakfast ready, Boss," Bao said.

"Get everybody fed and get on the trail," he told the Chinaman. "I'm going hunting for Griffin."

"Boy not here?" Bao asked.

"He went hunting for Dennis's horse, which must have slipped its picket during the storm." Karl didn't know why he'd lied about what had really happened. Except he didn't want any more trouble between Dennis and Griffin. Assuming he got Griffin back.

"When you get to the camp," Karl continued, "get Hetty and Grace settled at the house. If I'm not back with Griffin by tonight, you and Dennis can come looking for both of us in the morning."

Karl didn't give Hetty a chance to argue further, simply gathered the survival supplies he needed and headed off to saddle his horse.

As Karl was mounting, Dennis came out of the tent and asked, "Where are you headed so early?"

"Griffin's missing. I'm going to hunt him down."

"Wait a minute and I'll join you."

"Griffin went hunting for your horse. It's gone."

Dennis swore. "I knew better than to trust that brat to take care of him."

"That 'brat' went out into the storm to find your mount. I don't want to hear another word about it," Karl retorted. "Bao says there's more weather coming. Do your best to get everybody to the logging camp before it hits."

Before Dennis could say more, Karl kicked his mount and headed in the direction the wind had been blowing last night. With any luck, the horse—and the boy following it—hadn't gone far.

Chapter Thirteen

Hetty spent the first night in her new log home praying that Griffin would be found alive. Grace was inconsolable. She was certain her brother had frozen to death. Hetty was also worried about Karl. He knew everything there was to know about plants, but what did he know about unrelenting snow and ruthless wind and brutal temperatures? What were his chances of finding one little boy in this vast, hostile wilderness?

Instead of going to bed in what was clearly Karl's bedroom, Hetty had settled into one of the two willow rockers she'd found in front of the river-rock fireplace in the parlor. She'd wrapped herself in a blanket and kept vigil through the night. By the time dawn arrived, Hetty was physically and emotionally drained. The wind still howled, and icy fingers of cold slipped between cracks in the log chinking. Karl had not returned with Griffin. Even if he'd found the boy, Hetty knew they must be suffering terribly without shelter from the storm. Dennis and Bao had checked in with her this morning before they'd ventured out into the frozen wasteland to search for Karl and Griffin.

Hetty's heart physically ached. It couldn't be the fear

of losing Karl. She'd only known him a matter of weeks, although it hadn't taken much more time than that to fall in love with Clive. Except, she wasn't in love with Karl. She wasn't sure she could ever open her heart to another man. She was never going through that kind of pain again.

No, her heart must be aching for Griffin. He reminded her of her little brother, Nick, who was nearly the same age, even to the devilry the boy seemed always to get into.

"Mom?"

Hetty turned at the whispered word and opened her arms to Grace, who'd left the bedroom she should have shared with her brother last night and now crawled into Hetty's lap, wrapping her arms tightly around Hetty's neck.

"They didn't come back," Grace said against Hetty's throat.

"Karl's a very smart man. He's probably holed up somewhere with Griffin right now, waiting out the storm. They'll come riding up to the cabin as soon as the sun comes out."

"Do you really believe that?" Grace asked, lifting her head to look into Hetty's eyes.

"I want to believe it," Hetty said, unwilling to lie to the girl. "We mustn't lose hope now."

"I don't know how I'll live with myself if anything happens to Griffin," Grace said in a choked voice. "I don't know why I said what I did. I would never abandon him. Never! I was just so angry with him."

"It's only human to lose patience now and again with those closest to us." Hetty vividly remembered her twin raging at her after Mr. McMurtry died, blaming her for everything that had gone wrong. And yet, Hannah had gone off into the wilderness to find help when Hetty was wounded, begging her to stay alive, reminding Hetty that they were bound together forever as two halves of one precious whole.

"What if Griffin dies believing I don't love him?" Grace asked in an anguished voice.

Hetty rubbed Grace's back as though she were a much younger child and said, "You know better than that, Grace. Griffin knows you love him." As she'd known Hannah loved her, even when she was raging. As Hannah must have known she was loved by Hetty.

"But I said—"

"Griffin knew you were angry. The fact that he went out into the storm is proof that he loves you as much as you love him." Surely a just God wouldn't allow Griffin to freeze to death in the cold. Or remain lost forever . . . or until the snow melted in the spring, revealing his corpse. Hetty had lost too many people in her life already. She didn't think she could bear to lose any more.

Come back, Karl, and bring Griffin back with you safe and sound. Please, please come back.

Hetty closed her eyes and continued rocking.

The door burst open and a blast of frigid air flooded the cabin. Hetty shoved Grace off her lap and whirled to find Karl staggering through the doorway with Griffin in his arms.

"Griffin!" Grace cried.

Hetty met Karl's brown eyes beneath brows layered with ice and saw the angst there. Then she looked at the boy in his arms, whose eyes were closed and whose face was as white as the snow gusting through the door.

"I figured I'd better get him back here in a hurry, instead of waiting out the storm. He looked frozen solid when I found him," Karl said as he headed for the children's bedroom, on the right side of the cabin.

Hetty studied the child's closed eyes and his chalk white face. She looked desperately for a pulse at his throat but didn't see one. "Is he still alive?"

"His pulse is shallow, but he's got one," Karl replied.

Hetty hurried after him on one side, while Grace held on to any part of Griffin she could reach on the other side. Once they reached the bedroom, Hetty pulled the covers down on the twin bed that hadn't been used the previous night.

"Where's Bao?" Karl asked as he laid Griffin down.

"He rode out with Dennis at first light to find you."

Karl looked grim. "I'd better go look for him."

"You can't go back out into that storm!" Hetty cried.

"We need his knowledge to save Griffin's hands and feet," Karl said, turning to leave.

"Wait!" Hetty squeezed her eyes closed and thought back over the things Bao had taught her during the week before they'd arrived in Butte, desperate to recall whether he'd ever said anything about treating someone with frostbite or pneumonia or whatever else might be wrong with Griffin.

She heard Mr. Lin's broken English saying, *If skin not black, warm water—not hot—to thaw frozen fingers and toes.* He'd said to do something else if the fingers and toes were black, but Hetty couldn't remember what that was. She hurried to where Griffin lay on the bed and pulled the mittens off his hands. His fingers were a grayish yellow.

"His fingers are frostbitten," she said. "Take off his boots, Karl."

She turned to Grace, who was standing stock-still beside the bed, and ordered, "Go get the pot of water boiling on the hob." When Grace didn't move she said, "Now, Grace. Go!"

Grace sobbed and ran from the room.

"Did you have to yell at her?" Karl said. "She's scared."

"So am I!" Hetty shot back. "Get those shoes and socks off him."

When the first sock came off, Hetty saw the damage to Griffin's feet was far worse than to his hands. The little toe on his left foot, where his sock had a corresponding hole, was dark purple. "We need to defrost his fingers and toes with warm water. Not hot," she said, repeating what Bao had taught her.

"I'll go get some snow to cool the water from the hob," Karl said. "Can you finish undressing him?"

Hetty nodded, then began unbuttoning Griffin's coat. Before Karl got to the bedroom door she turned to him and said, "As soon as I've taken care of him, I want to check you for frostbite."

"I'm fine, Hetty," Karl said.

"We'll see about that when you get back," she said. "Now go. Get me some snow."

Hetty had kept water boiling on the fire to make coffee when Karl returned. After Grace set the pot of water on a rough pine side table, Hetty asked the girl to retrieve three bowls and as many dishcloths as she could find. "We can all work on warming Griffin at the same time."

Hetty parsed out the boiling water into the three bowls, then made it less hot with chunks of snow Karl had brought back into the house. She handed Karl and Grace each a cloth, took two for herself, and said, "We need to gently warm his flesh until the blood comes back into it. It won't be pleasant for him. It's going to feel like someone's stabbing him with needles, or like his skin is on fire. His flesh may blister. I don't know how long he'll stay unconscious. Let's work quickly, before he wakes up."

She stripped Griffin to his smalls and covered him with several blankets, leaving his hands and feet exposed. She wrapped warm dishcloths around both of his hands while Karl and Grace each worked on a wounded foot. As soon as the cloths cooled, they replaced them with warm ones.

They hadn't been working long when Griffin's eyes fluttered open. He moaned and writhed at the pain and mumbled, "Where am I? How did I get here?"

"Be still," Hetty said quietly, putting a hand to his chest to hold him in place when he tried to sit up.

"What's going on? What's all this?" he asked, holding up his cloth-covered hands.

He struggled to be free, but Karl said, "Lie still," in a firm voice, and the fight went right out of him.

"You're safe," Hetty said in a soothing voice. "We're in Karl's cabin in the Bitterroot. You were lost in the storm. Karl found you and brought you here."

"Mr. Campbell's horse?" Griffin said.

Hetty glanced at Karl, who shook his head.

Tears streamed down Griffin's white face as his gaze

focused on Grace. "I'm sorry, Grace. I couldn't find him. I tried. Really, I did." He began to cry in great, gulping sobs and to thrash on the bed, dislodging the warming cloths. The harder he cried, the more hysterical Grace became.

"Griffin, you need to lie still while we treat your frostbite," Hetty said sharply. The girl's crying wasn't helping. "Grace, go put some more water on the hob to boil. When it's hot, make us all a cup of coffee."

"Lie still, boy," Karl said in a stern voice, "if you want to save your hands and feet."

Griffin didn't move again or say a word of complaint over the next half hour, just shuddered and moaned as the blood slowly but surely returned to his fingers and toes. At least, most of his toes. The small toe on his left foot stayed an ominous dark purple.

When Hetty was certain Griffin's hands were warmed, she instructed Grace to continue to replace the cloths on his hands and feet with warm ones. Then she took Karl's still-gloved hand and led him to their bedroom.

She made him sit on the bed and one by one pulled off his heavy leather gloves. His hands weren't yellowish-gray, like Griffin's, but they were very cold and parchment white. "Oh, Karl," Hetty said in dismay. "You should have let me treat your hands sooner."

"They've been thawing while I worked on Griffin."

"Bao told me a way to warm them quickly," she said. "If you're willing to try."

"Sure," Karl replied.

Hetty sat down beside him on the bed, then reached for one of his hands and placed it under one of her arms, in the warmth of her armpit. She took his other hand and did the same thing with the other armpit. She was embarrassed to have him touch her so intimately, but she reminded herself that this had nothing to do with seduction and everything to do with saving a man's hands.

She looked everywhere except into Karl's eyes.

"How long does this cure take?" Karl asked.

She heard the humor in his voice and glanced up at him. "Until your hands are warm."

"Well, my heart's certainly pumping a lot harder than it was a minute ago, so I suspect that won't take long."

Hetty accepted the farce in the situation. Nevertheless, she felt breathless at the way Karl's hands grazed the sides of her breasts. She searched for a topic of conversation to make their closeness feel less awkward and said, "How did you find Griffin?"

"I headed in the direction the wind was blowing and prayed."

"So it was prayer that saved him?"

"More like blind luck," Karl said. "Griffin was sitting with his back braced against a ponderosa pine. I rode right past him without seeing him. Thank God he was wearing a scarf with some fringe. The wind caught the fringe, and I saw something red move out of the corner of my eye."

"Was he awake? Was he aware?"

Karl shook his head. "The kid was half covered in snow and looked frozen solid," he said in a voice rough with emotion. "If I hadn't seen him . . ."

His voice drifted off, and Hetty knew they'd come

within a hairsbreadth of losing Griffin. She glanced at Karl and saw his eyelids were sliding closed.

"You must be exhausted. You should lie down," she said.

His eyes opened and he stared at her.

"You're half asleep already," she said. "I don't want you falling on the floor and hitting your head." She managed a lopsided smile. "I don't want to have to treat you for a concussion." Bao hadn't yet gotten to that lesson.

He smiled back at her, then pulled his hands free, stood, and unbuttoned his coat. She took it as he slid it off his shoulders and laid it across a ladder-back chair in the corner. He stood where he was for a moment in his red-and-black-plaid wool shirt, apparently unsure what to do next. She hurried to pull the covers down on the bed and said, "Sit down and let me take off your boots."

"I can do it," he protested.

"Your hands aren't warm yet. It'll be quicker if I do it."

He sagged onto the bed with a groan, allowing her to see the full extent of his weariness.

Hetty untied both hobnail boots, grabbed the heel of one boot and tugged it off, then pulled off the other. "I should check your feet," she said, looking up at him.

"Go ahead."

She pulled off one sock, then the other. He moaned as Hetty prodded his feet. "They're not as bad as Griffin's, but you need to get them warmed up." She pulled the socks back on and ordered, "Under the covers."

She'd had a great deal of time to check out their bedroom, so she knew there were extra blankets in the chest at the foot of the bed. She grabbed a gray wool blanket and opened it just enough to add an extra layer of warmth around Karl's feet. Then she leaned down to untie her shoelaces, slipped off her shoes, and slid under the covers with him.

"What are you doing?" he asked, his brow furrowed in confusion.

"Your hands still need to be warmed." She turned on her side toward him, rearranging her skirt around her legs to avoid the ice-cold sheets. Then she placed one of his hands under her left armpit, reached for the other hand, and did the same thing on the right. Turned the way she was, the weight of her breast necessarily rested on Karl's wrist, and the weight of his other wrist necessarily rested against her other breast. There was nowhere to look except directly into Karl's heavy-lidded brown eyes.

"You can sleep if you like," she said.

He grinned, revealing the overlapping front tooth that she found so intriguing, and said, "I'm suddenly not the least bit sleepy. I can't imagine why."

She laughed, and that easily the awkwardness of the situation disappeared. Not the tension, just the awkwardness. She was very much aware of being in bed with Karl.

He hissed and wriggled the fingers of the hand closest to the bed. Hetty caught her breath as his fingers brushed her breast. "Are you all right?" she asked.

"I must be thawing out. It feels like a million pinpricks."

"Can you stand this a little longer?"

Karl met her gaze and said, "I could stand this the rest of my life."

Hetty was startled into laughter again. "Are you trying to seduce me, Karl?"

"Is it working?"

Hetty felt herself flush at his intent look. Of course. He was thinking about consummating the union. Hetty's mind skittered away from the possibility. Making love was the furthest thing from her mind at the moment. Or ought to be.

"I was worried about you," she admitted, because she needed something to say.

"Were you?"

"And about Griffin, of course."

"Of course."

He wasn't helping the conversation along, and Hetty struggled to come up with something else to say. "Grace was beside herself with worry. She was afraid Griffin might die thinking she didn't love him. I told her Griffin knew she loved him even though she was angry with him, that sometimes we get impatient with those we care about most." Hetty knew she was babbling, but she couldn't seem to stop.

There was no fire in the fireplace, so the room was cold enough for her to see her breath when she spoke. "I should get up and light a fire."

"Don't leave," Karl said.

The low, rumbling timbre of his voice sent a frisson of feeling down Hetty's spine. She realized she'd been looking into Karl's eyes all this time. And he'd been looking back.

Chapter Fourteen

Karl's hands were in agony. And his heart was in agony. He wanted to make love to his wife. Her mouth was only a few inches from his own, but he felt certain that if he made the slightest move to kiss her, she would flee. But the pain in his hands—and his heart—was relentless. He counted *one . . . two . . . three . . .* before his restraint fled.

He leaned forward, and his lips met hers. He felt Hetty trembling and gentled the touch of his mouth to entice her to stay with the kiss, to beguile her to stay with him.

The kiss became more than a meeting of lips. He was living a fantasy. Hetty's lips were soft and surprisingly willing. His tongue barely touched the seam, and her sudden gasp allowed him to intrude, tasting her sweetness. She might have fled then, except his hands were tucked into her armpits. Despite the pain, he used them to hold her in place.

Her upper arm moved as her fingers twined in his hair, and his hand was suddenly free to caress her. He turned so he could hold her breast more firmly, while his thumb found the peak. Karl moaned deep in his throat, but he wasn't sure whether the sound was caused by the soft weight of her breast in his hand or the excruciating reawakening of his fingers.

He grazed the inside of her upper lip with his tongue and felt her gasp again. This time she leaned into his body. Her fingers slid down to his nape and did something there that caused him to grow hard and ready.

He drew his other hand free to grasp her hair and angle her head for a deeper kiss. But he must have pulled her hair or done something else to break the spell, because an instant later, Hetty was out of bed and on her feet, staring at him with wide, dazed eyes, one hand on her heart, the back of the other against her gasping mouth. She was shaking her head almost in bewilderment.

"Oh, my. Oh, my."

Karl sat up and scooted toward her, but she extended her palm and said, "Stay where you are."

He stopped and held out his hands, wanting to draw her in again, wanting what had happened to continue to its logical conclusion.

The look on her face told him their interlude was over. Whatever enchantment had held her still for his kiss had dissipated like snow melting under the sun's hot glare. She was awake and aware and alarmed.

"It's all right, Hetty," he said in an attempt to keep her from literally fleeing the room. "We didn't do anything wrong."

"We can't be kissing like that, Karl."

"Why not?"

She seemed to struggle for an answer and finally said, "I can't feel like . . . I won't allow . . . I shouldn't be . . ."

"It was only a kiss, Hetty."

"With both of us lying in bed," she pointed out. "And the children needing us in the next room."

He wondered why she sounded so upset. "We're in our own bed, in our own room," he said. Maybe she'd suddenly realized that he'd been kissing and caressing her in broad daylight.

But that wasn't the reason she gave him for stopping. What she said was, "We hardly know each other, Karl."

He'd told her she could take all the time she needed to feel comfortable with him before they consummated their marriage. But he hadn't realized how much he would want his wife.

"You've had two weeks to get to know me. How much longer do you need?" Karl heard the impatience—and irritation—in his voice.

She must have heard it, too, because her face blanched. "Just . . . more time."

"How much more?" Karl persisted.

"Till Christmas," she blurted.

He could see it would have been fine with her if he never touched her again. He was wondering how he was going to keep his hands off of her for that long. He looked her in the eye and said, "So a month from now."

She caught her lower lip in her teeth and gave a jerky nod.

"Fine," he said. But he knew he was only postponing the inevitable. He would be the same man four weeks from now. But perhaps by then Hetty would realize there was a great deal more to him than what she saw on the outside.

The bedroom door opened at the same time as someone knocked on it, and Karl saw Grace standing in the doorway. He shuddered to think what she would have seen if she'd walked in a minute or two sooner. He saw from the blush that appeared on Hetty's cheeks as she met his gaze that she'd realized the same thing.

"Knock first. Wait for permission to enter. Then come in," Karl instructed the girl.

"Oh? Did I interrupt something?"

Karl glanced at Hetty, whose blush deepened. "Come on in," he said when the girl stayed by the door. "What do you want?"

"Is everything all right?" she asked, looking from Hetty, standing beside the bed, to Karl, sitting in his stocking feet on the messy bedclothes.

"I was trying to get Karl's hands and feet warm," Hetty explained as she crossed to Grace. "So I put them under my arms."

"In bed?" Grace asked doubtfully.

Hetty avoided Karl's gaze as she explained, "His feet needed to be warmed, too, and that seemed the easiest way to achieve both."

Karl wondered why Hetty felt it so necessary to excuse those mussed bedclothes. They were married, for heaven's sake!

"What do you want?" Karl asked again.

"I need to talk to Hetty," Grace said.

Hetty glanced back at Karl and said, "You should stay in bed and get some sleep. I'll wake you at suppertime." Then she put an arm around Grace's shoulders and left the room, closing the door behind her.

Karl was left sitting on the edge of the bed. Alone.

He was tempted to put his shoes back on and go out there and confront Hetty and demand . . . What? That she come back to bed and make love to him? Was that all he really wanted from Hetty? Her beautiful body in bed? Would that be enough to satisfy him for the rest of his life?

Karl had resigned himself to marrying a woman sight unseen, but he'd paid close attention to the letters his prospective bride had written. Those letters had been full of hopes and dreams. They'd been written by an intelligent, imaginative woman. He'd figured that if he and his wife had a love of learning in common, they would have a good basis on which to build a relationship to last a lifetime.

Those letters had influenced his immediate attraction to Hetty. But he was beginning to realize that there was a great deal he didn't know about his wife. She was as skittish as a virgin whenever he touched her. He wondered what her relationship with her previous husband—or husbands—had been like. Had she been a victim of violence? Her wound seemed to suggest it.

It had never occurred to him that his bride might have some aversion to sex, as opposed to sex specifically with him, when she'd borne two children.

Karl wondered whether Hetty was physically attracted to him. He didn't think so. On the other hand, when he'd kissed her in bed, she'd kissed him back. He wasn't mistaken about that. She must at least enjoy kissing him. Otherwise, she could have turned her head aside.

But Karl didn't trust himself to be objective where Hetty was concerned. He'd allowed a great many doubts about his new wife to go unchallenged, something he wouldn't have done if his wife hadn't been so beautiful.

He sighed and got back under the covers. He'd have to sleep on it. He needed to learn more about his wife. Whatever Hetty's hopes and dreams, she'd obviously been forced into this marriage by the need to care for those two imps. And he'd let himself get suckered into going along for the ride, all for the sake of a pretty— all right, an irresistibly beautiful—face.

Karl needed to find out if there was any chance of a happily ever after with his bride. He might be a plain-looking man, but in his dreams he was always Prince Charming. In the picture books, as in his dreams, the princess was always blue-eyed and blond and beautiful. Maybe that was why he'd fallen so quickly for Hetty.

Karl fell asleep wondering how he could get the real-life girl to fall as deeply in love with him as the princess in his dreams.

Chapter Fifteen

Hetty's mind was whirling with thoughts of what had just happened in the bedroom. What was it about Karl Norwood that made him so easy to laugh with? Why did she melt when he kissed her? Especially when, if anyone had asked, Hetty would have said there was absolutely nothing about her husband that might draw a woman's eye. Except for his brown eyes, which glowed golden in a certain light. And that overlapping front tooth, which made his smile do something strange to her insides.

Hetty freely admitted that although she'd been in love before, she had no experience with desire. But it seemed wrong to crave the touch of any man so soon after Clive's death. She'd believed the guilt and remorse she'd felt for inciting two men to fight and die would blight the rest of her life. It was disconcerting to find herself enjoying Karl's kisses. Reveling in Karl's kisses. Aching for Karl's kisses.

Hetty laid a hand against her stomach, which growled. Well, that explained the ache. She was starving. She couldn't remember the last time she'd eaten. Better to forget about kissing Karl, especially when she didn't deserve the kind of happiness that sort of intimacy portended. She'd had her chance at love, and her love had died. This was no love match, it was a marriage of convenience meant to save two destitute children.

Hetty felt a flush of shame that she'd let herself get so carried away. She needed to stay focused on what was important. Being a helpmate to her husband. Taking care of those two kids. Making a home for all of them. And getting supper on the table.

Hetty heard the children begin arguing loudly and forgot all about Karl's kisses. She hurried to their bedroom and found Griffin sitting up on the edge of his cot, pulling on a pair of socks over feet that had begun to blister.

"What's all the noise in here?" she asked in a quiet voice. "Karl's trying to get some sleep."

"Griffin's gone crazy!" Grace replied, her eyes wide with panic. She was standing beside his bed with her arms wrapped tightly around her budding chest, as though to keep herself from falling apart. "He wants to go back out in the snow and look for Mr. Campbell's horse."

"This is all my fault," the boy said. He hissed as he tried to pull a sock over his painfully frostbitten left foot.

"Oh, Griffin, no," Hetty said, her insides twisting as she imagined the excruciating pain of the rough wool rubbing against his blistered flesh. She sat down beside him on the bed and put her arms around his shoulders to stop him, leaving the sock hanging half off his injured foot.

He tried to shrug her off, but Hetty held on. "That

horse will probably show up here in a day or so all by himself. After all, he likely spent the summer stabled in the barn. He'll be able to find his way back home. Mark my words on it."

Tears leaked from Griffin's eyes, either from pain or guilt or both. He swiped at them, then glanced up at her and said, "Do you really think so?"

Hetty saw from the look in his eyes that he wanted to believe her. "Sure I do. Besides, you can't go anywhere until Bao gets back and has a look at that purple toe of yours." She reached down and eased the sock off as gently as she could, but she could tell from the way Griffin hissed in his breath that she was hurting him.

Once the sock was off, it was clear from the purple color and the lack of blisters that the little toe on his left foot was not responding to warmth as the rest of his toes had.

"Will Bao have to cut it off?" Griffin asked.

"No!" Grace cried, her arms coming free of her body to reach out in supplication. "Please don't let him do that, Mom."

"I don't know what Bao will decide to do," Hetty said in a soothing voice, grabbing one of Grace's hands and squeezing it reassuringly. "We have to trust him to know what's best."

Grace yanked her hand free. "But he can't cut it off! What if it makes Griffin limp?"

Hetty met Grace's tortured gaze and said in a calm voice, "We'll love him just the same."

The anxiety went out of Grace's face and her jaw firmed. "I certainly will."

"Toe not matter. Heart matter."

Hetty shivered at the sudden cold draft and turned to find Bao standing in the bedroom doorway, still wearing his snow-dusted coat. She shot him a relieved smile. "That sounds like something Confucius would say."

The Chinaman smiled back. "Not Confucius. Lin Bao."

Hetty laughed with relief that there was someone more knowledgeable on hand to care for Griffin. "It's good to see you back safe." She turned and saw that neither of the children was amused. Obviously, as far as they were concerned, frostbitten toes were not a laughing matter. Hetty would be sorry if Griffin lost a toe, but she was grateful more harm hadn't been done. And for that, they owed Karl thanks.

Bao shook the snow off his coat onto the planked wooden floor, then dropped his coat on Grace's bed and asked Hetty, "Boss okay?"

"He's sleeping."

"Found horse. Put in barn," Bao said to Griffin.

Hetty saw tears well again in the boy's dark brown eyes. She watched his Adam's apple bob before he croaked, "Thank you, Bao."

"Everybody okay?" the Chinaman asked.

"Karl has a little frostbite. Griffin's is worse," Hetty replied.

"Let me see hands and feet," Bao said as he crossed to the bed. He carefully inspected Griffin's hands and feet and said, "Ah."

"What does that mean?" Grace asked anxiously, her hands once more crossed over her chest.

Bao looked at Griffin, rather than at Grace, and

said, "Purple toe maybe dead. We watch. If not get better, must come off."

Hetty watched Griffin's features, which were finally getting some color, blanch again. "When will we know for sure?" she asked Bao.

The Chinaman shrugged. "Sometimes week. Sometimes month. Right now, need salve for blisters." He turned to Grace. "You nurse. I watch."

Grace looked surprised and her gaze shot to Hetty, who'd been Bao's student on the trail. "Shouldn't Hetty be doing this?"

"Your turn learn medicine." Then Bao turned to Hetty and said, "You make tea for boy with rose hips. Remember how?"

Hetty nodded. "If I can find the rose hips."

"In box by door," Bao said. "Second from top."

Despite the weather, Bao had unloaded the wagon when they'd arrived. Many of the supplies had ended up in the cookhouse or bunkhouse. The rest of the boxes and bags he'd dropped inside the door to the cabin.

Hetty hadn't unpacked because she'd been too worried to focus on anything except whether Karl would return, and if so, whether Griffin would be with him. In hindsight, doing something productive would have kept her from worrying so much. But it was another day, and her new family was back safe. It was time to go to work. Time to make rose-hip tea for Griffin. And time to make this house her home.

Hetty looked around with fresh eyes at the central room, which was divided in half. On the left, Karl had arranged a simple parlor around the river-rock fireplace on the back wall, with a couple of willow rockers set in front of the fire and a table between them.

To the right was the kitchen, with a stove on the side wall next to a copper sink. Roomy cupboards had been built above the sink, which had a pump handle to bring water into the kitchen.

The two small windows on either side of the front door were fitted with clear glass, and Hetty itched to make curtains to give them a more homey look and to provide privacy.

She'd only gotten a glimpse of the lumberjacks, but when the wagon had pulled up in front of the cabin, at least a dozen men had gathered around to ogle her and Grace. They'd nodded and touched the brims of their wool caps in homage, and she'd nodded back. They'd been frightening to behold. Unshaven. Long-haired. Bulbous noses. Blackened teeth. Tall men with enormous shoulders, and short, stout ones. Men with narrow faces. Men with sunken eyes and sun-browned skin, all of them blending into one jumbled horde.

Hetty told herself that despite their frightening appearance the ragtag throng weren't thieves or murderers. They were simply men hired to work with ax and saw during the snowy weather, when the cut logs could more easily be skidded down the mountain by oxen. They were also the men she was required to help feed and whose cuts she would be asked to stitch. Hetty wondered how she would ever have the courage to walk among them, let alone care for their hurts.

Grace appeared in the bedroom doorway looking shaken. "Bao said I should come help you unpack."

Hetty hurried to the girl and slid an arm around her waist.

"Griffin's in horrible pain," the girl whispered. "He was biting his lip to keep from crying out while Bao tended to him, but I could tell."

"It's too bad he's hurting, but I suspect he'll be back to his old cantankerous self before you know it."

"He's not cantankerous," Grace protested, coming yet again to the defense of her younger brother.

"Tell me that when he's driving you mad getting things for him while he's confined to bed," Hetty said with a smile. She gave Grace a comforting pat on the rump. "Come on. Let's get this stuff unpacked and make Griffin some tea."

"Griffin likes coffee better than tea."

"Bao suggested rose-hip tea," Hetty said. "We'll have to ask him if it has some medicinal purpose, so we'll know in the future."

Grace nodded. "I never thought of that."

"Let's see what's here before we start." Hetty looked through cupboards to see what was already on hand, so she would have some idea where to store things, while Grace surveyed the stack of boxes and bags by the door.

"Look at all this food!" Grace exclaimed.

Hetty was impressed herself. She'd known the wagon was full, but she'd never realized exactly what filled it. Fifty-pound bags of flour and cornmeal and rice and beans. Sugar! Salted pork and beef and lard. Canned peaches. Pickles and jellies and all sorts of relish in glass jars. Tobacco. And whiskey.

"Is Karl rich?" Grace asked. "Does this mean we'll never be hungry again?"

"Not for the foreseeable future, anyway," Hetty

said with a smile as she eyed the treasure trove they'd unpacked.

"I dreamed about a home like this," Grace said, running her hand along the kitchen table. "And a father like Karl." She met Hetty's gaze. "And a mother like you."

Hetty felt her throat swell with emotion. "That's the nicest thing anybody's ever said to me." She crossed and put her arms around Grace, hugging her tight, and felt Grace hugging her back.

Hetty's dreams had been about finding Prince Charming, not about raising children. It seemed she'd skipped a step somewhere along the way.

"I mean it," Grace mumbled, her face pressed against Hetty's bosom.

"Hey!" Griffin called from the bedroom. "I'm thirsty. Where's that tea?"

The two females looked at each other and laughed.

"You certainly called that right," Grace said.

Hetty had uncovered the rose hips long ago, but she'd forgotten about the tea in the excitement of opening boxes. "Coming up!" she called back to him.

She kissed Grace's forehead, let her go, and said, "You get the water from the hob. I'll get a cup and the rose hips. And we'd better get a fire going in that stove, so we can make something to eat. I don't know about you, but I'm starved."

Grace grinned. "Me, too! What should me make, Mom?"

"Didn't I see a book of recipes when we unpacked?"

"I put it on the shelf beside the sink," Grace said.

"Let's see what we can find that can be made up in

an hour or so and set some beans to soaking for supper."

It dawned on Hetty that she'd begun the rest of her life. This is what it would be like. Bao to provide Oriental wisdom. Griffin to have adventures that caused trouble. Grace to be a loving daughter. And Karl to protect them all and provide a home where they could live safely ever after.

Hetty took only a moment to realize that *safely* ever after was not exactly how the fairy tales went. What had happened to *happily* ever after? Hetty didn't allow herself to dwell on the thought. For now, being safe and secure seemed far more important than something as indefinable as happiness.

If her heart sank a little, she ignored it. There was work to occupy her mind, children to care for, and a new life to begin, with responsibilities and challenges. Happiness would have to wait.

"What's going on? What have I missed?"

Hetty turned and felt her heart career in her chest at the sight of Karl's rumpled brown hair and warm brown eyes. He smiled at her, and she felt herself smiling back.

Before Hetty could register her feelings, the front door burst open. A huge man with a hooked nose, small black eyes, and black hair sprouting from beneath a wool cap, stood in the doorway. "Better come quick, Boss. Trouble in the bunkhouse."

Chapter Sixteen

Karl's heart was pounding by the time he arrived at the bunkhouse, which was situated at the base of the Bitterroot Mountains on the western side of the valley. It was separated from the house by a wide, snow-covered meadow. The loggers had been hired by Dennis in Butte while Karl stayed behind in the valley to work on finishing up the house, barn, and bunkhouse. So he had no idea what to expect.

He found two men wrestling on the floor of the bunkhouse while the rest of the lumberjacks stood watching. Karl didn't hear the expected cheering for the man of their choice to win. It took only a moment to determine that Dennis was one of the two men in the fight, and that he was mercilessly beating the man beneath him.

That was why the logger had come running. None of them had felt he could interfere with the man who'd hired him.

Karl shoved his way through the crowd, put a hand on Dennis's shoulder, and had it knocked off with such power that it hit one of the men behind him in the face. Karl turned to apologize and was met with a fist in the nose that made him see stars. He tasted blood and realized his pummeled nose was bleeding.

The fellow next to the one who'd hit Karl muttered, "That's the boss," causing the man who'd hit Karl to make a disgusted face and say, "Well, I'll be a goat! There goes my job."

Karl didn't have time to spare for the logger's remorse. He turned back to Dennis, who was still whaling on the man he straddled, who was no longer capable of resisting. Karl didn't make the mistake of touching Dennis again, just got close enough to his ear to say, "That's enough, Dennis. Your man's down."

As though Karl's soft-spoken voice broke a spell, Dennis's bloodied knuckles fell to his thighs. He gave a huffing sigh and clambered to his feet, stepping across the downed logger.

Karl turned to the nearest man and said, "Put that fellow on his bunk. I'll send Bao out to tend him." Then he turned to Dennis and said, "Come with me."

As Dennis left the bunkhouse with Karl, he stared down the men around him, who shuffled off to find something to do.

They were outside before Karl spoke again. "What was that all about?"

"I told him to get out of my way, and he didn't," Dennis replied.

"So you hit him?"

"Of course."

"You couldn't have asked a second time?" Karl said. "Maybe he didn't hear you."

"Then he doesn't belong on a logging gang," Dennis replied. "The boss's word is law. When you're not on the mountain, I'll be in charge. When I say 'Jump,' those men need to answer 'How high?' or they're no good to me."

Karl planned to be on the mountain himself whenever his loggers were working, which meant there would never be a need for Dennis to take his place. "I'm the one they'll need to answer to, Dennis," he said quietly.

Dennis looked startled. "Are you planning to cut wood?"

"Why wouldn't I?"

Dennis laughed. "You don't have the shoulders for it."

Karl flushed. He wasn't particularly muscular, but he'd carried plenty of heavy packs across the Territory during his years of study. He was certainly fit enough to use an ax, though he would likely be sore and tired at the end of the day.

"Best leave the work on the mountain to me," Dennis said.

"This is my operation," Karl replied. "I'll handle it."

"You've got enough on your plate finding a site for that mill," Dennis said. "I can supervise the cutting."

And if he did, Karl was sure Dennis would tell Jonas he had. Which meant Karl's efforts to prove himself to his brother would come to naught. Karl had never been in charge of a dozen men before, certainly not men the likes of those he'd seen in the bunkhouse. He would never have considered using his fists to establish dominance over them, but Dennis seemed to think there was no other way.

Karl hoped he was wrong, because he planned to do things a different way. His own way. All he said was, "I appreciate the offer to help, Dennis, but I'm going to give it a go on my own."

Dennis snickered, making it clear what he thought of Karl's chances of succeeding. "Sure, Karl. Whatever you say."

Karl had forgotten about his bloody nose, which he'd swiped once or twice with the tip of his shirtsleeve where it hung out beneath his coat, so when he opened the door to the cabin he was startled by Hetty's, "Oh, no! What happened, Karl?"

Karl reached toward his tender nose and said, "It's nothing."

"Your nose is bleeding!" Hetty retorted. "Come with me."

She grabbed his hand as though he were a child and led him toward the kitchen table. Dennis followed along, winking at Karl and grinning as Hetty pulled off his coat and pushed her husband into a kitchen chair.

"Dennis's hands need attention," Karl said as he set his wool cap on the table.

"Bao can take care of Dennis," she replied, arranging Karl's coat on the back of his chair, never even glancing in Dennis's direction. Karl found it disconcerting to have her staring at his nose from four inches away. It was hard to focus with his one good eye.

"Bao needs to take a look at one of the loggers," he countered. "Bao!" he called.

Bao appeared in the doorway to the children's bedroom and said, "You call, Boss?"

"There's a man needs doctoring in the bunkhouse."

"On my way, Boss." Bao retrieved his coat and box

of medicines from the children's bedroom and left the cabin.

Meanwhile, Hetty pointed at Dennis, who was hovering by Karl's chair. "You sit, too."

Dennis set his coat on the chair back and sat down across from Karl, still grinning.

Hetty hustled around the kitchen, gathering hot water and dishcloths and scolding, "I just got through treating frostbite on your hands and feet, you've got an eye that's almost swollen closed, and now you've gotten yourself a bloody nose. You need to take better care of yourself, Karl."

"My feelings exactly," Dennis said.

She plopped a ceramic bowl of cold water in front of Dennis, forcing him to lean back to avoid getting splashed, and ordered, "Put your hands in there."

Dennis swore as the broken skin on his bruised knuckles sank into the icy water.

Hetty snapped, "Don't be a baby."

Karl smiled smugly. "Yeah, Dennis. Don't be a baby." Then he yelped as Hetty plopped a cold washcloth on his nose and snapped, "Tilt your head back."

"Hey! Be careful." He leaned away from her, holding the cloth more gently in place.

Her fists landed on her hips. "Why on earth did you get into a fight, Karl?"

"I didn't!" he protested. "Dennis swatted at me and I—"

She turned on Dennis, her mouth agape. "Dennis! How could you!"

"Karl snuck up on me, and I struck out to protect myself," Dennis retorted. "Besides, I didn't hit him in the nose. One of the loggers did that."

"Are your loggers so undisciplined that you need to use your fists to control them?" she demanded of both men.

"Better to let them know who the big dog is from the start," Dennis replied, pointing at his chest with a thumb.

"I thought Karl was the big dog," she said pointedly.

Dennis smirked. "Karl's a pussycat."

Karl felt the flush of humiliation stain his cheeks. It was bad enough to have Dennis make that sort of comment to him. It was a thousand times worse to have him say something so demeaning in front of his brand-new wife.

He'd thought that was the worst of it. But unlike on the trail, where Hetty had jumped to his defense, her lips pressed flat and she said nothing. He searched her face, wondering what she was thinking. But she kept her gaze focused on a sticking plaster she was manipulating in her hands.

He kept his one good eye focused on her face as she took the damp cloth away and gently dabbed at his bloodied nose with a dry cloth. Then she carefully placed the sticking plaster across the broken skin on the bridge and said, "Keep your head back until your nose stops dripping blood."

He wanted to say, *I'm as good a man as any other.* But Hetty would either believe the best of him, or she wouldn't. He wondered why she hadn't jumped to his defense this time. Why had she left that denigrating description of him as a *pussycat* unanswered? Unless she believed it.

Bao appeared at the door and said, "Need you, Boss."

Karl rose. "Be right there."

"Your nose is still bleeding," Hetty pointed out.

Karl swiped at his nose with his shirtsleeve and saw a red smear on the plaid wool. "It's fine." He grabbed his coat and cap and headed out the door without looking back.

Chapter Seventeen

Grace had vowed more than once that she was going to change her habit of eavesdropping. It just wasn't nice. But when the front door opened with a slam and a gust of frigid wind blew through, she came to the bedroom door—just to find out what was going on— and heard aggravated voices. Annoyed voices. Anxious voices.

She'd stayed hidden and listened, something she'd learned in the saloon growing up—where knowing which way the wind was blowing was literally a matter of life and death—until she could determine whether the situation required action on her part.

Hetty was chastising both Karl and Dennis. The two men had apparently been fighting again, only this time not with each other. It seemed Karl had gotten the worst of it. Again.

Grace's heart jumped to her throat when Karl abruptly left the house to attend to more trouble in the bunkhouse. It was like being hit in the face with a shovel to realize that her survival, and that of her brother, hinged upon Karl's survival. Hetty cared for them, but Hetty had nothing of her own. Having a home with a breadwinner like Karl was the main reason Grace had concocted the entire mail-order-bride scheme.

Grace had proffered a very high price to get herself and her brother to this log home in the Bitterroot Valley. She'd had a sick feeling in her stomach ever since she'd blurted to Hetty that she'd *paid* Mrs. Templeton to bring them along. Granted, her slip of the tongue had come when she'd been terrified that all was lost. But she'd been dreading the moment when Griffin recalled her words and asked, *Where did you get the kind of money it would take for the witch to bring us along?*

Because Grace had no answer that would keep her brother from figuring out how she'd gotten the cash to pay Mrs. Templeton. She couldn't bear for him to know what she'd done. He wouldn't understand. He'd despise her if he knew the truth, as he'd despised their mother.

But she'd only had one thing to sell. So she'd sold it.

Grace shuddered. The experience had been horrible. Degrading. Painful. She'd endured it because she'd known she was trading a few moments of her life in exchange for a better life forever after for herself and her brother.

It hadn't been easy talking herself into doing it. Grace had sworn, from the time she was old enough to know what her mother did for a living, that she would *never, ever* allow herself to become any man's plaything. In the end, she'd had no choice. But she would *never, ever* do it again.

That was easy to say. But that proud, defiant resolution depended on her and Griffin having a stable home in which to grow up, which included food on the table and a roof over their heads. It was appalling to realize that their future depended on the fortunes of a man who'd been beaten up twice in as many days and whose best friend had just described him as a *pussycat*.

"Hey! What the hell's going on out there?" Griffin demanded, sitting up in bed.

"Shush!" Grace jumped back inside and eased the bedroom door closed. She took one look at her brother and said, "For heaven's sake, wipe your nose!"

He swiped his long john sleeve across his runny nose and said, "Were Karl and Dennis fighting again?"

"You could use a hanky, you know."

"Don't have one."

"It's right there on the bedside table," Grace said.

"Oh." He started to pick it up and hissed as his blistered fingertips touched the white cloth. "I'll stick with my sleeve." He turned back to her and said, "I saw you listening, Grace. What did you find out?"

Grace shook her head. For a nine-year-old, her brother didn't miss much. "It was some kind of squabble in the bunkhouse. Karl got hurt."

"Again?" Griffin shook his head in disgust. "Karl wasn't the only guy looking for a mail-order bride that you wrote to, Grace. Why did you pick such a namby-pamby for a father?"

"Karl's not afraid to fight," Grace retorted.

"Maybe not. But he always comes out on the short end of the stick. One of these days, he's going to get his head handed to him. Why him, Grace?"

"His letters offered the most promise for a better life."

"Based on what?"

"For one thing, he didn't seem to care about looks." Grace was particularly sensitive on the subject because, with her garish red curls, impossible faceful of freckles, and baby fat that had stuck long past a time when it should have gone away, she knew what it felt like to be judged for her looks and found wanting. "Karl was seeking other, more important qualities in a bride, like responsibility and kindness. And he seemed to value education and intelligence."

Griffin snickered. "And yet, he got fooled by a thirteen-year-old girl."

Grace flushed. She hadn't told Griffin what she'd written in those letters. She thought maybe her notes had appealed to Karl because she'd poured out all her grown-up hopes and dreams for the future. Some of those plans—the ones that featured a loving husband and several children—would probably never come true now because of what she'd been forced to do to buy their passage to this new and better life.

But Karl had seemed willing to foster those dreams. Moreover, he'd shared several dreams of his own. Grace hadn't yet told Hetty about the hopes and fears Karl had put down on paper, but she'd kept all the letters, so perhaps that was something she ought to do.

She'd also kept copies of her own letters to Karl, where she'd written about her dreams of one day marrying a good man.

What good man would want her now?

Besides, her plans had changed. She would *never, ever* have to face a man across a marriage bed and explain why she wasn't a virgin, because she was *never, ever* going to let a man get that close to her again.

"I didn't want to join some make-believe family in the first place," Griffin muttered.

"You can't really complain. We ended up in a better home, with better parents, than we had any right to hope," Grace replied.

Griffin made a face that conceded her point, but said, "We were damned lucky we didn't end up spending the rest of our lives with that witch as our mother."

"I admit I didn't think that situation completely through. But you couldn't ask for a better mother than Hetty."

Griffin made another face. "She's pretty bossy."

"Someone needs to keep you in line," Grace said, sitting down on the bed beside her brother. "Speaking of which, you're going to have to try harder, Griffin."

"To do what?"

"To behave yourself." She saw Griffin was going to protest. "I should have done something about your behavior myself a long time ago. You've been running wild ever since Mom died two years ago."

Griffin swiped at his runny nose with his sleeve again. "You're not the boss of me."

"I know that. But these pranks have to stop."

Griffin dropped his chin to his chest and used his elbows to move around the muslin sheets, trying to pull them up around his waist. "You must hate me."

Grace scooted over and put her arms around Griffin, refusing to let go when he tried to wrestle out of her embrace. "I love you, you silly goose! Even when you're acting like an ass."

Griffin smirked at her. "All I have to do is crow like a rooster and grunt like a pig and you'll have a whole farmful of animals in your arms. *Cock-a-doodle-doo! Oink! Oink! Oink!*"

Grace wrinkled her nose and let him go. "You certainly smell like a barnyard full of animals."

Griffin laughed. "So do you."

"I wouldn't be surprised if Hetty—I mean Mom—starts in on cleaning us up as soon as she gets the house the way she wants it."

The grin disappeared from Griffin's face. "Just let her try!"

"You'll do as you're told," Grace said, ruffling her brother's lanky black hair. "Besides, a bath wouldn't hurt you."

Griffin held up his blistered hands and shot a look at his wounded feet. "Don't think I'm going to be getting into a tub anytime soon."

Grace felt her insides twist as she surveyed her brother's frostbitten extremities. Her gaze lingered on his little toe, which had turned nearly black. "I hope you don't lose your toe."

He shook his head in disgust. "I'm damned lucky I didn't freeze to death. I'm surprised Karl risked his life looking for me."

"Why wouldn't he?"

Griffin shot her a piercing look. "When did *anybody* ever do *anything* for us that they weren't paid to do?"

Grace held her breath, terrified that in the next instant Griffin was going to ask her where she'd gotten the money to pay Lucille Templeton. She quickly said, "I could tell from Karl's letters that he was a kind man. That's partly why I chose him. Apparently he intends to be a responsible stepfather, which includes looking for some crazy kid who trekked off in a blizzard to hunt down a horse that he let go in the first place."

Griffin flushed. "Fine. So Karl's kind. And responsible. He's also lily-livered."

"He is not!" Grace shot back. "No coward would have followed you into a blizzard, risking his life—"

"Only an idiot would do something that stupid," Griffin interrupted. "Admit it, Grace. The father you chose doesn't have a lot of common sense."

"Maybe not," she conceded. "But you can't deny he's intelligent."

"He's *book* smart," Griffin agreed. "What good is that going to do him out here in the middle of nowhere? We need a father who can use his head and not take risks that are going to get him killed. We need him alive, not dead."

Because Grace had come to the very same conclusion herself not five minutes before, she didn't argue. She simply said, "It's too late to do anything about it now."

Griffin met her gaze and said, "I suppose we better watch out for him."

"How are we going to do that? We'll probably both end up working around the house while he's up on the mountain."

Griffin's jaw firmed. "Guess I'm gonna have to get myself up on that mountain with him."

"Hetty will never let you go."

"Then you better convince her otherwise," Griffin replied.

"It's too dangerous, Griffin."

"No more dangerous than half the things I was into

in Cheyenne. Besides," he said with a wry smile, "you can count on Karl to keep a close eye on me."

Grace twisted the long curl at the end of one of her childish braids around her forefinger and said, "True." She furrowed her brow in thought. "I just don't see how I'm going to convince Hetty to let you go."

Griffin lay back down, using his elbows to pull the covers up around him. "You'll think of something, Grace. You always do."

Chapter Eighteen

Dennis couldn't believe his luck. Karl had been called back to the bunkhouse, the two brats were shut in their room, and he'd been left completely alone, at long last, with Karl's wife. The woman was already half in love with him. He'd felt the connection from the first moment their eyes had met in that hotel in Butte, when she'd blushed and lowered her startled gaze to avoid staring back at him. With a little effort, Dennis thought he could have her.

Hetty had trembled in his arms when he'd filched that kiss on her wedding day, and she'd been careful to avoid him ever since, a sure sign that she wasn't immune to his charms. He'd done everything he could along the trail to let her know he was a better man than Karl without ever coming right out and saying it. She'd been stubborn about supporting Karl, but he was encouraged by the fact that she'd felt she needed to defend her husband.

Dennis wasn't averse to cuckolding his friend. He just had to be careful not to let Karl find out. Karl might not be as strong or as experienced with his fists as Dennis was, but he had a surprising amount of grit and a great deal of pride. Karl Norwood would make a formidable enemy.

Unfortunately for Karl, he was weighed down by morals and rules for playing fair that had never troubled Dennis. If he was careful, Dennis could have what he wanted without Karl ever being the wiser.

Dennis wasn't a blackguard. He'd never taken a woman against her will. But what a woman freely gave, he was happy to take. That might be splitting hairs, but Dennis hadn't been born with all of Karl's advantages. He'd had to earn his way in life, which meant grabbing what he could get when he could get it.

Hetty took his wrist and eased one of his hands from the bowl of cold water in which they were soaking, surveyed his torn and bruised knuckles, and said, "Your hands look awful."

"They'll heal." Dennis was looking at Hetty and noticed she was biting her lower lip, clearly worried about something. About being alone with him? He said nothing, waiting to see what she would do.

A moment later she looked up at him with eyes as innocent and blue as a summer sky. And froze.

Dennis wondered about the apparent shyness—almost maidenly modesty—that caused her to suddenly lower her gaze. It seemed inappropriate in a woman with two children, and if Karl's suppositions were correct, at least two previous bed partners. Dennis found the guise—the pretense of innocence—particularly thrilling.

Perhaps Hetty had experienced sex but had never known passion. Dennis was an expert on the subject.

He would be happy to awaken her to that particular pleasure.

Hetty's perfect complexion turned rosy and she dropped his hand, which plopped back into the water. She glanced at him, then at her hands, which were gripped together, before settling them in her lap.

Dennis had a sudden thought. Was it possible Karl had never made love to his wife? Certainly Karl had kept his distance from his wife on the trail. What if considerate Karl had given his brand-new wife a reprieve from her wifely duties on the only night they'd spent alone together?

No wonder she was blushing. Apparently this rosebud was ripe for the plucking. He waited expectantly for the word of encouragement that was all he would need to act.

Hetty raised her head, looked him in the eye, and asked, "What's going to happen to Karl?"

Dennis almost hissed in disappointment. He pressed his lips flat for a moment to hide his chagrin that she'd chosen to discuss Karl, rather than a possible tryst with him. "What do you mean?"

"What if the loggers won't obey him?"

He watched as the flush moved from her cheeks to her throat. Was she uncomfortable criticizing Karl? Or very much aware of her attraction to him and the fact that they were alone?

She cleared her throat and continued, "Karl mentioned to me that he's never been a boss before. Do you think he'll be able to make the loggers do what he needs them to do?"

"You're worried—"

"Not worried, exactly," she interrupted. "I'm sure Karl will figure it all out. He's a very smart man."

"Yes, he is," Dennis conceded. With a wife determined to bolster him. It might be harder to get through Hetty's defenses than he'd initially thought. He pulled his hands from the water, held them out, and said, "Do you have a towel?"

She jumped up, like a rabbit escaping a fox, and retrieved a dishcloth from where it hung near a cupboard. He was standing when she returned, holding out his dripping hands so she could dry them.

She kept her eyes focused on what she was doing, but he pulled one hand free and reached out to tip her chin up, so he could look into her eyes, which were rife with confusion. "You don't have to worry about Karl because I'll be there to make sure nothing happens to him."

He felt the tremor that ran through her body at his touch. She dropped the cloth—or it fell—and she used that excuse to pull away. She stooped to pick up the cloth and returned it to the hook near the cupboard, keeping her back to him and fiddling with it as she said, "I don't think Karl needs a caretaker."

"Do you have any idea what we'll be doing up there on the mountain?" he asked.

She turned back to him, clearly curious. "Actually, I don't." She tucked her arms protectively under her breasts and kept her distance.

"Some of the men will be cutting logs with crosscut saws, some with axes. A couple will buck limbs. Someone else will skid logs back down the mountain through the snow with oxen. Once I get the mill up and running in the spring—"

She interrupted him to say, "Karl told me he's in charge of setting up the sawmill."

Dennis was unable to control the flicker of annoyance that crossed his face. "Karl and I have discussed the matter. The final say is his, of course, but he's been smart enough to defer to my experience in the past, so it's likely he will again."

Hetty lifted her chin and took two steps closer, so that no more than an inch or two separated them. "You make it sound like you're in charge. I was under the impression that Karl is running this operation."

The door was thrust open and Karl stood in the doorway, his eyes fierce, his fists bunched. He shot a frown at Hetty, who leapt back, putting a more respectable distance between the two of them. Karl focused his angry gaze on Dennis and said, "You better come."

"What's the problem?" Dennis glanced at Hetty to see her reaction to Karl appealing to him for help.

She hurried to Karl and asked, "What's wrong?"

"Stay out of this, Hetty," he snapped.

Hetty stopped short and gasped, clearly shocked at Karl's abrupt dismissal of her. She held out her hands in supplication. "Is someone hurt? Maybe I can help."

"There's nothing you can do," Karl replied harshly. He turned to Dennis and snarled, "Let's go."

As Dennis grabbed his coat, he caught a glimpse of the hurt look on Hetty's face and hid his grin of satisfaction. If Karl kept up this sort of behavior toward Hetty, his seduction of Karl's wife was a foregone conclusion.

Chapter Nineteen

The door closed, shutting Hetty out. Or rather, shutting Hetty in. She was still staring at the closed door a moment later when Grace joined her in the kitchen.

"What was that all about?" Grace asked.

"I have no idea," Hetty admitted. "Something must have gone wrong in the bunkhouse." And Karl had come to ask for Dennis's help in solving the problem. Hetty shuddered when she recalled the look on Karl's face when he'd opened the door and noticed her standing so close to Dennis.

She hadn't been flirting! She'd only wanted to find out everything she could about Karl's work. She didn't know how she'd ended up standing toe-to-toe with Dennis. Based on the lowering frown Karl had shot at her, he'd completely misconstrued what he'd seen. She had no desire to make Karl jealous. She knew better.

Hetty covered her face with her hands. She never wanted a repeat of the disaster she'd caused on the wagon train. She never wanted her behavior to give any man an excuse to fight, especially not Karl. She might not love her husband, but she liked and admired him. And her future, and that of the children, depended on the continuation of their marriage.

She felt Grace's hand on her shoulder and then heard the girl's tremulous voice asking, "What's wrong, Hetty?"

Hetty dropped her hands and snapped, "You know better than to call me Hetty!"

Before Grace could flee, Hetty caught her arm and pulled the girl into her embrace. "I'm sorry, Grace. I'm not mad at you. I'm mad at myself over something that has nothing to do with you."

Grace remained stiff and unyielding, so Hetty admitted, "I'm worried about Karl."

Grace looked up at her and said, "Me, too. What's happened now?"

"I have no idea. Karl completely shut me out."

"And you're going to let him get away with that?" Grace asked.

Hetty slid one arm down around Grace's waist and smiled ruefully. She was four years older than her stepdaughter, but in many ways, Grace was so much older and wiser. "Will you keep an eye on Griffin while I go to the bunkhouse?"

"Of course."

Hetty crossed to the antler coatrack by the door and slipped into her gray wool overcoat. She grabbed a wool shawl she'd inherited from Mrs. Templeton and began wrapping it around her head. As she opened the door, she turned back to Grace and ordered, "Don't either of you leave the house."

"We won't."

The sun glared off the snow, and Hetty squinted as she pulled on her knitted gloves, also courtesy of Mrs.

Templeton. She followed the dirty path trampled in the snow toward the bunkhouse across the meadow. The wind was brisk, and she tightened the shawl around her head. She could see smoke rising from the chimney at the cookhouse, a short distance from the bunkhouse. Apparently Bao was preparing lunch for the loggers.

Hetty was tempted to stop by the cookhouse and see if Bao had any idea what was going on. But when the trail split in two, she stayed to the right to go to the bunkhouse, afraid that if she stopped to talk with Bao she might lose her courage.

Karl should have told her what was wrong when she asked. She wanted to be his helpmate, but she couldn't very well do that if he didn't share his problems. She was going to be responsible for helping to feed these men and nursing their hurts. Karl should want her to meet them.

She hesitated at the bunkhouse door, wondering if she should knock. She heard angry voices inside and realized it was possible no one would hear her knock. She gripped the doorknob and pushed her way inside.

Hetty stopped short, overwhelmed by the atrocious body odor of a dozen men in a confined space who hadn't shaved or bathed in what must have been weeks or months, or maybe even years. She distinctly smelled tobacco and coal oil and licorice.

Her gaze shot to Karl and Dennis, who were standing in a corner confronting a curly-headed, dark-bearded mountain of a man. His face was ruddy with anger, and spittle flew from his lips as he argued with Karl.

Hetty saw the man mountain jab his finger toward a slight figure standing behind Karl. She took a closer look and saw that the giant had gestured toward a slender, towheaded boy who couldn't have been much older than Hetty was herself. The kid had a black eye, and he was using a dirty handkerchief to swipe at blood dribbling from both his nose and mouth.

It took her a moment to realize that the man mountain had blood on the knuckles of the hand he was using to point at the kid.

"Did you hit that poor boy?" Hetty hadn't realized she'd moved or even that she'd spoken until she found herself standing in front of the giant.

The muttering voices in the bunkhouse stopped as though someone had suddenly gagged them.

Karl grasped her arm, but Hetty held her ground and confronted the giant, her hands balled into fists to keep the men in the bunkhouse, whose eyes she could feel boring into her back, from seeing how they were trembling.

The giant's hand dropped abruptly and his ruddy face turned beet red as he looked down at her. "Yes, ma'am," he answered politely. "I surely did."

"Why?" she asked, her voice filled with anguish for the damage done to the boy's face.

"He wasn't following orders."

"What orders?" Hetty demanded.

"To make up my bunk," the giant admitted.

Hetty felt all the angry helplessness of living under the brutal tyranny of Miss Iris Birch rise up inside her. She hated bullies. Twisting free of Karl's hold, she whirled on him and asked, "How could you let this happen?"

It wasn't until she'd blurted the question that she realized the spot she'd put Karl in. She turned her head and scanned the faces in the room, but whenever she tried to meet a lumberman's eyes, he lowered his gaze to the ground. It was apparent that Karl had tried to fix the problem himself and hadn't succeeded. He'd needed someone bigger and stronger than himself—Dennis—to control this ruffian. Hetty's question had merely pointed out Karl's failure.

Karl put himself between Hetty and the man mountain and said quietly, "Go back to the house."

Hetty wished she could tell Karl about her years living in an orphanage under the oppressive hand of Miss Birch. She knew what it felt like to have someone force you to do their bidding. She'd spoken without thinking, but she'd spoken from her heart.

Before she could open her mouth to protest Karl's order, he added, "Take the boy with you and see what you can do to fix the damage to his face."

Hetty knew that if she didn't obey Karl, what little authority he had would be diminished even more. She turned to the boy and asked, "What's your name?"

"Andy Peterson, ma'am," he said with a distinctly Southern drawl.

"Come with me, Andy," she said. Then she turned her back on Karl and headed for the door. One of the loggers opened the door for her before she got there, and she simply marched out into the cold. She never looked back to see whether Andy was following her.

Her stomach churned. She hadn't wanted to cause Karl to lose face in front of his men, but she was very much afraid that that was what had happened as a result of her visit to the bunkhouse. She dreaded having to explain her behavior to him later.

Hetty got as far as the split in the trail that led to

the cookhouse before she stopped cold. Andy was following so close that he bumped into her. When she turned, she realized that the boy hadn't even stopped to get his coat and cap. He stood before her in his red long john shirt, his narrow shoulders shivering.

She looked up into the kid's beardless face and said, "Go to the house and tell my daughter, Grace, that she's to take care of your hurts."

"That's not necessary, ma'am," the boy said. "It's nothing. I can hang out in the stable till Buck cools off."

Hetty was tempted to let him go. But he was another lost child, another stray who needed her help. "Do as I say, Andy."

The boy shrugged. "Yes, ma'am."

Hetty stood where she was and let Andy pass her by. She needed some advice, and she knew where to get it. She turned around and headed right back in the direction from which she'd come. Only this time, she took the fork in the path that led to the cookhouse.

The cookhouse was both a lot warmer and a lot better smelling than the bunkhouse. The scent of bacon permeated the air, and Bao stood in front of an iron cookstove stirring a cauldron of what smelled like savory stew.

The Chinaman turned to her as she shut the door. The first words out of his mouth were, "Confucius say: 'When anger rises, think of consequences.'"

Hetty was surprised into laughter. "Is it so obvious that I'd like to dump that whole pot of stew on Karl's head."

He gestured her toward a seat on a bench long

enough to seat a half dozen men, which ran along one side of a wooden trestle table. "Sit. Have tea. Talk."

Hetty unwrapped her shawl and let it lie on her shoulders as she settled on the bench. Bao set a delicate china cup in front of her and poured tea from a white china teapot.

"This was going to be your cup of tea," Hetty said when she saw the small white cup and dragon-handled teapot.

Bao got a tin cup for himself and poured the rest of the tea from the teapot, then sat on the bench on the opposite side of the table. "Have tea. You talk."

Hetty wasn't sure where to start. If Karl had spoken to her before he'd left the house, she wouldn't have followed after him and put them both in such an awkward position. He must have been mortified when she'd chastised his man instead of letting him do it himself. When would she ever stop making stupid mistakes?

She felt tears welling in her eyes as she said, "How can I help Karl if he won't share his troubles with me?"

Bao pulled on his beard as he contemplated her question.

Hetty was waiting for the Chinaman to spout more wisdom from Confucius when the cookhouse door opened with a bang, letting in a stream of bright sunlight and a freezing draft. Hetty shivered and turned to see who it was.

Karl stood in the doorway, his feet spread wide. His face looked forbidding. He closed the door behind him and said, "We need to talk."

Chapter Twenty

Karl wasn't happy to find his wife sitting across the table from Bao having a cup of tea as though she hadn't a care in the world. Especially after that scene she'd caused in the bunkhouse. He couldn't believe Hetty had shown up as though she thought he needed rescuing.

He'd come here to remonstrate with Bao about his wife not trusting him to be able to handle his men, not to mention what he'd seen when he'd burst in on Hetty and his best friend at the house. Now, here she was usurping his relationship with the Chinaman as well.

"What the hell are you doing here?" he said in a harsh voice. "I sent you to the house to take care of that kid."

Karl could almost see Hetty's neck hairs hackle. Her back stiffened as she carefully set the delicate tea-cup back on its saucer. Then she turned to him and said, "Grace is perfectly capable of taking care of Andy. I decided to come have a cup of tea with Bao."

He stuck his bunched hands on his hips to keep from reaching out and shaking her. "What were you thinking, coming to the bunkhouse like that?"

She turned away from him, picked up her teacup, and took a sip in supposed indifference, but her trembling hands gave her away. She wasn't nearly so unfazed by his wrath as she pretended to be. "I thought it was time I met the loggers."

"Seems to me you already have one man eating out of your hand. I don't know why you'd need a whole bunkhouse full of them."

Karl didn't know where the jealous anger was coming from. This wasn't like him at all. He'd never been a jealous man. But then, he'd never had a beautiful woman for a wife before. He'd taken one look at Hetty standing with her breasts a hairsbreadth from Dennis's chest, looking up at his friend in a way he desperately wanted her to look at him, and he'd gone a little berserk.

Never had he felt such uncontrollable rage. He'd needed to get out of the house before he said or did something he would regret. So he'd whirled and fled.

Hetty gazed up at him from her seat on the bench with a wounded look in her eyes. "You're making a mountain out of a molehill, Karl. I don't know what you think you saw in the house, but nothing happened between me and Dennis."

Karl felt his heart plummet. The fact that Hetty felt she needed to deny that anything had happened suggested that there had indeed been something going on between the two of them.

"I've made my feelings about fidelity plain," he said. "I won't tolerate—"

"Stop right there!" The teacup clattered onto the saucer as Hetty rose to confront him. She stepped over the bench and took the few steps to stand toe-to-toe with him, her own hands perched aggressively on her hips. She lifted her chin and looked him directly in the eye. "I've already told you once, Karl, and I don't ever want to have to tell you again. I have never flirted with Dennis. I never intend to flirt with Dennis or with any other man. What you saw was perfectly innocent."

"What was it I saw, Hetty? Why were you standing so close?"

She looked him in the eye. "I was asking Dennis about you."

"What?"

"I wanted to know more about what you'll be doing on the mountain."

"You could have asked me," he said, hearing the childish petulance in his voice and hating it.

She flashed him an angry look. "I asked you what was going on when you came to the house to get Dennis and you ignored me. You dismissed me as if I were of no account. I'm your wife, Karl. I'm supposed to be your helpmate. I came to the bunkhouse because I wanted to help."

"I'll let you know when I need your help." He sighed and said, "I'd already stopped the fight, Hetty. I came to get Dennis because Buck—that's the giant's name—needed more information about where to start cutting wood tomorrow."

"You didn't have to fight Buck?" she asked.

Karl shook his head. "And I don't intend to fight him. Ever."

"Then how will you get the men to obey you?"

"By treating them with respect."

Hetty met his gaze and said, "What if that isn't enough?"

Bao rose from the bench on the other side of the table and said, "Confucius say: 'If you look into your own heart and you find nothing wrong there, then what is there to worry about? What is there to fear?'"

Karl had completely forgotten the Chinaman was in the room. He stared at Bao. "What did you say?"

"Must follow heart. Must do what you believe is right. If do that, all will be well." Bao crossed to the door, grabbed his coat from a wooden hook beside it, and left in a swirl of icy wind.

"Trust Bao to quote Confucius," Karl muttered.

"He's probably right. Or rather, Confucius is," Hetty said with a rueful smile.

Karl was glad Bao had left, because he had something very personal to say to Hetty, if he could get it out. "There's something I've been wanting to say to you."

When he didn't immediately continue she said, "I'm sorry for not trusting you, Karl."

"I guess that's something we both have to work on," he replied before he could change his mind about admitting that he'd been as guilty as she was. Karl separated her clasped hands and settled one on each of his shoulders, then set his hands at her waist. She made a soft sound of surprise as he pulled her close and laid his cheek against hers.

He held her for a moment without speaking, then said quietly, "I can't help acting a little foolish where you're concerned, Hetty. I never expected to have such a beautiful bride."

He felt her hand cup his cheek. "You never have to worry about me, Karl. I'm yours and only yours."

He wished he could believe her. He wanted to believe her. He turned his face to capture her lips and took what he wanted from his wife.

And felt her giving back.

Karl broke the kiss and pulled Hetty close to hug her, regretting that they were both still wearing coats. "I want to touch you," he said. "I want to feel your skin next to mine."

He felt Hetty press her cheek against his, which was rough with stubble, and grasp the hair at his nape. "Soon," she whispered in his ear. "Soon."

"It can't be soon enough for me," Karl said.

Hetty tensed in his arms, and Karl realized that if he wasn't careful, he would lose the gains he'd made today. He had to trust her to be as committed to their marriage as she said she was. He had to keep his newly discovered jealousy under wraps.

He needed to find Dennis and make it clear that he was going to do things his own way. Then he needed to go back to the bunkhouse and introduce himself to each and every one of those men and assign them jobs, so they understood he was in charge.

But he also needed to hold his wife.

Hetty was the one who finally broke their embrace. "I'd better go check on Grace. I sent Andy to her to get his face patched up. I'm sure she can handle it, but I don't like leaving her alone with someone I don't know."

Karl kept his arms around her for a moment longer, then released her.

She brushed a lock of hair from his forehead, then abruptly dropped her hand—and her gaze—as though she'd just realized what she'd done. She hurried to the door, opened it, then turned back to say, "Good luck in the bunkhouse."

"Thanks." He smiled confidently and waved, then muttered to himself, "I'm going to need it."

Chapter Twenty-one

"Somebody's at the door, Grace."

Grace was lying on top of her bed fully dressed down to her shoes and stockings, wrapped in a scratchy wool blanket, dozing, exhausted from lack of sleep and worry about Griffin. "You get it," she muttered, rolling over and tucking her chin down inside the rough wool.

Griffin snickered. "Sure. Just let me get my socks and shoes on."

Grace was suddenly wide-awake. "Don't you dare!" She grappled her way out of the confining wool, shoved herself off the bed, and tripped on the trailing blanket as she stumbled her way out of the room.

Griffin snorted and called after her, "I don't know who picked your name, Grace, but graceful you ain't!"

"I may be clumsy, but you're an idiot," she shot back. "At least I didn't wander off and get myself half frozen to death."

"Sticks and stones may break my bones—"

"They will if you don't shut up!"

Grace slammed the bedroom door on Griffin's laughter. Sometimes having a younger brother could be such a bother!

She yanked open the front door and stared at the lanky boy standing there, his face battered and bloody. He had corn-silk blond hair, a thin face with a blade of nose, and tawny golden eyes with flecks of black and brown that made her think of a lion.

Grace looked beyond him for Hetty, and when she didn't see her stepmother demanded, "Where's my mom? What's happened? What are you doing here?"

"Are you Grace?"

"Who wants to know?" she asked, eyes wary. The boy looked too young to be one of the loggers, but she had no idea what he was doing here if he wasn't one.

"Your mom sent me here. Said you could fix my face."

There was no doubt his face needed attention, but Grace had learned in a school of very hard knocks not to trust. She squinted at him and asked, "Why didn't my mom come with you?"

"Look, I'm freezing my butt off out here. Let me come in, and I'll tell you what I know."

All he had on was a red long john shirt, a pair of worn Levi's that hung so low off his bony hips that she wondered why they didn't slide right off, and scuffed brown cowboy boots. "Where's your coat?" she asked, her palm stuck on the doorjamb to keep him out.

"Your mom was in a hurry to get out of the bunk-house, so I left it behind when I followed her out."

"Why was she in such a hurry?"

He shrugged. "Don't think Mr. Norwood wanted her there."

"So where did she go?"

"Cookhouse, I think." The boy's teeth were chattering, and he shivered violently.

Grace stepped away from the door and said, "For heaven's sake, come inside!" The moment he was inside, she closed the door behind him.

The boy headed for the fireplace, making a *brrrrrr* sound with his lips, and briskly rubbing his arms. He glanced at her over his shoulder and said, "You're lucky you've got both a fireplace and a stove. We've only got a stove in the bunkhouse, and it's cold as a witch's tit out there."

When she scowled at his language the boy said, "Sorry, miss. Don't spend much time in female company."

"Who's out there?" Griffin yelled from behind the closed bedroom door.

"Nobody," Grace yelled back. "Go to sleep."

"I can hear you talking to somebody," Griffin said. "Who is it?"

"Name's Andy Peterson," the boy replied loud enough to be heard in the next room.

Grace shot the boy an exasperated look, then crossed to the bedroom door, opened it just wide enough to stick her head inside, and muttered to Griffin, "This is none of your business, so leave us alone."

"If you're alone with some guy, it *is* my business," Griffin replied somberly.

Grace felt cold inside. More than once Griffin had come to her rescue at the saloon, saving her from the unwanted attentions of some customer. "This is no drunken cowhand," she said.

"Maybe not, but you shouldn't have to deal with

any of that pond scum from the bunkhouse, either," he said. "Where's Hetty?"

"Shush!" Grace whispered. "You know better than to call her that!" Then, in a voice that showed her irritation with his suggestion that she was unable to deal with the troublesome kid who'd shown up at the door, she said, "If you'll keep your trap shut long enough, you little pest, I can find out what's going on. Believe me, I can handle this."

"But—"

"If I need you, I'll let out a shout," she interrupted. "Otherwise, give me a break and leave me alone!"

Grace pulled the door shut with enough force to rattle the planks. She turned once again to her visitor, who was now standing with his rear end toward the fire, his hands behind him, grinning from ear to ear.

"What's so funny?" she demanded, wondering if she had a smudge on her cheek and brushing at it and then at her flyaway red hair, which she suddenly realized was in wild tangles around her head.

"You're spunky."

"What I am is none of your damn business," she said, unsure whether he'd intended his comment as a compliment or a complaint. She saw the flare of shock in his eyes at her use of profanity and realized she'd better learn to curb her tongue, now that she no longer lived above a saloon. She huffed out a breath. "Sit down at the table, so I can take care of your face and get you out of here."

Grace crossed to the cast-iron stove, where a pot was kept boiling for rose-hip tea for Griffin, and poured some water from the blackened tin coffeepot into a bowl. Then she grabbed a dishcloth and the bowl and headed back to the table. She placed herself on the boy's left, where most of the damage to his face had been done. Then she set the bowl on the table, dipped the cloth into it, and wrung it out.

Hetty had taken care of all the wounded faces on the trail, but Grace would be lying if she said she didn't have her share of experience nursing the kind of cuts, bruises, and abrasions she saw on Andy Peterson's face. Soiled Doves working at the saloon had occasionally been beaten up by Johns, and her mother's numerous paramours had gotten into their share of bar fights. And of course, Griffin had been involved in more than a few skirmishes, several of which Grace had joined in herself.

"This may hurt," she said as she gently applied the warm cloth to the worst cut on his cheek.

He winced and said, "Ouch."

"Be still," she cautioned, laying a hand on the top of his head to keep him from moving. It was something she would have done with Griffin, but this interloper wasn't her brother. She was suddenly aware that she had her hand in this stranger's hair, and that it was soft and silky, not greasy like she might have expected. Nor did she see any lice.

That made two measly points in his favor. He was still a man. Still capable of hurting her. Still capable of making her life a misery if she ever gave him the chance.

"I hear your mom and Mr. Norwood are newlyweds," the boy said.

"So what?"

"Spunky. And touchy," the boy muttered. "I was making conversation."

Grace couldn't blame him for that. She was often lonely for someone to talk to who was closer to her age. "How old are you?" she asked.

"Sixteen."

Andy had looked young, but Grace was surprised to hear just how young he was. "You're only two years older than me," she blurted.

"You're fourteen?"

"I will be next month," she said, flustered by the sudden look of male interest in his eyes. To deflect his attention from herself she asked, "How did you end up here?"

"It's as good a place to be as any other."

"Do you have family somewhere?"

He hissed, and Grace realized she'd pressed a little harder on the broken skin across the bridge of his nose than she'd intended. "Sorry. I'll try to be more gentle."

He smiled. "You're gentle as pie, miss."

Grace glowered at him, suspicious of his praise because a man giving a compliment usually wanted something in return. "You haven't answered my question," she said. "About your family. Where are they now?"

"Lost a baby sister to pneumonia and had a baby brother who drowned. Two years ago the rest of my family—my mom and dad and older sister and younger brother—all died of smallpox at our ranch in Texas."

She searched Andy's face for the awful scars that smallpox left but didn't find a single one. "You didn't get it?"

"I was out rounding up cattle with my dad when some infected folks traveling through visited the house. By the time my dad and I got home, everyone was sick with the pox. My dad wouldn't let me in the house, but he went inside to nurse my mom. He got sick, too."

Grace felt a spurt of sympathy but smothered it. Life was hard. She didn't have emotions to spare on some saddle tramp. "How did you end up so far north?"

He shrugged. "I couldn't stay there anymore, so I buried them, drove the cattle north to market in Kansas, then started drifting. I ended up here."

She glanced at his slender shoulders and skinny arms and asked, "Are you going to be cutting logs?"

"I'm in charge of the skidding team."

She shot him a quizzical look. "What's that?"

"Once the logs are cut, they're attached by a chain to a harness pulled by a team of oxen. I drive the oxen, skidding—sliding—the logs back down the mountain."

"That sounds dangerous."

"It can be, but I know what I'm doing."

"What if the logs start slipping on the way down?" she asked. "What keeps you and the oxen from getting mowed over?"

"I told you, I know what I'm doing."

"You're only sixteen, and you're from Texas. Where did you get this supposed vast experience driving oxen in the snow?" Grace asked.

"What is this? I already got the job. I don't have to answer to you."

Grace realized her questions about the safety of his job were being provoked by her fear that he would be hurt. Not that she would admit that to him. She wasn't happy about admitting it to herself.

"Prickly," she muttered.

"Nosy," he retorted.

Grace found herself smiling behind his head, where

he couldn't see her. She liked him, but remained wary of him. "I could put a couple of sticking plasters on your face, if you like," she offered.

He reached up to tenderly touch the growing bruise on his cheek near the worst cut. "Better not. It'll just bring attention to the fact that Buck—he's the head logger—beat the tar out of me."

Grace took the bowl and cloth and crossed back to the copper sink, wanting to put some distance between herself and the boy she was finding so easy to talk with. "Why did Buck hit you?"

"He had some chores he wanted me to do, and I didn't move quick enough to do them."

Grace leaned back against the sink, drying her hands on a different dishcloth. "He sounds mean to me."

Andy shrugged and rose. "Most bosses I've had lash out before they think."

"Karl isn't like that."

Andy lifted a skeptical brow and winced when his raw face protested.

Grace reached for the wet towel again and hurried over to dab at his forehead, where blood still oozed from a scrape. Now that he was standing and she was so close, she realized how tall he was. Her head barely came to his shoulder. She was suddenly aware of his body heat—he was certainly warm now—and she could feel his gaze on her.

"I could spend the rest of my life looking into your eyes," he murmured. "They're beautiful."

Grace took a quick step back, her green eyes flashing. "Flattery is wasted on me, Mr. Peterson. And I have no respect for men who spout compliments, especially when they're not true."

"I wasn't lying. Your eyes are the prettiest thing I've seen since I got to this godforsaken valley."

"Get out." She pointed to the door, knowing from past experience that the flush of embarrassment was turning her red-freckled face into something freakish. "And don't come back."

He shrugged and headed for the door. He stopped before he opened it and turned back to her. "Do you like kittens?"

Grace made a moue of disgust. "Is that a trick question? Of course I like kittens. Who doesn't like kittens?"

He smiled and Grace felt her insides flip-flop.

"If you like kittens," he said, "there's a new batch of them at the barn. I can show them to you now, if you like."

Grace wanted to go see those kittens more than anything she'd wanted in a very long time. But she didn't dare encourage Andy to think she liked him or had any intention of spending time with him just for the fun of it. Because the truth was, she did like him and she would have loved spending more time talking with him.

She knew better. Liking this boy would surely lead to other, less savory activities with him, activities she wanted no part of. "I don't think I should," she said at last.

"Go see the damned kittens!" Griffin yelled from the other room. "You know you want to."

"Have you been listening all this time?" Grace shouted back, mortified.

"Of course I have," Griffin replied with a laugh. "Sounds to me like Andy's sweet on you, Grace."

Grace felt her whole face turning red, which she knew for a fact made her head look like a giant tomato. "Just for that," she yelled back, "I'm going to leave you in this house all alone, while I go to the barn and see those kittens!"

"Have fun!" Griffin called after her.

Grace grabbed her coat and scarf from the hooks near the door and said, "Let's go."

Andy held the door for her, and she marched through. She stopped just outside, turned to him, and said, "Don't get any ideas. I'm going to the barn to see those kittens, not for any other reason."

Andy lifted a brow and winced. "I didn't ask you to come to the barn for any other reason. But if I think of one between now and the time we get there, I'll let you know."

Grace strode away without looking back. The nerve of him! Suggesting that she thought he wanted to kiss her!

Grace felt a frisson of anticipation skitter down her spine. Andy's lips had felt pliant beneath the cloth she'd used to clean away the blood that had stained them. She wondered what they would feel like beneath her fingertips. She wondered what they would feel like against her own.

Grace's stomach heaved, and she felt nauseated. Kisses weren't all nice. Kisses weren't necessarily the stuff of fairy tales. She knew better.

She would see the kittens and return to the house. Period. She wouldn't allow herself to linger to talk with Andy.

"I've thought of another reason for you to be visiting the barn with me," he said when they were almost there.

Breathless because Andy's long legs had made it necessary for her to walk fast to keep up with him— not because she was expecting him to suggest a romantic tryst in the barn—Grace asked, "What reason is that?"

"You can meet my oxen, Oats and Barley."

Grace laughed with relief. Maybe if Andy kept his mind on kittens and oxen, she'd be safe with him. Maybe they could talk about subjects that had nothing to do with the fact that he was male and she was female. Maybe they could be friends.

Oh, Grace hoped so. She needed a friend to relieve the loneliness she felt, despite having a younger brother, and despite having a stepmother and stepfather. There were things she couldn't tell any of them. Things she could only share with a friend.

Andy had lost his family, too. Of course, he didn't know Hetty wasn't her real mother, and she couldn't tell him the truth. But she thought he would understand about feeling lonely even when other people were around.

Grace was still fantasizing about Andy as a friend when they reached the barn.

"Grace!" a voice called.

Grace turned and saw Hetty cutting across the meadow, making a path through the snow. She glanced at Andy and saw the guilt on his face and suddenly knew that he'd been thinking about showing her a lot more than kittens and oxen.

"I thought we could be friends," she said to him in a stricken voice.

"Grace, I—"

"What are you doing here, Grace?" Hetty asked as she joined them.

"I wanted to see the new kittens," Grace said.

Hetty shot Andy an admonishing look before she put her arm through Grace's and said, "You can see them another time. Right now I need you to help me get supper on the table."

Hetty took off for the house, tugging Grace along beside her.

Grace glanced back once at Andy, who stared back at her and shrugged. In apology? In frustration? She had no way of knowing.

"I see you got Andy's face patched up," Hetty said.

"He seems nice," Grace ventured.

"He didn't do anything to upset you, did he, Grace?" Hetty asked, a worried look in her eyes.

Grace stopped in her tracks. "No, he didn't. He was just going to show me the kittens, Hetty. That's the only reason I went with him to the barn."

"Grace, I'm not sure you can trust—"

Grace pulled herself completely free. "I wish everybody would stop trying to tell me what to think. I know what I'm doing. I've been taking care of myself for more years than I can count. I know what men are and what they do. You don't need to warn me off. I can handle Andy Peterson!"

She stomped away toward the house, her throat swollen with emotion, her eyes glistening with tears she refused to shed. The truth was, she couldn't trust *herself* around Andy Peterson. She liked him, which meant she wanted to give him her trust. And she knew exactly where something like that might lead.

"Damn, damn, damn," she muttered. She'd really wanted to see those kittens. She'd always wanted a kitten, the way Griffin had always wanted a horse. Her mother hadn't allowed her to have the kitten, and they'd never been able to afford a horse.

"Is a kitten too much to ask?" she wondered aloud.

There would be other chances to sneak away to the barn. By God, she would get there and see those kittens and pick one out for her very own. She had a birthday coming up, and when Hetty asked what she wanted, she was going to say, "A kitten."

She'd name it Blackie or Whitey or Ginger, depending on its color, and bring it into the house and give it all the milk it could drink and let it sleep on her pillow beside her head at night. Just see if she didn't!

She was sure Andy would help her. After all, he was the one who'd told her about the kittens in the first place. She would be forever grateful to him for that, even if he'd tricked her into coming to the barn with him. She could handle him. She could handle herself. She would never give another man the chance to take what she wasn't willing to give. Not even one she liked as much as Andy Peterson.

Chapter Twenty-two

Grace discovered that Hetty was absolutely right about how cantankerous Griffin would be once he began to recover. Her sympathy for her brother was dying a slow, but certain, death. Over the past three weeks she'd lost patience with Griffin's demands that she find him just the right piece of wood to whittle, that she sweep up the wood shavings, that she fetch the chamber pot, that she get him another pillow, that she fluff up his pillow, that she rearrange his covers, that she get him a cup of coffee—which he didn't even drink—and then a cup of tea—which he also didn't drink.

Grace had been holding on to her temper because she could see her brother was in a lot of pain as the blisters popped and his skin began to slough off and new skin began to grow in. The way he constantly fiddled with his dying little toe, touching it and worrying it, was getting on her nerves. Finally she snapped, "If you keep playing with that thing, it's going to fall off!"

To her horror, just as she said it, the toe fell sideways off his foot, hanging by a thread of dead skin.

"Oh my God, Griffin!" she cried. "I didn't mean it."

The expression on his parchment-white face was somewhere between sick and amused. "Bao told me it might do that," he said with a halfhearted smile. "I thought the whole thing would fall off. I didn't know it would hang there like that."

Grace stared at the thread of skin holding the blackened toe to his foot and said, "What do you want me to do?"

He handed her his whittling knife and said, "Why don't you cut it off?"

Grace had done a lot of favors for her brother over the years, but she'd finally reached a line she couldn't cross. She shook her head and said, "Let me get Hetty."

Griffin grimaced and said, "She won't have any more stomach for this than you do. Go get Bao."

"Don't touch it while I'm gone," she admonished. Then she fled the room, grabbed her coat and scarf, and said to Hetty, "I think it's time for Bao to come check on Griffin."

"Is Griffin all right?" Hetty asked, setting down the iron she was using to press Grace's calico dress.

"He's fine. He just needs . . ." Grace racked her brain for something she could say to keep Hetty from checking on Griffin and said, "Some more salve. I'll be back in a flash."

Once she was out the door, Grace ran pell-mell across the meadow. She shoved the cookhouse door open, saw Bao standing by the stove, and said between panting breaths, "You have to come quick! Griffin's little toe fell off. Not all the way off. It's just hanging there! He needs your help right away."

Bao remained unflappable despite her frantic plea. He said, "I go. You stir stew."

"Of course. Just hurry!"

It wasn't until Bao was gone with his box of medicines that Grace noticed that he hadn't been alone. Andy was sitting at the trestle table with a tin cup of coffee in front of him.

"What are you doing here? Aren't you supposed to be at work on the mountain?" It wasn't until after the words were out of her mouth that Grace realized how accusatory they sounded.

"I had a boil on my neck," he said. "It was bothering me, so Bao lanced it."

"Let me see." It wasn't concern for Andy that moved her across the room, it was mistrust. He'd said he had a boil, but maybe he was a malingerer. Better to know that about him before she started liking him any better.

Andy moved the collar of his navy wool shirt aside, and she saw a small white bandage above his red long john shirt. "Bao covered it with a sticking plaster, but you're welcome to take a closer look if you want. It's not a pretty sight."

"You should always take care of a boil right away. Otherwise it gets worse," she said.

"That's why I stopped here on my way up the mountain."

"So you're headed up there now?" Maybe he wasn't a malingerer after all.

"As soon as I get Oats and Barley harnessed. Want to come watch?"

She glanced at the pot of stew on the stove. "Bao asked me to watch the stew."

Andy rose and crossed to the stove, grabbed a mitt, and moved the pot off the heat and onto another part of the stove. "It'll be fine here for a while. I don't expect it'll take Bao long to clip off that toe."

Grace gagged and her stomach pitched at the image Andy had painted.

"Hey," he said. "You okay? Maybe you better sit down."

Andy crossed back to her, eased her down onto the bench he'd vacated, then sat down beside her. He pushed her head down between her knees and said, "Keep your head down. I don't want you fainting on me."

"I'm fine," she said, trying to sit up.

He kept the pressure on her nape. "Stay there a minute more. Just to be sure."

It was an ignominious position to be in, but Grace was forced to stay in it until Andy said, "All right. Come on back up. Easy now."

The truth was, her head felt a little fuzzy. She wasn't sure whether it was the thought of Griffin's hanging toe, or the fact that she'd spent the past minute being held down with her head between her legs by a boy she liked.

To Grace's dismay, when she'd put her head down, a riot of red curls had tumbled forward, and when she sat up again, they were still drooped across her face. She reached up to try and straighten them out, but Andy gently pushed her hands away and said, "Let me do it."

Grace stared at him wide-eyed, too shocked by the offer to stop him. His fingers sorted through her hair, gently twisting curls this way and that and brushing his fingers through the tangles until her face reappeared.

"You have the most incredible hair," he said. "It's so soft. And so curly."

"It's a rat's nest most of the time," she countered. "And those red curls are the bane of my existence. I'd give anything for hair as blond and straight as yours." She had the urge to reach out and brush his hair back from his face but resisted it. This wasn't her brother, whom she could handle freely. This was someone she barely knew.

"Your red hair makes you special," Andy said. "And those freckles are spots of brown sugar waiting to be kissed."

Grace bolted to her feet. "Keep talking like that and you're going to need a plaster on your nose as well as your neck."

Andy scooted a little farther away on the bench. "You don't like compliments?"

"I don't like false flattery."

Andy met her gaze. "I meant every word I said."

"We can't be friends if you're going to talk like that."

"Are we going to be friends?" he asked.

"I'd like us to be friends."

"But not more than that?" Andy clarified.

Grace shook her head. "No."

He rose and said, "Come on then. We better go."

"Go where?"

"To the barn."

Grace stared at him suspiciously. "You're awful quick to be running off alone with me to the barn."

"We won't be alone. The place is full of animals.

You can meet Oats and Barley and watch me harness them. And you can get a good look at those kittens."

Hetty had purposely been keeping Grace away from the barn so she wouldn't run into Andy. That also meant Grace hadn't gotten to see those kittens, which were getting older by the day. "All right," she said. "But no funny stuff."

Andy grinned and said, "I'll do my best not to make you laugh."

Grace made a face. "You know what I mean."

"I'm afraid I do," he said as he gathered his coat and cap and escorted her out the door.

Every second they were walking to the barn together, Grace half expected Hetty to show up at the front door to the house and call her inside. She didn't take an easy breath until she and Andy were closed inside the barn.

"What's that big sigh for?" Andy asked.

Grace couldn't tell him she was relieved to have escaped the careful rein Hetty kept on her, so she said, "I'm glad to have a chance to see those kittens at last. Where are they?"

"In the hayloft."

Grace glanced up at the hayloft, which was a dozen or more feet off the ground. "How are they ever going to get down from there?"

"When they're big enough, they'll figure it out," Andy said. "You want to go up?"

Grace didn't want Andy looking up her dress as she climbed the ladder to the loft so she said, "You go first."

He scrambled up the ladder lickety-split, and Grace did her best to follow quickly after him. When she got to the top, she felt him reach under her arms and lift her the rest of the way up, taking care that their bodies didn't touch as he set her on her feet.

"Thanks," she said, brushing at her dress to make sure she was decent. "You're pretty strong."

"You're light as a feather."

Grace frowned. "I don't appreciate you making fun of me."

Andy stuck his hands on his hips. "What are you complaining about now?"

"I've never been light as a feather. Matter of fact, I'm . . ." Grace couldn't get the words *pleasingly plump* to come out of her mouth, although that was the expression her mother had most often used to describe her.

"I like your curves, Grace. My dad always said the kindest women, like my mom, didn't have any sharp angles to them."

It took Grace a moment to realize that Andy's mother must have been *pleasingly plump*. Like her.

Andy squatted by the nest the mother cat had made in the hay for her kittens and gestured Grace over to him. "My dad told me it made him feel like he was a good provider when he held my mom in his arms and she wasn't all skin and bones."

"You must miss them a lot," Grace said wistfully as she dropped to her knees beside him.

"I do," Andy said quietly. "Which kitten do you like the best?"

The mother cat must have been out hunting supper, because the four kittens were sleeping curled up in a ball around each other. One was ginger, one was calico, one was black, and the tiniest one was black with white socks.

Grace reached out carefully and detached the smallest kitten from the rest of the bunch, then held the furry ball against her cheek. "I like this one."

"She's my favorite, too."

"I think I'll call her Socks."

"That's probably a better name than the one I gave her," Andy said sheepishly.

"What was that?"

He cleared his throat, and Grace saw a flush rise on his cheeks as he admitted, "Gracie."

Grace was startled into blurting, "After me?"

"Even though she's the smallest, she's just so . . ." Andy grinned at her and finished, "Spunky."

Grace found herself grinning back.

"And plenty nosy, too," he added.

Grace laughed. "Do the rest have names?"

He shook his head. "Naw. I only named the cutest one."

Grace knew how to scare off a drunken cowboy and how to stare down an insolent upstairs customer, but she had no idea how to respond to a young man who seemed to like and admire her. She felt flustered and couldn't think of what to say next.

Andy reached out and picked a piece of hay from the kitten's fur. He brushed a thumb across Grace's eyebrow, tracing the shape of it, then he slid his forefinger down her nose all the way to her bowed upper lip. He seemed fascinated by what he was doing, and Grace realized that her breath seemed to be caught in her chest.

The kitten mewed piteously, breaking the spell.

Grace realized she'd been like putty in Andy Peterson's hands. He could have tumbled her in the hay and taken her right there, and she wouldn't have made a squeak of protest.

It seemed there were some kinks she needed to work out if she wanted to be Andy's friend, but only his friend. This attraction thing was dangerous. She was going to have to do some thinking about how to deal with it.

She replaced the kitten it its nest, then lurched to her feet and marched toward the ladder.

"Grace? What's wrong?" Andy called as he followed after her.

"I've been gone from the house too long. Hetty will be worried about me."

"Don't you want to meet my oxen?"

"Another time."

He caught her hand before she could go down the ladder and said, "Let me go first, in case you slip. I don't want you to fall."

Grace glanced over the edge of the loft, which seemed a lot higher looking down than it had when she was climbing up, and felt a little dizzy. "All right," she agreed.

Andy hurried down the ladder. "All right, Grace. Come on down."

Grace felt frightened as she stepped over the edge of the loft onto the ladder, so she didn't look down as she descended the rungs. Near the bottom, her skirt caught under her shoe. When she let go of the ladder to try and tug it free, she lost her balance.

Grace screamed in terror as she plummeted, arms and legs akimbo. She was grasping for anything she could find to stop her fall, so when Andy caught her in his arms, she clung tightly to his neck with both hands.

"I have you, Grace," he said. "You're safe. I have you. Are you all right?"

Grace could feel Andy shaking. She leaned back to look into his face and realized his blue eyes were filled with fear—for her. She hid her face against his neck, afraid she might fall into those two deep blue wells and never want to come out again, and heaved a half sob, half sigh of relief that she wasn't hurt.

"I should have stayed right behind you when you came down," he said. "I should have been more careful."

She kept her face hidden as she said, "It wasn't your fault. I slipped and fell. You caught me, and I'm fine. That's an end to it. You can put me down now."

As he set her carefully onto her feet, Grace realized something. Andy might have narrow shoulders and slender arms, but he'd been plenty strong enough to catch her and hold her and keep her from harm.

"Grace, are you in there? I heard a scream. Are you all right? I've been looking everywhere for you. When you didn't come right back from the cookhouse I got worried."

Grace turned and saw Hetty striding toward them like a schoolmarm anxious to break up a schoolyard tussle. Except, she and Andy weren't even touching anymore. She was standing beside him as though nothing had happened.

But something had happened. Some *thing* had passed between them. She'd trusted Andy to catch her, and he hadn't let her down.

"I went up in the hayloft to see the kittens and slipped on the way down the ladder," Grace explained. "Andy caught me as I fell. I'm fine."

Grace wanted to laugh at the censuring look on Hetty's face, as though Andy was in the wrong somehow for being there to rescue her.

As Hetty escorted Grace out of the barn, Andy touched his wool cap with his fingertips in salute and said, "See you later, Grace. Maybe one of these days you'll get to meet Oats and Barley."

Grace took one look at Hetty's face and figured it would be a cold day in hell before her stepmother let Grace out of her sight again.

In days gone by, Grace might have gone along to get along. But since she'd met Hetty, she'd learned that there was more than one way to skin a cat. Not that Grace ever wanted to skin a cat. But when all was said and done, there was no way Hetty was going to stop her from being friends with Andy Peterson.

Chapter Twenty-three

After three weeks of sleeping in the same bed as Karl, Hetty knew his nighttime ritual, which should have ended with the two of them cuddled up together or engaged in other intimate activities enjoyed by newlyweds. Except, Hetty had asked for a reprieve until Christmas to get to know Karl, and Karl was holding true to his word, so they were on opposite sides of the bed.

That didn't mean their nights in the same bed hadn't been filled with hope on his side, and fraught with trepidation on hers. The palpable tension kept her awake most nights long after Karl had finally dropped off to sleep.

Tonight was different. Hetty felt relaxed and drowsy, even though Karl was still awake. She couldn't put her finger on exactly what had changed. She only knew that she was no longer quite so terrified of what Karl might do or say if—or when—he discovered she was a virgin. Oh, he was certain to be angry about the deception. But she'd learned some things about Karl Norwood today that had made her believe that, even if he discovered the worst, he might still be able to forgive her.

That reassurance hadn't come from anything Karl had said or done. It had come from a stack of letters Grace had given her.

Hetty had marched Grace back to the house after she'd found her stepdaughter in the barn with Andy, intending to give her a stern warning about spending time alone with rowdies from the bunkhouse, when Grace had turned to her and said, "I have something I should have given you as soon as you agreed to marry Karl."

Hetty had stared in confusion at Grace and asked, "What is that?"

Grace had raced to her bedroom and returned to the kitchen breathless and bearing a short stack of envelopes. "Here," she'd said, handing the papers to Hetty.

"What are these?"

"They're Karl's letters to his mail-order bride. The one he thought he was corresponding with in Cheyenne. I've put them in the order he wrote them."

Hetty gaped. "These are private correspondence. I don't think I should be reading them."

"They were meant for his bride," Grace replied. "You're his bride, Mom. He wanted his wife to know these things about him." Grace had blushed and added another stack of letters tied with ribbon. "These are copies of my letters to him. I made them for Lucy, so she'd know what I'd written, in case Karl asked, but she never bothered to read them."

Hetty very much wanted to read Grace's letters. It would give her a good idea what Karl had thought he was getting in a bride. But they would also reveal Grace's private thoughts and feelings. Hetty handed back the second stack of letters and said, "It doesn't matter what hopes and dreams you might have expressed to Karl. I have to look at his letters as though they were addressed to me and think of what I might have answered."

Grace gave a huge sigh of relief and said, "Oh, thank goodness!"

Hetty laughed, gave her stepdaughter a quick hug, and said, "Thank you, Grace."

Grace escaped to her room saying she needed to check on Griffin's missing toe. She'd also escaped Hetty's lecture, but Hetty knew there would be plenty of time for that later. Besides, she planned to keep Grace too busy in the house to find time for surreptitious meetings with any of Karl's hired hands.

Despite the fact that Karl had written the letters to his prospective bride, Hetty felt odd reading them. She justified opening them because Karl thought she already knew what they contained. Then she told herself there was no hurry to read them. But curiosity won out.

She stepped into her bedroom and closed the door, then sat down on the bed and opened the first letter he'd written.

Dear Mrs. Templeton,

It feels strange putting down my thoughts about marriage on paper. But I want to be sure we have a meeting of the minds before we meet in person.

How direct he was. How forthright. How honest. Hetty's conscience immediately smote her for all the deceptions she'd perpetrated on Karl. She was tempted to fold up the letter and put them all away. But maybe if she read Karl's letters, she could be a better wife to him, despite all the lies.

Karl continued, *First and foremost, I expect to deal honestly with my wife. If there are things that concern you, I expect you to speak up and name them. I will do the same.*

Karl had certainly done that, Hetty thought ruefully. He'd told her right off he valued fidelity. However, he hadn't blamed her for what he supposed were past transgressions. He'd simply expressed his desire that she remain faithful to him in the future. In hindsight, Hetty realized that Karl could have held what he thought she'd done in the past against her. But he hadn't.

That was her first inkling that Karl was willing to forgive, if not forget.

She read on: *I love learning about new places and things. I look forward to discussing whatever subjects interest you and hope you'll feel free to do the same with me.*

Karl had certainly shared his love of botany with her and the children in a way that made learning fun. She tried to think of a topic she'd suggested they should talk about, and realized all she'd ever spoken about to Karl was the children.

Which made her wonder what other interests she might have that she could share with him. Hetty's brow furrowed in thought, but nothing came to mind. Was she so frivolous, then? Was there nothing she could discuss besides Grace and Griffin?

She had the excuse that she couldn't share her past with him. But the truth was, her formal education had stopped three years ago, when her parents died. Her sister Josie was the reader in the family. Miranda had spent her days taking care of Nick and Harry. Hetty and Hannah had dabbled in poetry and fantasized endlessly about the knight who would ride into their lives on a white charger and rescue them from the detestable Miss Birch.

Hetty realized that Karl was getting far less than the wife he'd wanted. He'd clearly been expecting to marry an educated woman, someone who could have intelligent conversations on a variety of subjects by the fireside in the evening. Even when she'd been in school, Hetty hadn't been particularly interested in learning.

Before the Great Fire, she'd imagined a future where she married some successful banker or lawyer or businessman and spent her days at home loving and caring for their children.

She'd seen no point in spending her days with her nose in a book, like Josie.

It seemed, where Karl was concerned, there was far more to being a good wife than simply loving her husband and children.

Hetty read on.

I have one brother, but he's almost a decade older than I am, handsome and ambitious and successful at whatever he does. Though I admire and respect him, we're not close.

I would like our children to be born within a few years of each other, so they can be friends and play-

*mates, as I suspect your seven- and nine-year-old
children must be. I look forward to becoming a
good father to Grace and Griffin.*

What Hetty read into the first of those two para-
graphs was that Karl had essentially been raised as an
only child. Had he been lonely? Hetty couldn't imagine her life without the constant boisterous chaos created by her sisters and brothers. The six Wentworth
children had spent endless hours playing with each
other, teasing each other, fighting and making up with
each other, and driving each other crazy.

But she'd always known there was someone to talk
to, someone who would care. Someone who would
love her, no matter what she did.

Karl hadn't had that.

She reread that first paragraph and found a word she
would not have known was significant until she met
Karl. His older brother, the one he admired and respected, was *handsome*. Hetty wondered if, all those
years growing up, Karl's appearance had been compared to his older brother's by friends and family—and
females—and found wanting.

Hetty thought back to her own reaction on first seeing Karl. He hadn't been ugly, but he hadn't been
good-looking, either. She remembered observing wide-
spaced, serious brown eyes in an average face. His hair
was straight and brown, parted on the side so it fell
across his forehead. He wasn't short or tall or fat or
skinny. His shoulders weren't broad or narrow, but
somewhere in-between. He'd had no disfiguring marks
at all, nothing to distinguish him from a thousand
other men.

Hetty realized that, five weeks later, she saw Karl very differently. When he looked at her or the children in a certain way, golden flecks appeared in his plain brown eyes. She'd spent a lot of time observing his lips, especially since he'd kissed her, wondering how they could look so stern sometimes and yet feel so soft to the touch. She'd had her hands in his hair, so she knew how soft and springy it was. She often itched to brush aside that lock of hair that fell constantly on his forehead, making him look less like the learned man she was discovering he was.

Karl did have one distinguishing physical characteristic she found endearing: that overlapping front tooth. It kept his smile from being quite perfect. And she'd noticed something else. When Karl Norwood smiled, her heart leapt.

Hetty reread the sentence where Karl said he was looking forward to becoming not just a father, but a *good* father, to what he'd thought were seven- and nine-year-old children. What forbearance he must have exercised when he realized Grace and Griffin were older than the ages he'd expected them to be. She'd finally admitted they were nine and thirteen. Thank goodness he'd never made the children suffer for the lies she'd told.

Hetty's guilt caused her nose to burn and her eyes to well with tears. She'd treated Karl badly every step of the way, and he'd answered her with tolerance and understanding. She was keeping him at arm's distance in bed when he had the right to a wife who really *was* a wife.

She read the last two sentences of the letter through eyes blurred with tears.

I must close this now, to continue work on the home I'm building for us. I hope you will come to love this beautiful land as much as I do.

> *Your obedient servant,*
> *Karl Norwood*

Karl had written that he was building not just a *house*, but a *home* to share with his wife and stepchildren. Hetty had always suspected Karl loved Bitterroot, but there it was in writing. He'd supposedly settled in the valley to run a lumber project for his brother, but Hetty wondered now if Karl planned to live there always. It seemed he might.

Hetty let herself consider the possibility of staying in the Montana Territory for the rest of her life and realized that, if she knew her family was safe and well, she would be happy to remain here with Karl and Grace and Griffin . . . and the other children Karl wanted, who would be born close enough together to be playmates.

Hetty had folded the letter and returned it to the envelope by feel, because she hadn't been able to see through her tears. She'd learned a great deal from a single letter, enough to add layers of guilt to what she already felt. She'd been afraid to read more, afraid to see further into Karl's heart. At least, until she knew she could be the wife he wanted.

Hetty rolled over onto her side in bed so she was facing Karl. She smiled when she saw his brown eyes gleaming golden in the firelight. "Karl," she whispered.

"What is it, Hetty?" he replied in the rumbling voice that always made her insides tighten and tingle.

"Would you . . ." A frog got caught in her throat,

and Hetty took a moment to clear it before she tried again. "Would you hold me in your arms?"

Karl slid his arms around her as though she was made of eggshells that would crack if he held her too tight. When he was done, their bodies were still separated by several inches. Hetty realized he'd left the rest up to her. She could close the distance between them. Or not.

Hetty thought of Karl growing up without any brothers or sisters. No one to pull his shirttails or tie his shoelaces together. No one to take the blame when he cracked the teapot or offer to share the last piece of pie. No one to whisper secrets to when the lights were out. No one to bless him in nightly prayers.

She slid her arms around him until there was not one teeny-weeny bit of space separating them, so she could feel the heat of him and almost hear his racing heartbeat. His warm breath teased her ear, and she felt his voice all the way to the soles of her feet when he said, "This feels good."

It did. It really did.

"Good night, Karl," she murmured.

"Good night, Hetty."

She fell asleep with her head pressed against his chest, listening to the sound of his lonely heart.

Chapter Twenty-four

Over the next few days, Hetty made her way through all of Karl's letters. Even though it was phrased in different ways, one hope appeared in every one: *I'm looking forward to the two of us sitting in front of the fire in the evening sharing our thoughts.*

Clearly, Karl had sought more from a mail-order bride than someone to bear his children. Which was a good thing, because Hetty was still desperately avoiding that shattering moment when Karl might discover the truth.

But she loved lying in bed at night with Karl's arms around her as she fell asleep. She hadn't realized that by performing an act so Karl would feel less lonely, she would feel less lonely herself.

It was plain from his letters that Karl wanted more than a physical relationship with his wife. Hetty figured there was no reason why she couldn't begin sharing a bit of conversation with him before they retired for the evening.

Since she'd come to the valley, Hetty had been spending her evenings with the children, instead of Karl, because it was so easy to talk with them in the guise of caring for them, and so difficult, because of all the lies she'd told, to speak with Karl about anything at all.

Tonight, that was going to change.

The only problem was, Hetty had absolutely no idea what she should talk to Karl about. She couldn't tell him about her past, so discussions about her family were taboo. She was also intimidated by Karl's education and intelligence. What could she possibly tell him that he didn't already know?

Miranda had described both her behavior and Hannah's as flighty and scatterbrained, and her past actions seemed to confirm that. So she couldn't imagine what she and Karl Norwood would ever find to talk about. He was so smart. And she was so . . . pretty.

But Hetty was determined to try.

Dinner was over and the dishes were done. Grace had agreed to get Griffin into bed. Hetty's palms were sweaty, and her heart was racing. She'd taken special care to tame her hair in a sedate bun at her nape, although several curls had already escaped at her temples. She took off her apron, laid it across the back of a kitchen chair, then shook out her skirt to rid it of any flour from the biscuits she'd made for supper that might have caught on the hem.

Karl was already sitting in one of the two willow rockers in front of the fireplace in the parlor. If Hetty hadn't read his letters, she would never have realized that he'd been wishing all this time that she would join him there.

As though she did it every night, Hetty crossed to the empty rocker beside him, sat down, and began rocking. Too late, she realized she should have brought something with her to hold in her hands, like one of

Griffin's socks, which eternally needed to be darned. She knotted her empty hands in her lap, so Karl wouldn't see how they were trembling.

He glanced in her direction, but instead of speaking his head remained bowed, and he continued reading the book in his lap.

Why hadn't he said something? Where was the desire for conversation he'd written about in his letters?

Hetty bucked up her courage and asked, "What are you reading?"

He turned the book so she could see the tiny print. "It's Dickens."

Hetty had heard of Charles Dickens, but she wasn't familiar with much of his work. She didn't want to show her ignorance, so she replied with a neutral, "Oh?"

He smiled sheepishly and said, "It's *A Christmas Carol.*"

Hetty sighed with relief. "Oh." That was a story she knew.

"I thought it might be nice to read it to the kids in the days leading up to Christmas."

"What a wonderful idea!" Hetty had a feeling that neither Grace nor Griffin had experienced the joy of listening to a story being read to them before the fire. The Wentworth children had often gathered together in the evening to hear their father read, and those were some of her fondest memories of her childhood.

Hetty glanced sideways at Karl. It seemed he'd been plotting ways to get everyone together in the evening, not just her. She felt the tension ease from her shoulders.

She kept rocking. And waiting. But Karl seemed content to read his book. Hetty wondered petulantly if he'd used those sentences about conversation in front of the fireplace to fill up his letters because he didn't know what else to say. He certainly didn't seem inclined to talk.

When neither of them had said anything for a while, Karl asked, "Would you like something to read?"

"No. I'd like to talk." She heard the brusqueness in her voice and inwardly cringed. This was supposed to be a loving gesture, not armed combat. She was grateful when Karl closed his book and set it aside on the table between the two rockers. She attributed the look of concern on his face to the sharp tone of her voice when she'd spoken.

He focused his brown eyes intently on her blue ones. "I'm listening."

That was no help at all. That meant Hetty had to talk. What should she say? Should she ask him a question about his day or talk about hers? She pursed her lips and dived in. "How are things going on the mountain?"

"Better than I expected," Karl replied. "I think I finally convinced Buck—he's the giant you met that first day—that bruising faces is not the best way to get the loggers to work harder."

Hetty smiled. "How did you do that?"

"You don't want to hear about my work. I can tell something is troubling you. Is there some way I can help?"

He could help by answering her question, Hetty thought crossly. He'd written in his letters that he wanted to talk, and now getting him to talk was like pulling teeth.

"I was wondering if we could have a Christmas tree. At Christmas, I mean."

Karl smiled. "Of course. My mother always made a point of decorating our home in Connecticut. Garlands on the banisters. Pinecones on the mantel. A tree that reached almost to the ceiling, with beautiful colored-glass balls."

"That sounds a lot like my home growing up," Hetty replied.

"Where was that?"

Hetty's mind raced to decide whether she could tell the truth. Could she talk about the long-ago past and not get caught in a lie? "Chicago," she said at last.

"Do you still have family there?"

Hetty shook her head. "They're scattered to the four winds now."

"Sounds like you miss them," Karl said.

Hetty turned away to face the fire, so he wouldn't see the tears forming in her eyes. "I do."

"How did you end up in Cheyenne?" he asked.

Hetty took the leap and told the truth. "I came west on a wagon train." To keep him from asking more details about her past, she said, "What made you decide to study botany, of all things?"

He laughed. "That's a long story."

She looked into his eyes and said, "I have all the time in the world."

He looked thunderstruck, as though it had just occurred to him that here she was, fulfilling his dream of what married life might be like with his mail-order bride.

"I have a better idea," he said.

Before she could ask what it was, he stood up and

took the few steps to reach her. He caught one of her hands, pulled her to her feet, and said, "Let's continue this conversation in bed."

Hetty was startled into laughter. She almost blurted, *I thought you wanted to spend evenings talking to your wife in front of the fire.* Clearly, after surveying the situation, her highly intelligent husband had come up with a much better idea.

He grabbed the lantern and led her eagerly toward the bedroom, talking nonstop. "Did I ever tell you Dennis's father was the head gardener on my father's estate? I think I spent more time with Mr. Campbell than Dennis ever did. Mr. Campbell talked about trees and shrubs and flowers as though they were animate objects."

Hetty was still trying to figure out what *animate objects* were as Karl raced on.

"One summer he planted pink peonies along the terrace and had me keep a record of when the buds appeared and how large they grew and when they bloomed. Have you ever seen a peony, Hetty?"

Hetty was so entranced with what Karl was saying that she never noticed that, the whole time he was talking, they'd been undressing in front of each other. That was something they definitely hadn't done before.

Hetty flushed when she realized she was wearing nothing but her chemise and a skirt over her pantalets. She was in the act of unbuttoning her skirt, which would have left her in nothing but her pantalets. She raced to the wardrobe, grabbed a nightgown, and pulled it on over her head without putting her arms in the armholes. She removed the rest of her clothing within the concealment of the long flannel night-gown, listening raptly to Karl the whole time.

Karl was apparently oblivious to the fact that he'd stripped down to his long johns in front of her. "I think peonies are the most beautiful flower God ever made. Layers and layers and layers of petals. My mother used to say, with considerable disgust, that all those petals just made more places for the ants to hide." He grinned. "She never allowed a single one of those beautiful peonies into her house."

"What a shame," Hetty said. "If they're as beautiful as you say they are."

Karl grabbed her hands, which she'd finally poked through the armholes of her nightgown. "You can't imagine, Hetty. And the smell of them. Intoxicating!"

Hetty had never seen Karl so exuberant. His excitement was infectious, and she smiled back at him. "Will you plant some peonies here, Karl?"

He looked surprised at the proposal. "The growing season is short, but I don't know why we couldn't." He hugged her and said, "That's a great idea, Hetty. I would never have thought of doing it if you hadn't suggested it."

Seeing peonies through Karl's eyes had made her want to hold one in her hand, to examine its many petals, and to sniff its intoxicating scent—watching out, of course, for the ants!

Hetty realized Karl was still holding her close and that she could feel the male part of him, hot and hard against her body. How had he become aroused? All they'd done was talk!

Hetty wasn't sure what she should do now. She wasn't ready to do more than hug, but she didn't want to break the wonderful mood Karl was in. So she simply stood where she was. She slid her arms around Karl's waist and pressed her breasts against his chest as he leaned his bristled cheek against her neck.

"I'd forgotten how lovely the peonies were," Karl murmured against her throat. "Thank you, Hetty, for reminding me."

"You're welcome, Karl."

He took a step back and let her go.

Hetty tried not to look at the part of him that was now very obvious behind the fly of his long johns, but her glance flickered there long enough to see that he was fully aroused. He must have noticed her looking, because he turned abruptly and said, "The room is cold, Hetty. Get under the covers. I'll put out the lantern."

Hetty hurried around to her side of the bed and slid under the covers. The sheets were icy, and she shivered as she pulled the blanket all the way to her chin.

Karl added a few more logs to the fireplace, then put out the lantern before joining her in bed.

Hetty lay on her back staring at the flickering shadows on the log ceiling, wondering whether they would continue their conversation in bed, as Karl had suggested. Or not. And whether he would take her in his arms as was their custom now. Or not.

Hetty waited, but Karl remained silent. And a mile away on the other side of the bed. She was afraid she knew what he was thinking, but she decided to ask anyway.

"What are you thinking, Karl?"

"You don't want to know what I'm thinking."

"Yes, I do," Hetty persisted.

She felt him turn on his side toward her. "Come over here, Hetty. Where I can hold you in my arms."

Hetty hesitated maybe half a second. Then she practically threw herself into his embrace. Karl actually grunted as their bodies made solid contact. She snuggled close, her nose against his throat, breathing in the scent of him, which she thought must be as intoxicating as the peonies in his mother's garden.

"I always dreamed of moments like this," Karl murmured.

"Lying in bed together, you mean?"

"Sharing memories. Making memories." He chuckled and said, "I'll never forget the look on your face when you realized you were half undressed and I was standing right there in front of you. Did you know I could see the outline of your nipples right through your chemise?"

Hetty gasped. "Karl Norwood, how could you!"

He laughed and his arms closed more tightly around her. "This is what marriage is supposed to be like. I know it. I feel it."

Hetty stiffened in his arms as bile clawed its way up her throat. She'd felt the magic, too, but it couldn't last. And it might end much sooner than either of them hoped.

Because of the lies.

"Hetty? Have I spoken amiss?"

She shook her head. "I feel it too, Karl."

He pulled her close and whispered, "I'm glad."

Hetty leaned her head against his chest and listened to his steadily beating, not-quite-so-lonely heart.

Chapter Twenty-five

Karl couldn't believe he'd let Hetty talk him into bringing Griffin onto the mountain to work. She'd given him some cock-and-bull story about Griffin needing to spend his days around men, instead of being stuck at home with his mother and sister. It had done no good to mention that it had only been a few days since the boy's little toe had dried up and fallen off, that his hands and feet were barely healed, or that he was too young to be involved in such dangerous work.

Hetty had insisted, Grace had urged him to agree, and Griffin had argued, "I hardly have any limp at all. I want to go with you."

To Karl's surprise, Griffin had proved himself a quick study with a short ax. Maybe it was all his experience with a whittling knife, but Griffin could now buck the small limbs off a ponderosa pine as fast, or faster, than any of the grown men assigned to the job. He was more grudging about carrying the chopped-off limbs to a nearby slash pile to be burned later, but he did it.

Karl just wished everyone else was as committed to

getting the job done as his stepson. He spent a great deal of his time urging the men to give their best effort.

"Come on, Stefan," he said with a smile of encouragement, "put your back into it."

Stefan was working one side of a crosscut saw, with Buck on the other side, cutting the trunk of a downed 150-foot-long pine into 1,000-pound sections that could more easily be skidded down the mountain by Andy's 2,400-pound team of longhorn oxen. The crosscut saw was pulled by one man through the trunk of the pine, then had to be pulled—not pushed—by the other man in the opposite direction.

Stefan wasn't pulling hard enough or fast enough to keep the saw moving freely back and forth through the trunk. He stopped, mopped away the sweat on his sun-and-wind-ravaged brow with a red kerchief, and said, "If you think you can do better, Boss, you're welcome to come take my place."

Before Karl could take him up on the offer, Buck said, "Pull the damn saw, Stefan. The sooner we get this last section cut, the sooner we can quit for the day."

Stefan muttered an obscenity, but he tucked the kerchief back in his coat pocket, bent his back, and began pulling the saw with a great deal more energy than before.

Cutting down a tree had seemed like a simple job to Karl, until he'd learned all the variables that had to be considered. Where did you want the tree to fall? Did the tree lean? Was there a strong wind? Was the area where the tree would fall clear of obstacles, so it wouldn't lodge on the branches of another tree twenty feet off the ground on the way down? Was there plenty of open space—at least double its length—to swing an ax? And, most importantly, did you have a clear path of retreat when the tree finally fell?

There were dozens of mistakes that could be made, and Karl had seen most of them over the past month. Some of the loggers knew what they were doing. Others had lied about their experience to get the job. Karl was training them as fast as he could, but accidents happened every day.

One of the loggers didn't check his ax before he started swinging, and the loose head went flying. Another ruined the blade of his ax by cutting at roots on the ground and hitting a stone instead. A third left his ax lying on the ground, and another logger tripped over it and went flying.

It was sheer luck that no one had been seriously injured or killed. Karl spent most of his day keeping an eye on everyone and didn't get to cut wood himself as often as he would have liked.

But he loved the smell of the wood chips when he swung his ax and reveled in the flash of the sun off his blade. He had a heady feeling each time the straining muscles in his shoulders and back drove the razor-sharp ax deep into two-hundred-year-old wood.

The blisters he'd suffered in the beginning had healed, and he was now growing calluses on his hands and building muscles in his arms and shoulders. He wasn't as exhausted each day as he'd been during his first weeks on the mountain, either. He had energy left over now to lie awake in bed and imagine what it would be like to make love to his wife.

Christmas was only a few days away. The reprieve he'd promised Hetty was nearly at an end. It might be tonight or tomorrow or the next day, or it might be next week, but sometime soon, he would have the exquisite pleasure of joining their bodies and making them one.

That is, if she kept her promise.

Karl worried that Hetty would find some excuse to delay again. For the past month, he'd spent every night holding her in his arms. But she'd made it clear, with that definite, "Good night, Karl," that holding her was all she wanted.

She also kissed him before he left each morning, the sort of peck an old married couple might give one another, but she stayed out of range in the evening. She talked with him. She laughed with him. She teased him each night with the promise of what they might share. But whenever his touches became intimate, she bolted like a skittish filly.

He'd always been able to entice her back into his arms to sleep, but she never lingered there in the morning. He'd gotten into the habit of waking up before her so he would have a few moments to gaze on her face before she awoke and fled.

Karl had no explanation for Hetty's reluctance to make love to him. He thought she liked him. Maybe even a great deal. But there had been no encouragement in her eyes to consummate the marriage. He realized that sometime over the next few days he was going to have to take the bull by the horns—a particularly inappropriate metaphor, but the one that kept coming to mind—and do something about his sexless marriage.

Karl knew better than to let his mind wander to Hetty. Lumbering was far too hazardous an occupation to allow for daydreaming. He forced his frustrating thoughts about his wife to the back of his mind. He had to stay focused. And he had to make sure everyone else stayed focused.

He noticed one of the men pause to roll a smoke near a pine where a bucker was knocking a wedge into the notched hinge with a wooden maul, the last step before the logger made his final cuts to take down a massive pine.

Karl cupped his hands around his mouth and yelled, "Move your butt, Marty, before that tree flattens you like a pancake!"

Marty's head came up as he yelped, "Son of a bitch!" and scampered out of the way.

One more disaster averted.

Karl kept expecting the men to mutiny when he corrected them, but although they grumbled and complained, none of them had shouldered his ax and walked away. Everything he knew about logging, he'd learned from books. He'd supervised men before on his botanical research trips, but he'd been an expert on the subject. He was using his wits and a lot of bluffing to stay a jump ahead of the loggers.

Dennis had stood back and watched, waiting for the moment when things went to hell. So far that hadn't happened, and Karl was determined that it never would.

Dennis appeared at Karl's shoulder as though he'd been listening to Karl's innermost thoughts and said, "Feel like cutting down one more tree?"

Dennis had seemed surprised at how quickly Karl became proficient at getting his tree to fall exactly where he intended it to land. He'd gone so far as to create a competition to see which of them could get his pine cut first and land it closest to a predetermined spot.

Griffin stopped bucking limbs long enough to say, "Go ahead, Karl. You can take him."

At that moment, one of the lumbermen stood back and yelled, "Timmmmberrrrr!"

Karl listened for the *craaaccckkk* that signaled the tree had fallen forward on the notched hinge cut into its base, folding over toward the kerf on the other side. Both the notched hinge and the kerf were angles cut out of either side of the trunk which, along with the direction of the wind and the lean of the tree, determined where the tree would fall.

In all the weeks Karl had spent on the mountain, he hadn't gotten over the excitement of watching the enormous pines fall. He raised his eyes and shaded them from the glare of the setting sun on the snow as he watched the tree's majestic descent. The noise of cracking limbs was followed by the squawk and flutter of birds taking flight from nearby foliage.

Karl realized in the utter silence after the mammoth pine landed that the other lumbermen had stopped to watch as well. He wondered if they felt the same reverence as he did for the felling of the noble giant, or whether they'd stopped to keep a watchful eye on something that could squash them like a bug.

Karl heard Griffin say in a quiet, respectful voice, "Holy cow."

He turned to his stepson, met the boy's gaze long enough to share the wonder in Griffin's dark eyes, and said, "Yeah. Holy cow."

Griffin abruptly turned his attention back to the pine he was bucking as though the brief moment of togetherness had never happened.

Karl was frustrated by his lack of progress getting the boy to trust him. Griffin did his work and kept his distance. Maybe Hetty was right and the kid simply needed time to adjust to having a father. "You can finish bucking those limbs in the morning," he said.

At that moment, the final length of the felled log Stefan and Buck had been sawing separated into two pieces, which rolled apart.

Karl turned and yelled loud enough to be heard by the men who were spread out through the forest, "That's it for the day!"

He heard shouts of relief and name-calling between friends as each man shouldered his ax and began collecting bark to take back down the mountain for the bunkhouse stove.

"You mean you aren't going to take Dennis up on his challenge?" Griffin asked.

Karl was surprised into blurting, "You want me to?"

"You like doing it, so why not?"

Stefan rubbed his aching back with the knuckles of both gloved hands and muttered, "I'll lay a sawbuck that Dennis wins."

"I'll take that bet," Griffin said.

Stefan looked startled that his wager had even been heard, let alone accepted.

Karl wasn't happy, either. He was pretty sure gambling wasn't one of the things Hetty had intended for Griffin to learn by spending time with the loggers. "Where did you get the money to take that kind of bet?" he asked the boy.

"I'm earning a wage, aren't I?" Griffin replied.

Karl hadn't considered paying Griffin, but the boy was doing a man's work, and the loggers were earning forty dollars a month plus room and board. "Are you sure that's how you want to spend your hard-earned cash?"

Griffin nodded. "You can do it, Karl."

The thing was, Karl was pretty sure he *couldn't* do it. He was good, but he wasn't quite as fast as Dennis. In fact, Dennis had beaten him every single time they'd engaged in one of these matches. And he'd rather not have an audience.

"It's getting dark," he said. "You men should get started down the mountain."

"I've got four bits I'd like to bet on Dennis," one of the loggers said.

"Who's going to hold the cash?" Stefan asked.

"I will," Buck said. "Will you take that bet, Boss?"

"Come on, Karl," Griffin said. "I think you can beat him."

He was so surprised at Griffin's encouragement that Karl said, "Sure. Why not?"

By the time the betting was done, more than thirty dollars sat in the pot. Only one person besides Griffin had wagered against Dennis. Andy Peterson had bet a five-dollar gold piece that Karl would win.

Karl was surprised Andy had bet on him to win, because he'd been giving the kid a hard time ever since

Hetty had told him how the boy had lured Grace to the barn. Andy had never once gotten riled at Karl's probing questions about his intentions, and he'd worked hard and without complaint skidding logs down the mountain with his team of longhorns. As far as Karl could tell, there was nothing wrong with Andy Peterson. He just didn't want the Texan anywhere near his stepdaughter.

Karl turned to Griffin and said, "Want to come pick a tree for me?"

"Can I?" Griffin said.

"Sure," Karl replied.

"Is there anything I can do to help?" Andy asked.

Karl thought the Texan was probably having second thoughts about betting his gold piece on the boss. "You can help me figure out where to put the stake," he said at last.

If Karl angled the kerf and the notch for the hinge correctly and gauged the wind and the lean of the tree, the trunk of the falling pine should drive the pre-planted stake into the ground. In order to win the bet, he not only had to get his tree down first, he had to place it where he wanted it to go.

"This one, Karl," Griffin said, picking a pine with a trunk it would take three men to circle with their extended arms.

"I'll take this one," Dennis said.

"That's not the same size. It's a foot smaller around," Buck said. He pointed to a different pine. A larger pine. "That one's the same size."

Karl stared at Dennis, who looked chagrined. Karl was shocked. Was it possible Dennis had been choosing a smaller tree every time they competed? Surely not. And yet, Dennis didn't argue with Buck. He simply moved to the second tree.

Karl felt his heart lift. Lord have mercy. Maybe Buck had given him a fighting chance. Now all he had to do was take advantage of it.

Chapter Twenty-six

Karl leaned his head back to study the ponderosa pine Griffin had chosen for him to chop down.

"Slants pretty far to the left," Andy said.

"But most of the limbs up high are on the right," Griffin countered.

Karl weighed the right-hand-heavy crown of the tree against the significant slant of the trunk in the opposite direction and realized Griffin had chosen a pine that had balanced itself out.

Andy took off his glove, stuck a finger in his mouth to wet it, then held it up in the air. "Wind's from the south."

"But gusting from the west," Griffin said, pointing to a rustling spruce.

Karl glanced at the spruce, then at the pine boughs above him, judging the swirling breeze. He saw movement in the distance and watched as Dennis set his stake in the ground. No one would be shouting *Go!* The game began with the first ax cut by either man.

Karl heard a *thwack* and realized Dennis had begun. Karl didn't even have his stake in the snow yet.

"Run thirty paces in that direction," he instructed

Griffin, pointing with a gloved finger, "and plant my stake right between those two big pines."

"But Karl—" Griffin protested.

"Do it!" Karl freed his ax, which was embedded in a nearby stump. He ran his gloved hands up and down the smooth handle, then made a slow arc with the ax to make sure he had plenty of clearance to swing freely. "Take out that chokeberry for me, will you, Andy?" Karl said, gesturing with his chin at a small bush behind him.

Andy used a short ax he carried on his belt to chop off the plant at its roots. "Anything else?"

Karl heard the steady sound of Dennis's ax chopping wood and realized there was no time to waste. What else? What had he forgotten? He glanced around one last time, plotting his path of escape when the tree came down. By that time, Griffin had returned from placing the stake.

"All right, boys," Karl said. "Step back and join the crowd. I have work to do."

He waited one more beat, till he was sure both boys were safely out of range, then lifted his ax and made the first cut. *Thunk.*

He heard a loud *thwack* in reply.

Karl swung again. *Thunk.*

And again heard Dennis's *thwack.*

Karl formed his kerf with strong, steady strokes of his ax, cutting up, then down, chips flying as he created an angled notch across the trunk, aimed at the stake where he wanted the tree to land. Then he crossed to the other side of the tree, picked a spot higher on the trunk, and began cutting another notch that would act as a hinge. When he was almost done chopping down the tree, he would insert a wooden wedge in the notch to both slow down and steer the fall of the pine, so the trunk didn't bounce back and kill him.

Karl had no sense of time. He relished the endless rise and fall of his ax and the mighty labor required of muscle and bone. Sweat dripped from his brow, slid down his nose, and fell in thick droplets on the snow. Dennis's *thwack*s echoed back to him in the mountain air. They seemed to come faster and sounded louder than Karl's solid *thunk*s.

Karl heard guttural shouts from the gathered loggers egging Dennis on, but he refused to look at his rival to see whether Dennis was ahead or behind. Karl maintained a steady rhythm. He was nearly there. He set the wedge and was making his final cuts when he heard Dennis yell, "Timmmmbeerrrr!"

Karl didn't stop. He took another swing at the trunk. And another. And heard the telltale crack that told him the hinge was breaking. He yelled, "Timmmberrr!" and leapt backward along the escape route he'd chosen.

A moment later he felt his legs being struck out from under him. He was tangled with another body and spinning like crazy down the mountain over rough brush and stones. He came to an abrupt and painful stop wrapped around a pine stump.

Karl groaned. It felt like his back was broken.

"What the hell?" Karl looked down, still dizzy from the tumbling fall, to see who'd tackled him, and found Griffin's body wrapped tightly around his legs. The boy's eyes were closed. Karl reached out a hand—which he was happy to see he could move—and laid it on Griffin's head. "Griffin?"

The boy remained still.

Karl tried sitting up and was aided by Andy, who'd raced down the mountain after them. The rest of the loggers were soon gathered around.

"Are you all right?" Andy asked breathlessly.

"I think so," Karl said. "Check on Griffin."

Dennis was suddenly there to help brace Karl upright. "I can't believe what happened, Karl. That crazy tree came down all wrong!"

"What?" Karl was still dazed, still worried about Griffin, and unable to comprehend what Dennis was saying.

"The kid saved your life," Buck said. "Never saw anybody move that fast. Don't know how he figured out Dennis's tree was coming down the wrong way. You'd have been mincemeat if Griffin hadn't tackled you."

Karl put his hands under Griffin's arms, but before he moved him, he wanted to make sure the boy wasn't badly hurt. "How is he?" he asked Andy.

Andy's face was chalk white. "I can't find any broken bones, but his breathing is shallow. And he's not waking up."

Karl pulled his stepson up into his arms, cradling him like a baby. "Griffin," he said, gently patting the boy's cheek. "Open your eyes."

Griffin's eyes fluttered open, then closed and remained closed. Karl hoped the kid was only stunned, but he had an ugly-looking lump on his forehead. Karl realized it had gotten so dark he could barely see his hand in front of his face.

"Somebody fire up a lantern before we end up standing here in the dark," he ordered. "Andy, take your oxen and get down the mountain. Stop by the house and tell Mrs. Norwood that Griffin's been hurt. Make sure Bao has his medicine box handy when we get there."

"Got it, Boss." A moment later he was gone.

"Let me take the boy, Karl, while you get up," Dennis said.

"No!" Karl held tight to Griffin. "Just give me a hand getting on my feet."

Dennis shook his head at Karl's stubbornness but stuck his hands under Karl's arms and helped him onto his feet with Griffin in his arms. Dennis demanded a lantern from one of the loggers and held it high, so Karl could see his way as he carefully headed down the skid trail carrying the unconscious boy.

They hadn't gone far before Griffin opened his eyes again. The first thing he asked was, "Who won the bet?"

Karl was startled into relieved laughter. "Who cares? You're damned lucky to be alive. That was a fool thing to do, but thank you."

"Who won?" Griffin persisted.

"Dennis's tree came down first," Stefan called out from within the crowd of loggers following behind them.

"But it never came close to the stake he set out," Buck pointed out.

"What about Karl's tree? Where did it come down?" Griffin asked.

"Karl's tree hit his stake stone-cold center," Buck replied. "You won big, Boss. So did you, kid," he said to Griffin.

Karl heard respect in Buck's voice, but he wasn't

sure whether it was for him or the nine-year-old who'd rescued him.

Griffin wriggled in Karl's arms and said, "Put me down, Karl. I can walk."

"Be still," Karl ordered. "You've got a lump the size of a hen's egg on your forehead. Your mom's already going to give me hell for letting you get hurt. All I need is for you to pass out again and hurt yourself worse. I'd never hear the end of it."

Griffin's efforts to get free subsided, but Karl could tell from the tension in the kid's body how uncomfortable he was in Karl's arms.

Karl knew Hetty must be crazy with worry over her son, but when he stepped inside the cabin carrying Griffin, she looked amazingly composed. Only the white knuckles on her clenched hands, and her short, fearful glance at him, told him how really terrified she was.

Grace hovered at Griffin's side as Karl carried him to the bedroom, frantically touching any part of her brother she could reach. "What happened? What stupid thing did you do this time?" she asked in a shrill voice.

"Griffin saved my life," Karl said simply as he eased Griffin onto his bed. Hetty and Grace took up places on one side of the bed, as Dennis joined Karl on the other.

Grace's mouth hung slack in shock. "Griffin saved you?"

Karl nodded.

Grace turned to her brother and said, "Oh, Griffin, I'm sorry for thinking the worst of you. How did you get hurt? What happened to your head?"

"I bumped it," Griffin retorted. "Don't make such a fuss, Grace. I'm fine."

Bao entered the bedroom at that moment accompanied by Andy, who said, "I told Bao what happened."

Andy joined the crowd around the bed as Bao began his examination of Griffin.

"Bump is good thing," Bao announced when he was done. "Mean bleeding not inside head. You have headache?" he asked Griffin.

"Yeah," Griffin admitted.

Bao turned to Hetty. "Cold cloth on head. Keep swelling down." Then he turned to Karl. "Important you watch boy all night. Need rest, but no sleep. Must keep boy awake."

"I can do that," Grace said.

"We both can," Hetty said, settling a comforting arm around her daughter's shoulder.

"You can sleep in your mom's bed tonight, Grace," Karl said. "Hetty and I will sit up with Griffin."

Karl saw Hetty was surprised by his offer to keep vigil with her. She glanced immediately at Grace, who said, "I want to stay. He's *my* brother."

Karl wondered about the emphasis on the *my,* but before he could reflect on it, Hetty said, "Karl, you can't afford to lose a whole night's sleep. You still have work tomorrow. Why don't we take turns?"

Hetty smoothed Grace's flyaway curls from her brow and said, "You and I can take the first shift, Grace. Karl and I will watch the rest of the night till morning."

"When are you planning to sleep?" Karl asked Hetty.

"I can lie down on Grace's bed and nap if I get tired."

"Why can't I go to sleep?" Griffin asked Bao.

"Go to sleep, maybe not wake up," Bao replied.

"Oh." Griffin frowned and then groaned when his forehead protested the movement. A collective gasp arose as Griffin probed the enormous lump on his forehead.

"Don't touch it!" Grace cried.

"My head isn't even bleeding," Griffin said, as his hand came away from the bump. "What's the big deal?"

"If you could see yourself, you wouldn't ask that question," Karl replied. "Do me a favor and leave that lump alone."

"Must go serve dinner to lumbermen," Bao said as he packed up his box of medicines. "Boy too drowsy to stay awake, you call me. Otherwise, see you in morning." He bowed and left the room.

"I've got supper ready to serve, too," Hetty said. "Why don't we eat? Grace, wet a dishcloth with some cold water from the kitchen pump and lay it across Griffin's brow. By then, I'll have a bowl of stew ready that the two of you can share here in the bedroom."

Hetty turned to Andy and Dennis and said, "You're both welcome to join us for supper."

"Another time," Dennis said.

"I wouldn't mind keeping Grace and Griffin company," Andy replied. "If you don't mind, ma'am."

Karl frowned at the way the boy had finagled time with Grace, but Andy kept his gaze focused on Hetty, who hesitated only a second before saying, "I have no objection to that."

Karl shot a look at Grace, who blushed and hurried from the room.

"Let's get out of here and let Griffin get settled,"

Hetty said, waving her hands as though she were shooing flies, until everyone except Griffin and Andy were gone from the bedroom.

Karl stepped back to the doorway after Hetty passed him by and saw Griffin gesturing Andy over to him. Karl figured Griffin was going to warn the Texan to keep his distance from Grace. Instead, when Andy sat down next to Griffin, the two boys put their heads together and began whispering.

Karl heard Griffin exclaim, "He did it on purpose!"

Who did what on purpose? Karl wondered.

Hetty grabbed his arm and drew him away from the door, shutting the two boys in and shutting him out. "Griffin will be fine, Karl. You've done everything you can. Now leave the poor boy alone and come have supper."

As Hetty headed to the kitchen, Grace arrived at the bedroom door, wet cloth in hand, and slipped inside past Karl.

In the brief instant the door was open again, Karl heard Griffin say, "I tell you Dennis purposely offset that notch—"

Grace closed the door behind her, and Karl was left with an accusation he couldn't quite believe. Griffin had already locked horns with Dennis, and there was bad blood between them, which explained why the boy believed Dennis had felled his tree so it would crush Karl. Karl couldn't fathom Dennis doing something that potentially dangerous, not even as a joke.

But the fact was, Dennis's tree had come down in the only path Karl had open as an escape route.

Then Karl considered what Dennis would gain if Karl was "accidentally" killed. He would become boss of the project, a role he clearly believed he should have had from the start. That reason didn't seem good enough for what Dennis was supposed to have done because, if he didn't supervise this job for Jonas, he would supervise the next one.

On the other hand, if Karl was dead, Dennis would have a clear shot at wooing Karl's wife. The wife whom Karl had not yet bedded. He didn't delude himself that Dennis wanted to marry Hetty. She came with the burden of two half-grown children. But he had no doubt that Dennis would take advantage of Hetty's vulnerability in such a situation to seduce her.

Karl figured that last bit of speculation was his jealousy talking. But he made up his mind to keep an eye on his friend. And to find time to make love to his wife.

Chapter Twenty-seven

As Grace washed the last of the silverware she, Griffin, and Andy had used to eat their supper, she glanced over her shoulder and casually said to Hetty, who was sitting at the kitchen table having a cup of coffee with Karl, "Andy volunteered to stay and help me keep watch over Griffin until midnight." She set the spoons on the drain board, then turned completely, drying her hands with a towel, and added, "That way you and Karl can catch a few winks before you have to take over."

Grace could tell Hetty didn't like the idea, but to her surprise, Karl said, "Sounds fine to me."

Grace crossed to Hetty to give her a quick hug and said, "See you at midnight." Then she hurried back to her bedroom before Hetty could change Karl's mind.

As Grace closed the bedroom door behind her, she turned to the two boys and said, "We've got till midnight to figure out a plan."

Andy had shoved a ladder-back chair next to the bed so he could sit and talk easily with Griffin, who was sitting up with his back braced against a couple of pillows. Grace resumed the place she'd had before she'd left to take the dishes to the kitchen, sitting on the foot of her brother's bed.

"I'm still not sure I believe you," Andy said to Griffin. "Loggers make mistakes all the time."

"I watched him do it," Griffin said. "He took a long look at Karl before he started cutting. Dennis wanted Karl injured, maybe even wanted him dead."

"What I don't understand is why," Andy said. "Talk in the bunkhouse is that Dennis and Karl are lifelong friends."

Griffin shrugged. "I don't know why and I don't care. All I'm concerned about is keeping Karl Norwood safe. Grace and I don't intend to become orphans again."

Grace heard Griffin's slip of the tongue and glanced fearfully at Andy to see if he'd noticed. He had.

"Orphans?" Andy asked with a quizzical look.

Grace sought a way to cover the mistake, but Griffin simply said, "We kind of finagled our way into this family, and we don't intend to give it up."

"How did you—"

"Please don't ask," Grace said, cutting him off.

Andy said, "Good enough." He let the matter drop and turned back to Griffin. "How do you propose to keep Karl safe on the mountain?"

"I figure you can help me with that."

"What did you have in mind?"

"You could keep an eye on Karl during the trip up and down the mountain if you asked him to walk with you so you can get his advice on different subjects."

Andy frowned. "Like what?"

"Anything. Logging. Plants. He knows a lot about plants. You could even ask him for advice about how to woo Grace."

Grace was appalled by Griffin's last suggestion. "What if Andy doesn't want to woo me?" she blurted. "Have you thought of that? For that matter, what if I don't want to be wooed?"

"It's only pretend," Griffin said.

"Oh, really?" she snapped. That was even worse.

"I just thought Andy might want to talk to Karl about it," Griffin said.

She turned to Andy. "Did I miss something? What were you two discussing while I was in the kitchen?"

"Not this," Andy assured her. "I had no idea your brother was going to say that." He paused, looked her in the eye, and added, "But it's not a bad idea. Assuming you have no objection."

Grace was tongue-tied, completely unable to respond. It would have been awkward to discuss the subject of courting even if she and Andy were alone. It was especially trying with Griffin listening to every word she said. "I have no objection to a pretend romance," she said at last. "So long as you understand you're playing a part to keep an eye on Karl."

"It might be a very short conversation," Andy said to Grace with a rueful smile. "Karl might not consider me a proper suitor for his stepdaughter."

Griffin grinned. "Hell, Andy, it doesn't matter whether you are or not. In fact, Karl will likely spend the time explaining to you why you're all wrong for Grace. The point is, you'll be right there if Dennis sets another death trap for Karl like the last one."

"You seem pretty sure he will," Andy said.

"That son of a bitch pretends he's a nice man," Griffin said. "He's not."

"You really don't like him, do you?" Andy said.

Griffin shook his head, or tried to. "Whoa," he muttered as he raised a hand toward the knot on his brow. "That was a bad idea."

Grace jumped off the foot of the bed and rushed to his side. "Are you all right?"

"I'm a little dizzy," Griffin admitted.

"Why don't you lie down?" she suggested.

"I'm not supposed to sleep."

"There's no reason why you can't close your eyes and rest." Grace saw the worry in his eyes and added, "I promise I won't let you go to sleep, Griffin. Slide down a little," she urged as she rearranged the pillows under his head. She reached over and turned down the lantern so it wasn't so bright, and said, "Andy and I will be on the other side of the room."

"Keep thinking of ways to keep an eye on Karl," Griffin said as his eyes slid closed.

Grace pulled the covers up over her brother's chest and tucked them around him.

"Sheesh," Griffin murmured. "You'd think I was two years old."

"Shut up and go to—" Grace stopped herself and corrected, "Get some rest."

She and Andy left Griffin's bedside for the warmth of the fire that crackled in the stone fireplace on the other side of the room. Grace reached out to put another log on the fire, but Andy beat her to it. Instead of a couple of rockers, a long bench had been placed in front of the fire. Grace settled on the bench and gestured for Andy to join her. With their backs to her brother, if they spoke softly, they could carry on a conversation without being overheard.

"If you don't want to participate in this charade," she said when Andy was seated, "say so."

"I don't want to see Karl hurt."

"I'm sure there must be a lot of things you can discuss with him besides how to woo me," Grace said.

"Nothing as interesting to me."

Grace was startled by his answer, which suggested he really was interested in courting her. That possibility would have been exciting once upon a time. She was so tempted to let things follow their natural course. But she didn't want to hurt Andy. And she didn't want to be hurt herself. Which meant she should warn him off. But what excuse could she give?

Not the truth. Never the truth.

Grace felt Andy's gaze on her, but she refused to look up from her hands, which were twisted in her lap. "Don't start hoping for things that can never happen," she said quietly.

"Don't shut the door before you see what's behind it," he countered.

Grace looked up and felt her breath catch at the intense look in Andy's blue eyes. "You don't know anything about me."

"I know all I need to know."

Grace scoffed. "What's that?"

"You like me."

It was true, but Grace was reluctant to admit it to him. "So what?"

"So that's a pretty big deal. Especially since I like you, too."

"We're too young to be courting," Grace said.

"I'm in no hurry," Andy said. "I've got all the time in the world."

He reached out and separated Grace's hands and took one in his own. Grace knew she should pull free, but it felt nice to sit in front of the fire next to a boy and have him hold her hand, just like any normal girl her age.

Except, there was nothing normal about her anymore.

"The kittens are growing up," he said. "You should come see them again."

"I've wanted to come, but my mom's been keeping me busy in the house. You're lucky you can hold them anytime you like."

"No sense getting attached to them. Coyotes will probably get most of them before they're grown."

"That's awful!" Grace said.

Andy squeezed her hand. "Of course, they won't be able to get out of the loft for a while yet."

It took Grace a moment to realize Andy was teasing. "Oh, you! How could you scare me like that?"

Andy grinned. "I like to see your green eyes sparkle."

She yanked her hand free. "Just don't let anything happen to those kittens before I have a chance to get one."

"I can see I'm going to be doing an awful lot of guard duty. First your stepfather. And now your kittens."

"Griffin and I appreciate your help."

"I'm not doing it for Griffin," he said as he met her gaze.

Grace rose abruptly. In a voice that was all the more fervent because she was trying so hard not to be over-heard by her brother, she said, "Don't, Andy. Don't like me. Don't pay attention to me. Don't even think about courting me. Time isn't going to make a differ-ence. What's wrong with me won't change. Believe me when I say I'll never be any man's wife."

"But Grace—" he implored.

Grace could feel tears filling her eyes and burning her nose. "Leave. Now. Go back where you belong."

She expected Andy to argue with her. But he didn't.

He stood and said, "I'll keep an eye on the kittens for you. Come and see them when you can." Then he left the room, closing the door silently behind him.

"What's wrong with you, Grace?"

Grace turned at the sound of Griffin's voice. "Were you eavesdropping, you little creep?" She crossed to Griffin, who was leaning up on an elbow in bed, and said, "What's wrong with me is I don't appreciate my bratty brother trying to arrange my life."

"He likes you," Griffin said in a small voice. "I wanted to help."

"You can help by staying out of trouble. You can help by not being a nuisance. You can help by keep-ing your big nose out of my business!"

Griffin sank back down in bed and put the back of his arm across his face to hide his eyes.

Grace saw his mouth turn down and his chest move as though he was crying. Too bad if she'd hurt his feelings. He'd hurt her feelings, too.

Griffin deserved a comeuppance, but Grace couldn't walk away and leave him alone to cry. They were a team, Grace and Griffin. She needed him as much as he needed her. She would even do the awful thing again if it was ever necessary to keep him safe. That was how much she loved him.

Grace sat down next to her brother, swallowed over the painful lump in her throat, and said, "I'm sorry, Griffin. There are things about me even you don't know."

He lowered his arm and looked at her, his dark eyes bleak. "I know what you did to get us here."

Grace's heart skipped a beat. "What?"

"Lucy told me. She wanted to hurt me. She thought I'd be ashamed of you for what you did. But I'm not, Grace. I love you no matter what."

She heard Griffin swallow back a sob. Poor Griffin, trying so hard to be a man when he was barely a boy. Grace's throat ached with unshed tears. Tears were a waste of water. They weren't going to solve anything.

"Grace?"

Grace relented and bent to take Griffin in her arms. He grabbed her hard around the neck and held her tight.

"I was so scared, today," he said against her throat. "I thought for sure Karl was a goner. All I could think was how you might have to do that again. What you did. And I threw myself at him, because I don't ever want you to—"

Griffin sobbed, and Grace hugged him tighter as hot tears slid onto her freckled cheeks.

"It's okay, Griffin. It's all over. You don't have to

worry about Karl. After what happened today, he'll be watching out for himself a lot better than he did before. And he'll have you and me and Andy keeping an eye on him. Everything's going to be all right. We'll never have to go back to that other life. Karl won't let that happen, and neither will Hetty. We're safe."

Griffin sat back and scrubbed at his tears.

"Your nose is running," she said. "Let me get—"

Before she could offer him a hanky, Griffin swiped his nose with his sleeve.

"That's disgusting!"

Griffin shot her an unrepentant grin. "At least you know some things will never change."

"Lie down and shut up," she said, pulling the covers up over his chest.

"Gladly. Just don't let me fall asleep."

He was still a scared child and needed her reassurance. Still needed a mother and was afraid to let Hetty be one. Desperately needed a father and refused to let Karl be one.

"Trust me," Grace said, brushing at a dark curl on his brow. "I'm here, Griffin. I'll always be here."

"Till midnight, anyway," Griffin said with a smirk. "Then Hetty and Karl take over."

"Thank God," Grace quipped back. She settled onto her bed and lay staring up at the ceiling. She wondered how close it was to midnight. She hadn't realized how tired she was. She felt her eyes sinking closed. She would just rest for a minute. Then she'd get up and have a cup of coffee to keep herself awake.

She heard Griffin sniffle. She should get up and get him a hanky. But why waste the effort? He'd already have his nose wiped on his long johns by the time she did. She'd rest another minute. Then she'd check and make sure Griffin was still awake. He wasn't supposed to sleep, because he might not wake back up.

"Griffin? Are you awake?" she murmured.

"Uh-huh."

He was awake. He was okay. She could rest, just for a little while. She could . . .

Chapter Twenty-eight

Ever since Karl had come down from the mountain with Griffin in his arms, he'd been acting strangely. He was quiet. Brooding. Very unlike the open, talkative Karl whom Hetty had come to know and like over the past couple of weeks as they talked in front of the fireplace.

She stopped her rocker and asked, "Are you worried about Griffin?"

"Bao says he should be all right. We just need to keep watch overnight to be sure."

She waited for him to say more. To bring up another subject. But he stared at the fireplace in silence.

"Are you worried about Grace and Andy?" The Texan had left without a word right after supper.

"No."

Hetty searched for something she might have said or done to cause this sudden change in Karl's behavior toward her. She shied away from the obvious. He'd made it very clear over the past few weeks that he wanted to make love to her, that he was only waiting for a signal from her that she was ready to consummate their marriage. Which she hadn't given.

There was not much time left before Christmas, which was when the agreed-upon reprieve ended. Hetty knew she was only postponing the inevitable. But things had been going so well between the two of them that she hadn't wanted anything to upset the apple cart.

She was afraid that if they made love Karl would know—or somehow figure out—that she was a virgin, and that Grace and Griffin couldn't be hers. She wanted to believe it wouldn't matter to him that Grace and Griffin were no relation. But what if she was wrong?

It probably wouldn't have mattered if she'd told him the truth sooner. Hetty knew that now. But it was too late to go back and confess everything. And the longer she waited, the worse Karl was going to be hurt. But she didn't want their lovely evenings together to end, and she was very much afraid that they would when Karl discovered how she'd continued to lie long after she'd sworn she was telling the truth.

Hetty felt sure that something else besides Griffin's injury was bothering him tonight, but she was afraid to question him further. What if he *was* pondering the lack of physical completion in their marriage?

Hetty couldn't really blame him. Recently she'd found herself responding to Karl's increasingly ardent kisses in bed, then chickening out when his hands wandered to places that only husbands touched. Like the top of her thigh. Or the roundness of her belly. Or the tip of her breast, which tingled and became a tight bud when he caressed it.

Hetty had found those touches thrilling. And terrifying.

She wanted to do more, but she was too afraid Karl would discover her deception. Especially since she lost all sense of herself when Karl fondled her. It was as though what he was doing to her was happening to someone else. She had no idea what she was liable to do or say in the throes of passion.

Hetty was doing everything in her power *not* to fall in love with Karl. Her only experience with love had ended in disaster. She never wanted to experience that kind of pain again. She didn't dare fall in love with Karl before he knew the truth, because it was entirely likely Karl would reject her when he found out what she'd done.

And deep down, she didn't believe she deserved Karl's love, not when she'd married him under false pretenses. Not when he thought he was falling in love with a woman who didn't really exist.

She was simply going to have to buck up her courage and allow him to bed her. It wasn't fair to keep putting him off. She was still going to be a frightened virgin no matter when he bedded her. She might as well grit her teeth and take the plunge.

Karl leaned forward in his rocker, then reached an arm around toward the center of his back and flinched.

"I thought you said you weren't hurt in that accident today," Hetty said.

"It's only a bruise, I think, but it's been bothering me all night."

"Why didn't you say something sooner? Stand up and let me take a look."

"Why don't we go into the bedroom?" he said as he

rose. "That way I can stay warm by the fire when I take off my shirt."

Hetty had only intended to shove his shirt and long johns up out of his trousers to look, but maybe the source of his ache was higher up on his back. "All right," she said.

He grabbed the lantern from the table between their rockers and headed for their bedroom.

They were already in the bedroom by the time she realized Karl could just as easily have taken his shirt off by the fireplace in the other room. She figured he was probably worried about Grace finding him half clothed in the parlor.

Hetty closed the bedroom door behind her and turned to discover that Karl had dropped his plaid wool shirt on the bed and was already attacking his long john shirt. She admired the ripple of muscle along his spine and shoulder blades as he yanked the shirt up over his head. She noticed the dark bruise near the small of his back, but her eye was drawn away from it by the corded muscle across his shoulders.

Hetty let out a slow breath as Karl turned to face her. He'd never stripped down completely before. He'd always kept his long johns on when they went to bed. She stared at him, entranced.

When had his shoulders become so broad? When had his arms gotten so strong? When had his forearms become so lean and sinewy? How had his waist gotten so narrow and his stomach so flat?

Hetty felt her stomach flutter. She felt an ache lower down, a flood of feeling that made her knees go weak. Karl tucked his thumbs into the front of his trousers and long johns, dragging them down low enough to expose his hip bones.

She felt her mouth go dry.

This was Karl? This man with a visible rib cage and a washboard belly? With shoulders so broad she wondered if she could get her arms around them? With a belly so flat and hard she thought she could bounce a coin off it?

Hetty followed the line of downy black hair that started at Karl's navel to where it disappeared beneath the denim. The man part of him was straining against the fly of his jeans. For the first time in her life, she wanted to touch. Hungered to touch.

Her eyes skittered away and continued roaming his body, admiring what she saw. She looked up at last and met Karl's gaze.

His golden brown eyes had never looked so brilliant. His glance had never been so intense. "Hetty?"

Just the one word. Spoken with a yearning she could feel all the way to her bones. "Yes, Karl."

It took him a second to realize it wasn't a question. It was an answer.

In two strides Karl was across the room and enfolded her in his arms. His very powerful arms.

She laughed breathlessly. "You don't know your own strength, Karl."

He loosened his grasp enough to allow her a deep breath before he stole it away again by kissing her. His tongue plunged into her mouth, mimicking what he wanted to do to her body. Hetty felt like she was caught up in a whirlwind, dizzy and disoriented. She slung her arms around Karl's neck and hung on for dear life.

He broke the kiss long enough to say, "I want to feel your skin against mine." He didn't wait for her to undress, simply yanked on her cotton blouse. Buttons pinged like hail on the hardwood floor. He shoved the cloth down from her shoulders, blouse and chemise both, until her breasts were bared.

Before she had a chance to feel embarrassed, he lowered his head and suckled.

Hetty's knees turned to noodles.

She needn't have worried about falling. Karl held her close and took his pleasure. And gave it back to her again.

Hetty wanted to touch, but the only things she could reach were Karl's head and shoulders. She grasped his hair and bent her head to kiss his shoulder. It was salty, so she licked it. And then bit.

And heard Karl groan.

"Did I hurt you?" she asked anxiously.

"Do it again," he said. "Kiss me. Bite me. Love me."

Before she could reply, he was kissing her again, thrusting his tongue into her mouth and creating the most exquisite sensations imaginable. Hetty tasted him in return, and felt Karl's hold on her tighten.

Because she had no idea what to do, Hetty followed Karl's lead. When he lowered his head to kiss her belly, she leaned forward and flicked her tongue against his nipple. He made an approving sound, and she did it again.

She felt Karl stripping the rest of her clothes off, and in the spirit of giving as good as she got, she reached down to undo the buttons on his Levi's.

Hetty was careful not to look as Karl shoved them down to his ankles, along with his long john bottoms. He sat down to yank off his boots and socks, then slid out of his jeans. Hetty used the break to remove her shoes. Karl finished before her and knelt to rip off her stockings, the last item of clothing she had on.

Hetty was grateful there was so little light in the room, just the single lantern and the glow of coals in the fireplace.

She shivered, more from fear than cold, but Karl said, "Let's get you under the covers."

Hetty was happy to hide herself under the sheets, but Karl was beside her an instant later and once more took her in his arms. She felt the male part of him, hot and hard, pressed against her.

And panicked.

"I can't do this, Karl!" she said, fighting to be free of his embrace.

"Don't be afraid, Hetty. It's just me. Karl."

Hetty stopped struggling and hid her face against his chest, trying to control her panic. She had to do this sometime. It might as well be now. She'd gone this far. She should just let this happen.

But she couldn't seem to catch her breath.

"Easy now. Take a deep breath," Karl said.

"I can't!"

"You can. It's all right, Hetty. I have you. You're safe with me."

Hetty's whole body was trembling. With fear? With unquenched desire? She didn't have a clue. Karl was still talking, but she had no idea what he was saying. She sought out a source of comfort and ended up pressing her lips against his. His mouth was pliant as he kissed her back. Hetty slid her tongue along the seam of his lips, seeking succor.

Karl let her in.

Hetty felt Karl's hands soothing her, caressing her. Felt a dozen frissons of pleasure from the warmth of his touch. Felt her body ache where his fingers wandered and a yearning for . . . something more.

Karl turned her so she was under him, and she lifted her hips, seeking his warmth, wanting him close again. He slid his palms beneath her, and spread her thighs wide with his knees. She grabbed his shoulders and urged him down to her.

He paused with his face so close she could feel his warm breath on her cheek, looked into her eyes, and said, "My wife. At last."

Then he plunged himself inside her.

Hetty bit her lip to keep from screaming at the excruciating pain.

"What the hell?"

She froze. *He knows. Or suspects. I have to distract him. I have to keep pretending, or all is lost.*

Hetty slid her arms around Karl's neck, pulled him close, and whispered, "Please, Karl. Don't stop."

He remained still for another moment, then thrust his hips, seating himself to the hilt.

Hetty let out a cautious breath. That hadn't hurt as much. She gasped when he withdrew, expecting pain, but there was none. She tensed when he thrust again, but this time, not only was there no pain, it almost felt good.

She realized her fingernails were piercing Karl's shoulders and made herself relax her hands. She slid her hands upward into his hair, concentrating on the silky feel of it, trying to forget what was happening down below.

Karl's thrusts grew faster and stronger, until at last he threw his head back and made a guttural sound of exultation.

He slumped onto her body, then freed himself and turned over onto his back, pulling the sheet up to hide his nakedness.

So. It was done. She was his wife. Did he *know* the truth? Or did he only *suspect* it?

Hetty waited to hear what Karl had to say.

His breathing had returned to normal, but the sweat was still drying on his chest when he spoke. All he said was, "I love you, Hetty."

Hetty froze. She'd been expecting questions, not a declaration of love. She had no answer prepared for what he'd said.

She didn't want to lie to Karl. Or hurt him. She loved what he'd done to her. With her. How he'd made her body sing. At least, before that last part. But that didn't mean she loved him.

Hetty had done everything in her power *not* to love Karl Norwood. She was his mail-order bride, nothing more, nothing less. She liked him far too much to love him. Loving a man she was deceiving so completely was a disaster waiting to happen.

So she said nothing. But she was sure he heard her message loud and clear: *You might love me. But I don't love you.*

He got up and began dressing. "We'd better get moving. It's about time we took over for Grace. She must be pretty tired by now."

Hetty saw the closed look on Karl's face and knew

she'd hurt him. Badly. She should have lied. She was certainly good enough at it.

But it was too late now.

She needed to get out of bed and get dressed, but she was suddenly shy, aware of her nakedness as she hadn't been when Karl had been making love to her. She kept the sheet tucked up under her arms as she reached for her pantalets.

Karl already had his trousers back on and said, "I'll take the rest of my things and dress by the fire in the other room."

Then he was gone, leaving the door ajar.

Hetty sat slumped in the bed. She felt like crying. She was going to have to find some way to repair the damage she'd done, but she had no idea how.

You can offer to make love to him. He'll probably want to do it again. So do you, if you're honest. At least, you want to do the first part again.

Hetty was still pondering her options when she heard Karl yelling from the other room. Her blood froze when she made out what he and Grace were saying.

"Why did you let Griffin fall asleep?"

"I'm sorry, Karl," Grace replied. "He can't have been asleep for very long. Just wake him up."

"I've tried," Karl said. "I can't."

Chapter Twenty-nine

When Karl left the bedroom, he was angry. When he'd told Hetty "I love you," what he'd really meant was, *I forgive you for lying through your teeth. For not being who you said you were. For showing up with two children who cannot possibly be yours.* He'd been ready and willing to accept whatever story she told him and move on with their lives from there. Because the truth was, he'd somehow fallen in love with her, despite all the lies.

Except, she hadn't bothered with another story. She'd shot him a single guilty look and said nothing at all.

Karl had known when he married Hetty that his bride might never love him. But he hadn't expected it to hurt quite so much when she made it clear that she didn't.

He felt used. Hetty hadn't wanted a husband, she'd wanted a home for herself and those two kids. Having a husband was simply a necessary evil. She'd submitted to his lovemaking because he'd made it clear to her that making love was part of the deal.

Had Hetty really thought he wouldn't notice she was a virgin? He'd been stupid about a lot of things where she was concerned, but he was wising up fast. Who was Henrietta Wentworth Templeton? And where had she picked up the son and daughter she was passing off as her own?

Karl shoved open the door to the kids' bedroom intending to surprise them into confessing the truth, only to find them both sound asleep. Which was when he realized that the last thing Griffin should be was asleep.

He crossed the room in two strides, shook Griffin's shoulders, and said, "Wake up!"

The kid didn't move. He lay still as a stone.

Karl sat down on the bed, lifted the boy into his arms, and said, "Wake up, Griffin."

Grace sat up in the next bed, groaning and stretching and yawning. "What's wrong?"

"Why did you let Griffin fall asleep?" Karl demanded.

"I'm sorry, Karl. He can't have been asleep for very long. Just wake him up."

"I've tried," Karl said grimly. "I can't."

"Oh, no!" Grace climbed out of her bed and into Griffin's in a flash, crawling as close to her brother as she could get. "Griffin! Wake up!"

The boy's head lolled back over Karl's arm.

"What's wrong with him?" she cried. "Why isn't he moving? Is he dead?"

Griffin's eyes fluttered, and he licked his lips.

"He's alive!" Grace sobbed. "Griffin, wake up! You're scaring me."

The boy groaned and mumbled, "Stop shouting, Grace. You're making my head hurt."

"Open your eyes," Karl ordered. "Look at me."

Griffin blinked as his eyes adjusted to the glow of

the lantern on the bedside table. He lifted his head and finally focused his gaze on Karl.

Karl studied Griffin's dark brown eyes. The pupils seemed normal and both were the same size. "Do you feel dizzy? Or like you have to puke?"

Griffin started to shake his head, squinted his eyes closed instead, and said, "No. I just want to go back to sleep."

"Sorry, kid. You can't do that," Karl said. "Not until we're sure you don't have a concussion."

Karl had barely finished speaking when Hetty arrived in the doorway looking disheveled and frightened. She was barefoot, her tousled blond curls tumbling over her shoulders, her blue eyes luminous with unshed tears. She'd obviously grabbed the first thing she could find to cover her nakedness, because she was wearing that flimsy nightgown through which he could see the shadow of the pink nipples he'd so recently sucked.

Karl felt a flare of lust so strong that, if the children hadn't been present, he would have taken her then and there—against the wall, on the floor, on the bed—anywhere he could find a flat surface to have his way with her.

"Grace, go get in bed in your mother's room," Karl said.

"I want to stay with Griffin."

Karl's response was abrupt and unsympathetic. "Do what I said!"

Grace shot Hetty a fearful look and fled.

"She's just a child," Hetty said, stepping farther into the room. "It's not her fault she fell asleep."

"It's not Grace I'm angry with," he replied.

Hetty's face blanched.

"I'll stay with Griffin," he said. "You go keep Grace company."

Her eyes looked forlorn. She started to leave, but paused long enough to say, "I'll heat up some coffee to help you stay awake."

Karl's heart ached. He was going to have to figure out some way to fall out of love with Hetty. Because it hurt too much to love someone who didn't love him back.

"Why are you so mad?" Griffin asked.

"If I didn't owe you my life, I'd be a lot madder at you than I am," Karl shot back. He knew he shouldn't take out his ire on the kids. Hetty was the one who'd deceived him. Hetty was the guilty one. But he couldn't stop himself from asking, "Where did you and Grace meet Hetty?"

Griffin's mouth dropped open in shock before he recovered and said, "What do you mean?"

"I know she's not your mother."

"Did she tell you that?"

"Not in so many words. I figured it out."

"Don't blame Hetty," the boy said, laying an imploring hand on Karl's arm. "She only took Mrs. Templeton's place to help out me and Grace."

It took Karl a moment to process what Griffin had said. There had apparently been a Mrs. Templeton—the woman he'd corresponded with—but Hetty had taken her place. When? How? If Hetty wasn't Mrs. Templeton, then who the hell was she?

Karl's head was reeling. Who was it he'd married?

"Are you going to make us leave?"

The kid's plaintive question cut to the heart of the

matter. Was he going to throw them all out? And if he wasn't, where did he go from here?

Hetty stuck her head in the door and said, "Coffee's ready. Do you want me to bring you a cup, or do you want to drink it out here at the table?"

"At the table. Just give me a minute." Karl turned to Griffin and said, "I haven't made up my mind yet what I'm going to do. I suggest you sit here and think about how you'd feel if you were in my shoes and found out everyone you cared about had been deceiving you."

Karl was halfway to the door when Griffin said in a fierce voice, "Nobody ever gave a damn about me except Grace until Hetty came along. Don't hurt her. Or you'll have me to deal with."

Karl saw the kid had his jaw clenched in an attempt to keep the tears that had filled his eyes from spilling over. Karl swallowed over the sudden painful lump in his throat. "I have to do what I think is right."

"I mean it!" Griffin warned.

"I know you do." Karl left the room, determined to confront Hetty and get the truth out of her. But little pitchers had big ears, so he shut the door behind him, then crossed the house and checked on Grace. The lantern was out in the bedroom, but he could hear muffled sobs. He was tempted to try and comfort her, but he couldn't do that until he made up his mind how he was going to resolve the situation.

"Come sit down, Karl," Hetty called to him as she set a tin cup full of steaming coffee on the table.

"What if I don't feel like sitting?"

She set a second cup of coffee on the opposite side of the table and sat down in front of it. "It'll be easier to talk if we can look each other in the eye."

He scraped a chair back, dropped down into it, and leaned his elbows aggressively on the table. "I can see how looking me in the eye wouldn't be a problem for you, Hetty. You're pretty good at lying right to my face."

Even in the scant light from the lantern on the table he saw her cheeks flush. He couldn't be sure whether it was shame for what she'd done, or frustration at getting caught.

"Who are you?" he demanded.

"My name is Henrietta Wentworth."

"Not Templeton?"

She shook her head.

"What the hell is going on, Hetty?"

She focused her gaze on her hands, which were knotted before her on the table. He watched her swallow hard, but she didn't speak.

He reached across the narrow kitchen table and forced her chin up. "Look at me. Talk to me! Whose kids are those?"

She jerked her chin free, her eyes flashing, and said, "Mine!"

"They can't be yours," Karl retorted, grasping her wrist when she started to rise. "We both know why."

Hetty turned her eyes down and to the side, an admission that she'd been untouched before he'd made her his wife.

Karl felt an unutterable sadness. He hadn't insisted on having a woman who'd been untouched by another man. He hadn't thought it would matter to him that his wife had already borne two children. But the masculine exultation he'd felt when he'd realized the truth, when he'd known for certain that no other man had touched her and he was the first, had been something he'd never expected.

Her flush deepened as she sat back down. "The children needed a mother and I was available. I'm their mother now."

"Where did you find them?"

"I didn't find them. They found me." She tugged at her wrist and said, "You're hurting me, Karl."

Karl let her go and knotted his hands into fists, contemplating the beautiful woman sitting across from him. The beautiful, *deceitful* woman sitting across from him.

"You didn't expect there would be consequences if you were found out?"

"I didn't expect to be found out. How did you know—"

"I've never taken a virgin to bed, but I know what a hymen is, and I know when I've broached one."

She covered her face at such plain speaking. He waited her out. When she lowered her hands he said, "Let's start with how you hitched up with those kids. Did you meet them in Cheyenne?"

"I've never been to Cheyenne."

"You just said—"

"Do you want to hear what happened?" she interrupted. "Or do you want to yell at me?"

He clamped his jaw and waited. He watched a half dozen emotions flicker across her face before she began speaking. *Figuring out how to put the best face on her lies,* he thought bitterly.

"I was traveling west on a wagon train with two of my sisters—I come from a family of six children—

when we were attacked by Indians. I was wounded in the shoulder by an arrow."

"I've seen the scar," Karl said.

She put a hand to her shoulder where he'd seen the raised flesh that she'd kept constantly covered with clothing. "The savages went crazy when they realized Hannah and I were twins and let us alone. But they took my youngest sister Josie captive and stole the oxen pulling the wagon."

"I have to give you credit. When you make up a story, it's a corker."

"It's the truth!"

It sounded too farfetched to be the truth, but the anguish in her voice was real enough. "Where was the rest of the wagon train when all this was happening?"

"We were thrown off the train," Hetty admitted.

"Why?"

"Does it matter?"

He thought about that for a moment and said, "I can't believe a wagon master would abandon three women without a man to protect them."

"My sister Hannah's husband, Mr. McMurtry, was with us."

"What happened to him during the attack?"

"He'd died earlier that day of cholera."

"Helluva lot of bad luck, Hetty. Where's your twin? What happened to her?"

"I don't know," Hetty said. "I was dying, so she went to find help. She never came back."

"Then how did you get well?"

She hesitated.

Running out of convincing lies, Karl thought.

At last she said, "Bao found me and nursed me back to health."

Karl was stunned. Bao had been a part of this charade? He'd thought the Chinaman was his friend! He'd trusted Bao to travel to Cheyenne and return with his mail-order bride. He'd returned with a bride, all right. Just not the one he'd been sent to get. How had someone he trusted as much as he trusted Bao become a co-conspirator in this tale of betrayal?

Karl realized he was letting himself get distracted. There was still a big, unexplained hole in Hetty's story. "Where did you find the kids? Were they with the wagon train, too?"

Hetty swallowed hard and said, "They traveled from Cheyenne with your mail-order bride. Mrs. Templeton saw what she thought was an abandoned wagon along the trail and stopped to see if there was anything left inside. There was. Me."

Karl was trying to fill in the blanks between what Hetty had said and what she'd implied, trying to unravel the knotted string of truth she'd presented to him.

"So you're not the one who wrote those letters to me?"

"Grace did that."

Karl's lips flattened. "I was corresponding with a thirteen-year-old girl?"

Hetty nodded.

"How did the kids get involved with Mrs. Templeton?" he asked.

"Grace paid Mrs. Templeton to bring them along because she was desperate to find a home for herself and her brother. They'd been living upstairs in a saloon where their mother used to work."

Karl didn't have to ask what kind of work Grace and Griffin's mother had been doing. To clarify things in his mind, he asked, "So the children weren't related to Mrs. Templeton, either?"

Hetty shook her head.

"Poor kids," Karl muttered. It suddenly dawned on him that the *poor kids* he was feeling so sorry for were the same ones who'd manipulated him into this mail-order marriage. "If you're not the woman Grace planned to marry off to me, where is she?"

"On the way here, Mrs. Templeton fell off a cliff."

Karl snorted. "Of course she did."

"It wasn't my fault!"

Karl hadn't even considered the possibility that Hetty was responsible for Mrs. Templeton's death. Fortunately, he was too stunned to speak.

Hetty's chin came up as she said, "Mrs. Templeton was going to beat Griffin. Again. So I intervened."

"And pushed her off a cliff?" Karl said incredulously.

"I only punched her in the nose," Hetty protested. "She was trying to hit me with a heavy branch and lost her balance and fell."

"She couldn't *see* the cliff?" Karl asked.

"It was dark."

"Lord, lord, lord," Karl said, thrusting both hands through his hair in agitation. "I can't believe what I'm hearing." He frowned as he had a sudden thought. "And Bao went along with this . . . substitution?"

"Bao *suggested* it," Hetty replied. "I don't think he liked your mail-order bride."

Every answer Karl got made him think of more questions to ask. "Where did you come from? Where's the rest of your family?"

"My father was a banker in Chicago. Our home burned down in the Great Chicago Fire, killing my parents. My two brothers and three sisters and I ended up in an orphanage."

"Where's the rest of your family?"

"My eldest sister, Miranda, took my two little brothers, Nick and Harry, with her when she left Chicago to become a mail-order bride in Texas. We never heard from her again.

"It was awful at the orphanage without Miranda there to protect us from the headmistress. So Hannah decided to become a mail-order bride to Mr. McMurtry, who was heading west to the Wyoming Territory, and he agreed to bring me and Josie along."

"Lots of mail-order brides in your family," Karl said scornfully.

"We weren't left with many choices," Hetty shot back with equal scorn.

"I just realized something," Karl said. "We may not be legally married."

"I signed my full name to the church registry."

"Along with a false one," Karl pointed out.

"I'm your wife, Karl. We were married in church. We spoke words before God."

"You married me under false pretenses."

"Those two children still need a father. And a home. You can't throw them out," Hetty pleaded. "Grace will end up working upstairs in some saloon, and Griffin will end up in some awful orphanage. He'll be beaten and he'll run away and starve!"

She was painting an especially gruesome picture, but Karl could tell she believed every word she was saying.

"I would never have married you if I'd only been thinking of myself," she continued. "I had to save those children from a fate worse than death. I *had* to!"

"Why?"

"Because I know what it's like to be orphaned. I know what it's like to find yourself in an orphanage at the mercy of someone cruel. I could never condemn Griffin to that life, or Grace to the sort of life that faced her without my help. You see why I had to deceive you, don't you, Karl?" she said, her hands held out to him in supplication. "It wasn't for myself. It was for the children."

Why else would she accept marriage to a man as plain-looking as he was? She'd made love to him to be certain the marriage couldn't be annulled.

"I don't care about your motives," he said in a harsh voice. "You still lied to me. About everything."

She didn't bother denying it.

Karl finally knew the truth. It hurt even more than the lies had. His throat ached, but he forced himself to speak.

"What you did was despicable. How do you expect me ever to trust you again?"

"I'm so sorry, Karl," she whispered. "So very sorry."

"Why didn't you tell me sooner? You sat in front of that fire with me night after night and said *nothing*. You lay in my arms night after night, listening to my heart beat with love for you, and said *nothing*."

"I didn't know you loved me, Karl."

"I don't," he said flatly. "Not anymore. How could

I? I don't even know who you are. All you've done since I married you is tell one lie after another."

Hetty sobbed. "I'm sorry, Karl. I never meant to hurt you."

"A lot of good that does me," he snarled.

Karl felt like he might be sick. He could understand Hetty leaping before she took the time to think, accepting the role of mail-order bride to save those two kids. He could understand her believing that she needed to lie to him before she'd had a chance to find out the kind of man he was.

What he couldn't forgive was how she'd continued to lie to him long after she must have known, from their conversations in front of the fire and later in bed, that he'd never throw those two kids out in the snow.

Most of all, he couldn't forgive her for letting him fall so deeply in love with a woman who was unwilling to love him back. A woman he was afraid to trust and who was afraid to trust him.

Karl rubbed the nape of his neck. Tired and unhappy and confused. He needed time to think. He needed time to figure out exactly where they should go from here.

"Have you told me everything, Hetty? Is it all truly, finally out in the open?"

He saw the flicker of something pass over her face and realized there was indeed something more, at least one more secret she wasn't telling him. Karl gritted his teeth to keep from saying anything, waiting her out.

Instead of confessing whatever it was, she took a deep breath and said, "That's everything."

Like hell it is, Karl thought. *What else are you hid-*

ing, my devious wife? What other surprises do you have up your sleeve?

Suddenly he knew. It was something about Clive. The mysterious man in her past. Karl opened his mouth to mention the man's name and closed it again. He'd had enough pain for one night.

"Are you going to let us stay?" Hetty asked.

Instead of answering her, Karl said, "Looks to me like you didn't fare any better in this fiasco than I did."

"What do you mean?"

"You ended up with two kids you never wanted. And me."

"I was alone, Karl, without any way of taking care of myself. I would have needed to marry someone. I'm not sorry it was you."

"You're not?" He noticed Hetty couldn't meet his eyes. He waited for her to say more, but she didn't. "If you want out, tell me now."

"What about the children?" Hetty said, keeping her gaze focused on her lap. "What would happen to them if I left?"

His heart sank. If she wanted out, he would have to let her go. Maybe that was for the best. "I'll find somewhere for the kids to go."

He could see she was tempted to walk away. There was nothing here for her. Except two children she clearly loved.

She met his gaze again and said, "You can't put the children in an orphanage, Karl. They need a home. If you need to punish someone, punish me."

"How do you suggest I do that?"

"You could send me away," she said in a small voice.

"And leave myself without a wife? Without the helpmate I need to cook and clean the house and do laundry? Without a nurse for the loggers? Without a caretaker for those two kids? Without a woman to take to my bed? Or to give me more children?"

"But you can't want to keep me as your wife," she protested. "You've told me all the reasons that will never work. You won't ever be able to trust me. I've managed to destroy whatever feelings you had for me. You don't love me anymore."

"In order to punish you, I'd have to punish myself worse. I choose not to do that. I choose to keep you here. For all the reasons I mentioned, but especially so I have a woman in my bed. And a wife to bear me children."

"What if I don't accept your kind offer to stay?" she said bitterly.

He shrugged. "Then you're welcome to go. I'll make sure Bao gets you back to Butte. But take Grace and Griffin with you."

She gasped. And then said nothing for a very long time.

Karl was tempted to fill the silence that grew while she contemplated the future she could expect with a husband who despised her for what she'd done, versus the brutal existence she and the children would face on their own in a wilderness mining town.

He forced himself to wait her out.

When Hetty spoke at last, her eyes were bleak. He saw guilt and remorse. And something he hadn't expected, but which he found both exciting and promising. Defiance.

"I'll stay."

Karl felt his heart pounding in his chest. If they were ever to find peace together, they had a long road to travel. It was true he didn't know much about how to make a wife happy. Or how to make a woman fall in love with him. But he'd learned a few useful things from a life spent studying plants. Like, if he just waited patiently for it to grow, the smallest bud often became the most magnificent flower.

Chapter Thirty

Karl kept his distance from Hetty over the next week, rising early, then working late on the mountain and eating dinner with the loggers. He'd eyed Bao askance all week without mentioning the fact that, thanks to the Chinaman, he'd married a substitute bride. It was bad enough to have a wife he couldn't trust and a best friend who questioned his authority on the job. It was downright disheartening to discover that Bao didn't have his back.

Karl was still sitting at the cookhouse dining table long after the loggers had all eaten supper and headed back to the bunkhouse. He got up and rinsed his tin plate, fork, and spoon in the pot of hot water Bao had provided for that purpose, then set his clean plate facedown at his place with the silverware on top of it, as all the other loggers had done, ready for the next meal.

He knew he ought to head back to the house, but he was finding it harder and harder to resist the woeful look on Hetty's face. He didn't understand how he could be so mad at his wife and still yearn to sit and talk with her in front of the fireplace. It felt like he was the one suffering when he didn't hold her in his arms through the night.

But Karl didn't feel like he could do either of those things until he was able to forgive Hetty. And he couldn't forgive her because he was pretty damn sure she was still keeping secrets from him.

Bao came out of the kitchen and said, "You ready go home now, Boss?"

What Karl heard was, *You go home now, Boss*. Ordinarily, he would have taken the Chinaman's advice. Instead, he retorted, "Sounds like you want me out of here."

"Children miss you. Wife miss you. Time go home."

"Sounds like you're on their side, Bao. What happened to taking my side? What happened to being my friend?"

Bao crossed his arms and slid his hands inside his wide sleeves. "Why you so angry, Boss?"

"I know you let Hetty pass herself off as my mail-order bride when she was no such thing," Karl accused. "I know you not only went along with the scheme, you actually *suggested* it."

"You no like first wife," Bao said certainly.

"That's no excuse!"

"She selfish person. Pull girl's hair. Hit boy."

"They weren't her kids," Karl pointed out.

"No excuse. I save your life once, Boss. Responsible for you be happy, so give you pretty wife."

"Looks shouldn't matter," Karl argued.

"Matter she nice lady. Matter she like kids. Matter she make good wife."

"Hetty's lied to me from the moment we met," Karl countered.

"She only lie to save kids. I only lie so you marry proper lady."

"So, as long as you're lying for my own good, lying is fine?" Karl asked incredulously.

"She perfect wife," Bao said stubbornly. "Confucius say—"

"I don't give a damn what Confucius has to say," Karl interrupted angrily. "I want to know you aren't going to lie to me again. I want to know I can trust you."

Bao didn't look the least bit contrite. "Always do what best for you, Boss. Always."

Karl realized that was all the apology he was likely to get.

"Tomorrow you bring home tree for Christmas," Bao said. "You eat supper with wife and kids. You start over. You be happy."

Karl sighed. "I suppose Hetty told you to remind me she wants a Christmas tree."

"She mention want tree for kids. She love kids. She love you, too, you give her chance."

Karl's features darkened. Hetty had made it pretty clear she didn't love him, and he wasn't holding out a lot of hope that her feelings would change. But he missed his wife. He even missed the kids. He was going to have to start over sometime. It might as well be now.

He was almost to the door when he turned back to Bao and asked, "What was it Confucius had to say?"

" 'All good things difficult to achieve.' "

Karl snorted. "I can't argue with that."

"You win wife's love, you happy man."

Karl smiled ruefully. "I can't argue with that, either."

Chapter Thirty-one

Hetty was folding clean clothes in her bedroom when Karl appeared at the door and said, "I brought home an alpine fir to decorate for Christmas. I set it up next to the fireplace."

Hetty had desperately wanted a Christmas tree. But Karl had looked so forbidding over the past week since he'd discovered her deception, that she hadn't dared to ask him for anything. She felt a rush of pleasure that he'd thought of bringing home a tree without being asked.

"Thank you, Karl."

"I didn't do it for you. I did it for the kids. I have work to do in the barn. I won't be back till late."

"What about supper?"

"I'm not hungry." He turned and headed back out the door, leaving her alone.

Despite his threats to make use of the wife he'd paid to bring to Montana, Karl hadn't come near her in bed for the past week. He retired after she was asleep and rose before she was awake and headed up onto the mountain to spend his days cutting wood. He ate his meals with the loggers.

Of all the disasters Hetty had caused over the past year, and there had been many, hurting Karl was the worst. She'd felt so sad since their confrontation that it was hard to get out of bed in the morning. But she'd had no choice. She'd needed to be strong for the children, who were frightened by Karl's brooding silence. They still weren't sure he wasn't going to change his mind and throw them all out in the snow.

Hetty dropped the long john shirt she was folding and hurried into the next room to see the tree Karl had brought.

She found Grace and Griffin there before her, staring at the perfectly shaped fir in the parlor with wondering eyes.

Hetty breathed deeply, filling her lungs with the evergreen's pungent fragrance. The smell brought back memories of wonderful Christmases with her family as a child, when she'd been blissfully happy, unaware of all the tragedy to follow.

"You were right," Grace said, her smile stretching from ear to ear. "He brought us a tree."

"I didn't think he would," Griffin said. "I mean, not without me there to remind him."

Griffin had been ready to go back to work the next day after he'd gotten the knot on his head, but Karl had insisted the boy stay at the house until the swelling was completely gone. The bump was long gone, but Karl still hadn't okayed Griffin's return to the mountain.

"Just in time for Christmas tomorrow," Grace said. "It's a good thing we went ahead and made all those decorations, or we wouldn't have anything to put on it."

During the long days over the past week when both children had been stuck in the house with her, Hetty had kept them busy making the sorts of decorations they'd had on the Christmas tree at the orphanage.

She'd shown the kids how to use tin snips to cut tin can lids into flower petals, lifting one petal up and pushing one petal down to give it shape. Then they'd mounted small candles on the center of the lids with wax. Once the lids were attached with wire to the tree, they would reflect the candlelight, making it brighter.

They'd used brown paper and flour paste to make paper rings, attaching one ring to another to make an impossibly long garland to go around the tree. They'd attached red and green thread to different-sized pinecones, so they could be hung from the branches. They'd spent an entire evening stringing red chokeberries, so they could be draped around the limbs.

Hetty had insisted that the children each give up a stocking, which she'd hung by a nail to the mantel above the fireplace.

"What's that for?" Griffin demanded.

"Saint Nicholas needs somewhere to leave the gifts he brings for good little boys and girls when he visits on Christmas Eve," Hetty replied.

"Someone's coming to visit?" Griffin asked.

"Just wait. You'll see," Hetty promised. "When you wake up on Christmas morning, those stockings will be full of marvelous surprises."

"I've heard those stupid tales," Grace said, sounding far too jaded for her age. "Bad little boys and girls get sticks and stones and lumps of coal. Likely that's what'll you'll find in your stocking, Griffin."

"Sticks and coal will suit me fine," Griffin said with a smirk. "I can burn them in the fireplace to stay warm."

Hetty had been working furiously to make Christmas gifts for the children. She'd also been working on something to give Karl. She knew what he wanted most: a loving wife. She wasn't sure she could ever become the wife he wanted. And she had no idea where to start. She had no idea how to please Karl in bed, and she certainly hadn't been able to please him lately out of bed.

She hoped he would like the present she'd made for him. It had been started during the weeks when they'd spent their evenings together talking and their nights wrapped in each other's arms. And finished during this week of bitter silence.

She saw the children whispering together and said, "What mischief are you plotting now?"

"Nothing," Grace said quickly. "We need to talk to Karl. Will he be here for supper?"

"No. He's working in the barn tonight."

"We need to talk to him," Griffin said.

"You'll have to catch him tomorrow morning," Hetty said.

"Tomorrow's too late," Grace said.

Hetty chewed on her lower lip. Did she dare send the children out to the barn to speak with Karl? Was he likely to yell at them for disturbing him? Hetty realized she couldn't send them out there by themselves. She had to be there to intercede if Karl got upset with the children for showing up unannounced.

"We'll all go," she said.

"We need to talk to Karl *alone*," Grace protested.

"Either I go with you or you don't go," Hetty said.

"I'm sure you can find someplace private in the barn to speak with Karl."

Grace exchanged a look with Griffin, who nodded. "All right. Let's go."

The weather was cold but clear, and for once the wind wasn't blowing. Hetty made each of the children bring a lantern, and she carried one herself. She wanted the extra light to warn off any vicious predators that might be lurking in the darkness as she and the children crossed the meadow to the barn.

Not that Hetty had seen any vicious predators since they'd arrived in the Territory, but she'd heard enough stories about wolves and mountain lions to leave her with a terror of getting caught out in the dark alone.

Hetty heaved an almost audible sigh of relief when they reached the barn. She could hear hammering inside and wondered what was going on. It suddenly dawned on her that Karl might be making gifts for the children. Gifts that he didn't want them to see before Christmas morning.

"Griffin! Grace!" Hetty's call came too late. Griffin had already opened the barn door and slipped inside with Grace. She hurriedly followed them. The barn was warm from the body heat of the animals inside. She was struck by the acrid smell of ammonia, overlaid by the sweeter smell of hay.

The children headed straight for the light at the far end of the two rows of stalls on either side of the barn. Hetty could see Karl standing at a worktable. He'd turned at the sound of the barn door opening, and quickly covered whatever he was working on with a tarp.

"What are you guys doing out here?" he said, looking from the children to Hetty.

"We have to talk to you," Grace said.

"Alone," Griffin said, glancing over his shoulder at Hetty.

"Couldn't this wait?" Karl asked.

"No, it can't," Grace said.

Karl set down a hammer that he'd apparently forgotten he was holding, leaned back against the bench, and crossed his legs at the ankles. "I'm listening."

Grace turned back to Hetty and said pointedly, "We need some privacy."

Hetty backed up and then turned and walked to the other end of the barn to pet the horses, who'd poked their heads out over the stall doors. She'd often snuck out to the barn to feed them bits of carrot or dried apple, and as she passed, they stuck their velvet noses into her hand, looking for the promised treat.

"I didn't bring anything with me tonight," she said as she patted strong necks and rubbed soft ears.

She heard whispers from the threesome at the end of the barn, but no distinct words. A few moments later, Karl approached her with the kids trailing him on either side.

"Everything settled?" she said.

"We have a few things to do here," he said. "I'll bring the kids back when I come. You can go on back to the house."

"Oh." Hetty would have felt silly telling Karl she was afraid to walk back in the dark by herself. It wasn't far from the barn to the house. She had a lantern to show the way, and she could always run if something started chasing her.

"Is there some problem?" Karl asked.

"No. I'm fine. Don't keep the kids out too late. They'll want to be up early in the morning."

"I figured that," Karl said. "It being Christmas morning and all."

Hetty thought she saw a smile hovering on his lips, but it never settled there. She resisted the urge to confess her fear of being alone in the dark and left the barn, holding her lantern high.

She hadn't always been afraid of the dark. In fact, she'd never been afraid of the dark, until she'd been forced to spend two nights alone on the prairie in a Conestoga wagon. She'd lain there in the dark the second night, wondering if she was going to die all alone, and heard snuffling coyotes, or maybe wolves, prowling the edges of the wagon. She'd wanted to yell at them to go away, but her throat was too raw to speak. She lay there wondering if they'd figure out a way to get inside and eat her alive.

It had been a very long night.

Hetty heard snow crunch behind her and started running. She hadn't taken two steps when something grabbed her. She felt her wool shawl come off her head as she tore herself free. Then she was caught again. She dropped the lantern to claw at the hand grasping her breast through her coat. And the light went out.

She was alone with the most dangerous predator of all. A two-legged one.

Hetty opened her mouth to scream, but before she could, a powerful hand covered her mouth and nose, stifling the sound and suffocating her.

Hetty scratched and clawed for her life. She managed to free her nose, but her captor kept a firm grip over her mouth, preventing her from screaming for help.

"Cut it out! It's just me. Don't scream. I'm going to let you go."

Hetty stopped struggling and stood within the prison of Dennis Campbell's arms, panting like a fox run to ground by ravenous dogs. She waited until she felt his hands release her and whirled to confront him. "What do you mean by grabbing me like that? You scared me half to death!"

"I didn't mean to frighten you. I wanted to talk."

"In the dark?" she ranted. "How did you even know I was here?"

"I saw you and the kids traipsing out to the barn. I meant to catch up to you there, but I saw you leave, so I followed you."

"Why?" she demanded.

"I have a Christmas present for you and Karl. I wanted to ask if you'd put it under the tree."

Hetty had been expecting something much more sinister, especially the way Dennis had mauled her. Apparently he hadn't intended to assault her.

She felt like a balloon that someone had pricked, as all the air she'd gathered to fight with slowly seeped out of her. Her knees were threatening to collapse. "For heaven's sake! You could have stopped by in the morning and dropped it off."

"I wanted it to be under the tree when you wake up tomorrow morning."

Everything he said was perfectly plausible. It didn't explain why he hadn't called out to her, instead of sneaking up like that. It didn't explain why he'd man-handled her, groping her breasts and grazing her belly, while he kept her mouth covered to prevent her from crying out for succor.

She held out her hand. "Give it to me." She half expected him not to have a present with him, to have been making up a story for why he'd followed her.

But he reached into his coat and came out with a small package. "Here it is."

Hetty didn't want the present. Didn't want anything to do with Dennis Campbell. But she made herself take it. The package was small and light, wrapped in brown paper with a bow of brown string.

Dennis covered the hand in which she held the present with both of his hands, top and bottom. "I hope you'll like it. I thought of you when I bought it in Butte."

Hetty wanted free, but she didn't want to start a tug-of-war. "I thought you said this gift was for both of us."

"I think Karl will enjoy it, too, when he sees it around your pretty little neck."

Hetty had a sick feeling in her stomach. "You bought me a necklace?"

"A copper pendant. I hope you like it."

Hetty didn't want it. And she was sure Karl wouldn't like the fact that his friend had bought her something so personal. She tried to hand the gift back. "Thank you, but I can't accept this, Dennis."

Hetty had been so frightened, and then so relieved to discover her attacker was only Dennis, and then so concerned about how to give back a gift she couldn't possibly accept, that she hadn't noticed Karl and the children leaving the barn. She'd had no idea she and

Dennis were being observed, until she saw the three lights bobbing behind Dennis's shoulder.

"Take it back!" she said, trying to free herself from Dennis's hold. "I don't want it!" She had to get rid of the gift—and Dennis—before Karl reached them and misconstrued the situation. If Dennis would leave, she could grab her darkened lantern and run toward the lights in the house and Karl might never know they'd met up in the meadow.

She should have known Dennis wouldn't let her go. He was happy to cause trouble between her and Karl. She was inexperienced with men, but she was learning fast. Dennis had been pursuing her from the beginning. For some reason she couldn't fathom, he wanted to cause trouble between her and Karl. "Let me go, Dennis. Please. I want to go."

Dennis must have seen the lights bobbing out of the corner of his eye, because he held on until the moment Karl's light hit their joined hands and then quickly let go.

Karl arrived a moment later, saw Hetty's hand still extended, holding the gift Dennis had given her, and said, "What's that?"

Hetty felt literally sick to her stomach. "It's a Christmas gift from Dennis,"

"I didn't think you'd mind if I gave your bride a gift," Dennis said.

Hetty saw the muscle working in Karl's jaw and knew it was useless to try and explain that she hadn't asked for the gift, that she didn't want the gift, and that given a choice, she would have thrown it away.

"Good night, Karl," Dennis said as he picked up

his lantern and turned back to the bunkhouse. "Merry Christmas."

"Come on," Karl said to Hetty. "Pick up your lantern. Let's get back to the house."

"Karl, I—"

"Don't say anything. I don't want to hear excuses for why you were standing out here in the dark with Dennis Campbell."

"But I—"

Karl didn't wait for her. He simply headed for the house. Griffin kept pace with him, but Grace waited for Hetty to pick up her lantern and walked beside her back to the house.

"Dennis Campbell is a rat," Grace said.

Hetty was surprised into nervous laughter. "What?"

"I know you didn't plan to meet Dennis out here. If Karl stopped to think about it, he'd know it, too. But Karl isn't sure you like him, so it's easy for Dennis to make him jealous."

"I don't think Karl likes me enough to be jealous of Dennis."

"Karl's *in love* with you," Grace said.

Hetty stopped in her tracks. "How do you know that?"

"He's been besotted—head over teakettle—since the first time he laid eyes on you. I'm not as sure that he *loves* you," Grace said.

"What's the difference?" Hetty asked.

"A man in love with you wants to take you to bed. A man who loves you cares about you whether he can take you to bed or not."

Hetty wondered where a girl Grace's age had acquired that sort of knowledge. And whether she could possibly be right.

"Did you accomplish whatever you went to the barn to do?" Hetty asked.

Grace smiled. "Yep. Karl was a big help."

"Christmas has always been my favorite time of year," Hetty said. "How about you?"

Grace shrugged. "We never had a tree of our own. Sometimes the saloon would put one up. There was never much money for presents, but I always made sure Griffin got something."

Who made sure you got something? Hetty wondered. And realized it was likely nobody had. Hetty had been spoiled and pampered her whole life. There had been boxes and boxes of presents for her under the tree every year before the Great Fire. She at least had those memories of great Christmases in the past. She wanted more than anything to make happy memories for Grace.

"Maybe Saint Nicholas will show up with something for you this year," Hetty said.

"I know there's no Saint Nicholas," Grace said. "And so do you. I know you didn't have a way to buy anything for me for Christmas, Hetty, and I don't mind. Really, I don't. I'm just glad to know Griffin and I have a roof over our heads and food to eat and two parents to take care of us. That's really the best Christmas present of all."

Hetty slid an arm around Grace's shoulder and pulled her close. "I'm glad you're happy having me and Karl for parents. Don't worry about Griffin having a wonderful Christmas. I think Saint Nicholas just might surprise you both."

Chapter Thirty-two

Hetty didn't think Grace and Griffin would ever fall asleep. Griffin was excited by the prospect of a lot of gifts under the tree and had kept Grace awake with questions about what she thought they might find there in the morning.

Hetty had gone into their bedroom several times to shush them. "You know, Saint Nicholas won't come until you're sound asleep," she told Griffin as she pulled the covers up under his arms. She knew better than to try and kiss him good night, but she was able to brush a lock of dark hair from his forehead before he wriggled away.

"Is Karl still down at the barn?" Grace asked.

As soon as Karl had made sure she and the kids were safely back at the house, he'd returned to the barn, saying he hadn't quite finished what he was working on. Whatever that was.

"Yes, he's still out there," Hetty said. "You know, the sooner you go to sleep, the sooner it'll be morning."

Grace laughed. "The time's not likely to fly any faster just 'cause we're asleep."

Hetty tucked Grace more completely under the covers, then kissed her on the forehead. "You never know. Stranger things have happened on Christmas Eve. Now go to sleep!"

Hetty closed the door as she left the children's room and gasped when she turned and found Karl standing right behind her. "I didn't hear you come in," she whispered.

"I didn't want to wake the kids," he replied in an equally soft voice. "I had to finish wrapping up their gifts. I've put them under the tree."

Hetty stared at him, trying to tell whether he was still upset with her, but his brown eyes were caught in the shadows created by the candles on the tree and the single lantern on the table.

At last he said, "The tree looks nice."

"The kids helped me make the decorations. I left the candles burning so you could see it. We need to blow them out before they burn out."

Karl followed Hetty back to the Christmas tree. She leaned forward to blow out one of the candles, but he stopped her by slipping an arm around her waist from behind. "I dreamed of a Christmas tree like this, in my own home, with my wife and kids."

She looked over her shoulder and saw the wry twist of his lips. *Just not this wife and these kids,* Hetty thought. Her heart sank. She'd hoped the Christmas spirit might encourage Karl to forgive her. After Dennis's antics tonight, she was afraid Karl would never feel like he could trust her.

"We'd better blow out the candles," she said.

Karl leaned across her shoulder and blew out the closest candle. "Your turn," he said.

A frisson of feeling had run up Hetty's spine when she felt Karl's breath against her ear, but she ignored it and concentrated on blowing out the candle closest to her. Then Karl took his turn again. Hetty kept expecting him to let go of her as they moved around the tree extinguishing candles, but he didn't. Pretty soon, there was no light left in the room except the burned-down coals in the fire and the lantern on the kitchen table.

Hetty realized Karl hadn't even taken off his coat. Maybe he was planning on leaving again. She asked, "Are you finally done in the barn?"

"All finished." He pointed under the tree and said, "Where did those other gifts come from?"

"Those are Grace's and Griffin's presents for you and me."

Karl looked surprised. "They're giving me presents?"

"Why wouldn't they? You're their father."

"Where did they get them?"

Hetty shrugged and felt her breasts brush against his forearm. "Made them, I suppose."

"You didn't help?"

Hetty shook her head. "They were very secretive. I did give them brown paper and string to wrap them up." She hesitated and said, "My present to you is also under the tree."

"Along with Dennis's gift to you?"

Hetty felt her heart squeeze at the bitterness in Karl's voice. "I'd like a cup of coffee," she said, shoving Karl's arm away with both of her hands and moving past him into the kitchen.

"Pour one for me, too."

Hetty went directly to the stove and poured two cups of coffee. She brought them to the table and set them down, surprised that her hands weren't visibly shaking, because she was certainly trembling inside with exasperation and frustration. How was she ever going to undo the damage Dennis had done?

Karl took off his coat and hat and hung them on the rack by the door, then sat down across from her at the table.

"Dennis surprised me in the meadow," she blurted. "I wasn't expecting anyone to be there. When he caught up to me, I was scared and I dropped my lantern and it went out. That's why we were together in the dark."

"I didn't ask for an explanation, Hetty."

"I don't encourage him, Karl. I don't even like him. He—"

"That's enough, Hetty."

"I'm trying to tell you—"

"I don't want to hear it."

She scraped her chair back and ran to the Christmas tree and knelt down and searched for the small box Dennis had given her. She brought it back to Karl and threw it on the table in front of him. "I don't want it. Throw it away. Get rid of it!"

"Dennis is my friend. He'd be insulted if I did that."

"So you suspect me, but not him?" Hetty said.

"You must admit you've been lying to me pretty much nonstop since I met you."

"I told you why I did that!" Hetty said.

Karl rose and caught her by the shoulders. "Keep your voice down. You'll wake the kids."

Hetty pounded on Karl's chest with her fisted hands.

"You have to believe me. You have to give me a chance. You have to stop blaming me for everything. It's not my fault!"

"You're going to wake up the kids!" Karl hissed.

"I don't care—"

He scooped her up in his arms, carried her into their bedroom, and kicked the door closed behind him. He threw her on the bed and, before she'd even stopped bouncing, said, "This is all your fault! Every bit of it."

Hetty scrambled off the bed and stood toe-to-toe with him, ranting at him in a voice that wouldn't wake the children, "I may have a lot of flaws, Karl, but I'm not a cheater!"

"You cheated me the moment you took Mrs. Templeton's place."

"I didn't do that to hurt you."

"Maybe not, but you had plenty of chances to tell me the truth. And didn't."

"Fair enough. But I'm ready and willing now to do whatever it takes to convince you—"

Karl's kiss cut her off. His arms slid around her and pulled her close, so she could feel his muscular chest against her breasts. He caught her buttocks and held her tight between his legs, so she could feel the heat and the hardness of him.

Then his mouth was on hers again, his tongue seeking entrance. Hetty gasped at the exquisite feeling as his tongue intruded, tasting. She pushed her tongue into Karl's mouth and heard him make a guttural sound of pleasure. One of his hands captured her breast, while the other reached for her hand and carried it to the fly of his jeans.

Hetty wasn't sure what he wanted her to do, but his hand pressed hers against the man-part of him and then let go.

She could leave her hand there. Or she could remove it. Karl was giving her a choice. The kiss ended and Karl looked into her eyes.

"I want you, Hetty."

No longer *I love you,* but *I want you.*

Hetty felt sad and relieved at the same time. Sad because they'd both lost something. Relieved because she could honestly reply, "And I want you, Karl."

She didn't know where that sultry voice had come from. She traced the solid length of him beneath the denim with her fingers and saw him swallow hard.

"Hetty, I—"

She touched his lips with her fingertips, cutting him off. She saw the longing in his eyes and knew what he wanted for Christmas. She could give him the loving wife he'd bargained for. At least for tonight. She kept her other hand right where it was and said, "Make love to me, Karl."

It wasn't much in the way of instruction, but it turned out to be plenty. This night of love was a Christmas gift to Karl. The only thing she had to do was please him.

That turned out to be easier than she'd imagined, because everything she did caused appreciative sounds. Male hands returned the favors she granted, so that soon Hetty wasn't sure who was doing the giving and who was doing the getting.

"Karl," she moaned.

"What, sweetheart?"

"Do that again."

"Gladly. How does that feel?"

"Amazing. Do you like what I'm doing?"

He responded with a deep kiss that mimicked the ultimate act that all this foreplay was leading up to. Hetty wanted to feel her naked flesh next to Karl's. She unbuttoned his shirt and shoved it off his shoulders and reached for his long john shirt and pushed it off over his head. She kissed his throat and shivered as he did the same to her.

She ran her hands over his muscular shoulders and biceps. "You're so strong, Karl."

"And you're so soft," he said, cupping her breasts and teasing her nipples through her dress. "I want to feel you next to me."

He unbuttoned the dress and pulled it down off her shoulders, then hugged her tight. Hetty had never felt anything so *good*. She ran her fingers through his hair, liking the softness of it, then slid her hand down to his nape and played with the curls there. And heard him moan.

He was too impatient to take the time to completely undress, and Hetty was willing to indulge him. He grabbed a handful of her hair and used it to angle her head for his kiss, but the kiss only made her want more.

"Please, Karl." That sultry voice again. Begging. Pleading.

He let go of her hair so he could shove the necessary clothing out of the way, then toppled them both onto the bed and thrust inside her.

Hetty had been so focused on giving Karl pleasure

that it took her a moment to realize that there was no pain. And a moment more to realize that his hands were doing something to her down there that was making her body sing. And dance.

Her body undulated toward Karl, her hips moving in rhythm with his. The pleasure grew and changed, so it was almost unbearable.

"Karl!"

"Come with me, Hetty."

Hetty's body took over from her conscious mind as the pleasure crested like a giant wave. She could feel the pressure rising as the wave threatened to break. And then did.

Hetty clung tightly to Karl's strong shoulders, the only certain thing in an uncertain world. Then she felt Karl join her, his head flung back, his body taut as he gave a cry of exultation.

Karl slumped onto her, his lungs like bellows, his shoulders damp with sweat.

She kissed his throat between panting breaths and whispered, "Merry Christmas, Karl."

He chuckled.

"What's so funny?"

"We are." He moved away, pulling up his jeans and rebuttoning them. She felt bereft. And chilled. Her body, she realized, was damp with sweat, and she reached down to retrieve the covers. Before she could, Karl pulled her close and hugged her.

Suddenly, she was warm again.

"Why are we so funny?" she asked.

"This is not how I imagined Christmas Eve with my wife."

"What did you imagine?" she asked, her fingers finding their way to the curls at his nape.

She felt him quiver. He lowered his head to her shoulder, encouraging her to continue what she was doing. Hetty realized her Christmas present to Karl wasn't quite complete.

He needed more than sex. He needed love. Or at least, the appearance of it. Hetty could give him that.

She ran her hands through his hair, caressing him, giving solace to a wounded heart. She couldn't say *I love you.* Or she could, but it would be yet another of the many lies Karl had accused her of telling.

So she simply said, "Thank you, Karl. For making Christmas Eve wonderful."

He lifted his head and looked into her eyes and said, "Yes, it was, wasn't it? Thank you, Hetty."

How had she ever thought that brown eyes were uninteresting? Karl's eyes glowed with golden warmth. She saw that overlapping front tooth she always found so fascinating and realized he was smiling. She felt warm on the inside, where she hadn't even realized she'd been cold.

When Karl pulled away, Hetty asked, "Where are you going?"

"I think it's time for Saint Nicholas to make an appearance."

"I already filled the children's stockings."

"I think Saint Nicholas has some other stockings to fill."

Hetty looked at him quizzically, and his smile became a grin. "Now what's so funny?" she asked.

"Just wait till morning," he said. "You'll see."

Before she could stop him, he grabbed his shirt and was gone from the bedroom. Hetty lay back down and hugged herself, feeling like a kid on Christmas Eve, anxious and excited and wondering what wonderful surprise would be waiting for her when she awoke on Christmas morning.

Chapter Thirty-three

"Grace, wake up! Grace, it's Christmas morning. Wake up!"

Grace rolled over onto her back, opened her eyes, and realized it was still pitch dark. "You call this morning?" She turned onto her side, pulled the covers up higher on her shoulder, and mumbled, "Go back to bed, Griffin."

"It's Christmas morning," Griffin said. "The sun is up. I swear it is. Get up, Grace." He yanked the covers completely off her. "Let's go see what Saint Nicholas brought us."

Grace shivered and sat up to reach for the covers, but Griffin had jerked them all the way to the foot of the bed. Once she was sitting upright, she could clearly see a crack of yellow light over the windowsill. So Christmas morning had, indeed, arrived.

Griffin was hopping around like a rabbit on Easter. Wrong holiday, she thought glumly. Hopping around like a reindeer?

"All right. All right," she muttered. "Give me a minute to get some clothes on."

"I can't wait, Grace. Come in your nightgown. I'll bet no one else is awake yet."

"We can't open presents until Hetty and Karl are up," she said.

"Then let's get them up," Griffin urged.

Grace had heard Hetty and Karl arguing last night. It was the last thing she remembered before falling asleep. She'd gone to bed worried about whether they were still going to have a home on Christmas morning, and all Griffin could think about was what presents he might find under the tree.

The last thing she wanted to do was remind Karl Norwood what a pestilential brother she had. So maybe she'd better be the one to wake up Hetty and Karl. She would do it a lot more gently than her brother.

"I'm coming," she said, yawning as she stretched her arms high over her head. She noticed Griffin was shivering with cold, dressed only in his smalls and a long john shirt.

"Put some socks on," she ordered. "You'll catch cold in your bare feet."

"Anything to get you moving," he said, sitting down to pull on the pair of socks he'd left on the floor when he'd undressed.

Grace had worn her socks to bed because her feet were always cold. She had on a voluminous gray flannel nightgown and would have added a robe before leaving the bedroom, except she didn't own one.

"Let's go," she said. "But be quiet!"

Grace eased open the bedroom door and discovered Hetty and Karl already sitting at the kitchen table with a cup of coffee in front of each of them. Her mouth dropped open in astonishment. "What are you two doing up?" she asked as she crossed to Hetty.

Hetty smiled. "We've been sitting here at least a half hour. We didn't think you two sleepyheads were ever going to wake up."

Grace found herself smiling back. She turned to Karl and saw he was smiling, too. It was going to be all right. They weren't going to find themselves out in the cold on Christmas Day.

"Look at this, Grace!" Griffin shouted.

"What are you doing, Griffin?" Grace said as she hurried over to join her brother at the fireplace.

"Look at all this loot!" he said as he dumped his stocking onto the braided rug in front of the fire. He held up each item as he identified it. "Instead of sticks, peppermint sticks. Instead of stones, rock candy. And instead of coal, pecans!" Griffin beamed up at her. Smirked up at her was more like it, she thought as he added, "Guess I've been a good boy after all." He jumped up and tugged Grace's stocking free and handed it to her. "Empty yours, Grace. Let's see what you got."

Grace was aware that Hetty and Karl had left the table and were standing right behind her. She wanted to chastise Griffin for being so impatient, but she would have been reminding Karl that Griffin *was* impatient. So she held her tongue and dropped to her knees and dumped her stocking onto the rug.

"You got the same thing!" Griffin sounded disappointed.

"Of course I did," Grace said, soothing his ruffled feathers. "I've been every bit as good as you. It's only fair that we both get the same thing in our stockings."

"I better not find the same gift as you under the tree," Griffin muttered.

Grace glanced up to see if Hetty or Karl had heard Griffin grumbling. Both were still smiling. She stood and gave Hetty a hug, then met Karl's gaze and said, "Thank you very much. I love everything."

She shot a look at Griffin and jerked her head toward Hetty and Karl. Her brother stood and scuffed his sock against the rug and said, "Yeah. Thanks a lot."

"There are more presents under the tree," Hetty told him.

"I didn't see anything there for me last night before I went to bed," Griffin replied. Which meant he'd checked, despite Grace's warning not to be nosy.

"Saint Nicholas came during the night and left a few things," Hetty said.

Griffin surveyed the array of packages under the tree and asked, "How do I know which one is mine?"

"Your name is written on the package," Hetty said. "There are several under there for you."

Griffin looked at her with wonder. "Several?"

"I believe so," Hetty confirmed.

"Come help me, Grace." Griffin dropped to the floor in front of the tree and began sorting packages into piles, and Grace settled on her knees beside him.

"This one's yours, Grace," he said, setting an oblong package in front of her.

"This one's mine!" He stopped sorting packages and began opening the gift.

"Wait!" Grace said. "What about sorting everything first?"

"We can sort later," Griffin said. "I'm going to open mine now."

Grace turned to see what Hetty and Karl thought about this childish behavior and found Karl sitting cross-legged in front of the fireplace with Hetty right next to him, her skirt tucked under her, both watching expectantly.

"Go ahead, Griffin," Karl said. "Open it."

By the time he spoke, Griffin already had half the brown paper torn off. A moment later he was holding a tooled-leather knife sheath in his hand.

Grace kept her gaze focused on her brother's face as he carefully eased an incredibly shiny, incredibly sharp knife from the sheath. Griffin's gaze met hers, and Grace saw the sheen of tears in his eyes. He turned to Karl and said, "Is this really mine?"

"All yours," Karl said. "Merry Christmas, son."

Grace saw Griffin's jaws clamp on whatever retort he'd been about to give Karl for calling him *son*. Griffin kept his eyes lowered as he said, "Thanks, Karl."

Karl flinched when Griffin called him *Karl* instead of *Pa*, but Grace figured, all in all, things were going pretty well.

Griffin reverently set aside the knife and sheath, then reached under the tree and pulled out two badly wrapped presents—Grace had offered her help to wrap them, but Griffin had refused—and handed one to Hetty and one to Karl. "These are from me," he said gruffly.

Grace had been surprised when Griffin told her he had presents for Hetty and Karl, and even more surprised when Griffin had refused to show her what he was giving them. So she watched with equal interest as they surveyed their presents.

"You go first," Karl said.

Hetty hesitated, then carefully unwrapped her gift. She gasped and held out a carved miniature horse with a flowing mane and tail. "Oh, Griffin. It's beautiful!" She leaned forward to hug him, but he sidled away and said, "Open yours, Karl."

"I'm almost afraid to see what you carved for me," Karl said with a smile. "Probably a skunk."

Grace realized her brother's whole body was so tense he couldn't enjoy Karl's joke. Whatever Griffin had carved for Karl, he wanted Karl to like it. Grace held her breath, praying that he would.

Once Karl had the wrapping off his gift he sat perfectly still, staring at it. Grace was suffering from a lack of oxygen, but she didn't dare breathe. No one was breathing. No one was saying anything. Grace heard Karl swallow with a little gurgle. Then he focused his gaze on Griffin and said, "I have never, in my entire life, seen anything so wonderful."

Grace turned to look at Griffin, whose face had turned beet red.

"I tried to make it perfect," her brother said. "The mane isn't quite right."

"The mane is amazing," Karl said as he held up the carved horse head, its mouth wide as though the animal was screaming a challenge, mane flying, ears forward, nostrils flared, the strong neck proudly arched.

"I will treasure it always," Karl said.

Grace noticed that Karl made no attempt, as Hetty had, to embrace her brother. He simply looked at Griffin with appreciation. And maybe a little awe. Then he put out his hand and said, "Thank you, son."

Grace waited to see if Griffin would reach out and

shake Karl's hand, especially after he'd used that blasted word again.

Her brother hesitated so long that Grace thought maybe he was going to insult Karl after all. At last Griffin reached out his hand and took Karl's. They shook once, and Grace sighed with relief, figuring that was the end of it.

But Karl used his hold on Griffin to pull him close enough to give him a quick hug. Just as quickly, he released him. Griffin scuttled back to his spot by the tree and stared at Karl with a frown furrowing his brow.

Grace couldn't figure her brother out. Why carve such a beautiful present for Karl if he didn't like him? What did he want from Karl, anyway? If he wanted Karl's approval, he wasn't going to get it glowering at him like that.

To break the tension, Grace said, "I have gifts for both of you, too." Although hers weren't nearly as beautiful or original as the ones Griffin had made. She turned to her brother and said, "Can you find them under there?"

Griffin handed her the two small presents she'd wrapped with such great care. She handed a gift to Karl and said, "Why don't you open yours first?"

He untied the neat bow and took off the carefully folded paper, then held up the large leaf she'd encased in candle wax.

Grace could tell he had no idea what it was. "It's a bookmark. So you can mark your place when you're reading. It's *Populus tremuloides.*"

The smile grew on Karl's face as he met her gaze

and said, "The first leaf you asked me to identify on the trail."

Grace smiled back with relief. "You remembered."

"How could I forget the Trembling aspen?" He rose and, before she could object, grabbed her head between his large hands and kissed her on each cheek before letting her go. "Thank you, Grace. I'll keep it with me always."

Grace's stomach felt funny. It was doing all kinds of flip-flops, like a dying fish. She broke eye contact with Karl and turned to Hetty. "This one's for you."

Hetty took the tiny package, untied the bow, and carefully unwrapped the gift in her lap. She held up a delicate silver chain to which a very small silver butterfly was attached. "How lovely!"

"It's the only thing I owned that I thought you might like," Grace blurted.

Hetty suddenly looked unhappy. "Oh, Grace. I appreciate the thought, but I can't take this. You should keep it for yourself."

"I'm giving it to you."

"I can't accept it," Hetty protested, holding it out to Grace.

Grace didn't want to explain, but she was afraid Hetty would refuse the gift if she didn't. Her throat had a horrendous lump in it. Hetty had been a better mother to her during the past two months than her own mother had been during her entire life. She was nearly old enough to be a mother herself, and yet she couldn't help wanting—needing—a mother. Griffin didn't know how lucky they were to have Hetty fill those shoes, but Grace did.

She managed to rasp, "The necklace belonged to my mother. I want you to have it."

Grace saw the moment Hetty realized the significance of the gift. *Will you be my mother for now and always?*

Hetty's chin quivered and her eyes filled with tears. "Oh, Grace. I would love to have it. Will you help me put it on?"

Grace took the necklace from Hetty and leaned over to attach the clasp behind her neck. Hetty held the silver butterfly in one hand as she leaned over and kissed Grace on the lips. "Thank you, Grace," she whispered. "I will wear it always."

Grace put a hand to her lips. She had a mother. For now and always.

"Is the mushy stuff over now?" Griffin asked.

"Unless you'd like a kiss, too," Hetty said with a mischievous grin.

"Heck, no!" Griffin shoved the oblong box he'd first taken out from under the tree in Grace's direction and said, "Why don't you open your present? Who's it from?"

Grace glanced at the writing on the brown paper and said, "From Karl."

She took so much time carefully unwrapping the present that Griffin finally said, "Hurry up, Grace. What's taking you so long?"

Grace was savoring the fact that she had a present, let alone several presents, to open. Griffin didn't remember the years when there had been no Christmas, because Grace had done her best each year since he'd been old enough to know what Christmas was to provide him with some little gift.

She tried to recall a Christmas when her mother had given her a Christmas gift. She remembered getting a silver dollar once, but her mother had borrowed it back a week later. She remembered getting a pair of wool socks, but they were too big, made for a man, not a little girl. She remembered wishing for a special something—she had a specific something in mind—wrapped in bright paper with real ribbon to surprise her on Christmas morning.

Even though Grace had wished and hoped and prayed, she'd never gotten that special something. And now, here she was, opening a present, and wishing and hoping and praying it would be . . .

"Oh! Oh!" Grace sobbed as she stared down at the open box in her lap.

"Grace? I'm so sorry," Karl said. "I know it's not the sort of thing you probably wanted. I bought it when I thought you were younger. You probably don't—"

"I love her!" Grace cried, grabbing the doll from the box and hugging it to her chest. She could hardly see Karl through her tears. If she could have described the perfect doll, it would have looked like this one: a rosy-cheeked face, blue eyes and dark, painted eyelashes, long blond hair in two braids tied with ribbons, and wearing a frilly pink dress. She even had on black patent-leather shoes and white lace-trimmed socks.

Grace rocked the doll for another moment, then threw herself into Karl's arms, hugging him around the neck with one arm, while she held on to the doll with the other. It was every Christmas dream she'd ever had come true. "Thank you, Karl. Thank you, thank you! Julie's beautiful."

"Julie?" he asked in a gruff voice.

"That's her name." Grace pulled herself free of Karl's enfolding arms, suddenly self-conscious. She really was too old for a doll. In a few years, she'd be having babies of her own. Nevertheless, she found herself explaining, "I always said if I ever had a doll, I'd name her Julie."

Grace glanced at Hetty and saw the shock on her face. And realized what she'd revealed. *So I've never had a doll. What's the big deal? Lots of girls have never had dolls.* But it was clear from the stunned look on Hetty's face that she'd had a doll when she was a little girl and was amazed that Grace hadn't.

Grace sat back down, anxious to get the focus off of herself, and blurted, "What the hell else is under that tree?"

Chapter Thirty-four

Karl felt overwhelmed by the children's responses to his presents. He'd bought Christmas gifts in Butte that he'd thought his brand-new stepchildren would enjoy, worried that the boy's knife was too dangerous for a child his age, and wondering if the little girl already had a whole chest full of dolls and would find one more tiresome. Only to discover that Griffin revered his knife and sheath, and that Grace was receiving the very first doll she'd ever owned.

He was awed by Griffin's talent with a knife and wood. The carved horse head the boy had given him was exquisite. It almost breathed with life. In contrast, Hetty's horse figure seemed filled with energy, as though it might leap off the table if you set it down. Much like Hetty herself.

Karl still wasn't sure what to make of what had happened last night with his wife. He'd made love to Hetty, but she'd also made love to him. Maybe he was putting too fine a description on what had happened between them. He tried to remember the exact chain of events.

He'd said, *I want you.*

She'd replied, *I want you, too.*

Maybe love had played no part in what had followed, but there had been plenty of passion on both sides. Hetty had surprised him with her willingness to explore his body. To taste. To satisfy his craving to be touched. And to be tasted and touched in return.

Karl didn't realize his mind had wandered until he heard Grace say, "What the hell else is under that tree?"

"Grace!" Hetty said. "That's entirely the wrong kind of language for Christmas morning."

Grace flushed and said, "I'm sorry."

"Here," Griffin said, tossing a small gift at Karl. "This one's from Hetty."

Karl saw the grateful look Grace shot Griffin for drawing attention away from her use of profanity. Those sorts of slips happened more often now that their secret was out and they weren't trying to act like something they weren't. Karl appreciated the honesty, even though he felt the same way Hetty did about curbing the profanity.

The children were also no longer indulging in the pretense of calling Hetty *Mom*. Karl thought that was a shame, because as far as he could tell, Hetty had been—still was—a good mother.

"Hurry up and open your gift, Karl," Griffin said.

Karl smiled at the boy's eagerness. He'd been equally excited on Christmas morning when he was Griffin's age. But without family around, he'd seldom celebrated Christmas over the past ten years. He hadn't realized how much he'd missed the holly wreaths and spruce tree, the exchanging of gifts and the carol singing, which reminded him they hadn't done any of that yet.

Maybe he could talk Hetty and the kids into singing a song or two before the day was done.

"Did you fall asleep, Karl, or what?" Griffin said.

He'd been daydreaming again. "I'm untying this knot as fast as I can."

"Just push it off," Griffin said.

Karl laughed and did as he was told. He unwrapped the brown paper and discovered a small, framed sampler.

"Bao helped me frame it with pine from the mountain," Hetty said anxiously.

Karl held the embroidered cloth up so he could see it better in the dawn light. It took him a moment to decipher what it was. Two entwined bitterroot flowers delicately embroidered in white and pink and green thread, and beneath them, in green, the Latin name, *Lewisia rediviva,* and the date, 1874.

Karl was moved by the thought Hetty had put into the gift. Not one single flower, but two entwined. Not just any flower, but a bitterroot in perfect, full bloom. And the year of their marriage, the year of their first Christmas together, a promise of togetherness for the years to come.

Karl couldn't help feeling that there might be hope yet for a happy future with his mail-order bride. He turned to Hetty, swallowed over the knot in his throat, and asked, "How on earth did you know what a bitterroot flower looks like?"

"I found a picture in one of your books. Is it all right?"

"It's far more than that, Hetty. I think we should hang it over the fireplace." He got up and placed it on the mantel, then drew Hetty onto her feet and into his arms. He held her close and whispered in her ear, "It's perfect."

"Hey!" Griffin said. "Don't get sappy. We have more presents to open."

Karl laughed and let Hetty go. "I think we'd better sit back down."

"This big one says to Hetty from Karl," Griffin said.

Hetty dropped to her knees beside Karl's gift, which was too big to lift easily. She turned back to him with a childish look of delight on her face. "What is it, Karl?"

He didn't realize his heart was in his throat until he tried to speak. He'd thought of Hetty through every step of creating her gift, which he'd started making long before he'd discovered her deceit. He wanted her to like it. He made a *hmm*ing sound in his throat and said, "Open it and find out."

Hetty asked Griffin to cut the knots with his new knife, an act which he was delighted to perform. Then she ripped the paper off with relish, exposing the gift inside.

"Oh, Karl. Oh, my. Oh." She ran her hands over the oak he'd polished so lovingly. Over the entwined bitterroot flowers he'd carved into the lid of the hope chest. She looked up at him and smiled, her bewitching dimples contradicting the tears shining in her eyes. "It's beautiful."

"Look inside," Griffin said. "Maybe there's a gift in there."

"The box *is* the gift," Hetty told him with a laugh.

She glanced at Karl to confirm her statement, but he said, "Why don't you check and see?"

Hetty looked charmingly surprised, but she lifted the lid and looked. Her mouth opened in an O of surprise as she reached inside. She held up a tiny silk-and-lace dress.

"It's a doll dress," Griffin said in disgust.

"It's a christening gown," Karl corrected. "It was my christening gown." He met Hetty's rapt gaze and said, "I had my mother send it from Connecticut when I knew I was getting married."

"It's so tiny!" Grace exclaimed.

"You wore that?" Griffin said. "It's a dress!"

Karl laughed. "It certainly is. A dress a baby wears in church when it's christened."

Grace turned to Hetty, arched a brow, and asked, "Does this mean you're having a baby?"

Hetty flushed so pink her complexion became more like roses and cream than peaches and cream. She looked enchantingly flustered, glancing from Karl to Grace and back again. "No. I'm not."

Grace looked him in the eye. "But you figure she will be."

It was Karl's turn to blush. He felt the heat at his throat and said, "I'm looking forward to having a big family someday."

"What happens to us when you have all those kids?" Griffin asked, his eyes narrowed.

"I'll keep on loving and caring for you, just like I do now," Karl said.

Griffin looked flummoxed. Grace looked perplexed. It was Grace who spoke first. "You love us?"

They didn't make it easy to love them. But Karl had realized, when he was gathering the two presents they hadn't yet received—presents he and Hetty had discussed endlessly during the nights they'd spent lying in each other's arms—how much he looked forward to making the two children happy. Not to mention how much he'd gained in patience and forbearance from having Grace as a daughter and Griffin as a son.

"Yes, I love you," Karl said. "And your mother loves you." He was determined to refer to Hetty as their mother, whether the kids did or not. "Your mom has one more gift for each of you, but you have to come outside to see them."

"I'm not dressed," Grace protested.

"They're right out front," Karl replied. "Come and see."

Karl rose and reached for Hetty's hand to help her to her feet. He kept his arm around her as they headed for the front door and felt his own anticipation grow when he realized she was almost vibrating with excitement.

"Do we need coats?" Grace asked.

"Go ahead and grab them," Karl said.

"And shoes!" Hetty insisted. "I don't want either of you catching pneumonia."

Griffin raced into the bedroom and returned with shoestrings dragging. He grabbed his coat from the rack near the door and shoved his arms into it. "Let's get this over with. I want to try out my new knife."

Karl exchanged a conspiratorial smile with Hetty. If she was right, Griffin not only wouldn't be using his knife anytime soon, they'd be lucky to get him back inside the house before dark.

Grace took her coat with her into the bedroom and was in there long enough that Griffin called out, "Hurry, up, Grace. Christmas Day's wastin'."

Karl helped Hetty finish buttoning her coat before

slipping into his own. He opened the door wide and gestured both kids outside.

Griffin and Grace stepped onto the empty porch, then looked back at Karl and Hetty, who stood just outside the door.

"So where's this great gift you promised?" Griffin asked Hetty, his hands on his hips.

Andy came marching around the side of the house, carrying a black kitten with white socks. It had a bright red ribbon tied around its neck. "This is your gift, Grace."

Grace flew off the porch and met Andy halfway. "It's Socks!"

"I told your mom this is the one you like best," he said.

Grace took the tiny kitten from Andy and held it close to her heart as she turned back to Hetty. "You said I couldn't have a kitten for my birthday."

"The kittens were still too young to leave their mother then."

"Can I really keep her?"

"She's all yours," Hetty said, her smile almost as wide as Grace's.

Grace turned to Karl, her green eyes radiant, and said, "I mean, can I keep her in the house? Can she sleep on my bed?"

"That's up to you," Karl replied, his heart beating hard in his chest as he savored the joy he saw on her face. "She's your responsibility. You have to take care of her."

To his surprise, Grace walked back to Andy and whispered something to him that made the boy blush before he trotted away toward the bunkhouse. Then she turned and ran back up the steps to show her prize to Hetty.

"What about my gift?" Griffin demanded.

"There it is," Karl said, pointing behind the boy.

Griffin whirled and saw Bao leading a saddled and bridled brown-and-white pinto pony around the corner of the house. Bao stopped at the foot of the front porch steps. Griffin turned back to Karl and Hetty, his thin lips pressed flat with doubt, his dark eyes opened wide with hope. "What is this?"

"He's yours," Hetty said. "Karl will teach you how to ride him and how to take care of him. But you'll have to name him all by yourself."

For another second, the boy stood frozen. Then he threw himself into Hetty's arms, clutching her hard around the waist. "I never thought . . . How did you know . . . ? A pony!"

Hetty laughed and said, "Go and meet your pony."

Griffin glanced at Karl, but when he tore himself from Hetty's embrace, he headed away from him down the steps. Karl wasn't sure whether he felt relieved or disappointed that the boy hadn't come to him, but in any case, his throat was too thick with emotion to speak.

He noticed that Griffin slowed his excited steps as he approached the pony, so he wouldn't frighten the animal. Karl wondered how much the boy already knew about horses and how much he would have to teach him.

Griffin held his hand outstretched so the pony could smell his scent. Then he moved aside the pony's forelock and caressed its forehead. Griffin's hand moved slowly down to cheek and jaw before he reached out and stroked the animal's powerful neck beneath its mane. Karl could almost see the boy defining and confirming with his hands the equine muscle and bone that were so evident in the wooden horses he carved.

Finally, he wrapped his arms completely around the pony's neck and pressed his cheek against the pony's cheek. His voice was choked as he said, "Hello, Star. It's nice to meet you. I'm Griffin. We're going to be great friends."

Karl had traded with the Salish for the pony, and the animal had been hidden in a supply shed behind the bunkhouse for the past week. But it wasn't until Griffin named the pony that Karl realized the pinto had a distinct patch of white, a star, in the center of its dark forehead.

Griffin turned back to him and said, "Can I ride him, Karl?"

"As soon as you're dressed."

Griffin was already on the porch headed for the front door when Karl stopped him. "And your mother gets her birthday present."

He saw both children had completely forgotten about the plans they'd made with him the previous evening in the barn. He turned to Hetty and said, "Happy eighteenth birthday, Hetty."

Hetty stared at Karl in shock. "How did you know that today's my birthday?"

"The kids told me. They have a surprise for you."

Bao tied the pony to the hitching post in front of the house and stepped up onto the porch. "Cake burned. Must start over."

Hetty laughed and said, "It's enough to know that you baked one in the first place. Thank you, Bao."

"Not my idea. Kids' idea."

"That's why they came to the barn last night," Karl explained. "To see if Bao could bake a cake for your birthday."

Hetty focused her gaze on each of the children in turn and said, "I'm so touched that you remembered. Thank you."

"So sorry no cake," Bao said. "Confucius right."

Hetty smiled. "About what?"

"Confucius say: 'Success depend on preparation. Otherwise, sure to fail.' Wake up late. No time to finish cake this morning. Stove too hot. Cake burn. Will try again. Promise cake for supper."

"You're a gem, Bao. Thank you," Hetty said.

Bao turned to the children and said seriously, "I promise make cake. Now you give gift."

Griffin turned to Hetty and said, "We didn't have anything to give you for your birthday, so Grace came up with this idea."

"I know we aren't your kids," Grace said. "And now Karl knows it, too," she continued, holding out a palm to keep either Hetty or Karl from speaking. "But you're the only mother we have. So Griffin and I decided, if it's all right with you, from now on we're going to call you Mom."

"Yeah, Ma." Griffin must have seen Hetty's face contorting because he added, "I mean, if it's all right with you."

Karl saw Hetty's face crumple before she began to cry. He took her in his arms and heard her sob against his shoulder.

"You said she'd like it!" Griffin snarled at his sister.

"I thought she would," Grace protested. "Hetty, I'm sorry."

"Grace, Griffin, I'm not mad!" Hetty tore herself from Karl's arms and turned to face the kids, swiping at her wet face with the backs of her hands and smiling through her tears. "I'm crying because I'm so happy."

Griffin shared a bewildered look with Karl and shook his head in disgust. "Women!"

"You really don't mind if we call you Mom?" Grace said.

Hetty held her arms wide. "Come here, both of you."

Karl saw Griffin was clearly reluctant, but Grace shot him an admonishing look and he stepped close enough for Hetty to wrap her arms around both children.

"I love you both so very much. I can't think of a better birthday present." She showered both kids with kisses until the kitten in Grace's arms began to mew in protest.

"I think my kitten's hungry, Mom," Grace said. "Gotta go."

"Me, too, Ma," Griffin said. "Gotta get dressed, so I can go ride my pony."

Karl heard the door slam as the kids disappeared into the house. Hetty turned to share the moment with Karl, but he could barely see the joy on her face, his eyes were so clouded with tears.

Chapter Thirty-five

Even though Hetty had protested vigorously at Christmas that she wasn't pregnant, three months later, she was pretty sure she'd been wrong. She sat in one of the two willow rockers that had been moved onto the front porch, a shawl wrapped around her against the spring breeze, and chewed on an already short fingernail.

The courses that were supposed to have begun right after the New Year had never come. Nor had she bled in February or March. It was April, and Hetty could no longer deny the truth.

She was expecting a baby.

Hetty had spent a great deal of the past three months feeling nauseated. She would visit the outhouse first thing in the morning and lose the contents of her stomach, then walk around the rest of the day smiling as though nothing was wrong.

She wasn't sure why she was hiding her pregnancy from Karl. He'd said at Christmas that he wanted a large family. He might even be ecstatic at the news that she would be giving birth in the fall. Their relationship had improved a little since Karl had confronted her and she'd spewed the truth. But it wasn't as good as it had been before Karl found out she'd tricked him into marriage.

Hetty hadn't realized it at the time, but during that month before the truth had come out, Karl had shared himself totally with her. He'd allowed her to see into his heart, to share his dreams. In the three months since, that door had been shut. The vulnerable man who'd admitted he loved her was no more. The magic they'd shared had disappeared like a rabbit stuffed back into the hat.

Even though Karl hadn't been as open in their conversations in front of the fireplace, they still often made love afterward. The loving was sometimes tender, sometimes passionate, but never entirely satisfying. At least not to Hetty. Because Karl no longer held her in his arms through the night.

It was as though he could no longer bear the closeness to someone who'd lied to him so often and so long. It seemed to Hetty that, although her husband might have forgiven past transgressions, he hadn't forgotten them.

Quite simply, Karl didn't trust her. And if he didn't trust her, how could he ever grow to love her again? Hetty had racked her brain, but she had no idea how to regain his confidence.

Now she'd made matters worse by neglecting to mention that she was pregnant, something Karl surely had a right to know. The longer she waited to tell him, the worse the situation became. She kept putting it off because she didn't want him to withdraw from her any more than he already had. It was a conundrum for which she had no solution.

Except the truth. Sooner or later, she was going to have to bite the bullet and speak. And face the consequences, whatever they turned out to be.

"I'm done with hanging the wash," Grace announced as she stepped onto the front porch. "Is there something else you need me to do?"

Hetty and Grace had worked together boiling and scrubbing and wringing out the laundry, but when Grace had offered to hang it, Hetty had gratefully retired to the porch. Even now, she felt too tired to get out of the rocker.

"Stay where you are," Grace said, dropping into the willow rocker next to Hetty's.

They rocked in silence for a few moments before Grace said, "When's the baby due?"

Hetty's rocker stopped as she planted her feet and sat bolt upright. She stared at Grace aghast. "How long have you known?"

"Since the first trip you made to the outhouse to lose your breakfast," Grace replied. "And you haven't washed your rags in months."

Hetty leaned back in the rocker and set it to rocking again. "The baby's due in September."

"When are you going to tell Karl?"

"How do you know I haven't already told him?"

"Because I haven't seen him puff out his chest like a rooster and crow to all his friends that he's going to be a father."

Hetty smiled. "Is that what he's going to do?"

"Most likely," Grace said. "I heard what Karl said at Christmas. He wants kids of his own."

"He said he wants a big family," Hetty corrected. "He's pretty happy with the kids he already has."

Grace shrugged. "If you say so."

"I know so."

"Then why haven't you told him about the new baby?" Grace asked. "Pretty soon he's going to figure it out for himself. He's going to wonder why you didn't tell him sooner."

Grace wasn't telling her anything she didn't already know. Hetty was convinced that when she finally confessed she was pregnant, it was going to be a toss-up whether Karl was happy about the news that they were having a baby or upset that she'd kept it from him for so long. He might even be hurt that she hadn't shared something so special with him.

She was a little surprised that Karl hadn't already discovered the truth on his own. Her flat belly was a lot rounder these days, and her breasts were so sensitive it was all she could do not to wince when Karl caressed them.

"Why are you so anxious to have me tell him?" Hetty asked.

Grace shrugged again.

Hetty had a sudden thought. "Are you afraid Karl won't want you and Griffin once he has a child of his own?"

Grace's mouth twisted wryly. "The possibility has occurred to me."

"Karl isn't going to abandon you and Griffin, Grace."

The girl shrugged again.

Hetty found Grace's shrugs disquieting. The girl

usually said exactly what was on her mind. For some reason she was shrugging instead of speaking. "Why are you so willing to believe the worst of Karl?"

Grace shrugged.

Hetty laid a hand on Grace's arm. "Talk to me, Grace. I can't help if I don't know what's bothering you."

Grace jerked free and stood up facing Hetty. "What's bothering me is you!"

Hetty rose from her rocker, wrapped her shawl more protectively around herself, and said, "Me? What have I done?"

"Maybe *you* won't want us when the new baby comes," Grace accused. "Maybe you'll talk Karl into sending us away."

"Oh, Grace. That's never going to happen!"

"That's what you say now," Grace said in an anguished voice. "What's going to happen to me and Griffin when you have a baby of your own to love?"

Grace turned to run, but Hetty caught her wrist before she could get away, then wrapped both arms around Grace to keep her from escaping. When Grace struggled to be free, Hetty said, "You might resent this baby, but I don't think you want to hurt it."

Grace froze. She kept her eyes lowered and said, "I don't see how you could love us the same as a baby of your own."

"You're right," Hetty said. "I won't love you the same."

Grace's green eyes flashed up at her. "So I was right!"

Hetty brushed a flyaway red curl behind Grace's ear. "You're completely, totally wrong. I won't love you the same, I'll love you more. Because you'll not only be my daughter, you'll be the new baby's sister."

Grace frowned. "I never thought of that."

"Tell me this, Grace. Do you think *you* can love the new baby? I mean, you already have a brother to love," Hetty reminded her. "Do you think your heart can make room for one more? Another brother? Or perhaps a sister?"

Grace made a face. "I see what you're doing."

"What am I doing?"

"You're trying to show me that you can love more than one person at a time. But this isn't the same!" Grace argued. "The baby will be *yours*. You just picked me and Griffin up along the trail."

Hetty hugged Grace hard and let her go. "I'll always love you and Griffin. That's never going to change. No matter how many more children I have."

"*More* children?"

Hetty whirled at the sound of Karl's voice. "Where did you come from? Where's Griffin?"

"He decided to spend a little more time in the barn grooming his pony." His gaze swept from Hetty to Grace and back again.

"Am I missing something?"

Instead of answering him, Hetty said, "Aren't you back early?"

"Bear scare."

"What's that?" Hetty asked.

"Grizzly out of hibernation," Karl explained. "Dennis found tracks all around the area where we planned to start cutting this afternoon. It's not safe to work there until we can hunt him down."

"You're going bear hunting?" Hetty said in disbelief.

"Bright and early tomorrow morning," Karl confirmed.

"Isn't that dangerous?" Grace asked.

"We'll have guns," Karl said with a reassuring smile. "All the bear has is teeth and claws."

"And stealth and cunning," Hetty added.

"Aren't grizzly bears huge?" Grace asked, her eyes wide with fright. "I don't want you to get hurt."

"You're not planning to take Griffin along on this hunt, are you?" Hetty asked.

"I was. Yes."

"He's just a boy!"

"A growing boy. Soon he'll be a man. Besides, he wants to come."

"He wants to do a lot of things he shouldn't do," Hetty shot back.

"I promise I won't let anything happen to him, Hetty."

"What if that bear has different ideas?" Hetty realized her voice was rising, that she was overexcited, and that her stomach was starting to revolt. She put a hand over her mouth, but it was too late. She ran for the edge of the porch, bent over, and lost the contents of her stomach in the weeds.

"Grace, go get a damp cloth," she heard Karl say.

She was still retching, although there was nothing left to come up, when she felt Karl's hand on her shoulder.

"Hetty, what's wrong? I'm sorry. If you're so scared it makes you sick, I'll leave Griffin home."

Mercifully, the retching stopped. Grace arrived a

moment later with a damp cloth, which Hetty used to wipe her face, and a glass of water, which she used to rinse her mouth.

"Tell him," Grace said fiercely.

"Tell me what?" Karl demanded. "What the hell is going on here, Hetty?"

"I'm pregnant."

Chapter Thirty-six

Karl was shocked by Hetty's announcement, but not surprised that she was pregnant. They made love every night. Sometimes twice a night. Pollinate a flower and it would bear fruit.

Hetty had whirled and run inside. Karl followed her all the way to their bedroom, where he found her sitting on the bed with her back to him. Her shoulders were slumped. Her head was down. She flinched when she heard the door click closed behind him.

Karl still felt a little stunned. He was going to be a father. Hetty was going to bear a child. For real this time.

That was the crux of the problem. Karl was afraid to trust his wife. She was willing to lie. And she was good at it. How could he build a relationship with someone he couldn't trust? How could he share his innermost thoughts when she'd made it clear she didn't love him? And now they were going to be the parents of yet another child.

Hetty kept her face turned away when she spoke. "I know I should have told you sooner, but I couldn't quite believe it was true. When I did know for sure, I worried about what you would think, so I didn't say anything. I was afraid. . . ."

Karl stayed by the door processing what she'd said. Apparently she'd known she was pregnant for some time. She'd kept the news to herself because . . . she was afraid?

"Afraid of what?" he said, leaning back against the door, his arms crossed.

She peeked over her shoulder at him, took a long look at his crossed arms and the muscle working in his jaw, and turned away again. "Of what you're doing right now."

Karl was irritated because she was pushing all the right buttons to make him feel guilty. He had a right to be wary of his secretive wife. He had a right to feel frustrated that she'd kept her pregnancy to herself instead of sharing it with her husband the moment she knew. It was something they should have celebrated together.

This was wonderful news. Or should have been.

"Exactly what am I doing?" he said at last.

She grabbed the bedpost and used it to pull herself upright before she turned to confront him. "Are you happy about this baby?"

Karl was startled by the question. "Of course!"

Her chin came up and her blue eyes sparked. "Then why are you standing over there with your arms crossed and your jaw clenched? Why aren't you over here giving me a big hug and a kiss?"

Karl found himself captivated by her challenge. He crossed the room in three strides and stood looking down into her upturned face. Her absolutely beautiful face. Karl slid an arm around her waist and pulled her close, so he could feel the slight roundness of her belly, which held their child. His other hand captured her nape beneath her hair and angled her head for his kiss.

But he didn't kiss her. He simply looked into her eyes, which were brilliant with tears.

"Love me, Karl," she whispered.

He knew he should lift her into his arms and take her to bed and glorify the child growing inside her. But the bitterness won out. "I already tried that. It didn't work."

He watched the light die in her eyes.

He was on the verge of relenting when she thrust out her chin and said, "How long are you going to hold this grudge, Karl? I'd like to know. Till this child is three? Or six? Or till she's Grace's age?"

"How do you know it's a girl?"

"All men want a son, and since all I ever do is spite you—at least, according to you—it's sure to be a girl!" she spat.

Karl laughed and hugged her. And then kissed her, despite her struggle to get free. He felt the roundness of her belly and his heart faltered. He was happy about the child, but it wasn't enough to fill his hurting heart. He wanted Hetty's love.

He just didn't think he'd ever get it.

So what if she never loved him? So what if he was the one doing all the loving? They were married for better or worse. Now they were going to have a child together. He could hide his empty heart from his wife. At least until her feelings softened toward him. If they ever did.

"Karl?" she said. "Are you all right?"

"I'm fine." He managed a smile. "More than fine. I'm going to be a father!"

Karl sat down on the bed and lifted Hetty into his lap. She draped her arms around his neck and leaned her head against his shoulder. He placed his hand on her belly and asked, "How far along are you?"

She blushed. "She must have been conceived on Christmas Eve."

Karl counted the months. "So, September?"

She nodded.

"Tell me, Hetty, are *you* happy about this baby?"

"It'll be wonderful to have a baby sister for Grace."

"Or a baby brother for Griffin," Karl said.

"It's a girl," Hetty said certainly.

"We'll see." Karl nuzzled her neck, and she leaned her head back to give him better access to her throat. Karl was quickly changing his mind about making love to his wife, when he heard a hard knock on the bedroom door.

Hetty would have leapt out of his lap, but he tightened his arms around her to keep her in place.

"Who is it?" he called, expecting it to be one of the children and intending to tell whichever one it was to go away.

"It's me," Dennis said. "It's broad daylight, Karl. Leave your wife alone and come out here and talk to me. We've got a problem."

Karl stood abruptly, set Hetty on her feet, and marched to the door. He was surprised to find Hetty standing right behind him when he stepped out of the bedroom to confront Dennis.

"What is it?" he said, hands on hips to let his friend know he didn't appreciate being so rudely interrupted.

"It's that kid from Texas, that Andy Peterson," Dennis said.

Hetty stepped up beside Karl and asked, "What's wrong? Is he hurt?"

Dennis frowned at Hetty, then said to Karl, "That blasted kid had the nerve to tell me he wasn't going to take his oxen back up the mountain until we repaired the skid trail."

"What's wrong with the skid trail?" Karl asked.

"That Texan swears some of the timber we laid down to guide the logs downhill is coming loose in the spring melt. He's *demanding* that we secure it better."

"Have you checked it out?" Karl asked. "Is the platform loose?"

"Look, Karl, if we're going to stay on schedule, we need the men to be cutting logs, not spending their days repairing a few loose timbers that only affect one kid and his cows."

"Not cows," Karl corrected. "Two very valuable oxen. Not to mention a pretty nice young man. If anything happens to the three of them, we won't have a way to get logs off the mountain. Do the repair, Dennis."

"I don't think you understand the time we'll lose—"

"Just do it," Karl interrupted. "I understand precisely what's at stake here. That boy and his bullocks are more important to me than meeting some quota my brother set. Are we clear?"

Dennis sneered. "That's why your brother sent me here, Karl. Because you put people before profits. If there's one thing I've learned from working with Jonas all these years, it's that sacrifices have to be made."

"I'll be damned if I ever sacrifice a single person to the almighty dollar," Karl retorted. "I want that skid trail fixed, and I want it done today."

"Then you can do it yourself." Dennis turned and stomped out of the house.

Karl huffed out a breath and shoved an irritated hand through his hair. A moment later he felt Hetty's arms come around him from behind and hug him tight. He glanced over his shoulder. "What's all this?"

"You're right, Karl," she said fiercely. "And Dennis is wrong."

He loosened her hands and turned so he could take her in his arms. "He's right that we're going to lose time and get behind schedule."

"People are more important than schedules."

He sighed. "I agree. But my brother's going to end up disappointed in me."

She looked up at him and said, "I'm proud of you, Karl. I think you did the right thing."

Karl's throat ached. He hadn't realized how much her approval would matter.

"And not just because Grace is sweet on Andy Peterson," she continued.

Karl was jolted by the thought of that rowdy Texan with sweet, innocent Grace. All those questions Andy had drawn him aside to ask as they walked up the mountain, about how to woo a girl, suddenly made sense. "What did you say? Grace and Andy? I'll kill that son of a bitch!"

Hetty grabbed him hard around the waist to keep him from suiting word to deed. She laughed at him and said, "Whoa! They've done nothing but talk, and

I'm taking care of the matter. I never leave them alone together."

"Maybe I better have a talk with him anyway," Karl said, eyes narrowed.

"You'll only make him more determined to spend time with Grace than I think he already is."

"He's not good enough for her."

Hetty grinned at him. "You just told Dennis he was a pretty nice young man."

"That was before I knew he was stalking Grace."

Hetty laughed. "Karl, I had no idea you were going to be such a protective father." She put a hand to her belly and said, "I can't wait to see what a merry chase this little one leads you on."

Karl laid his hand atop hers, looked into her shining eyes, and said, "Neither can I."

Chapter Thirty-seven

"I forbid you to go on that stupid bear hunt!" Grace yelled as she entered the barn.

"You're scaring Star," Griffin replied as he stepped out of the stall where he'd been grooming his pony, closing the stall door behind him and wafting the pungent odor of fresh manure in her direction.

"You can't go, Griffin," Grace said. "I won't allow it!"

"I don't need your permission," Griffin said as he turned his back on her and walked to the other end of the barn.

"Don't walk away from me," Grace said, hurrying after him.

He set the curry comb and brush back where they belonged, then swiped his hands on his trousers and set them defiantly on his hips. "Karl said I can go, so I'm going."

"You might get killed. You might get eaten by a bear!"

Griffin laughed in her face. "Listen to yourself. Me and Karl and Dennis are going to be tracking that bear holding brand-new '73 Winchesters. Nobody's going to get hurt except that bear."

"You don't own a rifle."

Griffin crossed to his saddle, which was perched on a saddle tree near the supply chest, and pulled a Winchester from a brand-new leather boot attached to it.

"Put that down!" Grace shrieked. "Where did you get that?"

Griffin held the rifle in both hands, the bore aimed at the ceiling. "Karl gave it to me today. He said I need to be able to protect myself if we get separated tomorrow."

"Put it away! You have no idea how to load a rifle like that, let alone fire it," Grace scoffed. "You're more likely to shoot yourself than some bear."

Griffin shook his head. "You're wrong about that, Grace."

"Oh, really?" She crossed her arms over her chest to maintain some semblance of control, because everything Griffin said sounded preposterous and outrageous. "Where did you get all this experience with a Winchester?"

"Joe taught me how to shoot last summer," Griffin said as he returned the rifle to the leather boot.

"Joe? The bartender at the saloon? Why would he do that?"

Griffin leaned a hand on the horn of his saddle. "In case there was ever any trouble. He figured no one would suspect a kid like me could shoot. He kept an extra rifle under the bar." He puffed out his chest. "I was his backup in case he got into trouble."

Grace stared at her brother in disbelief. "You were only nine years old. What was he thinking?"

"I turned out to be a pretty good shot, if I do say so myself."

"This is crazy. You're just a little boy. You can't—"

Griffin squared his shoulders and said, "We haven't even been in the Bitterroot six months, and I've already grown an inch. I'm ten years old now, Grace. I have to learn how to be a man sometime."

"But—"

"Karl won't let anything happen to me." His lips twisted wryly as he added, "Ma would give him too hard a time if he did."

"I'll make a scene," she threatened. "I'll cry till my face is red. I'll beg Mom to make Karl leave you behind."

"If you love Karl, you won't do that, Grace."

Grace caught her breath. "Why not?"

"I'm not goin' on that bear hunt to hunt bear," he said. "I'm goin' on that hunt to protect Karl from Dennis."

"What?" Grace was so shocked that her rubbery knees gave up the ghost, and she plopped down onto a scratchy bale of hay. "You really think Dennis will try to kill Karl on the hunt?"

"It's too good an opportunity for him to pass up," Griffin said. "He can shoot Karl by 'accident' and blame it on the hunt. Or just not back him up if that bear attacks."

"But they're supposed to be friends."

"I think he's jealous of Karl."

"Jealous?"

"It's pretty obvious Dennis has always wanted to be the boss of this outfit. If something happened to Karl, he'd get the job."

"You're being ridiculous. No one kills someone for a job."

"I don't think that's all he wants," Griffin said. "I think he'd be happy to have Ma, too."

"She'd never marry Dennis."

"She would if she didn't have any other choice," Griffin said grimly. "She married Karl to save us, and she didn't even know him. She'd do what she had to do."

Unfortunately, Grace thought he might be right. Which only frightened her more. "You're just a little boy, Griffin," she said, her eyes stark. "How are you going to stop someone as dangerous as you say Dennis is?"

"By keeping a close eye on the son of a bitch. Now, if you don't mind, I'm starved. I'm goin' to the house and get some supper."

Griffin left the barn, closing the door behind him, leaving her sitting alone in the shadows. Grace stared after him. Her baby brother was growing up. When had he become so confident and sure of himself? That was all Karl's doing, she thought. Their lives would be a disaster if Dennis killed Karl. And she didn't want to think what life would be like for Hetty, who was expecting Karl's baby, if anything happened to him.

Grace wondered if there was anything she could do to help keep Karl safe. Maybe she should throw that fit after all and insist that both Karl and Griffin stay home tomorrow.

"Hey! Anybody in here?"

"Andy? Is that you?" Grace called out.

"It's me."

Since Christmas, she'd often crossed paths with Andy, but they'd never been alone. Karl or Griffin or Hetty had always been there. Nevertheless, she'd learned that Andy planned to settle down someday and build himself a homestead where he could run cattle, and she'd told him about her decision to study botany from Karl's books. He'd described the hill country west of San Antonio, where he'd grown up. She'd remained mute about her life in Cheyenne.

Grace never felt completely comfortable with the young Texan, probably because she wanted so much for him to like her, and she didn't see how he could possibly get past all of her physical flaws. She'd complained to him more than once about her impossible red curls, but he'd laughed and said, "I like them. They're wild and free. Like you."

It was hard for Grace to see herself as "wild and free," but she'd felt a knot in her chest loosen a little bit, so the next time they were together she was able to say, "Your eyes remind me of a lion." He'd laughed again and made claws of his hands and roared like a lion and said, "I might just eat you for supper. You're so sugar sweet, I figure you'd make a pretty tasty meal."

Being called "sugar sweet" had loosened that knot in her chest a little more, so she'd started looking forward to the few moments they spent together when they bumped into each other. She'd never gone so far as to arrange to be alone with him. He'd never asked for such a thing, and she'd been too shy to mention it.

But here they were, suddenly alone. Grace felt her heartbeat ratchet up. It seemed like she'd been waiting for this moment ever since Christmas. Now that it was here, she felt the urge to bolt. She made herself stay where she was. It was only Andy. They would talk and laugh together as they always had.

He could never be anything more to her because of what had happened in Cheyenne.

She watched the dust motes in the streaming sunlight disappear as Andy shut the barn door behind him. He crossed to the end of the barn where she was sitting and said, "What are you doing in here all alone?"

"Until a few minutes ago, I wasn't alone. I was trying to talk my idiot brother out of going on that stupid bear hunt."

"It's not stupid," Andy said as he sat down beside her.

Grace could feel the warmth of his thigh through her dress. She would have sidled away, except there was no more room on the bale of hay. Her heart started beating harder, and she could feel the red stain growing on her throat where a blush had started.

"Karl wants to cut trees right where that grizzly marked his territory," Andy explained. "It's him or us."

"That bear's got as much right to that mountain as you do," Grace said. "Why can't Karl find another place to cut?"

"Snow's melting off the mountain. We'd have to take time to make a new skid trail if we cut somewhere else."

Grace made a face. "Doesn't sound very fair to the bear."

Andy laughed. "Only you would worry about the bear, Grace."

"I mean it."

"That's what I love about you," Andy said.

He was still smiling, still laughing when he said it, but the words took Grace's breath away. She was staring into his golden eyes, waiting for him to realize what he'd admitted.

He sobered and reached for her hand and twined their fingers together. She realized for the first time how callused his hands were. He must not have shaved that morning, because a dark blond stubble shadowed his cheeks and chin.

He kept his gaze steady on hers as he spoke. "I'll be seventeen next month. I have the money from the sale of my family's ranch in Texas. Whenever you're ready, we can get married and settle anywhere you like."

Grace lowered her gaze and eased her hand free, knotting her hands in front of her so he couldn't take one again. "I can't ever marry you, Andy."

"I love you, Grace."

"I know. I'm sorry."

"Don't you love me anymore? You said you did on Christmas morning. Are you taking it back?"

Grace had been exuberant Christmas morning, filled with excitement over having a kitten of her own, which had carried over into an effusive thanks that had ended with the words, "I love you, Andy."

Now she had to explain away those words, which Andy had given a far weightier meaning than she'd intended.

She met his gaze and said earnestly, "I was grateful Christmas morning, because I knew it was you who told my mom I wanted a kitten. And you who picked out that particular kitten for me. And you who made sure that Socks was wearing a red ribbon when you put her into my arms, just as I told you I'd always dreamed."

"Then you didn't mean what you said?"

Grace swallowed hard. She'd never loved anyone—not Karl, not Hetty, not even Griffin—as much as she loved Andy. But she could never marry him. Because of what she'd done.

She lowered her gaze to her white-knuckled hands. "I meant it when I said it," she said in a small voice. "There are things you don't know about me, Andy. Things I can't undo."

"Nothing else matters if you love me," Andy said ardently. "Is it because you're only fourteen? I'll wait for as long as you want."

She shook her head. "It isn't that. I'd marry you to-morrow if I could."

Grace was so surprised when Andy raised her chin and kissed her—and she liked the feel of his lips on hers so much—that she let the kiss continue a very long time. She wanted it to go on forever. But it was unfair to lead him on. "Stop!" she cried. "Please, Andy. Don't kiss me anymore."

He looked abject as he let her go. "You didn't like it?"

She put a gentle hand to his cheek and looked into his eyes and said, "I loved it. But we can't be kissing like this, because I can't marry you. Not now. Not ever."

"Why not? Just tell me why," he pleaded.

Grace tried to think of a lie Andy would accept that

wasn't as bad as the truth. But her mind went completely blank.

Grace knew how much trouble all the deceit had caused between Hetty and Karl. She didn't want to lie to Andy. If she married him without saying anything about her past, he might never know she hadn't come to him untouched. But she would know. Keeping secrets from the start would eventually spoil everything. Better to tell Andy the truth and end it all now. But where should she start?

"I'm not really Hetty's daughter," she began.

"I know."

Grace gasped and her gaze shot to his. "How could you possibly know that?"

Andy untied the knot she'd made of her fingers and took one of her hands in both of his. "Griffin hinted as much the night he got that lump on his head. Since then, we've spent a lot of time together on the mountain, and he's told me everything."

Grace panicked. Surely Griffin hadn't told him *everything*. Surely he hadn't! She tried to flee, but Andy held on to her hand. "Let me go, Andy! I want to go!"

"Sit down, Grace," he said calmly. "Let's talk."

"Talking won't change anything!" she said angrily. "If you know the truth, then you know what I am. And why I can't marry you."

"I know you're the woman I love."

"You can't love me. I'm a whore! I've sold my body for money."

All the blood leached from his face.

And Grace suddenly realized that Andy hadn't

known this truth about her. Not until she'd just told him. He seemed to have forgotten that he was still holding her hand.

She tried to free herself, to run away and hide, but Andy held on. "You have to let me go, Andy. You don't want to marry someone like me."

He met her gaze and asked, "Why did you do it, Grace?"

"Does it matter? I did it."

She watched his Adam's apple bob as he swallowed hard. But what she'd told him wasn't going down easily.

"I'd like to know why you sold yourself for money," he said. "If you think you can bear to tell me."

She searched his gaze, looking for the condemnation she felt sure he was only waiting for an excuse to speak. But his lion eyes remained steadily, reassuringly, focused on her.

She took a shuddering breath and let it out. "I only did it once." She hurried to say, "Not that doing it just once makes my sin any less awful." Grace's heart hurt when she saw the pain in Andy's eyes.

His eyes said he'd heard enough. But his ragged voice said, "I'm listening, Grace."

She swallowed over the agonizing lump in her throat and said, "I did it to get the money to pay the woman who was supposed to be Karl's mail-order bride to bring us to Montana. I wanted a better life for my brother." She paused, then added with brutal honesty, "And a better life for myself. So you see, I didn't do it for entirely unselfish reasons."

"I don't think there's a selfish bone in your body, Grace."

Grace felt flustered. "Maybe you don't know me as well as you think."

"Do you love me, Grace?"

Grace felt the tears well and then spill from her eyes. "Does it matter?"

"It does to me."

"I don't want to hurt you, Andy." And marrying a fallen woman could do him no good.

"Then tell me the truth, Grace. Do you love me?"

"I love you more than my own life. I love you so much I want to die when I think of you leaving here and never speaking to me again."

He rose and pulled her, unresisting, into his arms. Grace felt his hand at her nape and his mouth at her temple. Then he kissed away the tears on each of her cheeks as he murmured, "I'm not going anywhere. Will you marry me, Grace?"

"I—"

His kiss prevented her from answering. When they came up for air he said, "Marry me, Grace."

"But—"

He kissed her breathless again and urged, "Marry me."

"All right," Grace said, panting with excitement and fear and hope. "All right, Andy. If you're sure this is what you want, I'll marry you."

Andy lifted her under the arms and swung her around and gave a Texas yell so loud the horses whinnied and sidled in their stalls.

Grace slung her arms around his neck and gave a whoop of her own, which was cut off as she gave back the kisses Andy had so generously given her.

Grace had a momentary qualm, wondering whether Griffin would feel betrayed by her decision, and what Hetty would think about her stepdaughter getting married so soon after her marriage to Karl. Then she was lost in the euphoria of being kissed by the man she loved, a man whose heart was big enough to forgive the unforgivable.

Chapter Thirty-eight

Karl had spent the rest of the day making sure that the skid trail got repaired. Hetty was lying in bed wrapped in Karl's arms listening to the wind whistle eerily outside the window. She watched mysterious shapes waver and change in the flickering light from the burned-down logs in the fireplace.

She felt safe in Karl's arms and frightened at the same time. Everything was happening too fast. In practically the same moment that she'd told Karl she was pregnant, Grace and Andy had come to the house and announced that they wanted to get married.

Hetty pressed her face against Karl's throat, inhaling the sharp, arresting scent that was uniquely his, and asked, "Don't you think she's too young to get married?"

"Andy has the means to support her. And they love each other." He paused and added, "But I think we can insist they wait at least until Grace is fifteen. It won't hurt for them to be engaged for a year. It'll give them both a chance to make sure they'll suit."

"Thank you, Karl. I don't want to lose my eldest daughter so soon."

She felt Karl's smile against her cheek as he admitted, "Me neither."

Hetty had been surprised when Karl told her just how much money Andy had stashed in a bank in Texas. The boy had apparently come to Karl first to request permission to marry Grace. When Karl had asked about Andy's prospects, he'd confessed he was rich.

Hetty was glad for her stepdaughter. Grace would never go hungry again. Or need to sell her body again. Hetty felt a shiver run through her. Grace had blurted that news in the excitement of telling Hetty, "He loves me. And he doesn't care!"

"About what?" she'd asked, smiling with happiness for Grace.

"About what I did to get the money to pay Lucy to bring us along." Suddenly, her face had looked stricken. "Are you ashamed of me? Do you hate me now that you know?"

Hetty was still trying to figure out what dastardly deed Grace had committed when Grace's subsequent questions made the answer clear. *Something shameful. Something worthy of hate.* It could only be one thing.

Hetty had been appalled. And dismayed. She'd struggled to keep any kind of judgment off her face and out of her voice as she replied, "I love you, Grace. The most important thing is, can you forgive yourself and move on with your life?"

"I can. Oh, yes, I can! Andy says it doesn't matter to him, and because he doesn't care, I don't ever have to think about it again."

Hetty thought about the tremendous sacrifice Grace had made for her brother. It wasn't so different from ne sacrifice Hetty's eldest sister, Miranda, had made, becoming a mail-order bride—selling herself, body and soul—to provide a home for their two younger brothers. Or the sacrifice her twin, Hannah, had made, marrying Mr. McMurtry so that Hetty and Josie could escape from the detestable Miss Birch.

Or the sacrifice she herself had made, accepting Karl as her husband to save Grace and Griffin from a fate worse than death. She was glad to have been a part of helping the two children escape the bitter life they'd led. Thanks to her, Griffin had a mother and father, and Grace had come to the Bitterroot and found Andy.

Hetty curled her body a little closer to Karl's, seeking warmth and comfort. "Grace says Andy's planning to build a cabin not far from here, so she can stay close to Griffin."

Karl chuckled. "Did you see the look on Andy's face when Griffin suggested that maybe he should come live with them?"

Hetty smiled against his throat. "I saw the look of relief on Grace's face when you spoke up."

"I just said what I believe. Griffin needs a mother and father for the foreseeable future more than he needs his sister."

Hetty felt one of his large hands settle on her rounded belly as he asked, "Have you felt the baby move?"

"I felt a flicker, like a butterfly wing brushing my belly, but on the inside. I wasn't sure if it was the baby, but I don't know what else it could have been."

"Your stomach acting up," Karl said.

She shook her head. "When I felt it, my stomach wasn't upset."

"Are you really happy, Hetty? About the baby, I mean?"

"Mmm." It was an answer Karl could construe any way he wanted. Hetty hadn't really considered her feelings in terms of happy and unhappy. She was still adjusting to becoming a mother to Grace and Griffin and now she was going to be caring for an infant. She had no idea how to nurse a baby or change diapers or any of the things she would be expected to do. Hetty wished she'd paid more attention when her brother Harry was a baby, but Miranda had been the one to take care of him at the orphanage.

"I'll need to build an addition on the house this summer so we'll have more room," Karl mused.

"A crib isn't going to take up much space."

Karl chuckled again. "I suppose not. But Griffin said something about being in the way when the new baby comes. He'll need his sleep if he's going to do a full day's work for me, and he won't get much rest with a squalling infant in his room."

"Hmm," she said again. Her thoughts felt jumbled. Like her life.

Karl twisted one of her curls around his finger. "You're awfully quiet tonight. Are you worried about something?"

She was tired of keeping secrets from Karl, but Grace's secret wasn't hers to tell. Better he should believe that she was thinking about the baby. "I'm just glad you finally know about the baby and that you're happy about it."

He let go of her hair and hugged her close. "I am."

One of her hands found its way under his long john shirt to his bare chest. His belly rippled with muscle, and she could almost count his ribs. "I like touching you, Karl."

"I like it, too," he said. "I wish I'd known you weren't feeling well these past couple of months. Bao probably has some remedy that would have helped."

"I was afraid he'd tell you if he knew."

"Well, I know now," he said. "I'm going to see if I can find a midwife or a doctor in one of the towns farther north in the valley to help with the delivery."

"You're thinking awfully far ahead, aren't you? The baby's not due until the fall."

Karl's fingers sieved through her hair. "I don't want to take any chances. It was hard enough getting just the right mail-order bride. I don't want to lose you, Hetty."

"Any more than I want to lose you." Which reminded her that Karl was headed off into the wilderness first thing in the morning to hunt down the most dangerous predator in the Territory. "Do you really have to go hunting that grizzly tomorrow?"

He nuzzled a spot beneath her ear. "Yes, I do."

She arched her neck so he could more easily reach her throat and said, "I mean it, Karl. I'm afraid you'll get hurt."

"I didn't think you cared what happened to me."

"Of course I care," Hetty said.

"So you care about me, you just don't love me."

Hetty sat upright in the dark, pulling her hair free of his grasp. Karl remained supine, but he tucked a hand behind his head to lift it off the pillow.

She stared down at him, her heart caught in her throat, and realized she'd been lying to herself all these months. *What a fool I am!*

It wasn't only the way Karl made her feel in bed that she loved. It was the way he made her feel when he looked into her eyes at the breakfast table. The way he'd taught Griffin to ride and helped Grace with the study of plants. The way he took care of his workers. The appreciation he showed her for cooking his supper and washing his shirts. And the way he noticed that the sheets smelled like fresh air when they'd just come in from the line.

She loved his plain brown eyes and his plain brown hair and his extraordinarily ordinary face. Except, in her eyes, there was nothing plain about Karl Norwood. No one else had brown eyes as warm as his. No one else had brown hair streaked with gold by the sun like his. And no one else's face had ever been so dear. Why had she been so reluctant to admit that her feelings had changed?

"I do love you, Karl. I do."

He sat up beside her. "I wish I could believe you, Hetty."

"Why wouldn't you believe me? It's the truth."

He sighed. But he said nothing.

"It's because of all the lies I've told in the past," she said. "That's why you don't believe me."

"That might have a little something to do with it. That, and the fact you've made this profession of love to keep me from doing something that needs to be done, no matter how dangerous it is."

"You really think I said I love you so you won't go hunting that grizzly tomorrow?"

"Yeah. I do."

"I take it back. I don't give a damn about you! I don't care if that grizzly claws you to shreds. I don't care if he bites your head off. I don't care if he eats you whole and spits out your shoes!"

Karl laughed and pulled her close, then lowered her to the bed, covering her body with his.

"This isn't funny, Karl. I told you I love you, and you're laughing at me. I'm serious!"

"I'm serious, too. About making love to my wife and the mother of my children. Let's enjoy tonight, Hetty, and let tomorrow take care of itself."

Hetty would have protested, but his mouth had already captured hers and his hands were doing magic things to her body that made it sing hosanna. She gave herself up to the pleasure of making love to her husband.

Karl was right. Words didn't matter. Feelings did. She would *show* him that she loved him. She would treasure him and pleasure him and be a wonderful wife and a perfect mother. Maybe then he would believe her. She had the rest of her life to convince him.

She pushed aside her worry about some stupid grizzly bear. Karl knew what he was doing. Karl was strong. Karl was invincible. Karl would shoot that bear dead.

Chapter Thirty-nine

Karl took the lead as he and Dennis and Griffin tracked the bear's spoor across the mountain. Before he'd left that morning, Hetty had asked him if he couldn't take Andy along, just to have one more rifle handy. Karl had held her close and explained that Andy had logs to get down the mountain, now that the skid trail was repaired.

She was also worried about Griffin and wondered if he shouldn't be left at home. Karl had promised to keep a close eye on the boy and reminded her, "He needs to learn, Hetty. And doing is the very best way of learning."

Throughout the day, Karl's mind kept wandering back to the previous night, to Hetty's confession of love and the lovemaking that had followed. Was it possible? Could she really love him?

"I've found something," Griffin said excitedly.

"Keep your voice down," Dennis warned. "We don't want to scare him away."

"I don't think that bear's been here since last fall," Griffin said, pointing toward a spot where bark was missing from a pine trunk. "Those claw marks are pretty old."

Karl studied the deep grooves in the bark, noting how high they reached. "I was impressed with the size of that grizzly's paw prints. Here's more proof that we're looking for a truly enormous beast," he said to Dennis. "I'd have to be standing on your shoulders to reach those upper marks."

"He'll make a nice rug," Dennis replied.

"If you can find him," Griffin muttered. "We haven't seen any sign of him for a couple of hours."

Dennis's eyes narrowed as he focused on Griffin. "We'll find him all right, even if we have to stay out here all night."

"I wasn't planning on camping on the mountain overnight," Karl said. "Especially with that bear on the loose."

"Build a big enough fire, and he'll keep his distance," Dennis said.

"You're willing to bet our lives on that?" Karl asked.

"Ma's gonna be worried if we don't show up at sundown," Griffin said. "We better get started home."

"If we go back now, we'll have to start over from scratch tomorrow," Dennis said. "We've got that bear on the run. We'll pick up sign again in the morning. I say we don't give him a break. We keep after him and put him down."

Karl leaned his rifle against the tree, then took off his flat-brimmed hat and ruffled his sweaty hair. The weather had been unexpectedly warm, which made trekking up and down the mountain hot work. The terrain was so rough, they'd been leading their mounts for the past half hour. "I don't know, Dennis. I didn't tell Hetty we'd be out overnight."

"Every day we don't cut wood is another day we get further behind," Dennis reminded him.

"We'll make up the time," Karl said. Once again, it was a question of men over money. Karl wasn't about to lose a logger to some grizzly prowling the mountain. He would face down his brother, if it came to that, but he was confident he could do this job the safe way and still get it done.

Throughout the winter they'd encountered only minor stoppages, caused by mishaps like missing saws and dull or broken axes, and minor repairs like Karl had insisted upon doing on the skidding trail. But Karl hadn't counted on illness decimating his workforce.

Since the beginning of spring, a quarter of the loggers had come down with a fever, accompanied by a bad rash that left them spotted like rattlesnakes. Karl had been told by the Salish to avoid the west-side canyons once the snow began to melt, but when they couldn't give him a good reason why, he'd ignored the advice. When his men came down with the spotted fever, he realized it had been a mistake not to heed their warning.

Despite Bao's best efforts to heal the infected men, within ten days, two of them had died. Panic had spread through the bunkhouse. Karl had been forced to double the loggers' wages to keep them working. When yet another man got sick and died, Karl had called off cutting entirely for several days while he looked for the cause of the illness.

Try as he might, he could find nothing different about the mountain terrain in spring except the prevalence of more animals—mountain goats, squirrels, and chipmunks—and he couldn't imagine how they could have anything to do with this sickness. Bao had pointed out a reddish spot on one man's arm, where he'd removed a tick, but Karl didn't see how something as tiny as a tick could be killing his men.

No one had gotten sick for the past two weeks, and Karl had been cautiously optimistic that they would catch up. And then the grizzly had appeared.

Karl remained undaunted. This marauding bear was only one more challenge to be met and conquered. He smoothed his hair and settled his hat back low on his forehead. "All right. Let's find someplace to camp that'll give us an escape route if that grizzly attacks."

"I think we should go home," Griffin said.

"I told you we shouldn't have brought him along," Dennis said.

Karl put a hand on Griffin's shoulder and said, "Dennis is right. If we go home, we'll lose too much time finding that bear's trail again in the morning. When we don't show up, your mom will realize that we've decided to stay out overnight."

"When we don't show up, Grace will figure that bear attacked us and we're all bleeding out somewhere on the mountain," Griffin retorted. "She'll do her best to convince Ma that they ought to ride to the rescue."

Karl smiled. "Hetty won't do that." But he wasn't at all sure that she would wait patiently for his return. Especially since he'd been too busy making love to her last night to explain that this hunt might take more than a single day.

"We'll deal with your mom when and if she shows

up on the mountain," Karl said. "Right now, let's get started setting up camp."

"You're going to camp here?" Griffin asked.

"Why not?" Karl said.

"That bear was marking his territory when he clawed that tree," Griffin said.

"How could you possibly know that?" Dennis asked sarcastically.

Griffin kept his gaze focused on Karl as he said, "I grew up in a Cheyenne saloon. Buffalo hunters, trappers, cowboys—all sorts of men came in there to have a drink and talk. And I listened. I'm telling you, Karl, we lost that grizzly's tracks a couple of hours ago, but we're in his territory for sure. That bear is probably closer than we think. We shouldn't stay here."

"It's getting dark," Dennis said. "Where do you propose we go?"

"We should head home," Griffin persisted.

Karl remembered what had happened the last time he'd ignored good advice. But Dennis was right about the time they'd lose if they abandoned the hunt now. "You said yourself those claw marks look old," he told the boy. "We'll build ourselves a fire, and we'll set a watch through the night. We'll be fine."

"Just because that bear hasn't made it back to this tree yet this spring doesn't mean he isn't coming," Griffin argued.

"Give it a rest, kid," Dennis said as he began untying his saddlebags. "We're staying."

Griffin shrugged. "Don't say I didn't warn you."

Karl hadn't planned to be gone overnight, but he'd taken the precaution of bringing along bedrolls and enough food for a couple of days, in case the hunt ran longer than expected. He'd hoped they could find and kill the bear in a day. But that hadn't happened.

The timing of the hunt was terrible. He wanted to be home with his pregnant wife. He wanted to lie beside her and hold her and talk with her, as they had last night, then turn her in his arms and make sweet love to her. He wanted to look into her eyes and see the love she'd said he would find there. He wanted her to say those three words again—and be able to believe them.

Karl hoped Griffin was wrong about Grace convincing Hetty to come looking for them. Surely Hetty would wait at least another day before she panicked. And surely they'd find that bear tomorrow and get back home tomorrow night.

Karl picked a flat spot where they could spread out their sleeping pallets. Then they unsaddled their horses and picketed them close in, where they would be safe from other nighttime predators, including cougars and wolves. Griffin collected dead branches for firewood and moved stones into a circle to contain the fire.

Once they'd made camp and collected and cut enough dead wood to keep the fire burning all night, they settled on the ground and Dennis handed out biscuits with ham, boiled eggs in the shell, and pickles.

"This feels like a picnic," Griffin said as he cracked his egg against a stone and began peeling it, throwing the shell into the fire.

"Kid thinks he's on a picnic," Dennis said scornfully.

"I've never been on a picnic," Griffin continued. "But if this is what it's like, Karl, I think I'd like to try it again sometime with Mom and Grace. I guess Andy would have to come, too, seeing as how he and Grace are engaged."

"I can't believe you're allowing that Texas kid to marry your stepdaughter," Dennis muttered.

Karl didn't rise to the bait and argue. He knew how it must look, letting Grace marry a skidder who made thirty bucks a month, but Andy had insisted on keeping his finances private, so Karl endured Dennis's outrage without comment.

A wolf howled in the distance, and Griffin scooted a little closer to the fire. And to Karl.

"Scared, kid?" Dennis said.

"Wolves don't bother me," Griffin said. "But I'm not ashamed to admit that grizzly has me worried. Bears have pretty good noses. This one might get a hankering for ham and biscuits."

Dennis laughed derisively. "And you know bears can smell ham and biscuits a mile off because you heard it in some saloon?" Instead of eating the last bite of his biscuit with ham, he threw it over his shoulder into the darkness.

"What the hell are you doing?" Karl said. "You want that bear to come looking for us?"

"Why not?" Dennis said. "We'll build up the fire so we can see him coming—assuming he can smell a mile and has a hankering for ham and biscuits. With any luck, we can finish this hunt up tonight and head home in the morning."

"I don't like the idea of my pony getting attacked by some ham-sniffing bear," Griffin said.

"Too late now," Dennis said. "Unless you want to see if you can find that bit of ham and biscuit in the dark."

Griffin snorted in disgust. "No thanks."

"That's enough, Dennis," Karl said angrily. "It's going to be enough of a challenge killing that bear in the daylight. I don't want to end up having to fight him in the dark."

"We can stoke up the fire, make it bigger," Dennis said.

"What happens when we run out of wood?" Karl said. "We didn't cut enough for the bonfire you're describing. Are you going out there in the dark to cut more?"

"You're worrying over nothing," Dennis replied.

"That grizzly is not *nothing*," Karl said. "He's a ton of teeth and claws."

"That I can put down with one bullet."

"Maybe not," Griffin said.

"Butt out, kid," Dennis snarled.

"Even if you hit that grizzly in the heart, it's going to pump a couple more times," Griffin said with relish. "His skull is so thick it's hard to get to his brain. You're going to need a couple of bullets—and a lot of luck—to put that grizzly down before he turns you into ground meat. One swipe of his paw can take off your head. His claws will rip your eyes out. His teeth—"

"That's enough, Griffin," Karl interrupted. "You've made your point."

Dennis exchanged a sardonic look with Karl. "That kid should be writing penny dreadfuls. I'll take the first watch."

Karl was surprised when Griffin laid out his pallet right next to his, but he didn't say anything. Maybe the kid was more scared than he'd said he was. What surprised him even more was seeing Griffin hug his rifle to his chest under the covers.

"You're liable to lose another toe if that gun goes off," Karl said as he settled onto his side.

"If I need this rifle, I'm going to need it in a hurry," Griffin said. "Besides, I don't have a bullet in the chamber."

Karl chuckled. "Good for you."

"Wake me up for my turn on watch," Griffin said.

"If you want, you can watch with me," Karl said.

"Don't you trust me?" Griffin asked.

How was he supposed to answer that? Karl wondered. "Did you ever think that maybe I wanted you to help keep me awake?"

Griffin yawned. "All right. Wake me when it's time."

Karl tried to sleep, but sleep eluded him. He kept thinking about that bit of ham and biscuit Dennis had set out as bait. What if it worked? He finally drifted off thinking of Hetty, of the softness of her breasts and the swell of her belly where their child was growing inside her.

He woke to the horrific sound of screaming.

Chapter Forty

When Karl and Griffin didn't return from the hunt by sundown, Hetty convinced Grace there was nothing to worry about. "Karl won't take any chances hunting that bear. If he's still out there on the mountain, it means they haven't found him yet."

"Or they've found that grizzly and it attacked them and they're lying mangled on the mountain, praying that we come find them before they die!" Grace retorted.

Hetty laughed at Grace's hysterics in an effort to downplay her stepdaughter's concerns, but a shiver shot down her spine at the thought of Karl and Griffin lying desperately injured in the woods, waiting for succor that wasn't on the way.

She allowed Grace to bring Socks and come sleep in bed with her in order to comfort the girl. But Grace's restlessness and the kitten's playfulness kept Hetty from getting any sleep. When she did finally manage to close her eyes, she had a nightmare where an enormous grizzly with a slavering mouth and razor-sharp teeth towered over Karl, who stood helpless in the shadow of the giant beast with no weapon to defend himself.

The next morning, both Hetty and Grace were sporting sunken, sleep-starved eyes and drawn, uneasy faces.

"At least let me send Andy after them," Grace argued as she poured a second cup of coffee for Hetty. "He could take Bao along, in case anyone needs stitches."

Stitches implied cuts from teeth and claws.

"Maybe we should all go," Hetty said as Grace set the cup of coffee in front of her.

Grace hugged her from behind and said, "Oh, Mom, thank you! I told Andy how we traveled all the way from Cheyenne to the Bitterroot with only Bao to protect us, and that spending a night or two on the mountain wouldn't scare us a bit."

Hetty knew the idiocy of running after two men and a boy who were perfectly capable of taking care of themselves. She was likely going to be in for a tongue-lashing when they met up with Karl and discovered everyone was fine. He'd probably send her right back down the mountain.

But what if he wasn't okay? What if something had gone wrong? What if he and Griffin and Dennis were lying somewhere on the mountain, bleeding to death? She knew the likelihood of all three being incapacitated was slim, but that gave her small comfort.

Hetty was startled by a knock on the door. As she rose, Grace said, "Stay. I'll get it. It's probably Andy again."

It was Bao, who had definite ideas about the wisdom of heading up the mountain. He stood across the table from Hetty and said, "Not good idea."

"Why not?" Hetty asked.

"Confucius say: 'Real knowledge is knowing one's ignorance.'"

"I think I've heard that one," Hetty said.

Bao arched a brow and continued, "I not know how to find grizzly, so let Boss track bear. You know how to find grizzly?"

"No," Hetty admitted. "But—"

"No but," Bao interrupted. "You stay home. Boss return. You here safe."

"What if he doesn't return?" Hetty demanded. "How long am I supposed to wait?"

Bao pulled on his beard, ran his hand down his long braid, then settled his silk cap lower on his forehead. "Not know."

Grace laid her hands on Hetty's shoulders and said, "Andy believes something might have gone wrong."

"Andy want to please you," Bao said. "Not know what happen for sure."

"Which is why we should go up there and make certain they're all right," Hetty urged. "Please come with us, Bao. Karl or Griffin or Dennis may need you."

Bao's face remained inscrutable for another moment. Then he said, "Not like idea. But go along."

"Thank you, Bao," Hetty said.

Grace hurled herself around the table to hug the Chinaman, who stood stoically immovable. "Andy's already got a mule packed with supplies," Grace told him. "Hetty and I can be ready in no time."

"We can?" Hetty said.

"I already have a bag packed for us," Grace said.

Hetty smiled at Grace, then rose and said to Bao,

"We'll meet you outside in half an hour. Will that give you enough time to put together whatever medicines you'll need?"

"All ready now," Bao said. "You stubborn woman. Know I lose argument."

"I suppose Confucius has a saying for that, too," Hetty said with a smile.

"Bao say: 'Hurry up and get ready. Day wasting.'"

Hetty laughed, but she was up and on her way in moments, and within the next half hour, the four of them were on the trail. Too late, Hetty realized that Andy had not been as willing to bring her and Grace along as her daughter had suggested. The young couple spent most of the morning's ride arguing about how dangerous it was for two women to be traveling on a mountain a grizzly claimed as its own.

"How do you know they stayed on this game trail?" Hetty asked when Andy dismounted once again to search for sign.

He pointed to a spot on the trail. "See those bear paw prints in the dust? They were following that bear, and this is the way that bear went."

Hetty's heart skipped a beat when she saw the size of the giant paw marks. "Are you sure that's the grizzly they're hunting?"

"Yes, ma'am. We saw marks like this around the logging camp. It's missing a claw on one of its toes." He pointed to a dried paw print, and sure enough, the third toe on the left paw had a claw missing.

"Those prints are huge!" Hetty said.

"Yes, ma'am. Are you two ladies ready to head back now?"

Hetty met Grace's frightened gaze and questioned with her eyes whether the girl wanted to continue.

"I say we go on," Grace said. "Karl and Griffin may need us."

"You might run right into that grizzly yourself, if they haven't found it yet," Andy warned.

"I trust you not to let that happen," Grace said.

Andy walked over to stand by Grace's mount, looked up at her, and said, "Maybe I don't want that responsibility."

"Please, Andy. I know something's wrong. I can feel it here." Grace put a fist against her heart.

Andy grimaced. "Guess you gotta trust your gut. All right. We better keep moving."

Soon the trail changed to softer ground, and even Hetty could see signs that three shod horses had passed that way. "How long ago where they here?" she asked Andy.

"Sometime early yesterday."

"They could be miles from here by now," Hetty said.

"Yes, ma'am," Andy said. "Most likely the distance they traveled up the mountain was why they didn't come home last night."

"So you're saying this is a fool's errand," Hetty said.

"You said it, ma'am, not me."

It was obvious to Hetty that Andy was merely humoring her and Grace, and that he thought they were wasting their time. Hetty wasn't so sure. She had that same strange ache in her chest that Grace must be feeling. Something was wrong. She knew it.

During the afternoon, Andy had no difficulty following the sign left by Karl, Dennis, and Griffin, even after they left the game trail. But as the day waned, and they didn't meet up with the three bear hunters on the way back home, Hetty's sense of foreboding increased.

Grace trotted her mount close to Hetty's and asked in a voice quiet enough that Andy couldn't hear, "What if we don't find them before dark?"

"Let's find the spot where they camped last night before we decide what to do," Hetty replied.

"Stop!" Andy called back to them. "Stay where you are."

Andy had been riding ahead, rifle across his arms, in case they encountered the grizzly. His cry of warning stopped Hetty, Grace, and Bao in their tracks.

Hetty felt her horse quiver and snort and sidle. Grace's horse whinnied and backed up.

"Whoa," Grace said. "Easy, girl." But her horse continued its agitated movements.

Hetty's heart shot to her throat. Was it the grizzly? Were they about to be attacked?

"Bao!" Andy shouted. "Get up here."

"Andy, be careful!" Grace yelled.

"I'm okay. Bao, get up here," Andy said.

"What is it?" Hetty cried. "What's wrong? What did you find?" Hetty spurred her mount to close the distance to Andy.

Her horse resisted her kicks and tried to turn around. "Come on!" she urged, using the reins to pull its head back in the direction she wanted to go.

Grace was more successful spurring her horse, and her mount passed Hetty and reached the clearing before her. "Oh, my God!" Grace cried.

Hetty couldn't see Andy, but she heard him say, "Goddammit, Grace, I told you to stay the hell away."

Then she heard Grace's anguished voice say, "What is that on the ground? Where did all this blood come from?"

Chapter Forty-one

Karl glanced over his shoulder to check on Griffin, who was riding right behind him, and asked, "How is Star doing?"

"He's favoring his right rear leg," Griffin replied unhappily.

"That pony's fine," Dennis said from his place third in line. "All that cougar did was scratch his flank."

"A few of those scratches looked deep," Karl countered. He wondered if Dennis's bit of ham and biscuit had been what attracted the cougar that had shown up and launched itself onto the back of Griffin's pony. It was the pony's scream of pain that had woken Karl from his fitful sleep.

Karl had reached for his rifle, but Griffin had a bullet chambered a second sooner. Both bullets had hit the cat—which was flying through the air, lit up by Dennis's bonfire—within seconds of each other. The cougar was already dead by the time Dennis located his rifle and pumped a third bullet into it on the ground.

Griffin was distraught when he saw the claw marks on Star's hide, and flung his arms around the skittish pony's neck, sobbing as though the animal had been killed, instead of slightly wounded. Karl had turned Griffin into his arms, and when he felt the boy trembling, hugged him tight.

Adrenaline was pumping through Karl's veins, but he kept his voice calm as he said, "Star's fine, Griffin. He nearly bucked that cougar to kingdom come. Another minute or two and Star would've stomped that cat flat all by his lonesome."

"Star's bleeding," Griffin had said, pulling himself free and turning back to survey his pony. "What if the bleeding doesn't stop?"

"Let's take a closer look at those scratches," Karl replied.

Once Griffin had something to do, he was able to follow Karl's instructions. Karl had made a torch so they could examine the pony's injuries and pointed out to Griffin that the wounds in the pony's hide were shallow and barely seeping blood.

"He'll be a little sore tomorrow, but he should heal up just fine."

"Too bad the wrong predator showed up," Dennis said. "Or we'd be heading home in the morning."

"If that bear had shown up, we'd have been up shit creek without a paddle," Karl said heatedly. "Where was your rifle, Dennis?"

"Right beside me."

"On the ground?"

"Did you expect me to sit there holding it all night?"

"If that had been the grizzly instead of a cougar—"

"I would have put a bullet into it," Dennis interrupted. "Just like I did with that cat. What are you so sore about?"

Karl shook his head in disgust. Dennis had plenty of experience dealing with men, but Karl had spent far more time in the wilderness. "Wild beasts don't give you a second chance."

"Does that mean you two yellow bellies are calling off the hunt?" Dennis demanded.

"I ain't no chicken," Griffin snapped. "Neither is Karl."

Dennis turned to Karl and said, "Are we hunting that bear tomorrow morning, or not?"

"We're hunting," Griffin replied.

"Shut your trap, kid. I wasn't talking to you."

Karl turned to Dennis and said, "Keep a civil tongue in your month when you speak to my son."

"What the hell?"

"And watch your language."

"Son of a bitch," Dennis muttered.

"Griffin and I will stand watch the rest of the night."

"I've got something to do first," Dennis said.

"What's that?"

"Skin that cat."

"That's Griffin's pelt," Karl said in a steely voice. "His bullet killed that cat."

"Prove it," Dennis retorted. "That pelt is mine!"

Dennis's hand tightened on his rifle, but before he could raise it to threaten Karl, Griffin said, "He can have that stinky old pelt. I don't want it."

Karl turned to the boy and saw anxious eyes looking back at him.

"I don't want it, Karl. Really, I don't."

"The kid doesn't want it, and I do," Dennis said. "Satisfied?" Dennis pulled a knife from the sheath at his waist and stalked toward the dead cougar.

Karl crossed to Griffin and lifted the boy's chin in his hand and looked him in the eye. "I don't know if you really didn't want that pelt, or if you didn't want me to end up fighting Dennis."

"I didn't want the stupid pelt," Griffin said. "I figure you could beat the crap out of Dennis Campbell if you really wanted to. But I couldn't trust him not to shoot you if he got pissed off because you gave me that hide."

Griffin turned and walked off toward his pony, leaving Karl with a great deal of food for thought. He'd never been happier in his life than when they broke camp the next morning and left the butchered remains of the cougar behind.

It was frustrating to realize, as the day wore on, that the grizzly was leading them in circles. By late afternoon, they weren't far from where they'd made camp the previous evening.

"Maybe it's time we headed back, Dennis. Griffin's mount isn't recovering as well as I thought he would. And we're not any closer to catching that bear now than we were yesterday afternoon."

"Quitting, Karl?" Dennis replied. "I should have expected it."

"Griffin and I are heading back," Karl said, refusing to be provoked. "You're welcome to continue on your own."

"If not for me, this whole operation would have been a bust," Dennis continued.

"By God, Dennis," Karl said, "When we get off this mountain I'm going to—"

The bear came out of nowhere.

"Pa, look out!"

Karl was so startled to be called *Pa* that his head shot around to gape at Griffin. By the time he looked back in the direction Griffin was pointing, it was too late. His horse crow-hopped and then reared, and Karl ended up flat on his back on the ground, a grizzly on four paws, carnivore's maw open wide and roaring defiance, not five feet away from him.

Karl's rifle was still in the boot on his saddle and his horse was long gone. From the corner of his eye, he saw Dennis riding hell-for-leather in the opposite direction. He was tempted to scuttle backward, but he knew any movement would set off the bear's predatory instincts.

"Take your rifle out of the boot, son. Slow and easy."

"My pony won't stand still," Griffin said in a trembling voice.

"You've got plenty of time. That bear's still thinking about what he wants to do." Karl had a pretty good idea that the first thing that grizzly was going to do was bite off his head.

He felt a fleeting fear of the future Hetty and their unborn baby would face if he got eaten by a bear, but didn't allow himself to focus on it. He needed to think clearly if he was going to survive.

Everything seemed to move in slow motion. The shaggy animal rose up on two legs, towering over Karl as Griffin urged his pony a step closer.

"Shoot for the heart," Karl said. "Now!"

Karl heard three quick shots and saw the bear drop down on four legs again and take an angry swipe at him with its paw.

Karl's face felt like he'd been licked with fire as he rolled away, launched himself onto his feet, and raced toward Griffin's pony. He threw himself onto the pony's haunches behind the saddle, spurred the animal, and yelled, "Let's go!"

He slung an arm around Griffin's waist as the boy yelled "Ha!" and the pinto ran for its life.

They hadn't gone fifty yards when they saw four riders coming toward them at a gallop.

"That's Ma!" Griffin yelled.

Karl glanced over his shoulder and said, "Don't slow down. That bear's still coming."

As the riders yanked their mounts to a halt to keep from careening into one another, Karl yelled, "Henrietta Wentworth Norwood, what the hell are you doing here!"

"Karl, your face is bleeding," she said. "You're hurt!"

"There's a wounded grizzly right behind us," Karl snapped at Andy. "Get these women out of here!"

The undergrowth was thick enough that it was difficult to get five horses turned around and headed in the opposite direction.

Karl heard the bear crashing through the underbrush behind them and said to Griffin, "Give me your Winchester."

"What are you going to do?" Griffin asked fearfully.

"Finish off that bear once and for all."

"Let him be, Pa. He'll die on his own. Let's just go."

Karl's arm was still slung around Griffin's waist, and he gave the boy a quick hug and said, "That's the second time you've called me Pa. I'd feel better about it if you hadn't been scared to death—both times—that I'm going to get myself killed."

"Now that I've got a proper pa," Griffin said, "I don't want to lose you."

"It's that bear needs to worry," Karl said, sliding off the pony's rump onto his feet. "Andy, get moving! I'll catch up with you after I kill that bear."

"Take my mount," Andy said, one leg already out of the stirrup.

Karl shook his head. "Horses are too skittish around this monster. I'm safer on foot. Griffin already put three slugs into him. I'm just going to make sure that grizzly's down for good."

As he turned, Karl realized that the grizzly had caught up to them. It was tangled up in the underbrush, but it would only take a couple of swipes from those powerful paws to set it free.

Karl turned to Hetty, his heart in his eyes, and said, "I love you."

"Karl, wait!" Hetty clambered off her horse and ran to him, throwing her arms around his neck. "I love you, too. Please come with us!"

"I love you, too, Pa," Griffin said, coming off his horse to join Hetty.

"Me, too, Pa," Grace said as she slipped off her horse and slid her arms around Karl from behind.

Andy said anxiously, "Better break it up, folks, or that bear is going to have himself a Norwood sandwich for lunch."

"Get mounted and get out of here," Karl urged, pulling Hetty's arms from around his neck, easing Grace's arms from around his waist, and forcing Griffin to let him go. "Let me take care of that bear, and I'll come join you in a little while."

Karl's heart was filled with love. And pumped so full of adrenaline that he was afraid it would burst from his chest.

"Get them out of here, Andy," he ordered in a harsh voice. "Take care of them, Bao."

Then he turned and headed into the underbrush.

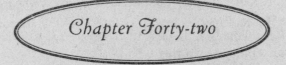

Chapter Forty-two

Karl could feel Hetty's eyes on him even after he disappeared into the undergrowth. He quickly checked the Winchester to make sure Griffin had left a bullet in the chamber, then shoved his way into the maze of mountain greenery.

It took Karl a moment to realize that the bear had stopped dead in its tracks. He peered through the foliage and saw that instead of shoving forward, the grizzly was backing out. Once the beast was in the clear, it lifted its nose high in the air, apparently hunting for the scent of something on the wind.

Karl turned his face into the breeze and discovered Dennis sitting on his horse on the other side of the clearing, his back to the bear.

Karl realized with horror that the grizzly must have caught the scent of that bloody cougar pelt Dennis had salvaged and tied into a roll on the back of his saddle. Karl opened his mouth to shout a warning but realized his cry would only turn the bear back in his direction. And toward Hetty and the children.

So he remained silent.

Karl stalked the bear as the bear stalked Dennis,

hose gaze was focused on the ground in front of
im as he slowly walked his mount forward, pains-
takingly searching for something.

He's hunting for a blood trail, Karl realized. *Something to lead him to my body and Griffin's remains.
He needs to know what happened to us so he can tell
Jonas and my father he did everything he could to
save us from that bear.*

Karl kept his Winchester ready, hoping he could get
a clear shot at the bear before the grizzly caught up
with Dennis. Karl was impressed with the way the
beast stayed out of Dennis's sight line.

Dennis's mount must have caught the bear's scent,
because it began to sidle and jerk its head up and
down, anxious to be free of the constraints that kept
it from running.

"Easy, boy," Karl clearly heard Dennis say. "It's all
right. Whatever's up there is already dead. It's no threat
to you."

At that moment, the grizzly gave a terrifying roar
and charged, landing on the gelding's haunches. Karl
saw the bear take a savage swipe at Dennis's shoulder
with its claws, leaving bloody furrows. Dennis went
flying and landed facedown on the ground.

The horse kicked the bear in the chest with both
hind hooves, and as the grizzly backed off, the horse
galloped away, stirrups on the empty saddle flapping.

Before Karl could draw a bead on the bear, it disappeared behind a tree, where he had no shot.

"Dennis, don't move!" Karl called out. "Lie still."

"If I do, he's going to eat me alive!" Dennis shouted
back in terror.

"Your only chance is to stay where you are. Don't

budge an inch," Karl warned. "Pretend you're dead. I'm going to move where I have a shot at him."

Dennis didn't say anything more, because the bear had started lumbering in his direction. Karl moved as quickly as he could in Dennis's direction, desperate for a shot at the grizzly before it reached the man on the ground.

Karl had the rifle to his shoulder, taking aim behind the bear's shoulder where its heart should be, when Dennis suddenly leapt to his feet and darted for the closest tree. Karl took the shot he'd lined up, but the bear bolted after Dennis with lightning speed.

Karl ran forward and yelled, "Run, Dennis. Climb!"

But there were no trees with branches low enough for Dennis to reach. He'd shinnied only six feet up a narrow-trunked pine when the bear swiped at Dennis's ankle with its enormous paw and knocked him from the tree.

Dennis fell straight into the jaws of the behemoth.

He screamed. And screamed again. And then was silent.

Karl emptied his rifle into the grizzly as he ran forward, closing the distance between himself and the bear. "Dennis!" he yelled. "Dennis!"

"Karl! Stop! Don't!"

Karl was astonished to hear Hetty's voice calling out to him. And terrified, because if she was within shouting distance of him, she was within shouting distance of the grizzly. He took a second to locate her—and Andy and Bao and Grace and Griffin—in a nearby stand of trees, before he turned his attention back to the bear.

He realized the animal was slumped on the ground. All he could see of Dennis was an arm, sticking out beyond the grizzly's enormous girth. Karl ran forward and slowed a half dozen feet from the bear. He circled the behemoth with his rifle at the ready until he was certain it was no longer breathing. Then he tried shoving the grizzly off of Dennis, but the bear was too heavy.

"Andy, Bao, come quick!" he yelled.

As the two men galloped their horses toward him, Karl shouted orders. They tied ropes around the bear's head and rear paws, dallied them around their saddle horns, and using the strength of both horses, hauled the grizzly off of Dennis.

By then, Hetty and the children had reached the spot where the bear had fallen.

"Stay on your horses," Karl ordered. He didn't want them seeing the kind of gore he expected when Dennis's body was revealed.

Bao quickly examined Dennis, then looked at Karl and shook his head.

Karl crossed to where Dennis lay and looked down at him.

"There's hardly a mark on him. What happened?"

"Suffocated," Bao said as he arranged a blanket in which to wrap Dennis's body.

"Then this is my fault," Karl said flatly. "For shooting that bear so it fell on him."

"It's Dennis's fault for running away and leaving you to die, Pa," Griffin said. "And for not lying still like you said."

Karl frowned. "You saw what happened?"

"We were standing right there," Grace said, pointing to the concealing underbrush. "We saw it all. You did everything you could, Pa."

"The children are right, Karl. You couldn't have done more than you did. You saved Dennis from being eaten alive by that grizzly."

Hetty was off her mount before Karl could stop her. She stopped in front of him and surveyed the shallow claw marks the grizzly had left on his cheeks. "Oh, Karl. Your face."

He wouldn't look ordinary anymore. He'd carry the scars from this day forever after. He opened his arms, which suddenly felt as if they had no strength, and closed them around the woman he loved. "Let's go home," he said.

"Wait, Karl!" Griffin said.

Karl was instantly alert. "What's wrong?"

Griffin stepped off his pony, pulled his brand-new knife from the scabbard, and said, "I've got a bear to skin."

Hetty stuck her nose against his neck and shuddered.

"It's all over, Hetty," he said, rubbing her back soothingly. "You don't have to be scared anymore."

She leaned close and said, "I love you, Karl."

Karl looked into her eyes and saw the truth staring back at him. He hugged her tight and whispered, "I love you, too."

Epilogue

It was still hard for Karl to accept that Hetty loved him. He supposed there had been too many lies in the beginning for him to accept that everything had turned out so right in the end. But Grace and Griffin were calling him Pa, and he was soon to be the father of a third child, who would be arriving in a matter of months. Having a family to love was so much better than he'd ever imagined it could be.

So he was more than a little disturbed when, one month after the bear hunt, a man dressed in a black suit and a black duster and wearing a black bowler hat knocked on his front door and asked if he could speak with Miss Henrietta Wentworth.

"Who are you?" Karl demanded.

The man doffed his hat and said, "Excuse me, sir. I'm a Pinkerton. Can you direct me to Miss Wentworth?"

"There's no one here by that name," Karl said, knowing full well whom the detective wanted.

"Perhaps I was misled," the Pinkerton said. "I was told that Miss Henrietta Wentworth traveled to the Bitterroot last fall."

"Miss Wentworth is now Mrs. Karl Norwood. My wife."

The Pinkerton smiled and returned his hat to his head. "I saw how the church register was signed, Mr. Norwood. I'm not entirely sure you're married to Miss Wentworth. I'm still checking into the legalities of the matter."

The last thing Karl wanted to hear was that he wasn't married to Hetty. He managed not to snap when he asked, "What is it you want with my wife?"

"I've been hired by her eldest sister to find her."

"Her *eldest* sister?" Karl said. "Not her twin?"

"Her twin, Mrs. Flint Creed of the Wyoming Territory, is also seeking Miss Wentworth, but the Pinkerton Agency was employed by Mrs. Jacob Creed, who resides in South Texas."

"Both married sisters have the same last name?" Karl said. "How is that possible?"

"They married brothers, one living in Texas and the other in Wyoming," the Pinkerton said. "Could I speak with your wife, Mr. Norwood? It's my duty to inform her that her sisters are searching for her, and to give her information on how she may contact them."

"Karl? Who's at the door?"

Karl turned to find Hetty standing behind him, looking adorably rumpled, as though she'd just gotten out of bed. Which she had. He'd kept her there making love to her after they'd woken up, and told her he'd make breakfast while she slept in. Except, those plans had gone to hell when this stranger knocked on the door.

"It's a Pinkerton," Karl said bluntly.

"Why don't you invite him inside?" Hetty said, tying her robe more tightly around her nightgown.

The Pinkerton removed his bowler again. "How do you do, Miss Wentworth? I have a message for you from your sister."

Hetty's eyes lit up. "Hannah? Then she's alive? Please come in! And it's Mrs. Norwood," she said.

The Pinkerton's eyebrows rose at the correction, and he shot a look at Karl, who couldn't help smiling back smugly. Then the detective stepped inside and allowed Hetty to usher him to the kitchen table. She offered him a seat, which he took.

"Please tell me," Hetty said anxiously as she sat down at the table across from the detective, "how is Hannah?"

"Happily married to Mr. Flint Creed of the Wyoming Territory and the mother of a little girl named Lauren," the Pinkerton reported.

"Karl," Hetty said, reaching out a hand, which he crossed the room to grasp. "She's alive! She's married and a mother. I didn't kill her!"

The sudden tears in Hetty's eyes gave evidence of the burden of guilt she'd carried. Karl couldn't believe this was really happening. Hetty was being offered the chance to reunite with her family.

"I'm also delighted to report that your eldest sister, Miranda, is married to Mr. Jacob Creed, and that along with your younger brothers, Nicholas and Harrison, is living on a ranch in South Texas," the Pinkerton said.

Hetty's grip on Karl's hand became painfully tight. He took a step closer and laid a comforting hand on her shoulder.

"What's going on out here?" Griffin asked as he entered the room barefoot, dressed in his smalls and a long john shirt, and rubbing sleep from his eyes.

"We have company," Hetty said. "Go get dressed."

Griffin froze where he was, his eyes frightened. "I know who you are," he said, pointing at the stranger. "I've seen your kind before, dressed all in black and with that bowler hat. You're a Pinkerton!"

"Yes, my good man, I am," the Pinkerton confirmed.

"Grace, get in here!" Griffin shouted. "There's a Pinkerton in the house."

A moment later, Grace appeared in her bedroom door, wearing wool socks without shoes and tying a robe Hetty had made for her. "What does he want?" she asked her brother.

From the anxious look his children exchanged, Karl had the feeling they were guilty of more in the past year than deceiving him. "Who else did you scam?" he asked.

"Griffin only did it for me, Pa," Grace said. "And I snuck the money back where it belonged as soon as I found out."

"Come here, both of you," Karl said sternly.

Grace grasped Griffin's hand, and they took the few steps necessary to face Karl.

"I won't ever do anything like that again, Pa," Griffin said. "Please don't send us away!"

Karl reached out to enfold both children in his arms and hugged them close. "I'll take your word that both of you have given up your lives of crime. I'm not sending you anywhere except into the bedroom to get dressed."

"What about the Pinkerton?" Griffin asked, eyeing the stranger suspiciously.

"He's here to give your mother some good news. He's found her missing family."

Grace left Karl's side and rushed over to hug Hetty. "Mom, that's wonderful! I'm so happy for you. Are they coming to the valley to see us?"

"I don't know if they have plans to come here," Hetty replied. "I certainly can't travel south until the baby is born, and I can figure out how to pay for my passage," Hetty added, looking at Karl.

Karl grimaced. Hetty was well aware of the fact that, instead of profiting from the work he'd done over the winter, he'd been left high and dry by his brother. He'd met Jonas's quotas for lumber, only to have Jonas inform him that he'd failed to work out financing for a railroad into the valley to haul the lumber out. Until Jonas could figure out a way to economically get lumber out of the valley, the entire logging project was on hold.

Since both Hetty and Karl loved the valley and wanted to stay there, Karl had been toying with the idea of ranching. The valley was ripe with long grass, and Andy had suggested they drive some longhorns up to the Bitterroot from Texas.

Which led Karl to say, "Andy and I are planning a trip to Texas to buy cattle. Maybe that would be a good time to visit your sisters."

"I believe the entire family is planning a reunion later in the fall." The Pinkerton handed a letter to Hetty. "The details are all there."

Karl watched Hetty take the letter reverently in her

hands. She looked up at him, her eyes glistening with tears of joy. "We're all going to be together again, Karl. Miranda and Hannah and me and—" She cut herself off and turned back to the Pinkerton. "What about Josie? Have you found her? Is she safe?"

"Your youngest sister, Miss Josephine Wentworth, is no longer a captive of the Sioux," the Pinkerton said. "She was bought by an Englishman who—"

"Bought!" Hetty exclaimed.

"Exchanged for a gold watch, actually," the Pinkerton said with a smile.

"So where is she?" Hetty asked.

"The Englishman was traveling abroad and took your sister along with him. I believe he's scheduled to return to Blackthorne Abbey, his home in England, by the end of the summer. We will be there, that is to say, I will be there," he corrected, "to inform him that Josephine's eldest sister is seeking her whereabouts, and to arrange for her return to the bosom of her family."

"This must be costing a fortune," Hetty murmured. "Who's paying your fee?"

"Your sister Miranda employed the agency, madam," the Pinkerton said.

"But we're orphans!" Hetty said. "We don't have—"

"You're all heirs to your father's fortune, which was not burned in the Great Fire, as was first reported. Unfortunately, your uncle Stephen absconded with a great deal of your father's wealth. Rest assured, we will find him." He winked and said, "A Pinkerton never sleeps."

Hetty jumped up and hugged Karl. "I can't believe this is happening. My family is safe! And we're rich! I can buy Grace a whole trousseau of dresses, and we can get Griffin a Sunday suit."

"I'd rather have a dog," Griffin said.

"Whoa!" Karl said. "Let's not put the cart before the horse. If I heard the Pinkerton right, your uncle has most of your father's fortune, and he hasn't been found."

"That is correct," the Pinkerton said.

"Aw, shucks," Griffin said. "Does that mean I don't get a dog?"

"We'll see about the dog," Karl said. "Meanwhile, let Hetty read the letter from her sister."

Hetty plopped back down in her chair, opened the letter, and began to read aloud.

Dear Hetty,

If you're reading this, it means the Pinkerton has found you at last. I'm living in Texas with my husband, Jake, his former father-in-law, a beautiful stepdaughter, and a feisty son who was born earlier this year.

Hannah is married to Jake's brother, Flint, who lives near Jake's other brother, Ransom, in the Wyoming Territory. Hannah has a daughter, Lauren, by Mr. McMurtry, and is pregnant again with Flint's child.

We decided to postpone reuniting until we can all be together, which means after we find Josie. We know she's alive, but we're concerned about the scoundrel who bought her from the Indians. It seems he's the black sheep of the family, even if he is the Duke of Blackthorne. There's no telling what he's done to Josie.

The Pinkerton has also told you by now that Fa-

ther's money wasn't burned up in the Great Fire after all, but we have to catch Uncle Stephen to retrieve it. The Pinkerton is authorized to provide whatever funds you need to make the journey here.

I love and miss you and look forward to the day when we can all be together again here in Texas.

Your loving sister,
Miranda

"Are you going to Texas, Mom?" Grace asked.

Karl was grateful Grace had asked, because he couldn't speak past the painful lump in his throat.

"Not right away," Hetty said, laying a hand on her very pregnant belly.

"But once the baby is born you'll be leaving the valley to rejoin your family?" Grace persisted.

Hetty turned to meet Karl's gaze, and reached out to grasp his hand. "My family is right here."

Karl pulled Hetty from her chair and held her tight. "I love you, Hetty."

"I love you, too, Karl." She shot him a mischievous grin and said, "And maybe, someday, you'll really believe it."

Karl thought of all the pain he'd felt, wondering if Hetty would ever love him. It was a sign of how certain he was of her love that she could now tease him about it. He looked forward to meeting her family and to having them meet his and Hetty's children. "I want you to see your family again," he said.

"And I want to see them." Hetty pulled Grace close as Karl reached for Griffin. "Maybe we can all go to Texas together in the fall."

"Does this mean I don't get a dog?" Griffin said.

Karl laughed and said to Hetty, "How did you pick these kids?"

"I lucked out," Hetty said. "They picked me."

"I guess we're going to have both a dog and a cat running around the house," Karl grumbled.

Griffin whooped. "I get a dog, Grace!"

Grace smiled and reminded Karl, "I'm taking Socks with me when Andy and I get married next June."

"June is a whole year off," Karl said. "I'm happy to enjoy the chaos until then."

"I'll be taking my leave," the Pinkerton said. "I'll be in touch, Mrs. Norwood, when I locate your sister."

Once the Pinkerton was gone, Karl sent an excited Grace and Griffin back to their room to get dressed. Then he pulled Hetty into his arms and hugged her tight—and felt the baby kick his hip bone.

"Charlene is kicking again," he said, placing his hand on her belly where he'd felt the kick.

She took his hand and put it on the other side of her belly, where he felt a distinct bulge. "Charles is making himself known, too."

Karl stared at her blankly. "What do you mean?"

She grinned and said, "I'd think a scientist like you would have figured it out by now."

"Figured what out?"

"I'm a twin, Karl. I come from a family filled with twins."

Karl felt poleaxed. "Twins? You're having twins?"

"I can't be sure. But I keep finding a foot over here." She pointed to one side of her belly. "And another foot way over here." She pointed to the other side of her belly. "What does that suggest to you, scientifically speaking?"

Karl laughed and wrapped Hetty in his arms. "Double the joy. Double the fun. And a whole lot more love."

Acknowledgments

I had the joy of visiting the Bitterroot Valley in the fall of 2012 to do research for this novel. I want to thank the individuals who invited me into their homes and shared their family histories in the valley with me, including Dale and Juanita Maki and Bill and Donna Kyle. A special thank-you to Ernie and Sherry Palin, with whom I had a memorable meeting at the Montana Café in Darby.

Helen Bibler gave me the idea to infect some of my loggers with Rocky Mountain Spotted Fever. The Flatheads and Salish didn't know why folks got sick and died when they spent time in canyons on the west side of the Bitterroot River in spring, but they stayed away and stayed safe. Rocky Mountain Spotted Fever, which was most often fatal at that time, was transmitted to humans by ticks found on animals like mountain goats, squirrels, and chipmunks.

For the record, the lumber industry didn't really get going in the Bitterroot Valley until the 1880s, but there were always small mills where lumber was cut.

I couldn't have begun my research without the introductions and directions (including maps) I got from

Pat Easley at the Bitterroot Valley Chamber of Commerce. Thank you, Pat! I also want to thank Tamar Stanley, director of the Ravalli County Museum in Hamilton, for making the Bitterroot Valley Historical Society tome *Bitterroot Trails,* a wonderful history of the valley, available to me.

A loving thanks to my writer friends Kat and Larry Martin, who provided bed and board in Clinton, so I could make my daily treks "up the valley" (which was really south) to Darby, where I set this book. You haven't really lived until you've watched wild turkeys and a herd of deer trek across the front lawn while you're having supper.

I also want to thank my editor, Shauna Summers, for her suggestions to make this a better book. You're a joy and a treasure!

If you've come this far along the trail with me, you're ready for the next installment of Wentworth family adventures. I'm already working on my next Bitter Creek novel, Josie's story, which is coming soon.

I welcome your comments or suggestions about my novels. You can reach me through my website at www.joanjohnston.com or through Facebook at www.facebook.com/joanjohnstonauthor.

Happy reading,

Joan Johnston

From beloved *New York Times*
bestselling author JOAN JOHNSTON comes
a sizzling contemporary Western romance
beginning another chapter in
the Bitter Creek series.

Three beautiful daughters
stand to lose their inheritance
and the only home they've ever known.

A prodigal son is determined to seize
the fortune he's been promised no matter
who stands in his way.

One estate will either be
divided by a family feud
or united by an unlikely love.

Look for it soon from Dell Books